...sion for travel has taken *New York Times* bestselling
... **Vicki Lewis Thompson** to Europe, Great Britain, the
... isles, Australia and New Zealand. She's visited most of
... America and has her eye on South America's rain
...ts. Africa, India and China beckon. But her first love is
...ome state of Arizona, with its deserts, mountains, sunsets
...—last but not least—cowboys! The wide-open spaces
... heroes on horseback influence everything she writes.
...nnect with her at vickilewisthompson.com, Facebook.com/
...ilewisthompson and Twitter.com/vickilthompson

...A *TODAY* bestselling author **Anna DePalo** is a Harvard
...duate and former intellectual property attorney who lives
... her husband, son and daughter in her native New York.
... writes sexy, humorous books that have been published in
...e than twenty countries. Her novels have won the *RT Book
...views* Reviewers' Choice Award, the Golden Leaf and the
...ok Buyer's Best. You can sign up for her newsletter at
...w.annadepalo.com

...arlet Wilson writes for both Mills & Boon Romance and
...dical Romance. She lives on the west coast of Scotland with
... fiancé and their two sons. She loves to hear from readers
...d can be reached via her website: scarlet-wilson.com

D0522795

Tempted by the Movie Star

VICKI LEWIS THOMPSON
ANNA DePALO
SCARLET WILSON

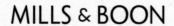

MIX
Paper from
responsible sources
FSC C007454
FSC

This book is produced from independently certified FSC™
paper to ensure responsible forest management

For more information visit: www.harpercollins.co.uk/green

Printed and bound in Spain
by CPI, Barcelona

MILLS & BOON

First Published in Great Britain 2019
by Mills & Boon, an imprint of HarperCollins*Publishers*
1 London Bridge Street, London, SE1 9GF

TEMPTED BY THE MOVIE STAR © 2019 Harlequin Books S. A.

In the Cowboy's Arms © 2017 Vicki Lewis Thompson
Hollywood Baby Affair © 2017 Anna DePalo
The Mysterious Italian Houseguest © 2017 Scarlet Wilson

ISBN: 978-0-263-27778-4

0819

IN THE COWBOY'S ARMS

VICKI LEWIS THOMPSON

To Mills & Boon authors everywhere—

In an uncertain world, our stories have given
pleasure, lightened burdens and changed lives.
We rock.

Chapter One

Broad-shouldered, lean-hipped men with square jaws and captivating eyes were a dime a dozen in Hollywood. After spending all twenty-seven years of her life in Tinseltown, Geena Lysander wasn't easily impressed. It was a testament to the beauty of Matt Forrest that her glasses fogged up whenever he walked into her office.

He was also a decent guy, and she didn't often come across someone who was both ethical and gorgeous. She'd been strongly attracted to him ever since they'd started working together six months ago. Several times she'd caught a flash of heat in his gaze that indicated he had feelings for her, too.

Once she'd thought he'd been ready to ask her out. When he hadn't, she'd decided it was for the best, considering their professional relationship. But that hadn't stopped her from wanting to kiss him, especially when he flashed one of his megawatt smiles.

Judging from the grim set of his mouth, he wouldn't be doing that today. Usually he came in wearing his signature hat, a chocolate-brown Stetson with a turquoise-studded hatband. He favored snug T-shirts, faded jeans and scuffed cowboy boots.

Not this morning. Instead, he'd pulled a generic baseball cap over his thick dark hair and covered his baby blues with aviator shades. He hadn't bothered to shave. She'd never seen that beat-up denim jacket before, either, and he'd turned the collar up even though it was seventy degrees outside. The jeans and the boots were the same, though.

Giving her glasses a quick polish, she smiled, then she put them back on and stood. "Hey."

"Ma'am." He touched the brim of his cap in greeting, but he didn't smile back.

If he'd intended to create a disguise, he'd failed. The paparazzi were experts at spotting celebrities trying to look like street people. And Matt, bless his heart, would look hot as sin no matter what he wore. "Any troubles on the way over?"

He shook his head. "Stayed with a buddy last night, which seems to have thrown them off the trail temporarily. Figured they might be watching my apartment building."

"I can send someone to check that out."

"I appreciate it, but I plan to avoid my place for a while so don't go to any extra trouble." Still no smile, and Matt was the kind of guy who looked for the humor in a situation.

She'd always cherished that about him and hated seeing him so down. He might have exercised poor judgment yesterday, but she understood how that could happen with a costar like Briana Danvers. He was so new at the game. One big-budget movie in the can and another scheduled to start shooting next month meant he was on his way, but he was bound to make a few rookie mistakes in the process.

That's what PR reps like her were for—to repair those little whoopsies.

He took off his shades and stared at her, his gaze bleak. "What now?"

"We'll work through it." As she sat down, she gestured to the chair in front of her desk. "Have a seat."

"Thank you." He lowered his muscular body onto the leather upholstery with a sigh.

"Heard anything from Harvey?" She wasn't crazy about Matt's agent, who headed up a big firm and always seemed to be unavailable or out of the country. But the guy had negotiated the original movie deal and Matt had been signed for another potential blockbuster that would begin filming in a few weeks, so Harvey was getting his client work. That was the bottom line.

"He texted me. Said I should relax, that it would all blow over."

"He's probably right."

"I hope he is, but this has really thrown me for a loop."

"I'm sure it has." And she was determined to help him sort it out, since Harvey had obviously dismissed the issue.

Pulling off his cap, Matt tunneled his fingers through his hair. "I never expected Briana to behave like that or say those things about me." The words were laced with pain.

Geena wondered if she should have seen this train wreck coming and warned him. Briana was seductive, both onscreen and off. The poor guy had probably become lost in the fantasy. "It's easy to develop feelings for a costar. You wouldn't be the first and you won't be the last."

"That's just it. I knew I couldn't let anything happen." He sat forward in his chair, his expression tense. "First of all, she's married, and second, her husband is Clifton effing *Wallace*, everyone's favorite, including my mom's. And mine, actually. He reminds me so much of the Duke."

High praise from Matt. Early on he'd told her that he knew all of John Wayne's movies by heart and repeatedly watched them for inspiration. "It's not the end of the world, Matt. Don't beat yourself up for being human."

"No, ma'am, I'm not." The chair squeaked as he leaned back and gazed at the ceiling. "I'm beating myself up for being stupid. A complete idiot."

Her heart went out to him. Had they not been separated by her desk, she would have squeezed his arm or given him a hug. Then she caught herself imagining that potential hug in far too much detail.

She cleared her throat. "It'll be okay."

"Eventually, I guess." He met her gaze. "I'm sure Harvey has a point. But being called a home wrecker is humiliating. I can take it, but I hate that my folks will have to hear such things."

"They're in Wyoming, right?"

"Yes, ma'am. But they'll have to face their friends and neighbors, and Sheridan's a fairly small town. They've been so proud of me..." His voice trailed off.

"Like I said, we'll handle it. The key is to appear contrite and apologetic. Then I can set you up with some visually appealing charity work, like organizing a benefit for a local animal rescue organization. Fans will overlook this, especially if you seem sufficiently remorseful."

He went very still. "Surely *you* don't believe I hit on her."

"What I think doesn't matter. The media is running a picture of you kissing her outside a café in Burbank. We need to—"

"I didn't kiss her."

"But—"

"*She* kissed *me*."

Judging from the mutual lip-lock Geena had seen in the picture, it was all semantics. "The specific details aren't important. To be honest, getting labeled as a bad boy isn't the worst thing that could happen, especially if we demonstrate that you regret your behavior. Up to now, I've promoted you as Hollywood's fresh new face, a handsome guy with a squeaky clean rep. But fans may like discovering you're not perfect."

His blue eyes lost all expression. "So you think I forced my attentions on Briana."

She would love to believe that he hadn't at least invited that kiss, even if he hadn't initiated it. The pictures were pretty damning. She understood why he wanted to put a different spin on the encounter, but that strategy could backfire into a he-said-she-said nightmare. "It makes no difference who started it. If we jump on the story right away we can take control of the narrative before it gets blown out of proportion."

"I see."

His icy tone made her blink. One glance at his face told her that a wall had gone up. She'd seen that protective shield a couple of times before and had thought the device would serve him well in a brutal business. But employing it against her was counterproductive. "Matt, listen. We can—"

"Sorry, ma'am." He stood and put on his hat and shades. "But I'm outta here."

"Wait!" She leaped up. "You can't leave now. It'll look like you're running away."

"That's fine with me." He turned toward the door.

"Where are you going?"

"Home."

The minute Matt stepped out on the sidewalk they were on him with their cameras, mikes and invasive questions. Must be a slow news day if someone had tracked him over here. Too bad he hadn't called a cab. None were in sight, either.

He shouldered his way through what felt like a mob, but was only five or six reporters, and sprinted toward the nearest bus stop. Three years of running all over town auditioning for commercials had forced him to memorize the public transportation system. There was a bus stop a couple of blocks from here. Thanks to a rigorous training schedule, he was in shape.

He outran the paparazzi and caught the bus right before it pulled away from the curb. After paying the fare he sank gratefully into a seat. Adrenaline plus the blast of A/C made him shiver as he ran through his options.

Going back to his apartment wouldn't work. Even if he made it inside without being accosted, he'd be a virtual prisoner in there until this thing died down. He believed it would. That was what he'd expected Geena to say.

She was a super-smart lady. A little nerdy, but he liked that about her. Tall and slender, she dressed in conservative suits and wore her brown hair up in an arrangement on top of her head. She had a sexy librarian thing going on that had fascinated him from the get-go.

When she was thinking real hard she took off her

glasses and stuck them in her hairdo. He'd envisioned her thinking hard about this mess and coming up with a plan that included hustling him out the back entrance of the building. Then she'd hire a car to spirit him away to some remote cabin in the mountains for a week or so.

He'd even fantasized that she'd take time off and go with him. They could strategize how to deal with this and…yeah, get cozy in the cabin. He'd allowed his brain to come up with an intimate scenario that would never happen, but it had been fun to think about.

Instead, she wanted him to publicly apologize for something he hadn't done and then become proactive by supporting animal rescue. He loved helping a good cause, and animal rescue was dear to his heart. His foster father had devoted his life to a well-respected practice as a large-animal vet.

But Matt balked at using homeless animals as a publicity stunt to prove he was a nice guy. Her plan sucked, but that wasn't the worst part. The real kicker was realizing that Geena believed he'd done what Briana had accused him of.

He felt like ending the relationship with her PR company ASAP, but that was a knee-jerk reaction. He'd give himself time to think about it before doing anything drastic. Aside from being attracted to her, he also liked her and admired that she'd built the company herself. She looked too young to be the head of the firm, and once he'd asked her how old she was. Turned out she was twenty-seven, same as him.

Being near her gave him a buzz, no question, and he'd caught her giving him the eye, too.

He'd debated asking her to dinner to see what might happen. He'd come close to doing it once, but he wasn't sure if asking his PR rep for a date would be an unprofessional move. Making that call wasn't easy in an industry where the lines seemed to blur, but in the end he'd decided to err on the side of caution.

When it came to Briana Danvers, though, his thoughts had been crystal clear. During the filming of *Preston's Revenge* she'd kissed him like she meant it, but he'd never for one second contemplated making a move in private, let alone in a public setting. If Geena thought he had, then she'd seriously misjudged him.

Being blamed for something he didn't do was a hot button. His mom used to do it all the time. Thanks to some counseling, now he could handle the issue if he didn't respect the person doing the judging. But he respected Geena and it bothered him that she thought he could have made a move on Cliff Wallace's wife.

So much for his fantasy of spending a few days in a cabin with her. If she wouldn't help him get the hell out of Dodge, he'd take care of it himself. When he'd told her he was going home, he'd meant Thunder Mountain Ranch where his foster parents lived. They'd saved his bacon when his mom had left him years ago, and ever since then he'd considered them his true family along with his foster brothers.

Rosie and Herb Padgett had been a godsend for many boys caught between a rock and a hard place. But these days, instead of taking in foster kids, they'd opened a residential equine academy for older teens. Much as he wanted to go home, showing up when classes were in session was inconsiderate, especially now that he was a hot item in the scandal sheets.

He used to wonder if he'd ever be famous enough to appear on the cover of the magazines in racks at the grocery store. Thanks to Briana, now he was. They'd plastered that picture everywhere, and one tabloid had dredged up a stock photo of Cliff looking outraged. It'd implied that had been Cliff's reaction. Probably had been, and Matt hated that.

If he could hide out at the ranch for a few days, he wouldn't have to keep seeing those tabloids. A quick check of the Thunder Mountain Academy site on his phone brought good news. The spring session had ended two days ago and summer classes wouldn't start for another week. That meant everyone would be busy preparing the cabins and the rec hall for the next batch of kids.

He could help with that, but first he had to get on a plane. He hadn't paid attention to what bus he'd used to escape the reporters, but this one wouldn't take him to the airport. A few transfers would confuse his pursuers if he still had any, and he could make plane reservations on the way.

His tickets, one to Denver and a separate one on a commuter to the Sheridan County Airport, cost a ridiculous amount. Then again, he was making a ridiculous amount, enough for first class on the LA to Denver leg. He'd considered that briefly, because he didn't fit comfortably in coach, but flying up front would only draw more attention.

Besides, he hated spending money on something so transitory as a bigger seat on the plane. He preferred investing in more permanent pleasures. He'd sunk a good portion of his earnings into a fixer-upper ranch not far from Thunder Mountain. He'd bought it sight unseen as a sanctuary from the craziness of LA, not knowing just how crazy things could get.

Rosie and Herb had checked out the place before he'd signed the papers and they'd assured him it would be beautiful once he gave it some TLC. Although he wouldn't have much time to do that on this trip, he couldn't wait to see it.

Too bad he had to be back in LA so soon, but some publicity gigs for *Preston's Revenge* were scheduled next week, and after that he'd start shooting the new movie. He hoped to God Briana had settled down by the time they had to make a joint appearance. If not, those events would be awkward as hell.

After the relative tranquility of the bus ride, he stepped into the chaos of LAX with trepidation. He scanned the crowd for reporters and then decided he was being paranoid. He wasn't a big enough deal for them to stake out the airport. No one paid attention to him until he had to hand over his driver's license going through security.

The woman's eyes widened. "Aren't you—"

"Yes, ma'am. Please don't react."

"Wouldn't dream of it, honey." She gave him a smile and stamped his boarding pass.

Okay, so maybe not everyone in the world thought he was a scumbag who'd tried to steal Cliff Wallace's wife. In the gate area he spotted several people reading the tabloid that had caused the most commotion because the headline screamed HOME WRECKER in large type. He kept his head down and hoped for the best. A couple of teenage girls snapped some pictures, but he could certainly live with that. Even if they posted them online, the paparazzi couldn't get to him here.

He checked his phone and saw several texts from Geena, although she hadn't tried to call him. He appreciated that. He texted back that he was on his way to Sheridan and would be out of touch for a week or so.

Then it occurred to him he should let Rosie know he was coming. In all the chaos he'd forgotten to do that. She was somewhat psychic, but figuring out he was flying home today might be beyond her powers. He sought out an area that was slightly less noisy and called her.

She answered immediately. "You've been on my mind all morning. How are you, son?"

Her caring voice almost made him lose it. No scolding, no exclamations of horror, no tears. She only wanted to know that he was okay. "I'm fine, Mom. I'm coming home for a few days, if that's okay."

"Of course it's okay! When will you be here?"

He checked his arrival time. "I have a long layover in Denver so I won't make it for dinner. Looks like I'll land about nine or so tonight."

"Cade and Lexi will pick you up."

"Great. Can't wait to see them." His foster brother Cade Gallagher had moved back from Colorado two years ago and reunited with his high school sweetheart, Lexi Simmons. They'd both worked hard to make Thunder Mountain Academy a reality.

"The truck's new, so look for the academy logo on the door. Oh, Matt, I'm so glad you're coming home. I feel the need to see you."

"I feel the need to see you, too." He swallowed a sudden lump in his throat. "Gotta go. We're about to load."

He disconnected and stared at the floor while he pulled himself together. Six months ago he'd called Rosie with the life-changing news that he'd been given the male lead in his first big-budget film. She'd whooped and hollered for a good five minutes before she'd been able to speak rationally.

What a beautiful moment that had been. He'd cherished the idea that she could brag to her friends about her son the movie star. He'd loved giving her something special to celebrate after all she and Herb had done for him. And now that shiny moment had been tarnished.

At least his folks were in Wyoming, far from the ugliness. He never wanted it to touch them. Their privacy meant everything to him and he'd protect it at all costs.

Chapter Two

Matt had no trouble spotting the ranch truck as he stood in the cool night air outside the Sheridan airport waiting for his ride. Cade drove up in a tan, four-door long bed with the Thunder Mountain Academy logo on the door. Lexi wasn't with him, after all, so Matt climbed into the front seat and grasped Cade's outstretched hand.

"Hey, Matt." A straw cowboy hat shadowed Cade's face, but his subdued greeting telegraphed his concern. "No luggage?"

"Nope." Matt closed the door and fastened his seat belt.

"At least you stayed ahead of the peasants with the pitchforks." Cade put the truck in gear and pulled out.

"Barely. Nice truck."

"Mom likes me to drive it whenever I come to town. She thinks it's good for the academy's image."

Matt leaned back against the seat. "Yeah, until some derelict gets in."

"Now that you mention it, you do look a little rough around the edges, bro. Is the scruff for your next role?"

"The scruff is for lack of a razor, although I figured it also might keep people from recognizing me."

"Oh."

"So, where's Lexi?"

"She thought we might need some brotherhood moments so she's waiting at the ranch with Mom and Dad."

"Wow." Lexi's understanding touched him. "That's... really nice of her."

"That's my lady. She has it all going on."

"You're a lucky guy."

"Yes, yes, I am." Cade stopped at a red light and took a deep breath. "And since she's given us the chance to talk, let me say this whole thing bites. I mean, one damn kiss. It's not like you were boinking that woman in the middle of Sunset Boulevard. And wouldn't you know some jackass would be there with a camera."

"Of course he was." In spite of his exhaustion, Matt's anger flared to life. "She hired him to be there."

"What?"

"She set me up." Matt's stomach clenched as he said it out loud for the first time. "I can't prove it yet, but the long layover in Denver allowed me to think through all that's happened and I've put the pieces together. I realize everything started on the last day of shooting when she propositioned me."

"Aw, hell. Seriously?"

"Afraid so. I've never told anyone about it, though, so keep it to yourself."

"Goes without saying."

"Anyway, she was a little drunk, but not that drunk. She said Cliff wasn't man enough for her anymore."

"Anymore? They've been married for like three years, tops!"

Matt shrugged. "Who knows what their relationship is like? She promised we'd be discreet and no one would ever have to know. I turned her down as nicely as I could, but—"

"Now she hates you with the heat of a thousand branding irons."

"Sure looks that way. She invited me to lunch yesterday, supposedly to apologize for her inappropriate behavior. Instead, she kissed me in front of witnesses and then told the media I was the aggressor."

"Holy shit on a swizzle stick."

"Yeah." He glanced over at Cade. "But now that I'm out of paparazzi range it should die down. Without me to harass they'll focus on some other poor slob. At least, that's my plan. And I'd like to forget Briana Danvers while I'm here, so let's talk about something else. You still have that gray tabby cat?"

"You remember Ringo?"

"Absolutely. He was one of the highlights from that quick visit last year."

Cade chuckled. "Ringo's living the life. Ever since Lexi moved into my cabin he prefers staying there with us instead of patrolling the barn looking for mice. He's turned into a feline couch potato."

"Smart cat."

"Smarter than we are, that's for sure. Listen, you may want to forget about Briana, but I'm just getting started thinking about her and I want justice." Cade smacked the steering wheel. "Here's an idea! We'll call a press conference so you can tell your side. We can't let her get away with this crap."

His brother had his back. The heaviness lifted from Matt's shoulders and he smiled for the first time in twenty-four hours. A press conference in Sheridan, Wyoming. That would be a first, especially if they could get any members of the press to show up, which wasn't likely.

"I don't know how to organize a press conference," Cade continued, "but I'll bet you do. Or you know people who know people. We can make it happen."

"Look, it's a good impulse and I appreciate the moral support, but a press conference won't work for a lot of reasons."

"What she's done is *wrong*, damn it! It's character assassination and you need to defend yourself."

"I doubt I can. She's a very good actress who knows her camera angles. She orchestrated that kiss so I'd look guilty as charged. Even if I try to tell my side, hardly anyone will believe me."

"They might if you tell them about the proposition."

"Not doing that."

Cade groaned. "I should have known you wouldn't. You're too noble for your own good, buddy. She doesn't deserve your overdeveloped sense of chivalry."

"It's not her I'm thinking about. It's Cliff Wallace. I respect the hell out of the guy. He has lousy instincts when it comes to women, but like I said, Briana's a very good actress. He may eventually find out the truth about her, but not because of me."

"You had some love scenes with her, right?"

"Oh, yeah."

"Hot?"

"Yep."

Cade was silent for a while. Then he cleared his throat.

"Let me just say I respect the hell out of *you*, cowboy. A lot of guys would have taken her up on that offer."

"Not if they were members of the Thunder Mountain Brotherhood." Matt took great pride in being a part of the group Cade had started years ago with Damon Harrison and Finn O'Roarke, the first three foster boys. Now every guy who'd lived at the ranch was included.

"True."

"And not if they'd been raised by Herb and Rosie."

Cade grinned. "Also true. And for the record, Mom's been informing everyone that the tabloids got it wrong. You never would have behaved that way."

"God, I love that woman."

"Don't we all." He looked over at Matt. "Are you planning to tell her everything you just told me?"

"Probably not."

"I wouldn't, either, unless you want her to buy a ticket to LA and open up a can of whoop-ass on Briana. She's already put a couple of DVDs in the trash compactor."

Matt chuckled at the image of Rosie listening to the crunch as the DVDs bit the dust. "That's why I had to come home, so I could hear stuff like this. Mom's destroying DVDs and you're ready to call a press conference. It's a far better reaction than what I got from my PR rep this morning."

"Which was?"

"She wanted me to publicly show remorse for my behavior."

Cade met that comment with several choice swear words. "So, did you fire her?"

"Not yet. She doesn't know me that well and the photo convinced her I'd forced myself on Briana."

"Did you tell her you hadn't?"

"Yeah, I said it was the other way around—that Briana kissed me—but Geena didn't think it mattered who kissed who. I'm supposed to suck it up and be apologetic."

"That's her name? Geena?"

"Geena Lysander."

"Well, this Geena person should have believed you. She should have taken your side. Apologize, my ass."

"In a way, she was trying to take my side. She kept telling me it would be okay and we'd fix this." He thought of the earnest light in her eyes as she'd laid out her plan. She had pretty eyes, and when they took on that special gleam, he had the urge to kiss her. Like that would ever happen.

"Well, you're not apologizing."

"Nope. I'll just hide out for the next few days. My phone's been off for hours and I'm growing fond of that mode. I might leave it off."

"But you're a big-deal actor now. Don't you have to stay in touch with your peeps?"

"My peeps are all right here in Sheridan. You, Lexi, Rosie and Herb. Plus Damon and Philomena. How's their baby doing, by the way?"

"Sophie's cute as hell, bright red hair just like her mother's. And Jake Ramsey moved back to town. He's working at the fire station and engaged to Amethyst Ferguson. Remember her?"

Matt laughed. "Doesn't everybody? I can't hear 'Santa Baby' without remembering her sexy performance back in high school. I thought she'd be giving Taylor Swift a run for her money by now."

"Turns out she'd rather stick to performing locally."

"You know, after what just happened, I get that."

"Please don't tell me you're hanging it up because of this nonsense."

"No, I'm not. I'm starting a new movie next month."

"Awesome! I don't think I heard about that."

"It came up pretty fast, and I kept meaning to call Mom but then this thing hit." Matt let out a weary sigh. "But I'll hang in there. I love acting. Always have."

"The ultimate escape." Cade glanced at him. "Do you remember telling me that?"

"I do, actually. School plays were great when I was a kid, but this…you can completely disappear into the role. You don't have to worry about what to say because they hand you a script. You don't have to wonder how everything will turn out, either. It's all written out."

"Sounds damned appealing. It's a wonder more of us didn't get into that line of work. Perfect way to forget about things you'd rather not remember."

"Sure is. But I need a break. I'm ready to unplug, at least for the next week or so. Let's talk about your wedding. Third weekend in August, right?"

"Yep."

"I want all the deets, bridegroom."

"You won't be bored?"

"Not a chance." He settled back, ready to hear about something positive for a change.

Once Cade got started on the subject of his upcoming nuptials, he barely stopped for breath. Matt got a kick out of his excitement. By the time they turned down the dirt road leading to the ranch, the humiliation of the past twenty-four hours seemed unimportant compared to Cade's obvious joy in marrying the love of his life.

The tabloid blitz had loomed large back in LA, but moonlight shining on the massive bulk of the Bighorns put everything in perspective. Cade parked in the circular gravel drive in front of the low-slung ranch house and Matt swung down from the cab. Lamplight coming through the windows allowed him to see Rosie, Herb and Lexi sitting in the Adirondack chairs lined up on the long porch.

They called out a greeting as they started down the steps. Matt hadn't shaved or showered in two days, but nobody seemed to care. Arms outstretched, they gathered him close. Coming home had been the right thing to do.

As the crow flew, Sheridan didn't seem that far from LA. Geena wished she could get there by crow, because clearly traveling by passenger plane would take all flipping day. The layover in Denver was ridiculous, but it gave her plenty of time to think about where she'd gone wrong with Matt Forrest.

And she'd gone very wrong with him. She'd also underestimated Briana Danvers's thirst for publicity. Somehow the woman had learned that Matt had left town and she'd made a huge deal of it, calling his departure an admission of guilt.

That was exactly why Geena had wanted him to stick around, but she'd handled the situation poorly. Because she'd dealt with her fair share of clients caught in compromising situations off the set, she'd assumed Matt fell into that category. She'd expected him to agree with her plan to contain the damage. Instead, he'd stormed out of her office.

So she'd gone into research mode. A friend had sent her the dailies from *Preston's Revenge*. The scenes between Briana and Matt were off the charts, but did that mean he'd aggressively pursued her?

She was less and less sure about that. Briana was married to a revered but aging Western movie star. What if she'd been captivated by Matt? He claimed that she'd initiated the kiss.

And, unlike other clients, he seemed horrified by the

drama that photo had created. Some stars were thrilled by any publicity at all, even if it was potentially negative. Not Matt. He'd chosen to hide out.

It might have been a workable strategy except that Briana obviously planned to keep stirring the pot. Matt needed to fight back or he was liable to be forever labeled with Briana's taunt of *run, Forrest, run.*

No other celebrities were doing something stupid this week, so the gossip mags were hungry for anything Briana fed them. The situation reflected poorly on Geena's firm, which she'd started only three years ago, but that wasn't why she'd decided to make a trip to Sheridan. She couldn't bear to stand by and watch Matt take a beating.

So she'd booked her flights to Sheridan, a place that was not easy to get to. But she'd brave a puddle jumper if that's what it took to talk to Matt face-to-face.

He wouldn't be happy to see his PR rep, though. She reminded herself of that as she drove her rented SUV down some of the darkest roads she'd ever seen. Thank God for her GPS or she'd surely have ended up in some pasture staring at an angry bull.

She almost missed the turnoff to Thunder Mountain Ranch. At the last minute she saw it, thanks to a small spotlight trained on the carved wooden sign. A second sign hung below it proclaiming this the *Home of Thunder Mountain Academy.*

She had no idea what that was about, but the ranch was listed as Matt's home address so she'd forge on. Presumably his parents, Rosie and Herb Padgett, lived here. He'd probably changed his last name to something less jarring than Matt Padgett, which was smart marketing.

The dirt road leading to the ranch was even darker than the highway. If she'd spent the night in Sheridan, she could have tackled this road first thing in the morning. But Matt would have an easier time turning her away in broad daylight. A gentleman didn't send a lady back out into the night after she'd traveled all day to see him. And Matt Forrest was a gentleman.

She'd allowed the turmoil Briana had created to obscure that basic fact. Briana might be irresistible to the majority of males out there, but despite her famous allure, Matt would never succumb to it in a public place. Such behavior would have violated his personal code of conduct, one that probably had its roots right here on this extremely authentic-looking ranch and in all the John Wayne movies he'd memorized.

Arriving unannounced with a small overnight case in the passenger seat was cheeky. She planned to leave it there and see what happened after she knocked on the door, but in movies ranch houses always had spare bedrooms. Staying in the same house as Matt would help the cause, since she didn't expect instant cooperation.

The SUV's tires crunched on a layer of thick gravel as she navigated the circular drive and parked by the front door. Hers was the only vehicle there, but several more were down by a large hip-roofed barn. The Adirondack chairs lined up on the long front porch were empty, but when she stepped out of the car, she heard country music coming from the house. And laughter, both male and female. It seemed she'd arrived in the middle of a party.

Well, that made sense. His folks had probably decided to celebrate his success and ignore the scandal. No wonder he'd wanted to come back to that kind of love and support.

She paused beside the SUV. Her arrival would be about as popular as Maleficent crashing a baby shower. On the other hand, having lots of people around might be a good thing. She was fine with crowds. Growing up with a Hollywood star for a mom, she'd learned to handle herself in any circumstance, no matter how bizarre or awkward.

She was still debating what to do when the front door opened and a redheaded woman came out holding a baby who looked to be about five or six months old. A tall guy tugged on the brim of his cowboy hat as he followed her out and started to close the door.

"I still say she said my name," called someone from inside, someone who sounded a lot like Matt.

Laughing, the cowboy swung the door open again. "You're dreaming, bro!" he called back.

"Aw, come on, Damon." The redhead was busy fiddling with the baby's blanket and obviously hadn't spotted the SUV yet. "Let Uncle Matt have his little fantasy."

"You heard her," the guy named Damon said as he closed the door. "She was saying *ma-ma* like she always does. She—hello, who's this?" He put a protective hand on the woman's shoulder and looked in Geena's direction.

She moved away from the vehicle and came toward them. "My name's Geena Lysander and I'm here to see Matt Forrest, but apparently I'm interrupting a celebration."

"Geena Lysander," the woman said. "Your name came up tonight. Aren't you his PR rep?"

"Yes, and I'm here to discuss—"

"Let me stop you right there, ma'am." The tall cowboy descended the steps. "From what I understand, he's not interested in having any more discussions. He came here to get away from all that, so I'm afraid you've made a trip for nothing. My wife and I can lead you back into town and get you settled in a hotel room, though."

Despite Geena's height, augmented by four-inch heels, she had to look up to meet his determined gaze. Judging from the set of his jaw, he planned to do whatever was necessary to keep her from going up to the front door. Clearly he intended to protect Matt from the likes of her.

As she debated her next move, the door opened again and Matt stepped out holding a pacifier. At first he looked confused by her presence, but gradually his expression hardened into a mask of anger.

She despaired of getting through to him but she had to try. "I realize you're not happy to see me."

"No, ma'am, I'm not."

"But we need to talk."

Instead of responding to her comment, he gestured to the SUV. "Is that your vehicle?"

"Yes. I rented it."

"No worries, bro," Damon said. "We'll lead her back to town and help her find a hotel room."

Matt shook his head. "I appreciate the offer, but this is my deal and I'll handle the problem." He gave the pacifier to the redhead. "Found this on the sofa and thought you might need it. You two head on home with Sophie. I'll grab the keys to the ranch truck and make sure Geena has a place for the night." He glanced over at her. "And a plane reservation in the morning."

"We're not in a rush," Damon said. "We'll hang out here until you fetch the truck keys."

"Listen, you don't have to stand guard over me." Geena glanced toward the baby, who was starting to fuss. "I promise to stay right here while Matt gets those keys. I'm sure you'd like to get home."

"We would. Sophie's hungry." The redhead jiggled the bundle in her arms. "I think you can stand down, cowboy. Geena doesn't look dangerous."

"Okay." Damon faced Geena and touched the brim of his hat in farewell. "Ma'am."

"Bye." She felt wistful as she watched them walk toward the vehicles parked near the barn. She couldn't remember a time when anyone had stood between her and a potential threat. Must be nice.

Chapter Three

Geena had solid brass ones. Matt would give her that much, but nothing else. She'd made it as far as the driveway, but she wasn't coming any closer than that. Once he'd escorted her to a hotel in town, he'd fire her like he should have done yesterday. Then she'd have to fly home because she wouldn't have any reason to hang around.

He stepped inside the house and paused to take a calming breath. Barreling in looking agitated would provoke a bunch of questions. He'd like to do this with as little discussion as possible. He'd already talked about the subject more than he wanted to.

During dinner Phil had asked whether he had publicity folks doing damage control and he'd described his meeting with Geena. He wasn't surprised that Damon had been ready to escort her straight back to town, but that wasn't his responsibility or Phil's.

The living room furniture had been moved aside for

dancing, and now that Damon and Phil had left, only four people occupied the floor. Cade and Lexi were teaching some elaborate new move to Herb and Rosie. Matt hated to break that up, but it couldn't be helped.

As he approached the group, Cade glanced at him. "How about you partner with Lexi? I know this already."

"I'd be glad to, but I have a little errand to run. Can I borrow the ranch truck for a couple of hours?"

Herb looked puzzled. "Certainly, but I can't imagine what sort of errand you'd have to run at this hour."

"Don't pry," Rosie said. "Maybe he's heard from an old girlfriend."

Cade nudged back his hat. "That would be a trick, since he made such a huge deal about turning off his phone for the next week." His voice softened. "What's up, bro?"

"We have an uninvited guest and I need to escort her back to town."

Rosie blinked. "A woman's outside? Did some star-struck fan follow you here?"

"No, she's not a fan. Look, if it's okay, I'll just get the keys and take care of this."

"Hang on," Cade said. "If it's some damned reporter, let me go out there with you. I'm sure between the two of us we can convince her to get lost."

Matt sighed. He probably should have spit it out in the beginning. "She's not a reporter, either. It's Geena. If I can borrow the truck for a couple of hours, I'll—"

"Great." Cade started for the door. "I'm delighted she's here and she's not going anywhere until I've told her ex-actly what I think of how she treated you."

"No!" Matt blocked Cade's progress. "Nobody's going out there except me. All I need is the keys to the truck. She doesn't know the area so I feel an obligation to make sure she gets back to town okay and has a hotel room. Then I'll make damn sure she knows that she has to leave in the morning."

"Matt." Rosie sent him a look of reproach. "The woman traveled all the way from Los Angeles to see you. I realize you're annoyed with her, but shooing her away after she's made that kind of effort isn't good manners."

He stared at his foster mother. "She showed up uninvited. That isn't good manners, either."

"True, but two wrongs don't make a right. Sending her back where she came from might give you temporary satisfaction, but it's not the gracious thing to do."

"But—"

"Is she an evil person?"

"No."

"Has she deliberately harmed you in any way?"

Matt sighed. He'd lived with Rosie long enough to know where this was going. "No."

"Then you need to take the high road, son. Invite her to join us and I'll offer to put her up."

Every instinct told him that this was a bad idea. "I don't want her here, Mom." He clenched both fists. "Whatever nastiness happened in LA stays in LA. I don't want you and Dad involved. Or anyone in my family, for that matter."

Rosie studied him for a moment. "I understand that and I appreciate your desire to protect us. That's very gallant. I can tell you're very angry that she's come here, but let's think about why she did. Her job is to make you look good, right?"

"Supposedly, but I don't like her plan or the fact she came to my home uninvited. I'm going to fire her."

"Do you have a replacement lined up?"

"Not yet."

"Considering you need a PR person to guide you through this incident, you might want to hold off ditching the one you have. I agree that you shouldn't apologize for something you didn't do, but she's on your turf now." Rosie smiled. "You don't agree with her plan for handling things, but now you have a golden opportunity to change her mind."

Cade nodded, a gleam in his eyes. "And I have a golden opportunity to give her a piece of mine. Yeah, let's invite her in. Can't wait."

"Cade Gallagher." Rosie pinned him with her gaze. "You will not ambush someone who's a guest in this house. In fact, I'm going out there to issue the invitation myself. You boys stay right here. And once she walks through that door, you'll be on your best behavior with her at all times. Is that clear?"

"Yes, ma'am," Matt and Cade said in unison.

Lexi's muffled snort was the only sound in the room as Rosie turned and left.

Geena reasoned that she hadn't completely lost out. Matt was enough of a gentleman to make sure she found her way back to Sheridan and that she had a place to stay. While she could handle everything herself, she'd accept his help because it would give her a chance to accomplish what she'd come for.

Sometime during their interaction she'd apologize for assuming he'd accosted Briana. Then she'd make her case for having him come back to repair the damage to his reputation. Grabbing a few moments on the fly wasn't ideal, but at least her trip wouldn't be completely wasted.

God, he'd been angry, so angry that his blue eyes had glittered like a pair of Fourth of July sparklers. The effect had been thrilling, actually, seeing him go into protector mode concerning his home and family. Now wasn't a good time to think about it, but that cowboy turned her on.

When the front door opened she expected him to come out bringing all his Matt Forrestness with him.

Instead, a plump woman with blond hair walked out on the porch and down the steps. She approached and held out her hand. "Hello, Geena. I'm Rosie Padgett, Matt's foster mom."

"Foster mom?" Geena heard herself and cringed. "Sorry, that was rude." She accepted Rosie's firm hand-shake. "It's just that from the way Matt talked about you, I thought he was your son."

"He is. They all are. Many years ago Herb and I started taking in boys with nowhere else to go. Most of them ended up calling us Mom and Dad, which pleases us no end. We couldn't have kids of our own and now we're blessed with a huge family. We love it."

"Wow. So this ranch used to be a foster home?"

"Sure did, although once again, the boys usually dropped the word *foster* after they'd been here awhile. The ranch was just home."

"That's wonderful." She was beginning to realize how little she knew about Matt. But she doubted Rosie had walked out here to give her a quick history lesson.

"It has been. Listen, I know you've had a long trip. I'll bet you could use some food and something to drink. Why don't you come in?"

Whoa. Talk about falling down the rabbit hole. "Uh, because Matt doesn't want me to?"

"You're right, he doesn't. He's embarrassed about the mess with Briana Danvers and hates how it's affected his life. He made the trip without going back to his apart-ment because he didn't want to be waylaid. He asked me to shop for him today so he'd have a few clothes and some toiletries."

"Poor guy."

"He's hurting, that's for sure. And he doesn't want any of it touching his family." Rosie paused. "But unless you have paparazzi hiding in your SUV, I can't imagine how bringing you inside would involve us in the scandal."

"I promise I'm not dragging a gaggle of reporters behind me. Sheridan isn't the easiest place in the world to access by air. Matt's not a big enough story to warrant suffering through long layovers and tiny planes."

Rosie laughed. "I love that about this town. But in spite of the inconvenience, here you are."

"Because I really have to talk to him."

"I'm sure you do. Just because Matt doesn't go online doesn't mean I haven't. I've sent that woman an email letting her know what I think of her shenanigans, not that she'll ever see it."

"No, she probably won't. I'm sure her PR people filter out the negative ones. I do the same for my clients. If I thought this would go away I'd ignore her, but she's escalated the attack. That's why I need to discuss it with Matt."

"Then let's make that happen. You're lucky we were having a party or we all might have been in bed."

"Oh! I didn't think of that!"

"I'll bet nobody goes to bed at ten in Los Angeles."

"Not anyone I know. Plus it's an hour earlier there. I forgot about the time change, which isn't like me. I apologize."

"As it turns out, it doesn't matter. But I should warn you that ranch folks get up at dawn so we don't tend to be night owls unless it's a special occasion."

"Then I won't stay long. And I really don't need someone to lead me back to town and find me a hotel. I can manage."

"No reason for you to do that. We have plenty of room."

Geena was stunned. "You're suggesting I stay here?"

"I am."

"I don't think that's a good idea."

"Actually, it's a fine idea. I assume you have a bag with you?"

"Yes, but—"

"Then let's get it." Rosie started toward the SUV.

"Wait a minute. Matt will hit the roof. I knew he'd be upset but I had no idea how upset. After I talk with him I'll drive into town like he suggested. I don't want to cause problems."

"Trust me, there will be no problems."

"You're sure?"

"Absolutely sure." Rosie opened the passenger door and reached for the overnight bag.

"Oh, no, let me get it." Geena edged her out of the way. "It's bad enough that I arrived unannounced and uninvited. I won't have you schlepping my luggage." She pulled out the small carry-on and closed the door.

"The way I figure it," Rosie said as they started back toward the porch, "you came unannounced because you had to. If you'd told Matt, he would have met you at the airport and sent you right back."

"Guaranteed."

"I realize there's a crisis here, and it's a shame you and Matt don't see eye-to-eye on how it should be managed."

"Yes, it is."

"Just so you're clear on my position, I agree with him that he shouldn't have to make a public apology. He didn't do anything wrong."

"I know that now." Geena lifted her bag so it would clear the steps. "It's one of the things I want to tell him."

Rosie glanced over, her expression eager. "You have proof?"

"Unfortunately not. But when I started thinking about what a gentleman he is, I knew he wouldn't have deliberately embarrassed a woman in public."

"Ah. That's a good start. You're beginning to see who he is under the pretty packaging."

Geena choked on a laugh. "Excuse me?"

"Don't tell me you haven't noticed that he's a beautiful young man, because I won't believe you."

"Okay, I've noticed."

"I'm sure that Briana noticed, too. I have a feeling we don't have the whole story, but like you said, Matt's a gentleman. We might have to get the info out of Cade."

"Cade?"

"One of Matt's brothers. He's inside with his fiancée, Lexi, so you'll get to meet both of them, plus my husband, Herb. This is all working out for the best." She opened the door. "After you."

A knot of anxiety settled in Geena's stomach as she walked into the living room carrying her overnight bag. Sure, she was good at handling awkward situations in the world of glitz and glamour. Somehow it was easier when a large number of the participants had an agenda, often a self-serving one.

She hadn't spent much time around people who weren't jockeying for a spot on the next rung up, people who got up at dawn to feed the chickens or whatever it was they found to do at that hour. She'd never set foot on an honest-to-God ranch, let alone a ranch that used to be a foster home.

Had she ever known someone who'd been a foster kid?

If so, they hadn't told her about it. Matt hadn't told her, either. He'd obviously considered it private information and she respected that.

The comfy-looking living room furniture had been shoved against the wall, probably to create a dance floor. Even without a fire in the fireplace, the room had a cozy, lived-in feel. She could imagine how much it would appeal to a homeless boy.

The good-looking, dark-haired cowboy standing next to a woman with short brown curls had to be Cade, the one most likely to have the inside scoop on what had gone down between Matt and Briana. The woman must be Lexi, who fit right into the casual setting in her jeans, boots and long-sleeved yellow T-shirt.

Cade wore a cowboy hat indoors, like Matt always did. Apparently that was the custom around here, although the older gentleman wasn't wearing one. She pegged him as Herb, Rosie's husband.

For one awful moment there was total silence in the room. It made her realize that the heels, nifty black jacket and pencil skirt she'd worn on the plane were out of place on a working ranch, but she didn't own Western wear and she'd wanted to look professional.

Matt was the first to move. "Let me take that." He came forward and divested her of the bag.

"Thank you."

He gave her a curt nod. "You're welcome. Mom, where should I put it?"

"The green bedroom's all made up."

"Right." He disappeared down a hallway.

"Hi, Geena." Lexi walked over to shake her hand. "I'm Lexi Simmons and this is my fiancé, Cade Gallagher."

Cade touched the brim of his hat. "Ma'am." The greeting, polite but with no warmth, was identical to the fare-well Damon had given her a while ago.

"I'm Herb, Rosie's husband." The wiry guy had kind eyes and a firm grip. "Welcome to Thunder Mountain."

"Thank you." She swallowed a lump of nervousness. "I'm glad to be here."

"And we're pleased to have you." Rosie said it as if daring anyone to contradict her.

Geena couldn't remember when she'd felt less sure of herself. "Look, you were all doing something before I barged in here, so please continue."

"We were working on a dance step," Lexi said. "I don't suppose you'd want to learn—"

"Why not?" Geena nudged off her heels and put them in a corner.

"Before you get into that," Rosie said, "are you hungry? Can I make you a sandwich?"

"I'm starving." Her hunger pangs wouldn't allow her to say anything but the truth. "I headed out here as soon as I picked up the rental." Her gaze swept the room. "I knew it was late, although I didn't realize how late. I apologize for that."

"Then let me fix you something. Any issues? Food allergies?"

"I'll be grateful for anything, but let me make it myself. I don't expect to be waited on."

Rosie waved her off. "Tomorrow I'll put you to work, but tonight relax and enjoy yourself. What do you want to drink?"

"Water, please."

"That's it? How about an adult beverage?"

Geena considered where she was and what they might have on hand. Under the circumstances, alcohol would be welcome. "A beer would be great."

Matt came back at that moment. "I'll get it. You can sample my brother's brew." He said it with enormous pride before leaving the room.

"Cade?" She glanced to him. "You make beer?"

"Oh, no, not me. That would be Finn O'Roarke. He has a microbrewery in Seattle. Very successful." His gaze issued a challenge. "We have a lot of talent in the brotherhood. Brewers, lawyers, horse trainers, firefighters. You name it, we got it."

"Impressive. You called it a *brotherhood*. What's that all about?"

"Nothing." Matt arrived and handed her an open bottle of beer and a glass before turning to glare at Cade. "Absolutely nothing."

"Yeah." Cade exchanged a glance with Matt. "Just a figure of speech. Not important."

Geena didn't push it, but her PR instincts were telling her that if Matt belonged to a group calling themselves *the brotherhood*, she needed to pay attention. A public apology for the kiss didn't interest her anymore, now that she knew Matt would have to lie in order to make one. But apparently he had a rich tradition of family and loyalty.

She could work the heck out of that angle. Fans would love to know that he was part of a close-knit group of foster brothers who'd grown up on a working ranch. Talk about wholesome. She wasn't sure what would be the best promo vehicle to get the story out, but it probably didn't matter. Judging from his reaction so far, he'd never let that story be told.

Chapter Four

Matt hadn't wanted Geena anywhere near his family, and yet here she was, and damned if she didn't fit in much better than he could have predicted. Barefoot and wearing a tight skirt that restricted her movements, she still managed to execute the dance moves Cade and Lexi taught her.

Worse yet, she was very appealing doing it. No, not just appealing. The glasses paired with her excellent sense of rhythm created a dynamite combination of brains and sexy moves.

In the months he'd known Geena he'd had many inappropriate thoughts about her, even though mostly she'd sat behind her desk while they talked. She wasn't behind her desk now, and every time she wiggled her hips, his johnson gave a twitch in response.

She was making inroads with his family members, too. His mom had defected immediately and he wanted to know what those two had talked about outside. Lexi and Herb had both warmed to her, as well. Cade had been a holdout for quite a while, but her willingness to learn the new dance step was slowly winning him over.

Then Rosie brought in Geena's sandwich and everyone took a break. Matt fetched some chips and more of Finn's beer from the fridge in the rec room. That was another thing. Earlier, Geena had put down the glass he'd brought her and was drinking from the bottle like everyone else. It was a small thing, but small things added up. She was easy to be with.

While Geena ate, the group lounged on the displaced furniture and talked about Thunder Mountain Academy. Matt hadn't wanted Geena to know anything about that, either, but it was a logical topic because several chores were in the works during this break between sessions.

Geena seemed fascinated by every aspect of the program. Matt's family softened even more in response to her enthusiasm. It wasn't artificial enthusiasm, either. That was a quality he'd liked about her from the beginning. Hollywood was crawling with fakes, but Geena never pretended to be something she wasn't.

Perfect example—she could have arrived all duded up in an effort to present herself as a cowgirl. Instead, she'd worn the type of clothes he'd always seen her in. This was his first glimpse of her bare toes, however. She'd propped her feet up on the coffee table and he couldn't help noticing her sea-blue polish. And her delicate ankles and shapely calves.

He looked away. The situation was complicated enough already.

"Do you ride?" Lexi asked her.

"I don't know the first thing about horses." Geena finished off her sandwich. "I take that back. I know what a Clydesdale is because I've seen the commercials. My hat's off to whoever came up with the idea of using them to market beer."

Lexi smiled. "Yeah, everybody loves those big ol' horses, me included. I just thought you might be a rider since you're so interested in the academy."

"I wouldn't mind trying it sometime, but I'd be a total beginner."

"Want to try it while you're here?"

Matt bit back a groan. That was so Lexi, eager to introduce the uninitiated to the wonders of horseback riding. That was why she was such a good teacher, but in this case he wished she'd zip her lip.

"I'd love to, but all I brought to wear was stuff like this." Geena gestured to her skirt and jacket.

"I can find you some clothes and boots," Rosie said. "I've stocked up on spare items for the students."

"I don't know. I'm pretty tall."

"So are some of the girls we get here. I try to be prepared when pants get ripped and kids come with expensive boots that shouldn't be worn to muck out stalls."

"So they have to be financially well-off to attend?"

"At first they did." Herb hadn't spoken much but this was a favorite topic of his. "We're working on changing that. We already have one scholarship opportunity thanks to Ben Radcliffe, a local saddle maker who conducts a class every semester. We're looking for more sponsors. There are plenty of kids who would benefit but don't have the tuition."

"I'll offer a scholarship," Matt said. "I can probably handle two or three if the money stays good. I can't believe I haven't thought of it before."

"That's brilliant." Geena smiled. "Too bad we can't

get it organized this week because a picture of you with
a recipient would be—"

"Not happening." Matt gazed at her and wished they
didn't always have to be on opposite sides of this particular fence. But she didn't seem to get his need for privacy.
Maybe he'd have to fire her, after all. "The scholarships
would be anonymous."

She frowned. "You'd be throwing away a great PR opportunity if you do that."

"And keeping my personal life separate from my public one. That's always been important to me, but after
what happened two days ago, it's critical."

Her shoulders slumped. "That makes it tough to do
my job."

"I know. But that's the way it has to be."

"It's okay. I'll think of something else. I—" She stifled
a yawn. "Sorry. It's been a long day. I guess the beer and
food made me sleepy."

"I'm sure you're exhausted." Rosie switched into
mothering mode. "You should get some rest. I know what
I said about getting up at dawn, but you don't have to."

"Oh, no, I want to." She glanced at the grandfather
clock in the corner. "When is dawn, anyway?"

That got a laugh. Even Matt couldn't help grinning.
She was such a city girl. But she was also game for anything, which meant she'd get along fine in this new setting. Resilience was a valued commodity around here.

"It's around five fifteen," his dad said.

Her eyes widened. "That early?"

"But you don't have to get up then," Herb continued.
"We do because the horses need to be fed and turned out
to pasture. Rosie likes to organize the food for breakfast,
but we don't eat until after six, so you'll have some extra
time to ease into the day."

"Well, um, I never eat breakfast."

"You'll want to eat this one." Lexi glanced over at Cade. "Nobody fixes a better breakfast than Rosie. Am I right?"

"Except for you, sweetheart."

"Nice try, Gallagher." Lexi gave him an affectionate nudge. "Flattery will get you nowhere. You're still responsible for fifty percent of the cooking at our house."

Cade sighed. "But I'm still no good at it."

"You're improving. That's what's important."

"You're both invited down here in the morning, though," Rosie said. "It's not every day we see Matt at the breakfast table. But Geena, you're excused. I'll have the coffeepot on until at least eight, so if that's all you need, come in and help yourself. We don't force food on anyone."

"I'll be there at six and I'd love to have your breakfast. I'll also get up at dawn to watch Herb feed the horses. I've never seen anybody do that except in the movies."

Herb smiled. "It's not all that exciting."

"Maybe not to you, because you do it every day. Me, I get up, get dressed, hit the drive-through at Starbucks and head to my office. Feeding horses at five thirty in the morning is exotic."

"Then you're welcome to show up at dawn."

"Great. Thank you." She turned to Matt. "Listen, before I toddle off to bed, can I have a word with you?"

His mom stood. "We can leave you two alone so you can talk."

"Heavens, no! You're all settled in. Matt and I will step out onto the porch." She glanced at him. "Okay with you?"

"Sure." He shouldn't have had that last beer. He was feeling way too mellow and he had to stay sharp. But refusing to have a chat on the porch would seem rude and his mom would call him on it.

Geena walked out there barefoot and that charmed him. He didn't want to be charmed any more than he wanted to have sexy thoughts about her. He needed to be tough and uncompromising as he sought to protect his family from…he was no longer clear what that was. He hadn't wanted any part of his life in LA to intrude on his life here, and yet Geena had inserted herself into his inner circle and the sky hadn't fallen.

After he closed the door, she turned and leaned her slim hips against the porch railing. She looked tired, which was understandable. The trip from California was taxing, especially for someone who wasn't used to long layovers, little planes and country roads. She'd probably fare better traveling to New York or London than making her way to Sheridan, Wyoming, home to folks who climbed out of bed at the crack of dawn.

He found a spot to lean against the front wall of the house so they'd both be standing. He suspected she hadn't taken one of the Adirondack chairs because she doubted she'd have the energy to pull herself back out of it. A cricket chirped nearby and a breeze stirred the tall pines not far from the house.

Geena sighed. "This is nice."

"Yeah." A little too nice. Even though his family was just beyond that door, he knew they wouldn't come out. They understood this was private

That left him with a feeling of intimacy he'd never experienced with Geena. They were truly alone for the first time since she'd arrived. He began thinking about how she'd feel in his arms and how her lips would taste. Did she have a lover? After watching her dance, he could easily imagine that she did.

She closed her eyes and took a deep breath. Apparently she was in no rush to begin the conversation, but unless they started talking he would continue with his inappropriate thoughts. If he walked over and kissed her, would she resist? Or would she part her lips and invite him in?

Finally he had to say something, anything, to keep him from acting on his fantasy. "You picked up that dance step pretty fast."

She opened her eyes and smiled. "Thanks. I should be able to, after fifteen years of ballet and tap."

He liked having another key to her personality. "When was this?"

"My mother enrolled me when I was three. Voice and acting lessons, too, so I'd be a triple threat. She named me after Geena Davis. I was supposed to be a star."

"I didn't know that." Not surprising. What he didn't know about Geena was seriously out of proportion to what he did know. "What happened?"

"A common story." She gave a little shrug. "I can dance and sing okay but I have no talent for acting. If I'd been movie-star beautiful that might have made up for my bad acting, but I'm not."

"I think you look nice." That just popped out. Hadn't meant to say it *at all*.

"Thanks." She smiled and took off her glasses to polish them. "But I would have had to be a real knockout to succeed. Luckily, along the way I discovered that supporting the careers of other actors makes me happy. I've hung out with them all my life, so opening a PR business was a no-brainer. Mom wasn't too pleased with my decision, but she eventually came to grips with it."

"That's good." He sometimes wondered if the woman who'd given birth to him would come out of the woodwork and claim his success was all because of her. "I'll have to admit that I've never seen one of your mother's movies."

"Sad to say, they were forgettable. She blames the scripts and the directing. Personally, I think she's better at creating drama offscreen than on. I was afraid she'd end up with her own reality TV show, but fortunately we were all spared that. She finally gave up trying to draw attention to herself and moved to Italy."

He couldn't get a bead on whether she loved her mother or tolerated her. "Is that a good thing?"

"To be honest, it's a relief. She's exhausting to be around."

"Almost as bad as a day spent trying to get to Sheridan, huh?"

"In retrospect, it wasn't so terrible." She put her glasses back on and pushed away from the railing. "Anyway, I didn't want to go to bed without talking to you about something."

Ah, yes, bedtime. Between the dancing, the beer and finally being alone with her, he was losing the battle with his sexual attraction. She'd be in the bedroom next to his and that would make falling asleep a challenge. When he'd arrived, his mom had asked him if he wanted to bunk in one of the cabins for nostalgia's sake. Knowing he'd be interfering with the cleaning and preparations for the summer school kids, he'd decided not to.

Now he wished he'd opted for the cabin. His mom had obviously accepted Geena, and for all he knew Rosie had put them adjacent to each other on purpose. It would be like her to think it served him right for being so unwelcoming. He wasn't feeling unwelcoming anymore. Life had been so much simpler when he'd thought of Geena as the enemy instead of a sexy woman who might or might not be seeing someone.

She took another deep breath, which strained the buttons on her jacket.

He'd been fascinated by that jacket all evening. It revealed a slight bit of cleavage, and near as he could tell, she wore nothing but a bra or a camisole underneath. She didn't really need a blouse because the jacket provided decent coverage, but he'd thought about what he'd see if he unfastened the buttons.

He needed to get off this train of thought and buy a ticket on another one. Her outfit was no more seductive than any she'd worn in meetings they'd had regarding his career. But those meetings had taken place in her office and not during a cool evening when a silky breeze wafted over them bringing the scent of wild grasses and pine trees.

"You're upset because I invaded your territory." Her voice was soft and weary.

"That did upset me." He wasn't angry now but chose not to say that.

"If I'd only hoped to convince you to go along with my original plan, then coming here would have been obnoxious, but that's not why I booked those flights."

"Then why did you?"

"First of all, I realized that Briana isn't going to let go of this. If you haven't gone online then you might not know, but she's come up with a cutesy slogan and she's plastering it everywhere."

Okay, this topic might effectively cool his jets. "I'm afraid to ask what it is."

"Run, Forrest, run."

"Oh, for God's sake." Just as Geena had predicted, he'd been branded a coward. "That's sickening."

"I agree, but the plain truth is that you're not going to be able to ride this one out. She's portraying your silence and your absence as an admission of guilt and she's spinning stories about how you lusted after her during the filming of *Preston's Revenge*."

His stomach pitched. "That's a damned lie." So much for the seductive ambiance of the porch.

"I know it is."

"How?" Their discussion in her office came back to him along with the anger he'd felt at being wrongly accused. "You weren't there."

"No, but I—"

"Geena, you've always been a straight shooter before. Please don't twist yourself into a pretzel because you like my family and you want to smooth things over."

Her chin lifted and she met his gaze. "That is *not* the case and I resent your implication."

"And I'm suspicious of your sudden turnaround! How can you be so sure I'm telling the truth?" He took a step closer. "Maybe I spent every available moment on location trying to seduce her while she valiantly fought me off."

A flame burned in her eyes, which were definitely green, like he'd thought. "I'm trying to apologize, damn it. You didn't try to seduce her and you didn't kiss her outside that café. A gentleman wouldn't do those things. I allowed the photo to convince me of something I should have known wasn't true. But I finally figured it out."

This was turning into an effing roller coaster. "So you've decided I'm a gentleman?"

"I didn't just *decide*. You've demonstrated it from the beginning with your *yes, ma'am* behavior and your respect for everyone in my office, including the cleaning lady. She made a point of telling me that you showed up late one afternoon after we'd all left and you offered to carry out the trash."

"Who wouldn't?"

"Most people, Matt. So obviously you didn't initiate that embarrassing scene in Burbank and you didn't hit on her during the filming. It doesn't fit your profile. It's not you."

"God, that makes me happy. You can't imagine how happy." Vindicated. Damn, that felt good.

"Because I hadn't put that together, I insulted your sense of honor. No wonder you stomped out of my office. I'm surprised you didn't end our business relationship."

He smiled. "That was my original goal when I thought I'd be escorting you back to town. First I'd get you a hotel room and then I'd fire you."

"Good thing Rosie asked me to stay, huh?"

"I wasn't in favor of that, either."

"Yeah, she robbed you of your chance to fire me." She gazed at him with an expression that bordered on tenderness. "You can still do that if you want, although Rosie seems to think you need me."

The warmth in her eyes brought him right back to the thoughts he'd been having until the discussion turned ugly. Drawn by that warmth, he drifted closer, within touching distance. "I probably do need you. I have no idea how to deal with this fiasco. Anyway, I can't fire you with Rosie around. She'd give me hell for it. The others wouldn't like it, either. You made some friends in there."

"Nice to know." For some reason her glasses misted up. She took them off. "How about out here?"

He was a goner. "I've always liked you. That's why it bothered me so much that you believed I'd caused that scene."

"I've always liked you, too." She moistened her lips. "That's all the more reason I should have stopped to think before I jumped to conclusions."

The gesture caught his attention and he noticed her lipstick had worn off. He'd never seen her without it. Because of that, the natural pink of her bare lips was more arousing than if she'd stripped naked. The sweep of her tongue had left her mouth with a satin sheen that begged to be savored.

"Rosie thinks there's more to it."

"More to what?" While he'd been imagining how she'd taste, he'd lost track of the conversation. Lifting his gaze, he saw awareness in her expression and his heart pounded in anticipation. She knew what he wanted. Judging from the way she was looking at him, she wasn't opposed.

"The kissing incident." Her breathing quickened. "She doesn't think we have all the facts and you won't make those public because you're too much of a gentleman. I'm inclined to agree. There are lines you won't cross."

He searched her expression. "Apparently you admire that."

"I do."

"Then maybe we should head inside."

She swallowed. "We should?"

"Uh-huh. I'm guessing you already have someone in your life."

"Actually, I don't." Her voice was laced with tension. "Why do you want that information?"

"Because I'm two seconds away from kissing you and I'd hate to ruin my sterling reputation."

Color bloomed in her cheeks. "I promise your reputation's safe with me."

Chapter Five

Being kissed by Matt Forrest was the last thing in the world Geena had expected to happen to her in Wyoming. Being trampled by a moose had seemed far more likely, or being eaten by a grizzly bear.

But kicking off her shoes to learn Cade's new dance step had felt like kicking off the traces. She'd been under strain, too, and dancing plus a bottle of beer had relaxed her. She'd forgotten to be so darned professional, and like any good actor, Matt had taken his cue.

Licking her lips had been an innocent and unplanned move, but when those electric-blue eyes had focused on her mouth, game over. A powerful wave of lust had swept her brain clean of everything but the need to kiss and be kissed by the hottest cowboy she'd ever known.

He took off his hat and laid it on a chair. Then he reached for her. Cupping her face in both hands, he gazed into her eyes. "I've thought about doing this for months. How about you?"

She was so excited she could barely breathe. "Never crossed my mind." Sliding her hands up the soft cotton of his T-shirt, she felt the solid muscles underneath. The tactile thrill was more delicious than she could have possibly imagined.

"You're not attracted to me? I could have sworn—"

"I didn't say that." She rubbed her hands across his chest because she couldn't help herself.

"So you are attracted to me."

"Uh-huh." She began a slow massage and watched his eyes darken to navy.

"I should've asked you out. I almost did."

"What stopped you?"

His gaze searched hers. "I thought it might be unprofessional."

"And people talk."

"Tell me about it." He tipped her head back. "But tonight, after watching you dance, I don't really care."

"I don't much care, either." Her pulse raced as she anticipated the touch of his mouth. It looked sexy on screen but ten times more kissable in real life.

He leaned closer. "Glad to hear it." And he captured her mouth.

When he did, the takeover was complete. She leaned into him and ran up the white flag without firing a single shot. No doubt the guy had many talents or he wouldn't be finding success in the competitive film industry. But he could give a master course in the art of mouth-to-mouth contact.

He made the connection effortlessly, as if he'd already mapped the contours of her lips. And once he settled in, heaven help her. The movements of his mouth and tongue were subtle yet devastating. He teased, he sucked and he nibbled until she was ready to rip her clothes off because she wanted his brand of intense pleasure *everywhere*.

That tortured moan had come from her. Her panties were damp and she was clinging to him for dear life. Dimly she remembered they were on the porch of his parents' house and nothing she longed for could happen here.

Gasping in reaction, she struggled out of his arms and backed away. "You should have a license for that mouth."

His chuckle was low and sexy, although he was breathing hard, too. "You were giving as good as you got, lady."

"Okay, Forrest, the gloves are off. We're officially hot for each other."

"I noticed." He dragged in air. "I'm quick that way."

She pressed a hand against her thumping heart. "I'm… I don't know what's supposed to happen next. This is still highly unprofessional."

"Like I said, I don't care anymore."

"Honestly, neither do I. But I'm a guest in your parents' home. I'm not planning to embarrass either me or them."

"We won't." He retrieved his hat and settled it on his head. "But this isn't over."

"I hope not, but I'm a stranger in a strange land. I need a guide."

"Right." He paused. "The first thing you should know is that Mom put you in the room next to mine."

"Oh, geez."

"That might have been an accident but it might not. She could have done it because she was upset with me for being a jerk when you arrived. But I also feel obliged to warn you that when it comes to her boys, she's a matchmaker."

Geena gulped. "But she barely knows me."

"And that may not figure into her thinking at all, but

I might have mentioned you a few times on the phone. That could be enough to set her in motion."

"Oh." Knowing he'd talked to Rosie about her was flattering but she wasn't crazy about being the target of a matchmaking scheme, even if the proposed match was between her and Mr. Hotter-than-a-jalapeño.

"I'm really not sure what she's thinking. But she knows that you want the best for me, which is a big deal for her. I'm sure she appreciates your interest in the academy, too. You've made a good first impression."

"I'm glad, but let me be clear. After that dynamite kiss I'm eager to get even friendlier, but it's way too early to be picking out china patterns. Considering my background, I'm not sure that will ever be in the cards."

"I'll call your background and raise you mine. Not to mention the lousy odds of any Hollywood couple lasting more than a few years."

She grimaced. "Isn't that the truth? But it's good that we're on the same page, even if your foster mom has other ideas."

"You know, I shouldn't assume she wants to marry me off just because she has that reputation with her boys. She knows how important my career is, how much I want to make it as an actor. So forget what I said. For sure she wants us to get along for our mutual benefit, but that might be the extent of it."

"Even though she put us in adjoining rooms?"

"Yeah, she did." He shrugged. "I'm not sure what she had in mind when she did that, but in any case, it won't work for me. I'll take a bedroll down to the barn."

"Is that a veiled invitation to join you there?"

"No, ma'am, it isn't."

"Getting it on in the barn has a certain ring to it."

"Been there, but with country girls. I'm not subjecting you to that."

She looked him in the eye. "What if I want to be subjected to it?"

His reaction was all she could have hoped for. His eyes darkened and his chest heaved. But he didn't give in. "Maybe before you leave, but not the first time. For all you know you're allergic to hay. Or horses. Hear me out on this and don't get crazy on me."

"I'm already crazy, and it's your fault because you kiss like no man I've ever known."

"So I've been told."

She groaned. "You could have warned me! I wasn't the least bit prepared!"

"Oh, Geena." Moving closer, he pulled her into his arms. "We've started this thing between us and I promise we'll finish it. I bought a ranch, and I'm thinking that maybe we—"

"A ranch? A whole ranch?"

"I'm hoping it's a whole ranch. I'd hate like hell to buy half a ranch."

That made her laugh. "So, where is it?"

"Right down the road." He rubbed the small of her back. "I vaguely remember the place from when I lived at Thunder Mountain but I've never been inside the house. Rosie and Herb looked it over for me and said it was a good buy, although it needs work. I want to go see it tomorrow, so if you'd like to ride along, you'd be most welcome."

"I'm way ahead of you. I accept your invitation to visit your ranch."

"Excellent."

"Now, let me go or I'm liable to drag you into my SUV and drive you over there tonight."

He backed away. "You're good for my ego."

"You ain't seen nothin' yet."

His gaze swept over her. "We need to get back inside before I change my mind about the barn."

"I'm not allergic to hay. Or horses. I just remembered that I've been exposed to both at Disneyland. I'm good with goats, too." His laughter made her smile. "Well, I am. They came right up to me wagging their little tails."

"I'll bet they did. But please don't come down to the barn tonight. It's not an appropriate venue for what I have in mind, and anyway, I didn't anticipate this so I don't have supplies."

Supplies. He really was a gentleman. "Okay. I'll respect your wishes." She put on her glasses and tucked a few strands of hair back into place.

"Besides, you should get a good night's sleep after what you've been through today."

"What about you, bedding down in the barn? Surely you won't get a good night's sleep."

"Actually, I will. I love listening to the horses moving around in their stalls, munching on hay, making snuffling sounds. It's comforting. I used to do it all the time when I lived here. I'd pretend I was John Wayne, banished to the barn by Maureen O'Hara." He took a deep breath. "Ready to go in?"

"Do I have a choice?" Now she wished that nature had given her red hair so she could be Maureen O'Hara to his John Wayne.

He shook his head. "We've already been out here long enough to raise suspicion. And you must be exhausted."

"I used to be." She glanced at him. "But thanks to you, I'm all revved up again."

"Sorry about that."

"Are you really?"

He grinned. "No, ma'am."

"I didn't think so. When I first arrived and saw your face, I thought I'd made a terrible mistake by coming here. But it wasn't a mistake, was it?"

He met her gaze and his eyes crinkled with laughter. "If it was, I hope you keep on makin' 'em."

Dear Lord, his kiss had been enough to seduce her without adding country charm to the mix. Apparently being in this setting highlighted all his considerable attributes. She could hardly wait for tomorrow's trip to his ranch so she could sample every one of them.

The woman was hotter than the griddle at a Chamber of Commerce pancake breakfast. Matt was forced to call on his acting skills in order to appear in control as he walked back into the living room with Geena. He was congratulating himself on his smooth entrance when he tripped over a footstool and barely saved himself from a face-plant.

"I saw that!" Cade smirked at him. "It was totally the stool's fault."

His face heated. "I was…uh…"

"Distracted?" Lexi gave him an innocent smile.

"Poor guy's worried about Briana." Geena's color was high and she avoided looking at him.

"That's the truth." He appreciated her attempt to excuse his clumsiness but he could tell the rest of them weren't buying it. Even his dad, usually the last to catch on, wore a knowing expression.

His mom stood. "Briana's lucky I don't live in her town. Miserable woman." She turned to Geena. "I'm sure you're ready to crash. Let me show you where everything is. Your bathroom's down the hall and the shower has some idiosyncrasies you'll need to know about."

"I appreciate that, because I would love to take a shower before I go to bed."

Great. Now he'd picture her naked in the shower in the bathroom they'd be sharing during this visit.

"I'm going to turn in, myself," his dad said. "See everybody in the morning."

Once all three had left, Matt sank down on the sofa and blew out a breath.

Cade pushed back his hat and gazed at him. "I don't know if it was good or bad, but whatever happened out there sure has you going, bro."

"It was obviously significant," Lexi said. "You're one of the most coordinated guys I know. You took fencing lessons, for God's sake. You don't trip over footstools."

Matt rubbed the back of his neck. "I kissed her."

Cade nodded as if he'd expected to hear that. "Judging from the glazed look in your eyes, she kissed you back."

"Yes."

"Ah." Lexi chuckled. "What a wealth of information is contained in that one little word. So is it okay for the rest of us to like her, now that you're kissing each other? Because we all pretty much do."

"Yeah, sure." He had trouble collecting his thoughts when his brain had been hijacked. "Do you think Mom's matchmaking?"

"Good question." Cade scratched his chin where the shadow of a beard was starting to show. "Normally I would say yes, but I don't get that vibe from her. We talked about Geena while you two were out there smooching, but—"

"It was *one* kiss."

"Then it must have been a dandy." Cade studied him. "I'm happy for you."

"Me, too," Lexi said. "Earlier tonight, before she

showed up, I got the impression from the conversation that you haven't been dating anyone in the past six months or so."

"I haven't. After auditioning for every commercial in the world, it seemed, I was finally in demand, which was great but kept me really busy. Then this bonanza hit, but a role like that takes a hell of a lot of prep work."

"I'll bet." Compassion shone in her eyes. "You looked strung out when you arrived, but you're a lot perkier after stealing a kiss from your PR rep."

"As well you should be," Cade said. "Geena's great. I regret the nasty things I said about her before."

"But you don't think Mom's up to her usual tricks?"

"I don't think so." Cade turned toward Lexi. "Do you?"

"Why do I get the feeling you three are talking about me?" Rosie walked into the living room looking more amused than upset.

"Guilty." Lexi spoke up immediately. "We were wondering if you were matchmaking between Geena and Matt."

"I'm not." Rosie claimed her favorite chair before gazing at him. "I came out to tell you that I moved her to the room down by us. That way she can have her own bathroom." She paused. "And you won't be neighbors."

He was very likely blushing. "Okay." He calculated whether the added distance would help him sleep any better. Probably not.

"Should've done that in the first place, but I was feeling a little put out with you, so I thought it would serve you right to have her next door. I figured sharing a bathroom might force you to be more civil."

Cade snorted. "I don't think that'll be a problem anymore."

"I can see that." She smiled at Matt. "I don't want to torture you, son. Or her, either. She confessed the strong attraction between you two but said she would never take advantage of my hospitality."

"She said that, straight out?" He gaped at her.

"You sound surprised," Lexi said. "Don't you know people tell Rosie everything? I've never met anyone who inspires people to spill their guts the way Rosie does. It's a gift."

"They don't tell me *everything*." Rosie surveyed the group. "For example, nobody has bothered to mention why Briana Danvers orchestrated that photo op. It was clearly planned and executed for a reason. Appears to be the work of an angry woman, if you ask me." She speared Matt with a look. "I'm sure you have noble intentions, but she doesn't deserve considerate treatment after the way she's behaved."

"That's what I said when he—" Cade groaned. "Sorry, Matt."

Rosie nodded as she studied the two of them. "As I suspected, it all came out on the drive from the airport." She turned her attention to Matt. "Well?"

He shook his head. "Sorry, Mom."

"You don't trust me to keep it to myself?"

"Of course I do." He sent a pleading glance in Cade's direction, but Cade only spread his hands in bewilderment.

"Maybe you don't trust *me*," Lexi said.

"I'd trust both of you with my life. Trust isn't the issue."

Rosie leaned forward. "Then what is the issue? I want to help you get out of this mess but I feel handicapped because I don't know the whole story. I assume Geena doesn't know it, either."

"No, she doesn't."

"She probably should. It might be extremely important."

"I can't tell you what happened unless you promise that you won't take any action against Briana."

"Action?" Rosie blinked. "What kind of action would I take?"

"I don't know, but you both have to promise not to try and harm her by word or deed."

"Wow," Lexi said. "This is getting intense. Want us to sign something in blood?"

Matt sighed. "Your word is good enough."

"All right," Rosie said. "Lexi and I promise not to harm that horrible woman." She paused. "Or hire someone to do it for us."

Cade choked on his beer.

Rosie waited until he'd settled down before turning back to Matt. "What happened?"

As Matt described Briana's behavior, his mom grew very still, but her fists clenched and her eyes glittered with an unholy fire.

He finished the story and took a deep breath. "It's safe to say she's after revenge."

Rosie looked at him and her voice sounded deceptively calm. "I could strangle her with my bare hands." The even tone coupled with the ring of certainty was a chilling combination. She didn't get angry often, but when she did everyone knew to take a step back.

He cleared his throat. "Mom, you promised not to—"

"And I won't. She's not worth going to jail for. I wouldn't dirty my hands on that piece of trash. But poor Cliff."

"He's the one I'm protecting, not her."

"Just realize you won't be able to protect him forever.

I doubt you're the first and you won't be the last. He'll find out sooner or later. Probably sooner now that everyone and his dog is online."

"But Matt doesn't want to be the bearer of bad news," Lexi said. "I get that. Cliff Wallace seems like a great guy."

"From what I've read about him, he is." Rosie leaned back in her chair. "But I think he has a weakness for bad women. I should have known this one would be no different. She won't last, but in the meantime, she's caused problems for one of my own." She glanced at Matt. "There must be some way to put a hitch in her giddyup."

"Don't I wish," he said, "but I'm fresh out of ideas."

"We're all too tired to think about this now." His mom stood. "We'll tackle it tomorrow. But thanks for trusting me with the info."

"It wasn't about trust." He got up to give her a goodnight hug. "Cade and I were worried the mama grizzly might fly to LA and do a number on Briana."

"And wouldn't I love to! But I won't." She hugged him back. Then she said good-night to Cade and Lexi before walking back down the hallway.

"I think that went okay," Cade said after she left. "Sorry I slipped up, though."

"No worries." Matt continued to gaze at the darkened hallway as he debated whether his mom's room-juggling trick changed anything. "Once we got into the conversation about Briana, I knew she'd find a way to dig it out of me."

"Like Lexi said, it's her gift." Cade stood and came over to sling an arm around Matt's shoulders. "I notice how you're focused on that hallway and who's sleeping at the end of it."

"Just thinking."

"I know how that goes. I don't want to get all up in your business, but—"

"Yeah, you do." Matt turned to smile at him.

"Let's just say that Mom's maneuver with the room switcheroo is well meant, but I doubt it'll lower your stress level. I suggest an alternate plan. Lexi and I have a comfy sofa you can use tonight. That should keep you out of trouble for the time being."

"And we'd be glad to have you as our guest," Lexi added.

"Thanks, but I think I'll just head down to the barn and make up a bedroll in an empty stall."

Cade nodded. "That works, too. I remember you used to like doing that, getting into your John Wayne persona."

Matt lowered his voice and moved closer to Cade. "Buddy, this is awkward as hell, but I have a problem if things heat up in the next day or two. I don't have—"

"Say no more," Cade murmured.

His color high, Matt glanced over at Lexi. "Don't listen."

"Can't hear a thing."

"Got you covered," Cade said quietly.

"Thanks."

"All righty, then." Cade clapped him on the back. "We'll shove off. See you in the—well, hello, sunshine."

Matt glanced toward the hallway.

Geena stood there rubbing her eyes. Her glossy brown hair tumbled in waves over her shoulders and she wore a bright blue sleep shirt with a Captain America shield on the front. She put on her glasses and peered at them. "Why is everybody still up? I thought we had to be awake at dawn."

"We're in the process of leaving," Cade said. "Why are you up?"

Matt was grateful for Cade's response because he was incapable of making one. His tongue was stuck to the roof of his mouth as he noticed the drape of her sleep shirt and concluded she wasn't wearing a bra. That could mean she didn't have on panties, either. The ends of her hair were still damp from the shower.

"I was thirsty and needed a glass for water."

Lexi started for the kitchen. "I'll get you one. There's a pitcher of cold water in the fridge. You'd probably rather have that."

"Thanks, I would. I'll come with you. I need to know where things are." Her bare feet whispered over the hardwood floor as she followed Lexi.

Matt gazed after her, still at a loss for words. She was supposed to be tucked in her room with the door closed, not out here roaming around in a Captain America sleep shirt with nothing underneath but warm, sensuous, freshly showered woman.

"You poor slob." Cade regarded him with sympathy. "There's no way I could slip you those raincoats tonight. Want us to hang around for a few, make sure she goes back to her designated area?"

"That's okay. I can handle it."

"Yeah, that's what I'm afraid of."

Chapter Six

The hum of conversation in the living room had traveled through the air ducts to Geena's room. She hadn't been able to make out any of it, which had been maddening. For sure she was missing something and it might be important.

She'd been dying to know what they were talking about, specifically what Matt was talking about. What if he'd decided to reveal the backstory that had led to Briana's stunt? Damn it, now she wasn't the least bit sleepy.

She mostly blamed Matt's kiss, although to be fair she was still on California time and she never went to bed this early. But it was after eleven here and people were still in the living room talking, even though Rosie had said they generally weren't night owls. That meant something special was going on and she wanted to know what it was.

When she couldn't stand it another minute, she'd come up with an excuse to go out there. She would have put on a robe, but she'd packed so quickly this morning that she hadn't thought to bring one. The sleep shirt was cotton, opaque and reached to midthigh. It covered everything important and she didn't consider it seductive.

At least, she hadn't until she'd noticed Matt's expression once she put on her glasses. He'd looked as if someone had blinded him with a strobe light.

Sadly, she seemed to have caught the tail end of the party. After Lexi poured her a glass of water from the fridge, the two of them walked back to the living room. Geena had hoped that everyone would sit down and continue the discussion, but although Cade seemed ready to stay, Lexi insisted on leaving.

After they were gone Geena was alone with Matt. She realized that might not be the best combination, considering how Matt was looking at her. She should take her water and go, but she wanted to know what that conversation had been about and she believed in seizing the moment. "Part of the reason I couldn't sleep is that I heard you guys talking out here."

That startled him. "You did?"

"Through the air ducts. But I couldn't understand what you were saying."

"Oh. Yeah, I forgot about the air duct thing. Sorry if we kept you awake." He didn't look particularly sorry. The gleam in his eyes returned.

"If it's private family stuff, then never mind."

"It kind of was." His expression said clearly that he'd like to drop the subject and move on to other things, like maybe kissing.

She wouldn't object, but she had a point to make first. "Matt, if you were giving them the scoop on your history with Briana, then I deserve to hear it, too. We're in this together."

"Nice to know." He took a step closer and there was no mistaking the intent in those blue eyes.

The huskiness in his voice fired her blood and fogged her glasses, but she recognized a delaying tactic when she saw one. "As long as we're working together, your reputation is connected with mine." She took off her glasses and used her shirtsleeve to clean them. "If I let you go down in flames that won't look good for my firm. I don't want to make this all about me because my investment in the problem isn't nearly as big as yours. But I do have a stake in it."

"I hadn't thought of that." Taking off his hat, he ran his fingers through his hair.

After yesterday, she recognized the gesture as a sign of nervousness. He didn't like talking about this and he'd already been through it once tonight. "I'm sorry if this is difficult, but I need to know."

"I understand, but the more people I tell, the more likely it'll come out and I don't want that."

"You're my client. I won't betray your confidence."

He studied her for a moment and a smile tugged at the corners of his mouth.

"What?"

"Can't doubt the sincerity of someone wearing a Captain America shirt." He used his hat to motion her toward the sofa. "We might as well sit."

She took one end and he claimed the other, leaving at least three feet between them. It wasn't enough. She could feel the air crackling in that empty space every time she looked into his eyes.

He laid his hat, brim side up, between them.

She glanced at it. "Is that the neutral zone?"

"Yes, ma'am." His wink gave her goose bumps.

"I promise not to attack you."

"I can't make that promise." His gaze swept over her. "Not when you come out here looking like that."

"Sorry. I forgot to bring a robe."

"I'm not complaining, just stating the facts." His attention settled on the Captain America shield again. "I take it you're a fan?"

"Sure. He's an all-American good guy. Like you."

"Thanks for the reminder. It'll help me stay on my side of the hat." He pointed to the glass she held. "You're not drinking your water."

"The water was an excuse to come out here to see what was going on."

He sighed. "All right. Let's get this over with." Glancing away, he cleared his throat. "You probably won't be surprised to hear that Briana propositioned me."

She sucked in a breath.

"So you are surprised."

"I shouldn't be, but *damn her.*" The news made her sick to her stomach. The woman was a predator if she'd take advantage of a guy who'd just gotten his first big break.

"I'd hoped she was kidding around, but when I tried to make a joke out of it she set me straight real fast."

Geena's stomach churned. "That explains everything. You know what they say. *Hell hath no fury like a woman scorned.*"

"I did *not* scorn her." He tunneled his fingers through his hair again and swore. "God knows I wanted to. I was furious, but I was also humiliated. I wanted her to like and respect me for my acting, but you know what? I wonder if she was jealous of the attention I got. Maybe she thought that if we had sex she'd have some leverage, some power over me." He glanced over. "Does that make sense?"

"Unfortunately it makes perfect sense." Her heart ached for the loss of his idealistic dreams. Briana had ruined what should have been special.

"I knew that yelling would make things worse so I tried to be nice. I had to think of something that didn't sound insulting, so I made up a personal rule—never get involved with a costar. I don't have any damned rule like that. It sounds stupid and anal, especially coming from somebody as green as I am, but I tried to make it sound believable."

"But you still rejected her."

"I had to! But I swear I wasn't mean about it."

"Doesn't matter. Once she made a move, she put you in a no-win situation."

"Are you saying I can't win this fight?"

"No, I'm definitely not saying that." She considered telling him that he had all the ammunition he needed right here on this ranch—his background as a foster kid, his bond with his foster brothers, his amazing foster parents and his scholarship plan to support the new venture. All he had to do was turn her loose on this PR bonanza and everyone would forget about the stupid scandal as they soaked up Matt's touching past.

But she could predict his response to that idea, especially after a long and emotional day. Timing was everything. "We'll figure this out, and I'm grateful to you for taking me into your confidence. Obviously it's a painful episode and we don't have to bring it up again." She stood.

He got to his feet, too. "You can see why I don't want this to come out, right?"

"Yes, I do. Besides, it would be tacky and pointless to accuse her of trying to seduce you. That could really backfire on us."

"And it would hurt Cliff."

She sighed. "You're gonna have to let that one go. He married a toxic woman. That decision will come back to bite him eventually, and everyone who knows and loves him will hate seeing it happen. But it can't be helped."

"Rosie said basically the same thing." He scrubbed a hand over his face. "He was in Utah with us for a couple of weeks. He was great, always complimenting me on my work and encouraging me whenever I struggled with a scene."

"I'll bet Briana hated that. I'm guessing his primary job is telling her *she's* fabulous. No wonder she propositioned you. She could gain power over you and punish her husband at the same time."

"Guess so." He looked destroyed. "And now, if he believes Briana's lies, which he has to since he loves her, he must hate my guts."

She closed the gap between them. "Matt, I'm so sorry. We'll fix it."

"I hope so." His troubled gaze searched hers. "I'm glad you're here."

"Me, too." She reached up and stroked his cheek. "It'll be okay. I promise."

He muttered an oath and drew her close. "I shouldn't be doing this. But God, you smell good."

"I shouldn't be doing this, either." She slid her arms around his waist and nestled against him. Sure enough, her glasses misted and she couldn't see him. "Wait. I need to take off—"

"*Don't.* Once I see you naked I won't be able to stop."

"I meant my glasses." She pulled them off and held them in her hand.

"Oh. I could work around those."

"But they fog up whenever we…whenever I…"

"I'm not surprised." His gaze roamed her face. "We generate a hell of a lot of heat." He shuddered. "I need you, Geena. One kiss. Just one." And his lips came down on hers.

She held tight as his big body trembled with the force of his powerful emotions and his attempt to keep them in check.

His tongue thrust deep as he lifted her hips to meet the hard ridge of his erection. He pressed forward with an urgency that tightened her core as moisture gathered between her thighs. She whimpered, yearning for that connection that he promised with each stroke of his tongue but ultimately would deny her, at least for tonight.

And then, as if a storm had passed, he gently eased away. Keeping his hands at her waist to steady her, he raised his head and gulped for air. "Enough."

Breathing hard, she looked into eyes that glittered with passion. "Is it?"

"For now." He paused and took a breath. "It has to be." He let go of her and stepped back. "I shouldn't have started that. But I...it helps when I can hold you."

"I'm glad."

"But this isn't the place or the time. I'm going to the barn."

"Me, too."

Smiling faintly, he glanced down at her bare feet. "I think not."

"You can carry me." She felt safe saying that because of all his lovely muscles.

"Lady, you are temptation personified." He swallowed. "But I want you to stay here." He reached out and stroked her cheek with the tip of his finger. "Please. I'd rather not take a chance that we'd get so involved that a member of my family would find us in the morning, all tangled up together and naked as the day we were born."

"I guess you've had enough embarrassment for a while, huh?"

"Actually, I was thinking of your embarrassment."

A surge of warmth moved through her, warmth that had little to do with sex. "Thank you, Matt."

"Don't give me too much credit. I was this close to pulling off your sleep shirt a moment ago, despite what I said."

"But you didn't."

"You whimpered as if I was being too rough. That was enough to bring me to my senses."

"For future reference, I wasn't whimpering because you were being too rough."

"You weren't?"

"When I make that little noise it means I'm frustrated beyond belief and I'm hoping you'll take care of the issue immediately."

"Oh."

"Just FYI."

He picked up his hat and settled it on his head. "Probably a good thing I didn't know that." He touched the tips of his fingers to the brim. "See you in the mornin'." And he walked out the front door.

Geena's questions had been answered by the interlude with Matt, even if her libido hadn't been satisfied. Apparently answers were more important than orgasms right now because she slept soundly until her phone chimed at five in the morning. Dawn would break in fifteen minutes.

Obviously the birds outside her window hadn't gotten the memo. They chirped and chattered as if the sun had come up an hour ago. Must be the early birds determined to get that worm. Which was a gross image, now that she thought about it.

Ten minutes later, her hair in a ponytail and wearing a tiny bit of makeup because she'd be seeing Matt, she put on a pair of beige linen pants and a green silk blouse. Until Rosie coughed up some cowgirl duds, it was the best she could do. Her open-toed slides didn't seem appropriate, either, but at least she wouldn't go prancing down to the barn in four-inch heels.

As she walked through the living room she heard Rosie rattling pans in the kitchen, but she didn't stop to chat. She'd promised to be down at the barn by five fifteen and she would, by golly, honor that promise. Anticipation curled in her stomach the way it used to on Christmas morning when she was little. Those mornings might be the only times she'd been up at dawn.

Despite her mother's many failings as a parent, she'd always made a big deal about Christmas. She and her boyfriend du jour would be standing at the foot of the stairs, their arms loaded with gifts. Another big pile would be waiting under the tree.

On some level, Geena had known the truckload of presents stemmed from her mother's guilt because the rest of the year she'd left Geena in the care of Beatrice, the nanny. Beatrice had always spent Christmas with her family, so the holiday had been all on Geena's mom. When it came to extravagance, her mother had written the book.

But as Geena stepped out on the front porch, the commercial splendor of her childhood seemed tawdry compared to the scene spread before her. The ground sparkled as if diamonds had been scattered there, and she finally realized it was dew touched by sunlight. And, oh, the mountains! She'd driven in after dark and she'd been too worried about getting lost to notice the dim bulk of the range that stretched as far as she could see.

Shadows chased by the rising sun moved gently downward from peaks still tipped with snow. If she lived here she'd never get anything done. She'd spend all her time on the porch in an Adirondack chair watching the light shift on the mountain slopes.

A horse whinnied. She'd left her prescription sunglasses in her room, so she shaded her eyes with her hand as she glanced in the direction of the sound. The barn doors slid open with a soft rumble and Matt walked out to gaze up at the house. He was looking for her!

Her pulse raced at the sight of him framed in the doorway of the barn. He had on a white T-shirt, possibly the same one he'd worn the night before. After all, he'd slept down there. She waved and started toward him.

He waited for her, and she found that incredibly sweet. He could have ducked back in to help with the chores, but instead, he'd made welcoming her a priority. Too bad she couldn't get there faster, but her open-toed shoes weren't happy with the uneven terrain. She'd rather not embarrass herself by falling down on her way to the barn.

When she drew close enough, he called out a greeting. "You look great!"

"Not exactly Western wear."

"Doesn't matter." He walked to meet her. "You climbed out of bed and made it down here for feeding time." He hadn't shaved, and his rakish grin made him look like a certified bad boy.

If he had a rebellious streak, he kept it firmly in check. But last night she'd caught an exciting glimpse of his wild side. She liked it.

He wrapped an arm around her shoulders. "I like the ponytail. Sassy."

"Thanks."

"You impress me, Geena Lysander."

"That makes it mutual." If she could wake up to the sight of Matt in a snug T-shirt and jeans every morning, she'd have no problem becoming an early riser. He would inspire any woman to sacrifice a little sleep. "But I don't want to interrupt your work."

"Since I slept down here, I had some of it done before my dad and Cade came. They sent me out to see if you were on your way. And here you are."

"I hope I didn't miss everything."

"Oh, no. I shoveled stalls instead of feeding. I knew you wanted to watch that part. Let's go let them know you're here and then I'll introduce you around."

"But I already know Herb and Cade."

"I meant introduce you to the horses."

"Oh! Then I'd be delighted to meet them. I don't think I've ever been personally introduced to a horse. Like I said yesterday, I have no experience with them."

"Then we should change that. They're amazing animals." Matt paused before heading down the wooden barn aisle. "She's here!"

"Excellent!" Cade poked his head out of one of the stalls.

"Hey, Geena!" Herb walked toward them. "Come on back. I was about to feed Lucy and Linus."

"Then let's start with them," Matt said. "I promised to introduce her to everybody. She's never met a horse face-to-face."

Herb chuckled and reached into his pocket. "Then it's a good thing I brought carrots." He handed her six chunks. "Give them three apiece. Those two love their carrots."

She put the pieces in the pocket of her pants and decided not to worry if they left a stain. She'd have fun explaining it to the dry cleaner.

"I'd start with Lucy," Herb said. "She gets her nose bent out of shape if her son gets treats before she does." He motioned toward the last stall. "That's Lucy."

A golden horse with a white streak down her nose put her head over the stall door and whinnied.

"She's gorgeous!" Geena gazed at the sleek animal. "She looks just like Roy Rogers's horse!"

Matt glanced at her in surprise. "I thought you didn't know horses."

"I don't, but I know movies. My mother has a collection like you wouldn't believe." Then she noticed another horse, nearly identical, peeking out from the neighboring stall. "Two of them! Lucy and Linus. I see the family resemblance."

Herb folded his arms and beamed. "Amazing, isn't it? You don't always get a palomino foal just because you have a palomino mare, let alone one with a blaze that's almost identical. Linus just had his first birthday. He was born here last May."

"Wow." Geena stared at the young horse. "He looks pretty big to me. They must grow fast."

"He's big," Herb said, "but he's not nearly filled out yet. And he's still a kid at heart. You can go ahead and give Lucy her carrots whenever you want."

"Okay." She approached Lucy, who looked extremely interested in the hand she'd shoved in her pocket. "How do I do it?"

"One piece at a time and rest it on your palm." Matt

walked up to stand beside her. "Hold your hand flat, like this." He straightened out her fingers. "Perfect."

He'd only touched her fingers, yet she felt a zing in every cell of her body. "So, I just hold out my hand and she'll take it?"

"Yes, ma'am."

She was growing very fond of his country manners. Shoot, she was growing very fond of him. If they'd been in LA she might not have allowed herself to give in to this attraction, but circumstances had changed. She expected the dynamic to reverse when they went back. Once again he'd be in a goldfish bowl and they'd need to rethink their arrangement.

Then Lucy began to nuzzle her palm in search of the carrot, and she forgot all about what would or wouldn't happen in a week or so. A horse was eating from her hand. It tickled, making her giggle. She pulled out another carrot and repeated the process. "Matt, I love this."

His soft laughter danced along her nerve endings. "Knew you would."

Chapter Seven

Watching Geena feed carrots to Lucy and Linus caused a major shift in Matt's thinking. She wasn't dressed for hanging out in a barn, but despite that, she looked as if she belonged here. He'd figured she'd like the horses and he'd been right about that. Her uninhibited delight as she interacted with them for the first time was touching.

But until this moment he'd thought of her as a city girl getting a taste of country living. She might enjoy the visit, but without any prior experience to draw on she'd be a fish out of water. Not so. She already fit in, even without the right clothes or any knowledge of horse behavior.

Cade wandered down to join the group and then took her over to meet his sleek black gelding, Hematite. The horse had good manners, thanks to Cade's training, but Hematite didn't warm up to everyone. He warmed right up to Geena, though, leaning into her hand as she scratched his neck the way Cade had shown her.

Herb came over to stand next to Matt. "She seems to be having a good time."

"Yep."

"That incident with Briana is unfortunate and I wish it had never happened, but at least it brought us Geena."

"True." *It brought us Geena.* Like she was a gift. He was beginning to think she was.

"I like her, son. She's welcome anytime."

"I'm sure she'll appreciate knowing that." So did he. Over the years, he'd learned to trust his dad's instincts regarding people. His mom was no slouch in that department, either. Many times in the three years he'd lived in LA he'd wished one or both of them had been on hand to size up a situation.

Geena finished loving on Hematite, and she and Cade started back down the barn aisle. "Cade says it's time to turn them out into the pasture but he thinks I should meet Navarre and Isabeau first."

"Absolutely." Matt glanced at his dad. "Do you want to do the honors of introducing them?"

"You go ahead. In fact, if you and Geena could turn out all the horses when you're finished, that would be a big help. Cade and I have to go fiddle with the automatic watering system."

"Cade's going to help you?" Matt wondered if this was a joke. His brother had many talents, but dealing with mechanical malfunctions wasn't one of them.

"I know it sounds crazy," Cade said, "but I've developed a basic understanding of this pain-in-the-ass watering system."

"That said, I'm still planning to replace it." Herb grimaced. "Darn thing is always acting up. If you decide to put one in over at your new place, don't get this brand."

Matt laughed. "Okay. But I'm a long way from installing a watering system in the barn. I haven't bought a horse, yet."

"Just warning you in advance that this outfit manufactures lemons. Come on, Cade, maybe you can jerry-rig that confounded hose one more time." Herb started toward the back of the barn.

"I'm at your service." With a tip of his hat to Matt and Geena, Cade followed Herb.

"You'll have a horse on your ranch?" Geena's eyes lit up.

"At least two." Now that his brother and his dad were at the other end of the barn, he felt more comfortable putting his arm around her as they walked over to Navarre's stall.

"You must be planning to take people out riding. That sounds like fun." Her comment sounded wistful, as if she'd like that.

"You're invited anytime."

"I'll remember that."

"But, to be totally honest, that's not the main reason I'd buy two. Horses get nervous if there's only one of them. They're herd animals." He stopped in front of Navarre's stall and clucked to the dark chestnut. "Hey, boy. Come on over and meet Geena."

"Look at you, Navarre," she crooned. "You're a handsome guy, just like your namesake." She reached out to stroke the nose that Navarre poked over the stall door.

"I take it your mom owned *Ladyhawke*, too."

"She did, but I bought my own copy. I watch it every year or two. Now when I do, I'll think of this beautiful horse."

He hoped she'd think of him, too. No guarantees on that, though. A crisis had thrown them into close contact, but once the crisis was over, who knew what would happen? Maybe she'd fall in love with Wyoming and want to spend more time here with him, and maybe she wouldn't.

He gave her shoulder a squeeze. "Ready to meet Isabeau?"

"Sure. And there she is, right there waiting for us." She moved closer to the stall door. "Hi, Isabeau, sweetheart." She stroked the mare's glossy neck. "You're a dainty girl, aren't you?" She looked up at Matt. "Why aren't they in the same stall?"

"I doubt they'd want that." He tried not to smile because she was adorably serious with that question.

"Navarre and Isabeau don't like each other?"

"They do, but that doesn't mean they want to share a stall. As you can see, that would be close quarters. They enjoy having their own space."

"Were they ever in the same stall?"

"Truthfully, I doubt it. They might not mirror the *Ladyhawke* movie script, but they like each other. I'd go so far as to say they're devoted to each other. They're a good choice to take out for a two-person trail ride. If there's time, maybe we could…oh, wait. Lexi offered to give you a lesson. That's probably a better idea, to start with her. She's an excellent teacher and I want you to have a good experience."

"Are you offering to take me on a trail ride?"

"I was, but then I remembered about Lexi. And I'm sure your time here is limited. When do you fly back?"

"When we've figured out how to deal with Briana."

He stared at her as he processed the meaning of that statement. "You didn't buy a round-trip ticket?"

"Nope. We need a game plan and I don't see the point in flying home without one. I can't predict how long it will take to come up with something, so I didn't buy a return ticket yet."

"That makes no sense. You have other clients. You can't hang out with me in Wyoming and ignore them."

"I won't ignore them. I'll check in with Larissa on a regular basis. She's in charge while I'm gone, but I intend to keep tabs on things by phone and email. She'll let me know if anything major happens."

"I suppose most things can be handled that way."

"Most things." She gazed at him. "But not this issue."

"Because I turned off my phone. I'm surprised you haven't yelled at me for doing that."

"How could I? You turned it off because I wasn't being helpful. Cutting off communication forced me to dig a little deeper and figure out why you didn't want to talk to me. I knew we had to work it out in person, so here I am. The more time we can spend doing that, the sooner I can get back."

Now, there was a challenging puzzle. The more they were together, the less time she'd be here. "So a trail ride with me would suit you?"

"I'd love it, especially if I can take my phone to keep tabs on the office."

"Absolutely."

"You were right about horses being incredible animals. There's no doubt Lexi has a lot to teach me, but I'll bet I could sit on a gentle horse and ride down the trail without falling off."

"I'm sure you could. I want to put in some time cleaning cabins first thing today, but we might be able to pack a lunch and go out around noon."

"I'll help with the cabins. We can brainstorm while we're cleaning."

"Yeah, no." Laughing, he shook his head. "Not happening."

"Why not? Scrubbing and thinking go great together."

"I could be wrong, but I don't think my mom's going to let you muck out cabins. Just a guess."

"I know how to clean. My nanny, Beatrice, used to let me help her. It was fun, although Beatrice made me swear I wouldn't tell my mother."

"I'm sure you're amazing with a mop, but you're a guest."

"Uninvited guest."

"Trust me, nobody thinks of you that way now. You won't be allowed to clean."

She frowned at him. "I didn't come here to sit around like some princess while everyone else works."

"You feel strongly about this."

"Yes, I do. Your family needs us to help, not hinder."

"Then maybe we can work out a compromise with my mom. We'll offer to tackle a few jobs together in the morning, and then as a reward we'll pack a lunch and take off on a trail ride. She might go for that, especially if you tell her you like to clean."

"All right. We'll try that approach."

"Great. Now, let's get these critters out to the pasture."

"Will I get to see them run?"

"Linus will run, for sure. Sometimes he convinces Hematite to play chase with him. But let's start with Navarre and Isabeau. Want to help me lead 'em out?"

"Yes!"

So he fetched a couple of lead ropes from the tack room. She took to the process as if she'd been doing it her whole life. When all the horses had been turned out, he leaned shoulder to shoulder with her at the gate as they watched Linus and Hematite kick up their heels.

She followed their movements, laughing as they bucked and spun, gold and ebony coats gleaming in the sunlight. "So beautiful."

He studied her profile—the high, intelligent forehead, deep-set eyes and determined chin. She'd chosen to wear glasses instead of contacts, and he thought that suited her straightforward personality. Her smile dimpled her cheek and a breeze coaxed strands of her hair out of her ponytail to curl at her nape. "Yes, ma'am," he murmured. "Beautiful."

She glanced over at him, her green eyes filled with happiness. "Flattery will get you everywhere."

"It's not flattery. It's the truth."

"Thank you, Matt. I feel beautiful when you look at me like that. I also want to kiss the living daylights out of you."

"I'd be fine with it if I didn't see my dad and Cade coming out of the barn."

"I thought they might be, which is why I didn't lay one on you." She pushed away from the gate. "Let's go have some of that breakfast Lexi's so keen on. Where is she, by the way? I can't imagine her sleeping in."

Matt took her hand as they walked back to the house. "Cade said she's updating her website. She never seems to find the time, and she's added some new features to her riding clinics."

"Clinics, huh? Obviously there's more to her job description than just *riding teacher*."

"A lot more. She gives clinics all over, even out of the state. Sure you don't want to take a lesson from her before we go on a trail ride?"

"Let's do the trail ride as planned. If she's so busy she doesn't have time for her website, she might have trouble working me in."

"She'll make the time."

"I know she will. She doesn't seem like the type who

reneges on a promise, but a simple trail ride sounds easy enough unless you think I can't handle it."

"You can and it'll be fun." His body warmed with anticipation. She might be focused on discussing their PR problem on that trail ride, but he had some ideas that had nothing to do with business. Cade had brought a box of condoms down to the barn this morning. Matt had hidden it in the tack room behind some old blankets, but not before he'd pocketed a few.

He'd planned to take her over to his ranch, but he didn't know what he'd find there. Last night, desperate for private time, he'd thought a trip to his recently purchased ranch would be perfect. In the light of day he couldn't picture making out in dusty, empty rooms.

A trail ride had all kinds of things going for it, though—fresh air, wildflowers and grassy meadows. If he wanted to do a subtle sales job on Wyoming, a trail ride to a picturesque clearing he knew about and a picnic on a soft blanket should do the trick.

"I don't know how to explain it," she said, "but being around horses feels very natural to me. Maybe that's because of all the movies I watched, although somehow I never imagined that *I* could ride. My life was crammed with lessons aimed at making me a performer. My mom would have considered riding a hobby, like knitting or scrapbooking. I didn't have time for hobbies."

"How about now?"

"What a thought! I've been concentrating on building my business, but why not have some hobbies?" She glanced at him. "Do you have any?"

"Not yet. But I figure my ranch will qualify once I get everything set up."

"Oh, it will. I imagine it as a place to de-stress and get back to basics."

"That's exactly my vision. You just nailed it."

"Matt, I have the best idea."

"What?"

"Your ranch is nearby, right?"

"Yes, ma'am. I wanted to be close to my folks."

"That's perfect, then! We can ride to your ranch and have lunch there. Your first meal in your new home. Can we do that? I really want to see it."

"Uh, okay, but I don't know what shape the place will be in. The house is empty of furniture, far as I know, and I'll bet there's dust an inch thick on—"

"I don't care about that. We can open the windows to let in fresh air. I'll bet Rosie has a dustpan and whisk-broom we could take along. We'll clear a spot and spread a blanket on the floor. I would be so honored to be the first person you entertain at your ranch."

"And I'd be honored to have you." So much for his picnic in the meadow, but maybe this would be better.

"I think everyone needs a place to get away from the pressures of a job, but judging from my experience, actors may need it more than most."

"I wouldn't have thought so, but now I do."

"Do you regret getting into the business?"

"Never. I had some bad moments after the story broke, but it's my life. I love what I do."

"I've never asked why you chose this kind of work."

They'd reached the steps and he paused to glance at her. "No, you haven't."

"Is it the wrong question to ask? I can withdraw it."

He could smell bacon and coffee. He was hungry and wanted nothing more than to head on inside to enjoy the breakfast Rosie had prepared. But he and Geena were making a connection, and this would come up eventually.

"No, don't withdraw it." He held her gaze. "Just know that none of this can ever go in a press release."

"I would never repeat something you told me without your permission."

"Then I'll make it short, and then we won't have to talk about that anymore, either."

"Okay."

He took a deep breath. He hadn't told this story in a while. None of his new friends in LA had a clue he was a foster kid. "I never knew who my dad was and my mom didn't enjoy having me around."

Her green eyes clouded. "That's hard to imagine."

"Don't worry. Rosie got me counseling and I've accepted that it wasn't my fault. I was in the way of her delusional plan that a guy would come along and sweep her off her feet. Maybe it happened. One day she was supposed to pick me up from school and she never showed."

"Oh, Matt."

"I finally got a friend's mom to give me a ride home and I found a note that said she'd gone to look for a better life. She left the phone number for the foster care division of the town's social services and I called it. Rosie was still working in that department then, and she offered to take me. End of story."

Geena swallowed. "Have you ever heard from your mother?"

"No, ma'am, and I'd rather not." He tugged the brim of his hat lower. "At this point, by her standards, I'm rich and she might think she could cash in."

"I'd like to see her try!"

Geena's protectiveness made him smile. It also made him glad he'd told her. "Thanks for that."

"Maybe you should give me her name in case she has the nerve to contact you through me."

"Mindy's her first name, but no telling what her last name is now. It could have changed six times since then."

"If anybody named Mindy comes looking for you, I'll let you know." She gazed at him. "And I had the audacity to whine about my childhood."

"Money doesn't make everything okay. You had it tough, too. Don't forget that I ended up with Rosie and Herb, plus all my brothers. The way I look at it, my birth mom did me a favor. She went looking for a better life, and thanks to her *I* found one."

"I suppose, in a way, she did the right thing. She wasn't a positive influence."

"Except she was the reason I got into acting. Whenever the school put on a play, I was the first to stick my hand in the air. It was my favorite escape, a chance to pretend I was someone else."

"But when you came here, you didn't give it up. That much I do know about you from your résumé. You were in a ton of high school productions."

"By then I was hooked. If I could make an audience laugh or cry, or even get mad, I was thrilled. Now I'll have to go to my own movies to get that buzz."

"Or take a shot at live theater."

"Maybe."

She stood on tiptoe and brushed a kiss over his cheek. "Thank you for trusting me with your story. It won't go anywhere."

Pushing back his hat, he took her by the shoulders and gave her a quick, fiery kiss. Then he noticed that her glasses were fogged and began to laugh. "I see what you mean about steaming things up. Let me help." He gently took them off and pulled a bandanna out of his back pocket. "I hope I end up doing this a lot." He cleaned the lenses and carefully slid the glasses back into place. "In fact, I'd kiss you again right now, but it's almost time for breakfast."

"Can I have a rain check?"

"Lady, you can have anything you want from me."

Chapter Eight

She could have anything she wanted from Matt. Geena wished she believed it, but she knew his comment didn't extend to whatever she had in mind for his goodwill campaign. He'd made it clear that his foster-kid story was off the table. Now that he'd told her the details, she understood why.

As she tucked into what was possibly the best breakfast she'd ever eaten, she reviewed the situation. Before hearing that his mother had abandoned him, she'd hoped he'd consent to a heartwarming article or video interview about how Rosie, Herb, his foster brothers and this ranch had shaped his life. She'd discovered that trying to refute bad publicity never worked, but replacing it with good news almost always did.

Unfortunately, she couldn't use the Thunder Mountain angle. Once she opened that door, celebrity gossip magazines would dig for the story behind the story. An enterprising reporter might find his mother. Or his mother would contact him. Since he didn't want that, they'd have to take a different approach.

She had no idea what that would be, but the conversation at the breakfast table had shifted from the weather to what everyone planned to do after breakfast. That was her cue to propose the cleaning plan. She glanced across at Matt, who gave her a subtle nod.

Somehow, in the midst of taking seats at the round table, they'd ended up on opposite sides. Herb and Rosie sat on her right and Lexi and Cade were on her left. She focused on Rosie and went into her spiel.

Rosie listened politely as she sipped her coffee. At the end of the speech she put down her mug. "That's a wonderful offer, but here's the deal. I didn't expect either of you to be here during this time, so we have it covered. Matt needs a break and you probably have calls to make. I doubt your business has come to a screeching halt because you flew to Wyoming."

"No, but I'll check in with my office before we start. If I have issues to handle I might have to retract my offer, but nothing was critical when I talked with my assistant yesterday. And I really do want to help."

"I can see that." Rosie beamed at her. "But you and Matt are both excused from cleaning duty."

Matt looked at Geena, his lifted eyebrows clearly saying *I told you so*.

But she wasn't giving up. "You didn't expect us, but here we are, consuming food and taking up space. I'm sure I speak for Matt when I say that we'd feel a whole lot better about our unplanned visit if you'd let us do something for the cause. It won't be a chore for either of us to scrub down a cabin or two. If we hop right on it, maybe we can finish up all four this morning."

"Whoa, there, Geena, ma'am." Cade took off his hat and settled it more securely on his head. "Back up the bus. You gotta leave something for the rest of us. My lady purely loves watching me operate a vacuum cleaner."

Lexi sighed dramatically. "I'll admit it. Nothing's sexier than a man running a vacuum." She fanned herself. "Oh, baby."

"I'd never want to deprive you of that." Geena focused on Lexi, figuring she'd understand the situation even if Rosie balked. "Can we split the job, two cabins for you guys and two for us?"

"Sure, why not?"

"I like it." Matt lifted his coffee mug in Rosie's direction. "Over to you, Mom, but I hope you'll throw in the towel. And the mop and the broom while you're at it."

"Matthew Edward." Rosie frowned at him. "Young women who come to visit Thunder Mountain are welcome to help out a little bit because that's being mannerly. But they're not supposed to wash windows and mop floors."

"Oooh, she said your whole name, bro." Cade rolled his eyes. "Either she's touched or annoyed. It could go either way."

"I'm both." Rosie pulled a tissue from her pocket. "But mostly I'm touched." She dabbed at her eyes and gave them all a teary smile. "When I listen to the four of you arguing for the *privilege* of cleaning the cabins, it gets to me."

"I'll just bet it does," Cade said. "You're probably remembering all the years we tried to argue our way out of doing it."

Rosie laughed and dabbed her eyes some more. "Yes, you certainly did. Very creatively, too."

Cade looked over at Matt. "We were rotten, you know?"

"I know. We should have been more grateful, more willing to—"

"Now, hang on," Herb said. "We're talking about normal boys, here, right?" He put an arm around Rosie. "We would have worried if you'd all gone about your chores with a smile on your face and a song in your heart."

Cade chuckled. "Yeah, that would have been kind of sickening."

"I loved it all," Rosie said. "The arguing, the pranks, the roughhousing. The handpicked bouquets." She winked at Cade.

"Who knew that was poison ivy?"

Herb shook his head and sighed. "Everybody but you, son."

"So many great memories." Rosie looked at Matt. "I'll never forget when you had the lead in *Oklahoma!*"

"Yeah, that was epic," Cade said. "Lining up outside the auditorium an hour early to make sure we sat in front and threatening the younger guys with death if they goofed off during the performance."

"Instead, they were mesmerized," Rosie said. "So was I." She reached over and squeezed Matt's arm. "I knew then you'd make it. I'm pretty sure I told you so."

"Yes, ma'am, you did." Matt's voice was gruff with emotion as he held Rosie's gaze. "Always remembered it."

"Okay, okay." Cade pushed back his chair. "We need to break this up before I start bawling. You don't want to see that, Geena. It gets ugly. So, Mom, is Geena cleared to be part of the cleaning crew?"

"Oh, all right." Rosie got up from the table. "But not in that outfit. Come with me, Geena. While the rest of this bunch tidies up the kitchen, I'll find you some knockabout clothes."

Geena followed Rosie through the living room and

down the hallway. Rosie made a comment about the unseasonably warm weather expected that day and Geena responded to that, but she was more interested in the family pictures lining the hall. A quick glance revealed that most of them were group photos of teenage boys. An older one of a couple in wedding attire had to be Rosie and Herb, but nearby hung a recent wedding picture featuring the couple Geena had met the night before, the ones with the baby.

Rosie looked over her shoulder and paused. "That's Damon and Philomena. They have a baby girl now."

"I know. I met them last night...sort of."

"What do you mean, sort of?" Rosie walked back to stand with her in front of the photograph.

"I was waiting in the driveway debating whether to go up and knock on the door when they came out. They were friendly until they found out who I was. Then they politely offered to escort me back to town."

"Oh, dear. I suppose he was trying to protect Matt. They do stick up for each other. By the way, I called Damon this morning, told him you were staying here and that you were a very nice woman."

"Thank you, Rosie." Geena impulsively gave her a hug and then wondered if she should have. "You'll have to excuse me if that was overly familiar. I just—"

"I love getting hugs." Rosie smiled at her. "The more the better." She gestured to the wall of pictures. "My boys are all good huggers. Some of them came here with the idea that it was unmanly. They got over it."

"I wish I could have seen this place back then. It must have been something."

"I have videos. Maybe while you're here we could have a movie night."

"I would love that." Geena gazed at the two smiling

people who'd been so suspicious of her last night. "Do you have videos of little Sophie?"

"My first grandchild?" Rosie's blue eyes glowed with pride. "You know I do! I'm supposed to get a studio picture for this wall any day now, too."

"I guess you could end up with a lot of baby pictures, couldn't you?"

"I hope so. I'll start a new wall somewhere else in the house if I need to. Now, let's go find you something cool to wear. It'll be a scorcher today." She led the way into a master bedroom containing furniture that was probably as old as the marriage. It wasn't a fancy room, but the bed was neatly made with a white chenille bedspread and the surfaces looked freshly dusted.

"This is my stash of hand-me-downs." Rosie slid back the doors of a large wall closet tightly packed with jeans and shirts hanging from the rod and boots lined up along the floor. "Some kids leave stuff and friends donate things. Sometimes I shop at the thrift store. It's all washed and mended."

"This is amazing, Rosie."

"Thanks." She gave Geena an assessing glance. "I could let you go through them, but it'll be faster if you let me pull some things out. By now I'm pretty good at knowing what will fit and look good."

"All I care about is the fit. Looking good isn't a priority."

Rosie laughed. "Oh, yes, it is. Everyone functions better when they like the way they look. That was one of the first things I learned when I worked in social services. Get someone a decent outfit or two and their entire attitude changes." She quickly chose three shirts and three pairs of jeans. "Not that I think you need an attitude change. Yours is excellent."

"Why, thank you." Geena flushed with pleasure. "What a nice thing to say."

"I know quality when I see it." Rosie handed over the clothes. "Go into the bathroom and try those on while I sort through the boots. That's trickier. Are you about an eight?"

"Nine. I really appreciate this, Rosie."

"I appreciate you going the extra mile." She hesitated. "Nobody likes to be falsely accused, but Matt's more touchy than most. His birth mother used to blame him for all kinds of things he didn't do."

"I'm not surprised. Any mother who can walk away and leave her kid…"

"Did he tell you about that?"

"This morning."

"Good. Then he must trust you, because he doesn't share that with many people."

"I completely understand that he's a very private person. But I'm desperate to find a way to improve his image. I was hoping to use his background, but he doesn't want that for many reasons. Reporters aren't the only ones who could show up here asking questions."

Rosie nodded. "Right. There's Mindy. I've been worried about her ever since he landed that role. She could already be trying to find a way to contact him, but no point in making it easy for her." Rosie patted Geena's arm. "I know this is a knotty problem, but give it a little time. You've only been here since last night."

Geena laughed. "Funny, but it seems much longer. I feel as if I've known you for years."

"That's a lovely compliment." Rosie held her gaze. "I'm going to help you figure this out. Like I said, give it time."

Geena drew a deep breath. "Okay." She chose not to

mention that time wasn't their friend. Even as they stood there discussing the problem, Briana's PR machine was spewing out garbage about Matt. The longer he stayed in hiding, the more likely people would believe all those hateful lies.

After Geena changed into her borrowed clothes, she checked in with Larissa and took notes for the calls she'd make after she finished cleaning. The hour's time difference would be a bonus. Matt, Cade and Lexi had gathered the supplies and were heading to the porch by the time she left her bedroom.

She'd taken everything Rosie had chosen and put on the outfit she liked best. Rosie had also come up with a straw Western hat to keep the sun out of her eyes during the walk to the meadow. Geena had twisted her hair on top of her head and shoved the hat over it.

The boot-cut jeans were a little snug on her, but they were soft and amazingly comfortable. So were the boots Rosie had found. The button-front green plaid shirt was designed to tie at the waist, which gave it a sassy feel. A quick glance in the mirror confirmed that she was finally wearing something that fit the occasion.

Matt's wide smile told her she passed muster. "You look great."

"Thanks." She noticed he'd taken time to shave, which could mean there were kisses in her future. The thought warmed her all over and she worried that her cheeks were pink. Couldn't be helped. "What should I carry?"

"How about a bucket and a mop?" Cade handed them to her and then divided up the rest of the supplies. He was clearly the person in charge.

While Geena had been trying on clothes she'd asked Rosie to fill her in on Cade, whose function wasn't clear

to her. It turned out that besides being the ranch fore-
man and primary student chaperone, he also taught an
academy class in horse psychology. He and Lexi lived in
a new log home near the meadow and the pasture, and
Rosie had said they couldn't manage without him.

As they all started down toward the meadow, Cade put
a hand on Matt's shoulder. "Have you provided Geena
with any background on these historic log cabins, bro?"

"He has not," she said. "For one thing, I didn't know
they were made of logs. And there are four?"

"Now there are," Cade said. "But originally there were
only three. Damon and Phil built the fourth one last summer, so technically only the first three are historic. Especially the first one." He glanced at Matt. "Is it okay if
I tell her about the brotherhood?"

"Go for it."

"I should hope you can tell her," Lexi said. "She volunteered to clean cabins, for pity's sake. She's working
hard to save Matt's reputation. Geena's aces in my book."

Geena flashed Lexi a smile. "Thanks."

"So, the story of the brotherhood." Cade adjusted his
grip on a second mop he carried on his shoulder like a
rifle. "The first three guys Rosie brought home were
Damon Harrison, Finn O'Roarke and me. Damon's—"

"I know who Damon is," she said. "And Finn's the guy
who brews the beer we drank last night."

"Exactly. So we created the Thunder Mountain Brotherhood. We had a blood-brother ceremony in the woods where
we swore to be straight with everyone, protect the weak
and be loyal to one another for life." He stated the pledge
without a trace of mockery. He'd obviously believed in the
concept then and he believed in it now.

Geena's throat tightened as she imagined three homeless boys pledging to stick together through thick and thin. "That's very cool."

"We thought so, too, but unfortunately we were kind of exclusive. We claimed the first cabin and although it sleeps four, we wouldn't let anybody else in."

Matt shook his head. "Tell me about it. You acted like you were royalty."

"I know. We were obnoxious. But we finally grew up and realized that every guy who shared the experience of living here with Rosie and Herb should be a part of the brotherhood, so now it's official. Everybody's in." He reached over and punched Matt lightly on the arm. "I hope you weren't too traumatized by being excluded for a while, big guy."

"Nah. There's always the cool crowd and then the rest of us."

"Yeah, but today I'm just a lowly cowhand and you're a famous movie star."

Matt grinned at him. "Bite me."

"And get sued by your studio for damaging the goods? No, thanks." He turned back to Geena. "Anyway, that was life in the cabins. Never a dull moment."

"Yeah, and I loved it," Matt said, "despite being lorded over by three megalomaniacs. I used to pretend we were all living on the frontier."

"Which wasn't so far from the truth, considering we had to hike down to the bathhouse in the middle of the night to take care of business. Speaking for myself, I felt like Davy Crockett every time I made that journey."

Geena blinked. "You're kidding, right?"

"No, he's not." Matt looked over at her and grinned. "There's no running water in the cabins."

"Really? How could you manage without indoor bathrooms?"

"Oh, we had indoor bathrooms," Cade said. "We just had to go outdoors to get to 'em. Rain or shine, sleet or snow, down the path we would go."

"Sometimes we had to shovel first, like if we had six feet of snow," Matt said.

"And that was if you could get out your door to shovel." Cade shifted his mop to the other shoulder. "Once the snow was so deep we couldn't pry the doors open. I don't think you'd arrived yet, Matt. Dad dug us out or we would've had to climb out a window. I'll bet we had a good ten feet that year."

She couldn't imagine, but then she was a California girl. "I suppose there are bathrooms in the cabins now, though, for the academy students."

"Nope." Matt shook his head.

"No?"

"They have to do the same thing we did. It's tradition. Toughens them up."

She held out the bucket she was carrying. "So, you're saying in order to mop the floors we have to haul water from the bathhouse?"

"Yes, ma'am."

"Wow, this will be more of an adventure than I thought!"

"You really don't have to do this." Lexi came over to put an arm around her. "Offering to help was a nice gesture, but I'm starting to feel bad about having you do manual labor on your business trip. The three of us can handle it."

"Nice try, but there's no way you're getting rid of me now. I was the kid who never went to camp. I would have loved to—" She stopped in her tracks as the semicircle of four cabins came into view. Nestled in a grassy meadow, they did look as if a family of settlers might have constructed them. Tall pines ringed the meadow and wind sighed through the top branches, making a sound that was hauntingly familiar.

Benches surrounded a fire pit in the middle of the cabin area and the lingering scent of charred logs blended with the aroma of pine. She longed to sit on one of those benches, roast marshmallows and tell ghost stories. Then she'd pile into a cabin with her friends and zip herself into her very own sleeping bag.

"Like it?" Matt's question brought her out of her day-dream.

"I don't just *like* it. I *love* it." She realized everyone was watching her with a bemused smile. "This may sound ridiculous, but seeing this meadow is like finding something I didn't know I missed. I can't hear traffic noises or sirens or jackhammers. Maybe I've always needed a place like this in my life. I just didn't know it."

Chapter Nine

Matt had been bowled over by Geena's transformation from city girl to country girl thanks to Rosie's magic closet. Then she'd made those heartfelt comments as she'd stood gazing at the log cabins where he'd spent the happiest years of his life. She'd reacted to the meadow exactly as he had the first time he'd laid eyes on it. She was rapidly turning into the girl of his dreams.

Now he really wanted to take her over to his ranch so she could picture herself going there with him next time he came home. He wouldn't let himself plan too far into the future because that would be foolish. But if he'd found a woman who loved both the film industry and the rural beauty of Wyoming, they could have some fun together.

Once she'd finished exclaiming over the rustic beauty of the cabins and their setting, Cade handed out directions. "We only have one vacuum so we'll have to trade that back and forth. You two can take it first and we'll wash windows until you're done. Then you can wash windows and mop floors while we vacuum. We'll reverse the process for the next two."

"Got it." Matt said.

Cade settled his hat more firmly on his head. "You need to flip the mattresses and look for any items they left behind. After the fall semester we found somebody's credit card."

"Aye, aye, sir." Geena gave him a snappy salute.

Cade's eyes sparkled with laughter. "You'll do, recruit. See you in a few." He and Lexi headed off.

"Nice salute." Matt carried the vacuum cleaner, and Geena took the bucket and mop.

"Learned it in an acting class in case we ever had an audition for a military role. Did you take any classes or are you just a natural born talent?"

"I took community college courses while I was here and enrolled in a couple of acting studios once I hit LA. That was expensive, though, so mostly I watched Westerns because I knew that's where I could shine."

"Lots of John Wayne."

"Yes, ma'am. Plus Steve McQueen, Lee Marvin and every Western Cliff Wallace made. The man can act with his back to the camera. Brando could do that, too. Impressive." He hustled up the steps ahead of her so he could open the door.

"Thank you." She took off her hat and hung it on a hook by the door. "Nice setup."

"It is." Adrenaline pumping, he followed her in and closed the door because he knew from experience it was easier to vacuum that way. Yeah, right. That's why he'd closed the door, so they could clean more efficiently.

Now they were alone, more alone than they'd ever been. The intimacy teased him with possibilities as he

108 *IN THE COWBOY'S ARMS*

stood behind her, trying to breathe normally. Wisps of hair that weren't long enough to fit into her updo curled against the tender skin of her nape. God, how he wanted to kiss her there. Other places, too. Lots of other places. But they had a job to do and there was no telling how fast Cade and Lexi would finish up and come over here.

So he did what most guys did when they couldn't decide whether a move would be appropriate. He babbled about nothing. "Last year I managed a quick visit home after Damon and Phil added the built-in loft beds and desks. We just had regular bunk beds when I was here. This is better. Everybody gets a top bunk and their own private area."

"It's a great idea." She pulled her phone out of her pocket and laid it on the nearest desk. "So we're supposed to vacuum, flip mattresses and look for stray items. Does that cover it until we move into the next phase?"

"Yes, ma'am." She still had her back to him. He thought he'd detected a faint shiver and her shoulders seemed tense, but he could be imagining things. If she was determined to go straight into work mode, so would he.

She swallowed. "Do you want to kiss me first or—"

He put down the vacuum and spun her around so fast she squeaked. "I want to kiss you more than I want to breathe."

"I see." Her green eyes simmered with heat. "Then I won't be needing these." Slowing removing her glasses, she perched them on top of her head where they nestled against her glossy hair.

His heartbeat picked up speed. Shoving back his hat, he pulled her close. Her full lips parted on a sigh. He could almost taste their velvet softness "This is risky."

She wound her arms around his neck. "Is it?"

"Yes, ma'am." He slid his hands over the warm denim covering her backside. For someone so slender, she perfectly filled his cupped hands. His breathing hitched. "Once I start kissing you, I'm liable to forget about cleaning."

She pressed her sweet body against his. "I'll remind you."

"You do that." He took her mouth with the desperation of a starving man. He'd only had a few chances to kiss her, but it seemed that was enough to make him addicted to the supple movement of her lips and the erotic dance of her tongue.

She caught fire immediately and he dove into the richness that was Geena's mouth. His hat fell to the floor. He left it there. He might yearn for a peaceful meadow, but he craved this, to be engulfed in a passion that made him forget his problems, forget everything but the heat of her body and the sound of her moans.

He'd told himself to go slow, but they were alone in this cabin and he wanted…more. Heart pounding, he untied her shirttails and worked his way up the row of buttons. He gave her time to object, but instead she deepened the kiss.

When he'd breached the barrier of her shirt, he discovered the front catch of her bra. What a terrific invention. Anticipation made him clumsy but eventually he flipped open the clasp.

She gasped as his hand closed over her breast.

Breathing hard, he lifted his mouth a fraction from hers. "Do you want me to stop?"

"No."

That one word traveled like a flame along a fuse. Cupping her warm breast, he supported her with his arm and leaned down. His tongue grazed her nipple and she whimpered. Now he knew what that meant.

Slowly he drew her in and listened to the wild sound of her breathing as he hollowed his cheeks and created a rhythm with his mouth and tongue. Her soft whimpers turned into nearly incoherent words.

He lifted his head again. "What?" he murmured. "Tell me."

"I want you so much," she wailed. "But we have to clean!"

Clean. His passion-soaked brain struggled with the concept and finally delivered the bad news. He might have a bed available, although they'd have to climb a ladder to get there, which lacked class. He might have an erection as rigid as the logs used to build this cabin. He might even have a condom in his jeans pocket.

Didn't matter. Instead of making sweet love to Geena, he had to vacuum floors and flip mattresses. Life wasn't even remotely fair.

With a resigned sigh, he released her soft, inviting breast. He didn't dare let go of her completely, though. If she was anywhere near as jacked up as he was, she might lose her balance. He wasn't entirely confident that he wouldn't lose his.

She gulped in air. "I shouldn't have started this. I should have known we couldn't just kiss each other without…"

"Right." He swallowed. "But don't take all the blame. I had a hunch things could get out of control in no time."

"You did?"

"Yes, ma'am. But I was willing to take the risk because kissing you is my new favorite thing."

"Kissing you is mine, too." She took a shaky breath.

"Okay, you can let me go. I'm reasonably steady and I should put myself back together so we can get to work."

He did as she asked and edged away. But he couldn't stop looking at her, although he definitely should because his package strained against his fly. Her creamy breasts trembled with each breath and her nipples, the rich color of burgundy wine, remained taut and eager for his mouth.

Then she gathered all that bounty into the white lace cups of her bra and fastened the catch, depriving him of that particular view. But he still had the tantalizing sight of her unbuttoned blouse and the inviting shadow of her cleavage. He willingly suffered continued pain in his crotch.

Her fingers trembled slightly as she buttoned her shirt and tied the tails in a loose knot. Last of all, she retrieved her glasses from the top of her head and put them on. "All done." She took another deep breath. "Do you want to vacuum or flip mattresses?"

"Neither. I want to strip off all your clothes. Then I want to kiss you until we're both crazy with anticipation. Then I want to make love to you for as long as it takes for both of us to be so satisfied that we can't imagine wanting even one more orgasm."

A fire burned in her green eyes. "That sounds amazing. And we'll do that eventually, I'm sure. But right now, we have to—"

"Clean cabins. I know." He sighed. "I'll flip the mattresses. I'll be done first so I'll haul water and put it on the front stoop for later."

"But I want to haul water."

That made him smile. Apparently she really did look upon this as an adventure. He clenched his hands into fists so he wouldn't reach for her again, because she was just that appealing. "Okay. Want to split some kindling while you're at it?"

"Could I? That would be awesome!"

"Don't see why not." He picked up his hat from the floor and dusted it off. "In fact, there's a dead tree about fifty yards into the forest that Dad wants to cut down."

"There is?" Her eyes widened.

"Yes, ma'am." He stroked a hand over his face so she wouldn't notice his grin. "He mentioned it yesterday. When I fetch the ax from the barn, I could also gas up the chain saw. That way you could—"

"Now you're making fun of me."

"Just a little." He settled his hat on his head. "The thing is, if I don't tease you I'll just have to kiss you again. A woman who's excited about hauling water and chopping wood is tough to resist."

"So is a certain cowboy who took the time to shave before coming out here to clean cabins. I expected you'd still have the scruff."

"And I expected to steal kisses, so the scruff had to go. I don't like giving ladies whisker burn." He backed away. "But I'm staying out of the temptation zone until we get something accomplished. FYI, there's an outlet under each desk."

"Does this happen to be your cabin?"

"It was, in fact, although the built-ins change the look so it feels a lot different. But the outlets stayed the same. Oh, and the vacuum's old and cranky, but everybody's used to it so Mom keeps getting it repaired instead of buying a new one. It's sort of an heirloom."

"I like that." She leaned down and gave the canister vac a pat. "Don't worry, sweetie. I'll treat you with the respect you deserve."

He figured she was kidding, but as he turned over the

mattresses and checked for anything tucked in corners and crevices, he noticed that she used the vacuum efficiently but gently. She didn't bang it against the furniture or drag it by the cord. Every minute he was finding more reasons to like her, more reasons to make her a part of his personal life as well as his professional one.

The mattresses didn't take long and he only found some gum wrappers, a couple of small purple hair clips and a crumpled picture of a popular boy band. Obviously girls had been living in this cabin. Although he'd known all along that the academy was coed, he hadn't grasped the concept that girls might occupy the same cabin where he'd spent his pivotal teenage years. That was more of a shock than the loft beds.

Geena shut off the vacuum. "I found a gold anklet. At least I think it's an anklet." She dangled it from one finger. "Could be a bracelet. I'm glad I didn't suck it up. Her name's engraved on the little gold heart, which means Rosie can mail it back to her." She tucked the delicate gold chain in her jeans pocket.

"I don't think these are worth mailing, though, even if Mom found out who lost them." He showed her the hair clips.

"Nope. Those are easily replaced, but I'll take them. Rosie might want to add them to her stash. I don't know if she has hair doodads, but she might keep some on hand in case the girls lose theirs."

Matt handed them over. "I'll bet she gets a kick out of having girls around for a change."

"She and Herb never considered taking in foster girls, too?"

"Not that I know of. I think when they started with boys, it might have been simpler to stick with that."

"Probably." She shoved the clips in her other pocket

and gazed at him. "You know…" Then she blew out a breath. "Never mind. I should go get the water." She gestured to the vacuum. "Your heirloom awaits. I finished the left side of the room so the right side is all yours. Be right back."

"Wait. You obviously had something to say."

"There's no point. You won't like it."

"I might. You never know."

"Yeah, I do, but I might as well finish my thought. Finding that engraved gold chain brought it home to me that there were teenage girls living here last semester, girls who would go wild if they knew Matt Forrest had been on cleanup duty in the very cabin where they stayed."

A yellow caution light went on in his brain. "Maybe."

"No *maybe* about it. I realize you hate the negative publicity being generated, but—"

"Don't you hate it, too?"

"Yes, absolutely. I'd much rather see positive promo out there for all my clients. But the negative stuff's accomplished one thing. I guarantee most everyone knows who you are, including the teenage girls who lived in this cabin. They'd be super excited to discover you were here in the same space they so recently vacated."

"Even if they think I'm the kind of guy who would seduce a married woman?"

"Like I said before, bad boys are popular, too."

His gut tightened. "I don't want that kind of reputation."

"I know you don't. But I doubt you'd agree to a cute little story about the hot movie star who volunteered his time to clean cabins used by the students of Thunder Mountain Academy."

"You're right. I wouldn't agree to that."

"I can promise you the girls would be over the moon and even the guys might relish the idea that they had a connection to a celebrity, especially one who can ride and rope."

"They might, but I don't want reporters on this ranch invading Mom and Dad's privacy. Or Cade and Lexi's, for that matter."

"I understand." Her gaze was filled with compassion. "But you might end up having to make a choice. If you're determined to protect everyone's privacy, you may be stuck with the bad boy reputation."

The tightness in his gut turned into a slow burn. "I thought you said this was winnable."

"It is, but you may not be willing to do what's necessary to turn this thing around."

Bile rose in his throat. "I won't sacrifice my family for personal gain and that's final."

"I know. I'll be back soon with the water." She put on her straw hat, picked up the bucket sitting beside the door and left.

He turned on the vacuum because then he could swear as loud as he wanted. He'd arrived at the ranch at the age of twelve with a fair number of colorful words in his vocabulary. After hanging out with his foster brothers, he'd added quite a few more. None of the guys used that kind of language around Rosie and Herb, but down in the meadow late at night they used to turn the air blue and laugh like fiends.

This problem was no laughing matter, but swearing still felt like a cleansing activity. He worked his way through his entire repertoire before he started vacuuming. He didn't want to lose his temper with the machine after Geena had treated it with such loving care.

Maybe her assessment of his situation was wrong. But

she was smart and she was capable. Except for her initial reaction to the crisis, he'd been impressed with her grasp of the situation. Unfortunately that might mean she was right about his two choices. Too bad they were sucky and suckier.

Chapter Ten

Cade was on his way over to pick up the vacuum as Geena trudged back carrying the five-gallon bucket that she'd filled about two-thirds full. He didn't notice her and she was happy about that. The bucket was heavier than she'd expected, but she didn't want Cade to figure out that she was struggling and take it off her hands. Matt had given her credit for being strong enough, and she didn't want to admit she wasn't.

Now that she thought about it, chopping wood might not be as easy as she imagined, either. Much as she longed to be a country girl, she was still a city girl playing at country living. That didn't mean she'd have to stay that way, though.

Lugging the water had demonstrated that she was soft. She'd slacked off on her workouts at the gym, but that would change now that she had motivation to develop more upper body strength. She loved this place and wanted to spend more time on this ranch or one like it.

On the way down to the bathhouse, when she hadn't been burdened with a bucket of water, she'd had time to wonder about her visceral reaction to the meadow and the cabins. She couldn't be positive, but she had a vague memory of being in such a place with her father. She would have been less than three, because by that age her mother had taken over her schedule and packed it with activities to mold her into a superstar.

Sometime around then her dad had died while piloting his small plane. Prior to that he might have flown them to some remote spot for a vacation that she barely remembered. Apparently it had made a soul-deep impression on her, though, because she'd felt a connection to these log cabins from her first glimpse of them.

She was grateful for that epiphany and the trip to Wyoming that had made it possible. But her awakening to the beauties of ranching country didn't do anything for Matt's dilemma and she'd come here to help him. She'd had more thoughts about that but wasn't sure how to approach him with her ideas—or whether to approach him at all.

At breakfast, Rosie had talked about all the support she and Herb had received for the academy project. Matt's star power could contribute to the success of the school, perhaps really put it on the map, but reporters would have to be involved. He'd said he didn't want them invading his foster parents' privacy.

But she had no idea how Rosie and Herb felt about it. What if they'd gladly trade a little privacy for the publicity they'd get by aligning themselves with Matt's celebrity status? And what if they were reluctant to ask that of him because they didn't want to risk jeopardizing the privacy he found by coming here?

If it turned out that Matt was protecting Rosie and

Herb while they were protecting him, it was enough to give her a migraine. Or it should have been. But in this setting she couldn't imagine ever having a headache again. The air was blissfully smog-free and she didn't have to endure the cacophony of honking horns and the rhythmic thump of audio systems set to stun.

Los Angeles seemed a million miles away. She'd make those phone calls after this cleaning gig but she wasn't looking forward to talking with the client who'd thrown a tantrum because he hadn't been mentioned in *People* this week. Dealing with Matt wasn't easy, but she'd rather coax someone into the limelight than have to drag a client offstage with a shepherd's crook before they made a complete ass of themselves.

Cade was leaving the cabin with the canister vac in hand as she approached. He put it down and walked to meet her. "Here, I'll take that back for you."

"Thanks, I've got it." She pulled the bucket out of reach so fast she sloshed water on her jeans. Felt kind of good, actually.

His brows lifted. "A little possessive of that bucket, aren't we?"

"Yes. Yes, I am." Sweat trickled down her back. "I carried it all the way here and I intend to finish the job by myself."

"You have grit, Geena Lysander. I like that."

"Thank you." She lowered her voice. "Let me ask you something." She put the bucket down and swallowed a groan of relief.

"Sure."

"Has it occurred to you that linking Matt's name to the academy could be a good thing for business?"

His expression grew wary. "It might have." He moved

a step closer and spoke quietly. "But he needs this place as an escape and that could ruin it for him."

She decided not to address that particular assumption. It could be true, but maybe not if she planned her strategy in advance. "So the thought that Matt could be a draw has crossed your mind."

"Yes, ma'am, but we dismissed it immediately. I hope that's not the road you're heading down."

She noticed his use of *we*. "I'm not heading down any road. I'm still trying to read the map. Matt says he doesn't want your privacy invaded, meaning all four of you—Rosie, Herb, Lexi and you. According to what I'm hearing from him, it's not about his need for privacy. It's about yours."

"See, that's the way he is, always looking out for the people he cares about. Which means we need to look out for him. This situation has made him think that he'd be more of a hindrance than a help."

"But that's not necessarily true."

Cade tugged on the brim of his hat. "No, ma'am, but as long as he thinks it is, then Thunder Mountain can continue to be his sanctuary. Which is fine with us."

"When you say *us*, do you mean the four of you?"

"Uh, there's a few more than that involved."

"Who?"

He hesitated.

"If you don't mind my asking."

"Guess not. You've been trustworthy so far."

"Cade, I care about Matt. I'd never do anything to hurt him."

He met her gaze and seemed to be evaluating what to say. Finally he nodded. "Okay. Ever since Matt got this part, we've recognized his potential to help the academy. The primary group on site includes Mom, Dad, Lexi and me, plus Damon and Phil. Then there's Ben Radcliffe, who teaches saddle making for us, and his wife, Molly, who set up the curriculum. Finn's wife, Chelsea, is in marketing, so she immediately saw the possibilities, but she also knows that Matt's a private guy who cherishes this ranch. The upshot is that no one's said a word to him about helping to publicize the academy."

"So you guys are miles ahead of me. I had no idea."

"And now you know."

"I do. Thanks for trusting me with this."

"You can't tell him."

"I won't."

He smiled. "And now you'd better take that water where it belongs before he sends out a search party."

"Aye, aye, sir!" She snapped him another salute and picked up her bucket. She was pleased that he chuckled as she walked away. Cade was one of the good guys. In fact, they all sounded terrific and she wished she could meet the rest of the brotherhood.

When she reached the cabin, she left the bucket on the cement stoop and opened the door.

Matt had taken off his hat and had his back to her as he vigorously cleaned the inside of a window. He didn't turn around. "I was about to go looking for you."

"It was more of a challenge than I thought." But watching his tight buns flex inside well-washed denim and his back muscles shift beneath his white T-shirt was reward enough.

"Did you find the outside faucet?" He leaned over to rub a spot near the bottom of the window.

Lordy. "I did." She paused to clear the lust from her throat. "After I figured out that getting water from one of the sinks or from the shower wasn't practical, I went looking for a better alternative."

"Should've known you would." He gave the window one last swipe and turned around. "Did you run into Cade? He just left a bit ago with the vacuum."

"Yep, I saw him." She hoped her expression didn't give anything away.

"The windows over there were a lot dirtier than these, apparently." He gazed at her. "Which is lucky for us or Cade would have shown up a *lot* earlier to fetch the vacuum."

"You mean early enough to catch us...kissing?" Matt had done a lot more than kiss her, and she wouldn't mind having him repeat the process now that they were alone again.

"Yes, ma'am. Sorry about that. I forgot he's amazingly fast at windows."

"You also were looking proficient at the window-cleaning gig when I walked in here." She still had a buzz going. "How fast is Cade at vacuuming?"

His eyes darkened. "Too damned fast, I'm afraid." He tossed down the towel he'd been using on the window and came toward her. "Especially when you look at me like that. But I don't dare grab hold of you. I know what will happen." He reached out and brushed a damp strand of hair from her cheek and sucked in a breath. "There's something so sexy about a woman who's been outside getting sweaty."

She laughed, although her heart was pounding. "I can't imagine what."

"Can't you?" He brushed his knuckles lightly over her throat. "Your skin's already nice and warm, plus it's damp, which makes it so easy to slide my hand—"

"All right, I get it." She gulped and stepped back.

"Your glasses are fogged up again."

"I know." She quickly cleaned them on the tail of her

shirt. "You're right, we can't do this. Cade and Lexi will show up and find us rolling around on the floor."

"Rolling? Really?" His smile had a definite touch of wickedness. "I don't know about you, but I find it's a lot nicer if you stay put."

She groaned. "We need to start mopping this floor before I say to heck with what Cade and Lexi find us doing. Are you finished with the windows?"

"I'm finished with the inside. If you're willing to mop, I'll go take off the screens and do the outside."

"I'd rather have you do *me*."

"Yes, ma'am." He winked at her before scooping up the towel he'd dropped and snagging the spray bottle of window cleaner. "So would I." He went out the door, transferred the bucket from the stoop to the inside, and left her to work out her frustrations with some vigorous mopping.

Matt vowed that he'd concentrate on the windows. He'd taken off the screens without once looking inside the cabin. Then he'd washed an entire window while managing to ignore whatever was happening on the opposite side of the glass. Feeling noble and in control, he'd decided it wouldn't hurt to take a quick peek inside to see how Geena was coming along with her mopping.

He was still watching her when Cade clapped him on the shoulder, causing him to jump and drop the spray bottle. Luckily it was plastic. When he turned to confront a grinning Cade, he discovered Lexi was there, too, looking highly amused.

Matt glared at both of them, but mostly at Cade for startling him. "You shouldn't sneak up on a guy with a loaded spray bottle in his hand. I could've hit you in the face with a blast of window cleaner. That stuff has to be bad for your eyes."

"Couldn't resist, bro. But I regret to inform you that most women don't go for the Peeping Tom routine. If she catches you doing it, I guarantee she'll think it's creepy that you're staring in the window while she's mopping the floor. You'll lose points, bro, major points."

"But she's not just mopping. She's tap dancing while she does it."

"Are you kidding me?"

"Nope. Take a look."

Cade moved to the window. "I'll be damned. C'mere, Lex. This reminds me of those old black-and-white movies Mom likes."

Lexi walked over and stood on tiptoe. "I can't really see."

"Okay, here you go." Cade crouched down. "Get on my shoulders."

"You know, I don't think—"

"Do it. This is worth the price of admission."

"I hope she doesn't glance our way and see this." Lexi climbed on Cade's shoulders and he slowly got to his feet. "Oh, wow. She really is tap dancing. In cowboy boots, no less, and wearing her hat! I wonder if she has music. I can't hear anything. Maybe she has music on her phone."

"Maybe."

"Well, that's just cool. Look at her go! She's—uh-oh. She saw us. Now she'll probably quit."

Matt expected that, too. But after giving them a smile and a wave, she continued with her routine as she worked her way toward the cabin door. When she finished, she spun back toward them and bowed. They all applauded and Matt whistled through his teeth.

"Let's meet her at the door." Lexi hopped down and they walked around to the front of the cabin.

Geena came out holding the bucket with the mop handle sticking out of it. She was breathing hard and her cheeks were bright pink. Matt couldn't remember ever seeing a prettier sight, and he'd spent three years in the land of gorgeous women.

They all clapped and cheered, which made her roll her eyes and laugh. Setting down the bucket, she executed another little dance step on the concrete stoop and swept off her hat in a dramatic gesture, dislodging the pins in her hair. It tumbled out of its arrangement.

"That was *awesome*," Lexi said. "No wonder you caught on to the dance moves so quickly last night. You're a pro!"

"Sadly, I'm not. I haven't tapped in a while, so I'm pretty rusty and so out of shape."

Matt picked up the bucket and mop. He was willing to argue that point. He loved her shape. And her hair, which hung in glorious waves to her shoulders. He longed to comb it back with his fingers, cup her head in both hands and tilt it so he could kiss that smiling mouth.

"Would you please hold this for a sec while I fix my hair?" She handed him her hat.

"Sure." He felt like telling her to leave it down because it looked sexy that way. He thought better of saying that out loud.

Drawing a deep breath, she retrieved the scattered pins and used them to anchor her hair on top of her head again. "The mop reminded me of a number we put together when I was taking dance. We combined moves from the Gene Kelly mop dance and Fred Astaire's routine with a broom. You may not have seen either of those since they're from really old movies."

"I have," Cade said. "So have Damon and Finn. When we first came to the ranch, before the cabins were built, we used to sit in the living room and watch those musicals with Mom. She's crazy about them. She'd go nuts if you did a tap number for her."

"I'd probably be too self-conscious to give a planned performance. I don't even have the right shoes." She took back her hat and put it on.

"That's what made it so impressive," Lexi said. "You weren't wearing tap shoes. Did you have music playing?"

"Just in my head. I thought nobody was watching. Then I saw you guys at the window and my training kicked in. My dance teacher drummed into us that you never stop in the middle of a number when you have an audience. No matter what, the show must go on."

"I'm glad you didn't stop." Matt had been smitten before, but after that dance routine he was completely dazzled. He could manage a two-step and a waltz without a problem, but he didn't have the dedication to learn something as complicated as tap. Consequently, he admired the hell out of someone who'd had the determination to get good at it.

He had to laugh when he thought about the earnest conversation he'd had with Geena on the porch last night. They'd both announced that now was not the time to have a serious relationship. He'd been of a similar mindset when he told Cade and Lexi he didn't want Rosie launching into matchmaking mode.

On paper, the timing of his sudden interest in Geena couldn't be worse. His career was finally off to a promising start, but the film business was notoriously unstable. An actor could go from fame to obscurity in the blink of an eye.

Asking someone to share the ride when the journey

was wildly uncertain wasn't fair. His head knew that, but his heart wasn't listening. He was falling for this amazing woman at an alarming rate and getting serious sounded like a terrific idea. If Rosie had any advice on how to turn a temporary fling into something more permanent, he was ready to hear it.

Chapter Eleven

The four of them ended up working together on the last two cabins, which was fine with Matt. He got a kick out of the way Geena interacted with Cade and Lexi, as if she'd known them forever. They treated her the same way. Apparently they recognized qualities in each other that made friendship easy.

Besides, he'd given up the idea of more sexy interludes with her during this cleaning gig. Too much risk of being interrupted and he was feeling increasingly grubby. Before he held her again he needed a shower and a closer shave than he'd managed early this morning.

On the way back to the house Cade got into a conversation with Geena about old movies, and that gave Matt a chance to mention the upcoming trail ride to Lexi.

"Should be fun."

"I've never taken someone out who hasn't been on a horse. Is that a stupid idea? You were planning to give her a lesson and I don't want to jump the gun if you think she needs a lesson first."

"Cade mentioned that she seemed really comfortable with the horses this morning. I'm not saying a lesson wouldn't be helpful at some point, but greenhorns take trail rides all the time without any prior experience." Lexi smiled. "She has to be coordinated or she wouldn't be able to tap dance."

"What's that?" Geena called over to them. "Are you two talking about me?"

"Yes, ma'am." Matt glanced at her. "I wanted to get Lexi's opinion on our trail ride plan. She thinks it'll be fine."

"Good, because I think so, too, especially if we meander over to Matt's ranch and meander back."

Cade laughed. "Considering you're taking Navarre and Isabeau out in the middle of a warm day, you won't get them to do anything *but* meander."

"And that's perfect for a beginner like me. If Lexi and I can find the time for a lesson while I'm here, great. After I know more I'll try going a little faster."

Lexi pulled out her phone and consulted the screen. "How about first thing tomorrow morning? I don't have anything scheduled until ten." She grinned. "And now that you're used to getting up at dawn, we could work in a quick lesson before breakfast."

"That would be great. Thanks."

"Lexi's phone reminded me of something," Cade said. "Geena, you'd better take yours on the ride."

"I would, anyway, in case my assistant needs to get in touch."

"That's good, because last I heard, hotshot here stowed his in the bottom of a dresser drawer."

"No worries, bro." Matt looked over at him. "I'd already planned to unearth it for the ride."

"Well, good. Is the battery charged?"

Matt sighed. "Yes, Cade, the battery's charged."

"I'm delighted to hear it, because a gentleman would never take a lady on a trail ride without bringing his fully charged phone in case of an emergency."

"You won't have an emergency," Lexi added quickly. "But it's always good to be prepared."

"Have either of you seen my new place?" He didn't want to spoil the ambience by taking Geena to see peeling paint and rotting wood.

"Sorry, bro." Cade shook his head. "Haven't had the time. Mom and Dad said it has a lot of promise and that you got a good price on it."

"Is that code for *it's a dump but with a ton of work it'll be reasonably okay*?"

"I don't think it's a dump," Lexi said. "They wouldn't have let you buy it if they thought that. But I wouldn't expect it to look like a page out of a guest-ranch brochure, either."

"No worries," Geena said. "It's exciting that you bought a ranch, regardless of what it looks like."

"Yeah, it is." He hadn't cared what it looked like, either, until he'd invited her over there. But he wouldn't worry about it. How bad could it be?

"I have a question," Cade said. "Assuming you get it fixed up and maybe buy yourself a couple of horses, who's gonna take care of the place while you're in Hollywood being famous?"

"I'll need to hire someone. Got any ideas?"

"I might. Let me give it some thought."

"I wouldn't mind having somebody lined up before I go back."

"And when will that be?"

"Not sure yet."

"Don't forget you have that appearance for *Preston's Revenge* next week," Geena said.

"Right."

"And I booked you into two morning talk shows after that."

He nodded. "They're on my calendar." At one time he'd been excited about those publicity gigs.

"Don't worry." Her voice softened. "We'll schedule some coaching sessions before you do any of it. But I'll need my video equipment to do it right. I'd like you back in LA by Monday, at the latest."

"No worries," Cade said. "We can locate a caretaker for the ranch before then." He turned to Geena. "Can you stay until Monday?"

"I can if I absolutely have to, but I'd hate to think this issue will drag on that long. Surely we'll find a way to put a cork in it soon."

Matt blew out a breath. "Or I could just accept my new image as a bad boy and move on."

"Whoa, what?" Cade stopped walking and stared at him.

"It's an option. I don't have to apologize because that kind of guy wouldn't. If I give up worrying about my white hat image, I also don't have to put my family in front of a camera to testify that I'm some kind of paragon. Like I said, it's an option. I'm thinking about it."

Cade shook his head. "Well, you can stop thinking about it. We're the Thunder Mountain Brotherhood." His eyes took on a steely glint. "When someone attacks, we don't just roll over."

"We also don't put our loved ones in harm's way." Matt held his gaze. "If you think that by staying silent and taking the rap I'll be dishonoring the brotherhood, then I'll resign from—"

"Aw, hell, I didn't mean that! I'm asking you not to give up, okay? I swear we'll find a way out of this that will work for everybody."

"Like what?"

"I don't know yet. But remember that you're not alone and I'm not just talking about the folks, Lexi and me. The brotherhood is with you, all of us, and I'm thinking we may not have tapped into that firepower like we should be doing. Let me make some calls, see if we can set up a Skype thing tonight."

Emotion clogged Matt's throat and he had to clear it before he could speak. "That…that would be…"

"Fun?"

"That, too." He smiled. "Thanks. Even if nothing comes of it, I—"

"Something will come of it." Cade took a deep breath. "But I'd love for you and Geena to take a nice ride over to your new ranch and forget all about it for a few hours. Think you can do that, cowboy?"

Matt looked into his brother's eyes and saw a strength and determination that gave him more hope than he'd had in days. "Yeah, we can do that."

An hour later, Geena had made her phone calls and dealt with the prima donna. Although he was difficult to work with, he was a popular actor and gave her fledgling company a lot of street cred. Matt had the potential to do the same thing, which was why she'd agreed to work with him. And, bonus, he wasn't a prima donna.

She envisioned great things for him in the future, which would be good for both of them. Having a personal relationship added an element of risk, though, and she wasn't blind to the danger. If they developed issues, that would affect their business arrangement. She'd decided to think positively on that score.

For now, their personal relationship was uppermost in her mind because she was on her way to his ranch and riding a horse for the first time in her life. Except something about that felt familiar. Watching Isabeau's ears flick back and forth, and listening to the creak of the saddle triggered a memory.

They'd left the ranch property single file but now rode side by side down a dirt road that Matt had told her belonged to the Forest Service. Tall pines shaded a strip along the edge, but the sun was directly overhead. She felt it on her back and shoulders, but she was a California girl who was used to it.

She'd worn another pair of the jeans Rosie had loaned her, but she'd decided her white stretch tank would work for the ride if she slathered on sunscreen. She was also glad for the straw hat.

Lexi had given her a few pointers when she'd mounted up. She was supposed to keep her heels down and her back straight. Although she held the reins loosely in one hand, she had Lexi's permission to hang on to the saddle horn with the other as much as she wanted if it gave her a sense of security.

It did. At first the sensation of sitting astride a large animal had been unnerving and she'd hung on for dear life. Gradually, though, she'd become used to the rocking motion and she'd relaxed her grip on the horn.

As they rode, Matt described the scene in winter when everything was covered in a blanket of snow. Last semester the academy students had reconditioned an old sleigh under Phil's supervision, and now sleigh rides had been added to the list of activities. A white Christmas wasn't guaranteed in Wyoming, but Matt was hoping for one this year, and time off so he could spend the holiday at Thunder Mountain.

Geena loved hearing details like that and secretly hoped he would invite her along on such a trip. But she suspected he was making small talk because he'd promised to banish negative thoughts for the rest of the afternoon. Cade hadn't made her promise, but she'd do her best, too.

Cade's plan to rally his brothers brought tears to her eyes every time she thought about it. No matter what happened as a result, she'd never forget the love and pride in his voice as he'd reminded Matt that the Thunder Mountain Brotherhood had his back.

"You're looking good over there," Matt said. "How does it feel?"

"Believe it or not, like I've done this before."

"But you said you'd never ridden."

"I haven't, not like this. But Isabeau's head bobbing in front of me is very familiar."

"A pony ride, maybe?"

"No, I wasn't sitting on the horse. I was in somebody's lap." She glanced over at him. "You know what? I'll bet when I was very little, like, maybe two and a half, my dad held me while we went riding. I think the two of us might have taken a vacation together. I'm guessing there were log cabins and horses. That would explain the déjà vu."

"Where is he now?"

"He crashed his private plane when I was about three. No survivors."

"Damn."

"It's sad, and I sure wish it hadn't happened, but the truth is I barely remember him. He and my mom had already divorced by then. I'd love to ask her if he and I went on that kind of vacation, but she gets weepy when his name comes up."

"So, she still misses him."

"Yep. Once I went in her closet to try on her shoes and found an old love note from him tucked in the toe of sparkly red heels I'd never seen her wear. It's cool to know they were once in love, even if they didn't stay together."

"That is cool."

She heard the wistfulness in his voice and regretted having mentioned it. He didn't know who his father was, let alone whether his mom and dad had been in love. Likely not. Time to leave the past and concentrate on the present. "I have to say you're looking quite manly mounted up on your trusty steed."

"Oh?" He seemed to mentally pull himself back from wherever her story had sent him. "Thank you, ma'am." He winked at her and touched the brim of his Stetson. "Mighty kind of you to say so."

Her heart lurched. He was such a great guy. She'd never forgive Briana for making a move on him and creating this horrible scenario.

"Something wrong?" Matt's voice cut through her thoughts.

"No, why?"

"You're scowling."

She slowly breathed out and relaxed her facial muscles. So much for honoring Cade's wish that they could forget the problems and enjoy the afternoon. "Sorry."

"Care to tell me what you were scowling about?"

She turned to him with a sunny smile. "No."

"Okay."

He probably knew what she'd been thinking. What a waste. The day was beautiful and she was riding alongside a gorgeous cowboy who truly deserved to wear a white hat, even though currently his was brown. He'd showered and put on a clean white T-shirt and jeans. She suspected, from the scent of cologne drifting her way and the nick on his square jaw, that he'd shaved again.

"How much longer is the ride?"

He laughed. "Is that a version of *Are we there, yet*?"

"Kind of. I have a strong urge to kiss that little spot where you cut yourself shaving."

"Only that one spot?"

Just like that, he'd managed to jump-start her libido with a single teasing question. "Um, now that you mention it…"

"If you hadn't been so keen on seeing my ranch, we'd be making out on a picnic blanket this very minute."

"Where?" The eagerness in her voice was embarrassing, but she couldn't help it.

"A grassy meadow I know about. We passed it a ways back."

She glanced over her shoulder.

"No, ma'am, you can't see it from here and we're not heading back. We're closer to my ranch than we are to the meadow, and I have some special places I want to kiss once I get the chance. Wanna hear where they are?"

"Better not." Whew. She squirmed in the saddle and Isabeau snorted. "Hey, cowboy, you'd better dial back the sexy before I swoon and fall right off this horse."

Matt's low chuckle sent shivers down her spine. "You started it." He looked over at her and smiled. "It won't be long now. The back entrance is up yonder." He pointed to a weathered gate between two thick posts.

"I see it." *Up yonder.* She didn't remember him using phrases like that in LA. Being here really brought out the country in him and she loved that, too. "So we're going in the back way?"

"That's the best route for horses. If you're driving you take the paved road to the front gate. Either way, it's not too far from Thunder Mountain."

"Who knows you bought this place?"

"My family, you, the bank and the real estate agent. I'm guessing some other people in town know because word gets around when a ranch is bought or sold."

"You didn't tell any of your friends in LA?"

"Nope. They're still struggling financially, like I was six months ago. Mentioning that I'd bought a ranch seemed like bragging. I didn't bring it up."

That was so like him, thinking of someone else's feelings instead of his excitement about a major purchase.

"It'll be a while before I'm ready to invite anybody here, anyway." He halted Navarre in front of the sagging gate and swung down from the saddle. "Let's hope the house looks better than this gate." He took a key from his pocket and opened the padlock on a thick chain wrapped around both the gate and the post.

He gently pushed the gate inward as the hinges squeaked and the wood groaned. Then he stepped back and motioned her forward. "After you."

She nudged Isabeau in the ribs the way Lexi had shown her and the mare slowly trudged through the opening. Then she looked back at Navarre and whinnied. "She's not liking this," Geena said.

"I know she doesn't. Hey, Izzy, it's okay. We won't leave your boyfriend behind." Matt led Navarre through and closed the gate.

"See? You do think of them as a couple." Geena turned in her saddle so she could watch him mount up. So smooth. She'd love a video but her phone was in her saddlebag and he wouldn't want her to take one, anyway.

"Hard not to think of them as a couple with those

names. But as you can probably tell, Izzy's not a very liberated lady. Now that we're headed down a one-lane path, she'll want Navarre to lead."

"Fine with me. You should get the first look at your ranch house, anyway. You must be excited to finally see it."

He pulled alongside her and tipped back his hat. "Not nearly as excited as I am about what's going to happen when we get there."

She gulped. "Careful. I might swoon."

"In a few minutes you can do that all you want. I've been thinking about how this will likely play out."

"I thought…" She drew in a quick breath. "I thought we'd decided to clean off a spot on the floor and put down the blanket." It was tied behind his saddle and she'd been extremely aware of it the entire ride.

His hot glance traveled over her, igniting fires wherever it touched. "Let's be honest. We'll never make it into the house, let alone have the presence of mind to sweep the floor and lay down a blanket."

"Oh." Her brain turned to mush. "So what…what should we do?"

"Tie the horses, take this blanket—" He gave it a quick pat. "And find a nice patch of grass."

"Out…outside?"

"No one will be there but us." His gaze searched hers. "But if you don't want to—"

"Yes." She was very nearly panting and could barely speak. "I want to."

Chapter Twelve

Matt almost pulled her off her horse so they could execute the plan right then and there. But that would lack significance. He wanted her desperately, but this wasn't just about sex.

He gave the brim of his hat a determined downward tug. "Then let's go." He tapped Navarre with his boot heels. Snorting, the horse set out at a brisk walk, and Matt looked over his shoulder to see how Geena was handling the faster pace. "You okay?"

"Never better!" She'd tightened her grip on the saddle horn but she hadn't lost either of her stirrups. Some of her hair had escaped from under her hat and her skin was flushed a becoming shade of pink. She was smiling.

He co uldn't stop looking at that smile. Emotions crowded his chest until he wondered if it would break wide open from the pressure. Even when he faced forward again so he could see where the hell he was going, her smile stayed with him. He thought of what was about to happen and his hands began to shake.

It seemed he was nervous. As the leading man in a major motion picture, he'd made pretend love to a big-time movie star in front of a stage crew and several cameras, but he was afraid he'd mess this up. He'd also made love for real with several women since losing his virginity at seventeen, but he'd never felt as if his whole future depended on it. Maybe taking her on a blanket outside wasn't a good idea.

Maybe he should wait for a bed, clean sheets and a cool breeze through curtained windows. Because when it was all over, he needed to see that smile. He wanted that more than anything he'd ever wished for in his entire crazy life.

He was so absorbed in his inner debate that he rode right past the fence enclosing a pasture before he realized what he was looking at. Not much of the fence was still standing, so maybe he could be excused for missing it.

At that point the horse trail ended and he rode into an open space between the barn on his right and the house about thirty yards away on his left. *His house.* He'd never owned anything of value except an old pickup he'd sold before he'd left for LA.

He pulled Navarre to a halt and pivoted the horse in order to watch Geena coming toward him on Isabeau. Damn, that woman was so beautiful it made his throat hurt. And there was that heart-stopping smile again, one that he returned because, just like that, his doubts were gone.

What happened in the future didn't matter anymore. She was here today, and as eager to be his lover as he was to be hers. That was more than some men were given in a lifetime. His heart pounded and heat rushed to his groin. Debate over.

Her green eyes sparkled. "Just think, Matt. This is your land."

"Hard to believe."

"The barn looks sturdy."

He laughed. "Nice way to put it." He angled his head toward the house and turned Navarre back in that direction. "Let's go see if the house looks sturdy, too." Along the way they passed some clumps of weeds but so far not much in the way of grass. He hoped they'd find some in the front yard. Although he'd seen grass growing in the pasture, that wasn't the ambience he was after.

"I'm sure the house is sturdy," she said. "Like Lexi said, your folks wouldn't let you buy a place that had major structural flaws."

"And it wasn't like I could afford a showplace. Not if I wanted acreage to go with the house and barn."

"How many acres do you have?"

"Almost twenty-five."

"That sounds huge!"

"Not by Wyoming standards. But it's fine for me and a couple of horses."

"And whoever you hire to watch the place while you're gone."

"True." If he wanted horses, someone would have to live on the ranch year-round. Funny how he'd imagined bringing her back here in a few months for some private time, but unless he asked his hired hand to take off for a couple of days, he and Geena wouldn't be alone, after all.

They were now, though. Except for the birds chattering and the low sigh of a breeze, the place was quiet. Intimate. He looked over at her and she was looking right back. Her throat moved in a slow swallow.

"Nervous?"

"Some. Mostly excited."

"Me, too." As they approached the house from the side, he could see the large tree in front near the porch. In the picture it had been leafless, but now it was budding out in response to the warm weather. And, hallelujah, under the tree was a nice little patch of spring grass that might not have been there a week or two ago.

He spared a quick glance for the house, which looked fine, as Geena had predicted. It had been painted recently, but mustard yellow wouldn't have been his first choice. Didn't matter. Paint was cheap.

He rode up to the side railing of the porch and dismounted, anticipation making him stumble slightly. Navarre looked back at him. "Yeah, I know. Pathetic."

He turned to Geena, who'd pulled Isabeau to a stop. "You can park her next to Navarre. I'll help you down." He looped Navarre's reins loosely around the railing.

"I can get down by myself."

"Yes, ma'am, I know you can." He walked around to Isabeau's left side, took the mare's reins and wrapped them around the railing. "But you might need me to steady you a little bit, in case you're shaky." What a laugh. If anyone was shaky, he was. He needed to touch her. The sooner he could do that, the sooner his world would start making sense again.

"You could be right about that." She held tight to the saddle horn and swung her leg over Isabeau's rump.

Spanning her waist with his hands, Matt guided her descent until she had both feet on the ground. Then he didn't want to let go.

"Matt, I'm okay. You can—" She gasped as he spun her around.

"To hell with the blanket." He scooped her into his

arms and carried her over to the grass. Her hat fell off somewhere along the way, but she didn't seem to notice.

Instead, she wound her arms around his neck. She was breathing fast, and little puffs of warm air tickled his throat. He couldn't look down to see if she was okay with this because in his current state he might run smack into the tree trunk.

Somehow he managed to lay her on the fragrant grass without injuring either of them. He was coiled tight as a buckboard spring, but as he looked at her lying there, he realized he should find a safe place for her glasses. Leaning over her, he gently removed them, took off his hat and dropped her glasses inside.

"Thanks." Her voice was husky.

"Anytime." Setting his hat aside, he looked into her eyes. "If you—" He paused to suck in some air. "If you want me to get the blanket, or if you want anything to be different, you'd better tell me now."

"I want *you*." She grasped his face in both hands and pulled him down for an open-mouthed kiss that fried what was left of his brain.

Operating solely on instinct, he pushed up the stretchy cotton of her tank and found another front-catch bra under there. Instead of taking anything off, he simply moved the material aside. Then he broke away from her kiss so he could savor her beautiful breasts.

She moaned and arched into his caress, and at last she begged for more. She was very specific about what she wanted and he loved that she was so bold, loved that her hunger matched his. His cock swelled in response.

First her boots had to go. Next he pulled off her jeans and panties in one smooth motion. Earlier, caught in the frenzied dance of anticipation, he'd fumbled the simplest tasks, but now he was extremely focused.

His gaze swept over her as he knelt in the grass. He wanted the bra and tank top out of the way, too. "Lift your arms."

Holding his gaze, she raised them over her head and he removed the last of her clothes. She lay there panting as the scent of crushed grass and arousal flowed around them. Sunlight filtered by the new leaves created a dappled pattern on her smooth skin—pale where the sun's rays had been blocked by her swimsuit and golden where the sun had been allowed to kiss her.

"You look...like a goddess."

"I feel like one." Her green eyes glowed with passion. "And I command you to strip down, cowboy."

Wordlessly he reached back, grabbed his T-shirt with both hands and pulled it over his head. The slight breeze felt good on his bare chest.

She brushed her fingers over his chest hair. "They didn't make you shave."

"No." His heart thudded wildly. How had she guessed he was sensitive there? "They were going for—" He gasped as she gently pinched his nipple. "Historical accuracy."

"I'm glad. I like this look." She ran her fingertips down the strip of dark hair that disappeared under his belt buckle. "But you're still overdressed."

"I can fix that." Soon his boots and socks were history and he shucked his jeans and briefs in record time. But he remembered to take that all-important item from his pocket before he tossed his pants aside. He tore open the packet and rolled on the condom.

At last. Moving over her, he flattened his palms on the cool grass and settled between her thighs. His voice was tight with the strain of keeping himself in check. "You probably think I'm crazy."

"Not crazy. Creative." Her voice trembled, but her hands were steady as she caressed his shoulders and the tense muscles of his back. "You turn me on, Matt."

"Lucky me." He eased forward.

"Lucky us." She welcomed him with liquid heat and delicious friction that made him groan with pleasure.

His first impulse was to hide his reaction to the intense feeling of connection as he slid into her. He was good at hiding his emotions. Usually it was the safest course of action.

But this time, when she so obviously trusted him, it seemed wrong. Looking into her eyes, he masked nothing as he slowly began to stroke.

Neither did she. He drank in the passion, tenderness and joy shining in her gaze. And, ah, she was so eager. Her soft moans of pleasure told him that she wanted this with every fiber of her being. Gradually he picked up the pace.

Her fingertips dug into the muscles of his back as she rose to meet him. "Matt… *Matt.*"

"I'm here." He pushed in tight and paused, his gaze locked with hers. "Right here."

"I know." Her body grew taut. "I *know.*" She began to quiver and her eyes darkened, but she held his gaze as her climax swept through her. Gasping his name, she arched upward as if inviting him to plunge deeper.

His control snapped. With a roar of triumph, he thrust hard into her pulsing channel and welcomed an orgasm that electrified every muscle from his scalp to his toes. He nearly blacked out from the force of it.

Panting, he fought to keep himself braced on his outstretched arms. Gradually his vision cleared enough that he could see her face again. His wish had been granted. She was smiling.

* * *

In Geena's experience, happiness was difficult to pin down. No more. Happiness was looking into Matt's blue eyes and seeing the wonder of their shared climax reflected there. Happiness was feeling soft, damp grass against her bare skin and a gentle breeze brushing her heated cheeks. Happiness was realizing that today, in this place, with this man, she'd discovered a human connection so strong that she'd never again settle for less.

"I love it when you smile like that." He traced her lower lip with the pad of his thumb. "I almost hate to kiss you and give up my view of that smile." He leaned closer. "But I will."

"Please do." Oh, yes, and happiness was kissing someone who put his heart and soul into it. She did the same, which made for a kiss that was long, satisfying and… arousing? Incredibly, she wanted him again. Judging from the evidence, he would be happy to comply.

Lifting his head, he gazed down at her. "You're powerful medicine, lady. I feel like I'm seventeen again."

"Not me. I never had this much fun when I was seventeen."

"Come to think of it, neither did I. I was clueless."

"I'm here to tell you that's no longer the case."

"Thank you, ma'am. Is that a green light?"

"That's a hell yes."

"Hallelujah." He brushed a quick kiss over her mouth. "Don't go away."

"Not a chance." After he left she watched the tender green leaves above her dancing in the sunlight. She hadn't felt like dancing since she'd quit at eighteen. Until today. Until Matt.

Then he was there, moving between her thighs, his gaze warmer than the sun.

Her pulse rate shot up. "That was a fast turnaround, cowboy." Stroking both hands down his back, she cupped his firm buns.

"I was highly motivated." He nibbled on her mouth. "Didn't want you to get bored and leave."

"Like that was going to happen."

"You never know. But it's too late now." He entered her with one swift thrust. "Gotcha." Then he captured her low moan of surrender with an open-mouthed kiss.

The first time had been wonderful. She'd doubted that he could improve on something so perfect, but she hadn't stopped to think that he'd have more staying power the second time around. Lordy, did he know how to use staying power.

He drove her to the brink of insanity and then slowed the pace, teasing her with a leisurely yet erotic motion that kept her at a fever pitch without sending her over the edge. When she began to beg, he finally ramped up the action and she was enveloped in a whirlpool of pleasure. She expected him to follow her there, but instead he kept going.

"Matt?" Gasping, she looked up.

"You're amazing." His breathing was labored but his smile was filled with joy. "I'm having...the time of my life." He gulped for air. "Wrap your legs around me. You're going to come again."

She followed his directions, and sure enough, she swirled into another orgasm. Then he claimed his release, shuddering as a cry rose from deep in his throat. His chest heaved and his biceps trembled, but he remained braced on his outstretched forearms.

Tightening her hold on him, she tugged gently. "Come here."

He shook his head but there was no mistaking the yearning in his eyes. "I don't want to crush you."

"You won't. Lie with me."

A hint of vulnerability flashed in his eyes, but he eased down until he was nestled against her. Sighing, he laid his head on her shoulder. "Tell me if I'm too heavy."

"You're not." She combed her fingers through his damp hair. "You're perfect."

"You are, too."

She listened to his breathing as it slowly evened out. She had no idea what came next in what seemed to be turning into an actual relationship. Sure, making love always changed the dynamic. But she hadn't expected it to change her entire view of the future. Now she couldn't imagine hers without Matt.

Chapter Thirteen

As they lay together, sated and relaxed, Geena's stomach growled.

Matt chuckled. "I heard that. I'll fetch our lunch." Easing away from her, he made short work of the condom and stood, six feet three inches of sculpted manhood.

Despite their recent activities, the sight had the power to dazzle her. She worked regularly with gorgeous movie stars. But she didn't get naked with them. She sat up and looked around for her clothes. They were scattered everywhere.

She untangled her panties from the wad of denim that was her jeans. "We should get dressed and eat lunch in the house."

"Let's not get dressed and eat right here."

"And then what?"

He winked. On Matt, a wink looked really good. "We'll have dessert."

"Are you by any chance putting off the moment when you walk into the house you bought?"

"I'm putting off the moment when you get dressed."

She got to her feet and stood facing him. "Flattering as that is, I can't shake the feeling that you're reluctant to go inside."

"After all the great things that happened out here, the inside of the house has lost its appeal."

"I get that, but you have to take a look sometime. Your family will expect to hear your thoughts on the place."

He shoved his fingers through his hair. "The idea of buying a ranch sight unseen sounded like a bold move back in LA, especially when Mom and Dad gave it their approval. But what if I hate it?"

"Then you renovate. Aren't you expecting to do that, anyway?"

"I am. Damon and Phil are all set to do the work. But I've never bought a house, let alone figured out what needed to be done with it."

"That's all the more reason to go inside. I don't pretend to know anything, either, but we can't talk about what we haven't seen. You have to start somewhere, get a general idea. Then you can bring Damon and Phil over and work out the specifics."

"Okay." He started pulling on his clothes. "That's another thing I have to decide. They're refusing to charge for labor. Just materials. I need to come up with a way to compensate them that doesn't involve giving them a check."

"How about tickets to the premiere?" She dressed quickly. She'd always been eager to see the house but Matt had been a powerful distraction.

His laughter had a bitter edge. "Yeah, right."

"Why not? That's a huge gift, especially if you fly them over."

"Is it? Months ago I set aside a bunch of money so I could treat anybody who wanted to be there. That was before this nastiness happened. Now I wonder if anyone will want to come or even if they should."

"Of course they'll want to come." Her heart broke for him, but this wouldn't be the only time he'd have to face ugliness. Hollywood was filled with gossip and innuendo. She spoke softly. "Matt, I know this is awful, but unfortunately it's part of the job."

"I know. I just didn't expect it first time out of the gate when my family is so excited for me. Eventually I'll get used to the way things are. They will, too. But I hate that it's spoiled something that was so shiny and new."

"Are you sure it has? I haven't been here long but I've already seen what the people in your family are made of. They won't let something like that keep them from celebrating your big moment. I'll bet nothing's spoiled in their minds. They love you."

Sighing, he picked up his hat and walked over to her. "You're right." He grimaced. "You'd think by now I'd believe in their loyalty." Handing over her glasses, he put on his hat. "Thanks for reminding me."

She hadn't meant to chide him but he'd taken it that way. Stepping closer, she touched his arm. "You've been sabotaged by someone you respected, someone you trusted. That would mess with anybody's head, but when you've dealt with something similar in the past, it has to be even more devastating."

He gave her a long look. "Yes, ma'am, that about sums it up." His gusty sigh of impatience was followed by a quick shake of his head. "But my past is no excuse. I've had the counseling. I spent more than ten years living at

Thunder Mountain Ranch. Everything that was broken has been fixed. At least, I hope to hell it has. Otherwise I have no business…"

"What?" The haunted expression in his eyes made her stomach churn.

"I have no business wanting to be with you."

"I want to be with you, too." Her grip tightened on his arm. "I love how I feel when we're together. And I'm not just talking about the sex."

"Neither am I. You're…you're magic." His jaw tensed. "But I'm starting to see a pattern. When I'm focused on you, everything's fine. Then I think about the injustice of it all, I lose my cool. That's not a good sign. Maybe I've been kidding myself. Maybe I'm still the same screwed-up kid I used to be."

She fought panic. "I'm sure you're not."

"Easy for you to say when you don't know what I was like. Any little thing would set me off. If somebody even suggested I'd made a mistake, or that I'd taken what wasn't mine, I lashed out."

"But you haven't lashed out."

"No, because I switched from lashing out to shutting down." He paused. "Does that ring a bell?"

She remembered the moment in her office when suddenly there was an invisible wall between them. "But you had a reason. I wasn't being—"

"Doesn't matter whether I had a reason. It's a bad coping mechanism and I'm supposed to be over it. I caused a problem for you by reacting that way. You had to make this whole damn trip because of my behavior."

"And I'm not the least bit sorry I flew out here! Are you?"

"No." His gaze softened. "I probably should be, but

I guess I'm pretty selfish. What we've had together has been incredible. I'm glad you ran after me."

"Me, too. And I wish you weren't making it sound like what we've had together is going away."

He cupped her face in both hands. "I could be a bad bet, Geena."

"Let me decide that, okay?"

"Not so easy." He brushed his thumbs over her cheeks. "You'd need a hell of a lot more background in order to make an informed decision."

"Then fill me in, catch me up."

"Don't know if that would work. Whenever I'm with you I'd rather kiss than tell."

"Okay by me." She sensed that the telling would be hard for him. "A lot of kissing, a little telling."

"Considering what happened today, I'd want to go way beyond kissing."

"So would I. I don't see a problem here."

"The sex is really good."

"Still no problem."

"It's likely to interfere with your judgment."

She met that comment with silence, unwilling to admit he had a point.

"See? You know I'm right. That means I should back off, at least until I know whether or not I have my act together."

"What if I don't feel like backing off? This is a two-person activity, you know."

"Are you threatening to seduce me?"

"I believe so, yes."

"Then you'll probably succeed and that won't get us anywhere."

"That's your opinion. I maintain it gets us all kinds of places, paradise being one. I like it there."

He held her gaze for several seconds and the struggle in his blue eyes was obvious.

"Tell you what," she said softly. "Let's go look at the house. We'll have lunch. We'll talk. And then…we'll see."

He took a shaky breath. "Okay."

Matt opened the front door and ushered Geena into the entry hall of his house. "This feels weird, like I'm trespassing."

"You'll get used to it the longer you're here." She walked straight ahead through an arch into the dim living room, where olive-green drapes covered a window. "Let's check out your view." She reached for the cord on the drapes and paused midmotion. "You should open them."

That made him smile. "This isn't the opening of a Broadway show. Go right ahead."

She pulled the cord and the drapes slowly parted to reveal a smudged picture window with a view of the Bighorns. "Bingo! I thought you might have a view of the mountains from this side of the house. The window's old as the hills, which is why there's so much dust on the floor. Look, you can see our footprints."

Sure enough, there were his large ones and her smaller ones. But not dainty. There was nothing fragile about Geena, and he needed to remember that. She'd survived living in Hollywood with an overbearing mother and she'd come out of that determined to do her own thing. She wouldn't allow him to selfishly mistreat her. That was a comforting thought.

Next they explored the side of the house that contained three kid-sized bedrooms and a small bathroom tiled in pink with green fixtures. The grout was stained and the faucets were corroded. Geena went in and barely had room to turn around. She glanced at Matt. "Any ideas?"

"A few. Most of them involve a sledgehammer."

She grinned at him. "See? Now you're getting the idea. Destroy the bathroom and start over. Enlarge it. Maybe knock out a wall between two of the bedrooms and put in another bath."

He nodded as he envisioned the changes. "That would make a big difference. Right now it seems cramped and dated." Worse yet, it reminded him of the kind of crummy places he'd lived in with his mother.

"Plus it would feel more like yours because you'd be putting your stamp on it."

"True. Okay, let's go see the other side. Maybe it's better."

It was. The kitchen appliances needed updating but he liked the black and white tile on the counters. Creating an arch between the kitchen and dining areas would open up that space. Finally they walked into the master bedroom and adjoining bath.

"This is nice." She turned in a slow circle in the middle of the bedroom. "You have views of the mountains through the west windows and a shade tree on the east side in case you want to sleep in."

"If I have horses I won't sleep in." But if he had Geena in bed with him, he'd have a conflict. Without a doubt he'd wake up wanting her.

"Right. Up at dawn, in bed before ten."

Yeah, something would be up at dawn, all right. The early bedtime appealed to him, though. With a woman like Geena, he might suggest they climb in around nine. "That schedule must seem really strange to you."

"It would in LA, but not here. This morning was gorgeous, and having animals depending on you is a great reason to swing your feet over the edge of the bed at dawn. It's a lot more exciting than fighting rush-hour traffic."

"Or catching the four-forty-five bus to the studio for a five o'clock makeup call."

"You could afford a car service now, Matt."

"I know." He gave her a crooked smile. "Old habits die hard and the bus feels familiar. I can afford a better apartment, too, but moving takes time and I haven't had much to spare. When I get back I'll look into hiring a car service, though. It would be more convenient, especially at that hour in the morning."

"I don't know how you can deal with those early calls. Either you or the makeup artists."

"It goes with the territory. I love acting, and if it can pay enough to maintain this ranch, I'll be a very lucky man." But the ranch wouldn't be much fun unless he had someone who'd enjoy it with him. He'd never craved solitude, maybe because he'd spent so much time alone in the first twelve years of his life.

The idea that he'd be living here by himself, or at best with a hired hand, hadn't occurred to him. He'd impulsively decided that a small ranch would be both a good investment and an excellent getaway. Yes, he could invite his family over, but he might end up spending most of his time at Thunder Mountain.

"Why the frown?"

Geena's question penetrated the fog of his increasingly negative thoughts. He looked up and his first instinct was to stonewall. Oh, boy. He took a deep breath and vowed to say what was on his mind. "I was thinking that buying this ranch could be a mistake."

She studied him for a moment. "Why?"

"For one thing, it's a lot of house for one person.

Or even for two, taking into account the hired hand. If Damon and Phil do the renovations you and I just talked about, it'll be a very nice house, too."

"Yes, it will."

"What if, after all that, I don't really want to be here?"

"Where would you want to be instead?"

He shrugged. "Over at Thunder Mountain. That's home."

"I know." Her gaze gentled. "I'll bet very few people walk into a vacant, unfurnished house, especially one that hasn't been lived in for months, and feel like it's home."

"I guess." Damn, but he wanted to hold her. She was sexy as hell but she also offered comfort. He wanted big helpings of both. He was about to take a step toward her when her stomach growled so loud it made her laugh.

"Sorry. I was about to say that if you just give it time, your feelings about the house might change."

"They might, but let's drop the subject and eat our lunch. We were supposed to bring it in here and we didn't. I'll go fetch it."

"Would you please bring my phone in, too?"

"Sure thing." As he headed out of the room, he vowed to get a grip on his emotions. Although her kindness and understanding made him want to wrap her in his arms, he really shouldn't do that until he had a better handle on what he was all about.

He retrieved her phone first and tucked it into his pocket. Then he pulled a lunch tote and two stainless steel water bottles out of Navarre's saddlebags and remembered that Rosie had put some chunks of carrot in there for both horses. So he fed them carrots and discussed his misgivings about continuing a relationship with Geena. Although they were great listeners, they didn't offer any solutions.

Even so, he felt more in control when he walked back into the house carrying lunch plus the blanket he hadn't bothered with earlier. Now it could serve as their table-cloth.

The minute he came through the door he heard a rhythmic clicking sound. When he realized what it was, he smiled. Sure enough, when he arrived at the double doors leading into the master bedroom, Geena was humming to herself while she danced around the perimeter of the room.

He leaned in the doorway, tipped back his hat and watched her. This house wouldn't be too big if she lived in it. Her sunny personality would fill every corner of every room.

She stopped when she noticed him.

"I thought you were supposed to keep dancing when you have an audience."

"That's the general rule, but in this case the audience is bringing lunch and I'm starving."

"I apologize." He handed over her phone. "We should have eaten a long time ago."

"Not if that meant skipping all the fun stuff." She glanced at the blanket.

"I brought this in so we'd have a tablecloth."

"Okay." She gave him a sunny smile. "If you don't mind, I'll check my messages while you set things up."

"Absolutely." He spread out the blanket.

"Well, that figures." She sighed.

"What?" He set the tote and water bottles on the blanket.

"One of my clients doesn't think we're getting him enough attention in the press. I thought I had it handled this morning, but apparently the reporter I contacted hasn't followed through."

"Do you need to follow up?"

"I'll have Larissa do it." She keyed in a reply to her assistant before sitting cross-legged on the floor next to the blanket. She laid her phone nearby. "Let's eat."

"Gotcha." He chose the opposite side, unzipped the tote and took out both sandwiches. "We have cookies for dessert."

"Yum."

"Mom never packs a lunch without putting cookies in it."

"Speaking of her, I've decided that if she'd enjoy seeing me dance, I'll do it. That's why I was practicing just now. Well, that and the fact that you were taking forever. I thought you'd be right back." She unwrapped her sandwich and bit into it. "Mmm."

That little moan had a predictable effect on his package. He took a deep breath and concentrated on unwrapping his sandwich. "Mom added some carrot pieces so Navarre and Isabeau could have a snack."

"Aw. That's adorable. If I'd known that I would have come out with you."

"I didn't remember until I opened the saddlebags. Anyway, I think dancing for her is a great idea. She'll love it."

"Good. Then I'm committed to making that happen." She finished another bite of her sandwich and put it down so she could open her water. "Just FYI, today is the first time I've danced in almost ten years."

"I never would have guessed."

"A professional would be able to tell in a minute. But I can feel it coming back, which is gratifying. I only mention the long layoff because you're the reason I felt like trying a few steps."

"Me?" He stared at her in surprise. "Why?"

"My mother's expectations sucked out the joy of dancing for me, which is why I quit the minute I had the guts to tell her I wasn't going to follow her plan for my future. Now do you understand?"

"No, not really. Unless you're saying because of me you've decided to go pro, after all."

"Not even close. I never want to become a professional dancer or singer. But being with you brings me joy. Dancing is my way of expressing that."

He stared at her. "No one's ever said something like that to me before."

"I thought you should know."

His throat tightened. "Thank you. That's…special."

"Yeah, it is." She smiled at him and picked up her sandwich. "Your turn to talk."

"About what?"

"Tell me about your mother."

Chapter Fourteen

Geena had expected the wall to come up between them, and it did. The process was both fascinating and sad. In the blink of an eye, Matt went from open and vulnerable to closed off and protected.

She ate her sandwich and waited to see if that would change. He continued to eat, too, and she wondered if they'd finish the meal in silence and ride back to the ranch without talking. She hadn't *asked* him to tell her about his mother. She'd practically ordered him to.

But fair was fair. He'd said she needed more background info, so she'd made up her mind not to discuss superficial things during their very private lunch. If she couldn't eat her sandwich off his six-pack abs, an image she'd cherished ever since they'd planned this trip, then she might as well search for a crack in the wall.

"Looking back on it, I realize she must have been an addict."

Geena had her water halfway to her mouth, but she put it down and glanced over at him. He wasn't looking at her, though. She doubted he was seeing anything in this room.

For a split second she wished she hadn't asked this of him. It was obviously very difficult. But if they were ever going to have a future, he had to start talking.

"She was always frazzled, distracted, not quite there." He heaved a sigh. "The day she didn't pick me up from school I thought she'd just forgotten. It had happened before." He paused to drink. His throat moved in several long swallows.

She longed to go to him and wrap an arm around his shoulders, but she didn't dare. That might stop the flow of words in favor of something that was easier for him—touch, physical pleasure. "Did she have a job?"

"She had jobs, or I guess she did. She was gone a lot. She got money somehow."

Geena immediately thought of prostitution but she wasn't about to say so. No doubt Matt had thought of it, too.

"There was never enough food in the house. She'd buy a loaf of bread and tell me not to touch it, so I wouldn't. Then half would be gone and she'd accuse me of eating it. She'd eaten it, but she'd been high and couldn't remember. Good thing I got free lunches at school, although in the summer…"

"You went hungry." Grief for that desperate little boy warred with white-hot anger directed at his mother.

"Yes, ma'am. But that wouldn't have been so bad if she'd only…" He turned toward her, and the pain reflected in his eyes took her breath away. "She didn't like me much."

"But she was an addict. She didn't even like herself, so how could she—"

"I know. The therapist said that, too. My mother wasn't capable of loving or even liking me. When she blamed me for everything and accused me of stuff I didn't do, that was her issue, not mine."

"Right."

"Damn it, Geena." He took off his hat and tunneled his fingers through his hair. "I've been through all this." Cramming his hat back on, he pushed himself to his feet. "I thought I was done with it."

She stood and watched as he began to pace like a caged animal. "I'm no therapist, but I can take a guess at what might be going on."

He turned to face her. "All right."

"You worked all this out and accepted that not everyone was like your birth mother. In fact, you haven't run into anyone remotely like her until you landed this movie role."

"I don't buy it. Briana's nothing like my mother. She's rich, successful, has a great husband. Maybe she drinks a little too much but she's not an addict. I'd have figured that out after working so closely with her."

"She may be more accomplished than your mother. Life has obviously given her more advantages. But from what you've told me, they have one big thing in common. They are completely focused on themselves. People they're in contact with are either an asset or a liability."

He gazed at her as if letting that sink in. "I was a liability to my mother."

"Absolutely. You required attention and resources and you were too young to bring anything to the table." Geena thought of her own mother. "If she'd operated in the environment where I grew up, she would have exploited your looks and talent. She would have made you a child star."

"So, you're saying I was lucky?"

"No." She hesitated to move any closer because this was important and shouldn't get tangled up in their physical attraction. "If you're lucky, then you have one, maybe even two parents who love you for yourself, not for the glory you bring to the family unit."

"Then I definitely was lucky because I ended up at Thunder Mountain. Mom and Dad are happy that I've made it this far, but they're happy for *me*, not because they'll get something out of it."

Dear Lord, she hadn't thought of that. Rosie and Herb couldn't ask Matt to help publicize their academy because he might think they were exploiting him. His link to them was pure, without commercial value.

She admired the hell out of the concept but it made her job that much harder. "You're really fortunate to have Rosie and Herb in your corner."

"And you."

"It's not the same. You pay me for my services."

"Do I pay you enough to suffer through that long layover in Denver?"

She smiled. "Point taken."

"Face it, Geena, this entire trip to Wyoming has been a bust. You can't justify it on a spreadsheet except under the heading Client Rescue Missions."

"I don't always think in terms of spreadsheets." She wasn't thinking of them now, for sure.

"That's one of the many things that makes you special." His gaze was warm at first, friendly and appreciative. Then gradually it darkened. The space between them seemed to shrink and the air grew still and hot.

The fire in his gaze made her burn with longing.

They'd talked this through, so what could be the harm in using that blanket for its original purpose?

She reached for him just as her phone chimed with a text from Larissa.

He backed up a step. "Your phone."

"I'll get it later."

"Get it now. See if it's important."

"Okay." With an impatient sigh, she turned and scooped up her phone. Then she let out a groan.

"What is it?"

"She can't get in touch with the reporter and the client is threatening to leave the agency if we don't make something happen in the next twenty-four hours. I'd let him leave but he's high profile and the agency's new enough that we really can't afford to lose him."

"Can you fix it?"

"Yes, but I'll need my laptop with my files to figure out where I can call in a favor."

"Then let's go back."

They talked about the renovations to the house on the return trip and she hoped he hadn't given up on keeping the place. No wonder he was worried about whether he'd made a mistake by buying it, though. After living for years with a critical woman who'd falsely accused him at every turn, he was sensitive to being judged for his personal decisions.

Fortunately for his career, he could take criticism directed at his acting ability. But Briana had attacked his character. With the unerring instincts of a bully, she'd hit him where he was most vulnerable.

When they arrived back at the barn, Cade happened to be coming out of it. "Hey, good timing. Just turn the reins over to me and scoot inside."

Matt objected because he obviously took his cowhand responsibilities to heart. It made Geena smile to watch the two brothers argue over who would take care of the horses.

Matt glanced at her. "You need to get going, though."

"I do, or I'd get in on this and help with the horses." She looked at Cade. "A client's throwing a hissy fit and I have to intervene."

"Will it take long?"

"I hope not. Why?"

Cade shoved back his hat. "Damon and Phil will be here in about an hour or so for our Skype powwow," he said.

"I should be finished by then."

"Great. You're gonna love this get-together. We've got us a Thunder Mountain think tank."

"Sounds good." She turned to Matt. "I'll be working in my room. Fingers crossed I can handle this quickly, but in case I'm still in there when people start arriving, would you please come get me?"

"Be glad to."

"See you both then." She gave Matt's arm a quick squeeze before starting for the house. On the way there she called Larisssa, who sounded a little panicky. "Don't worry," she said. "I'm at the ranch now and I'm on it."

Nearly an hour later, she shut down her laptop with a sigh. Disaster averted. She stood and stretched while she tried to decide whether to take her makeup case into the bathroom.

Matt's tap on her door answered that question. "Be right there." She quickly put on lipstick and ran a brush through her hair. Good enough. She hurried over to the door and opened it.

Matt stood there, eyebrows lifted. "Success?"

"Yes, thank God. He's being interviewed even as we speak and it'll run this weekend. He's thrilled and he's promised to recommend the agency to everyone he sees."

Matt laughed. "That's a little over the top."

"He won't do it, but at least he won't badmouth us, either, which is a relief."

"That's great news." He paused. "Ready for the next event? Damon and Phil are here."

"Okay. Good." Remembering her last meeting with Damon gave her an uneasy feeling in the pit of her stomach.

"I hope you don't blame him for the way he acted last night."

"Of course not. He was protecting you. In fact, I envy that. My mom kept me so overscheduled I didn't make lifelong friends who'd stick with me through thick and thin. My mom isn't the protective type, either, so I've been pretty much on my own."

"Well, you're not anymore."

She glanced at him in surprise. "What do you mean?"

"I've spent the last hour down at the barn grooming and feeding horses. Gave me some time to think. I don't know if I'm destined to be your lover, but I'll damned sure be your friend because you've been one hell of a friend to me. I'll always have your back, Geena." His gaze held hers. "Always."

"Thank you." She swallowed. "No one's…no one's ever said that they…anyway, thanks." She felt silly getting choked up about it, but he'd given her something she hadn't realized she'd been missing.

"You're welcome." His voice was low and tender. He likely hadn't expected such an emotional reaction from her, but his expression indicated that he understood why. "Let's go." He held out his hand.

"You want to walk in holding hands?"

"Yes. I want Damon and Phil to know that I…" He paused as if uncertain how to finish the thought given what he'd just said.

"That you have my back?"

He smiled. "Exactly."

"In that case, I'll be proud to hold your hand." She slid her fingers through his and the contact traveled through every part of her. She looked into his eyes. "Do you feel that?"

"If you're asking whether I get a buzz whenever I touch you, the answer is yes."

"Then maybe we shouldn't hold hands."

He gave her fingers a light squeeze. "Yes, we should." Then he grinned. "Unless you won't be able to control yourself."

Ah, how she'd missed that grin. "I can if you can."

"Then let's do this."

When they walked into the living room, everyone glanced in their direction and then, almost in unison, they looked down at Matt's hand linked with hers. It sent a powerful signal.

Rosie and Herb gazed at each other and smiled. Lexi gave Geena and Matt a subtle thumbs-up. Damon and Phil came straight over as if determined to set things right immediately. Phil carried their redheaded baby, who wore a shirt and shorts today.

"My apologies, ma'am." Damon touched his fingers to the brim of his hat. "I wasn't very hospitable last night."

"No apologies necessary." Geena absorbed the innate kindness in his brown eyes. "I showed up uninvited and you were protecting Matt."

"Yes, ma'am. But I was so focused on Matt's situation that I didn't even introduce Phil. I mean, Philomena."

Phil propped the baby on her hip and smiled at Geena. "Please call me Phil. Sophie's in a much better mood than she was last night, so this is a better meet and greet, anyway. Sophie, this is Geena Lysander, Uncle Matt's friend."

Geena gazed into the baby's wide blue eyes. "Hello, Sophie."

The little girl studied her with great interest as if trying to decide if this new person was someone she wanted to know. Apparently the answer was yes, because she held out both chubby arms and leaned in Geena's direction.

Phil laughed. "I guess you've made a friend, but you don't have to take her if you don't—"

"I'd love to hold her." She let go of Matt's hand and gathered the sweet-smelling baby into her arms. "But just to warn you, I don't know a thing about babies."

"That's what you said about horses, too." The affection in Matt's voice was unmistakable, which was both gratifying and embarrassing. Tipping back his hat, he beamed at her. "Turns out you're a natural."

"I'm guessing babies are harder to figure out than horses."

"Definitely," Phil said. "We didn't know anything about them, either. Rosie and Herb weren't baby savvy and neither was my stepmother. My dad ended up giving us all a crash course, since he was the one who'd raised me."

"Somehow we've managed, but sometimes it gets ugly." Damon grimaced. "Sophie loves her bath but she's slippery as an eel. Picture Phil soaked to the skin while she tries to keep the baby in the little bathtub. Meanwhile, I'm on the phone asking my father-in-law about diaper rash. Oh, and now Sophie's teething, which is a whole new circle of hell."

Matt clapped him on the shoulder. "Builds character."

"I'll remind you of that when you're getting up for feedings at two in the morning."

"Yeah, you would, too."

Geena doubted that anyone else had seen Matt's first reaction to Damon's teasing remark. The flash of anxiety in his blue eyes had been momentary, but she'd caught it. She could also guess why Damon's comment had hit a nerve. Matt didn't know if he was fit to be a husband, let alone a father.

Damon was too focused on his daughter to notice Matt's subtle mood swing. "She keeps us hopping." He paused to reach over and stroke her cheek with one finger. "But I love this little bugger."

During the conversation Sophie had been trying to grab Geena's glasses. Tucking the baby securely against her side, she managed to get them off and hand them to Matt. When she turned back to the little girl, Sophie grabbed a fistful of Geena's hair and yanked hard.

"*Ooh*, that smarts." She managed not to yell, or worse yet, swear.

"Uh-oh," Phil said. "Here, let me—"

"I've got it." Matt took Sophie's tiny fist and dropped mini kisses on it while he gently uncurled her small fingers. "Come see your uncle Matt," he crooned as he lifted her away from Geena's hair and into his arms. "See if you can pull my hair. Betcha can't."

Sophie must have sensed a challenge in his words, because she immediately knocked off his Stetson.

"That'll teach you, bro." Damon scooped it up and dusted it off. "But I'll have a talk with her about the sacred nature of a cowboy's hat. Otherwise she'll get herself in trouble messing with the Stetson."

"Ah, doesn't matter." Matt settled her in the crook of

his arm. Keeping his attention on the baby, he reached for Geena's glasses, which he'd hooked in the neck of his T-shirt, and gave them back to her while he continued his conversation with the little girl. "Like your daddy said, I dared you and you took me up on it. You've got game, Sophie. I predict a bright, shiny future's in store for you."

Those baby blues gazed at him as if mesmerized.

Sophie wasn't the only one caught in a net of adoration. Geena put on her glasses so she could more fully enjoy the sight of this tall, muscular cowboy sweet-talking an adorable baby. It was PR gold, but that wasn't why her breath caught and her pulse raced.

If someone had asked her five minutes ago to describe her perfect dream of the future, she wouldn't have been able to say what it was. But now she'd seen it.

Chapter Fifteen

"So, what about the house?" Damon looked at Matt and Geena as he asked the question. "Do you have a handle on what needs to be done?"

Geena decided to keep her mouth shut. She had no idea how Matt felt about the house at this point.

"I'm not sure I'm ready to answer that." Matt tickled Sophie's nose and she laughed.

"No worries," Phil said. "It might take several trips over there to think it through. If you want us to go with you next time, we'd be glad to."

Matt glanced up. "No rush. In fact, I'm wondering if I should have bought it in the first place."

Inwardly, Geena groaned. Matt was pulling back, re-evaluating his dreams. Not good.

"You are?" Damon's eyes widened in surprise. "Last night you were all about the ranch. You couldn't wait to go see it."

"I know, but I've been rethinking the concept. I'd hate for you and Phil to invest time in it when I'll only be able to enjoy the place sporadically. Besides, when I come back, I'll want to be here, not sitting over there by myself."

Both Damon and Phil looked confused, and Geena understood why. He'd walked in holding her hand, a clear indication they were a couple, and now he was talking about being alone in that house. His behavior wasn't making any sense but that wasn't surprising. His thoughts must be in turmoil.

He was saved from having to give them a better explanation when Ben and Molly Radcliffe arrived. Geena was delighted for the interruption. Matt was liable to dig himself into an even deeper hole if he kept talking about a future that was obviously unclear to him.

He introduced her to the newcomers and she liked them both on sight. Molly taught at the community college and had set up the academy curriculum. Ben was a saddle maker who offered academy students a chance to learn the basics of his trade. Molly talked Matt into giving up Sophie, and soon afterward, Cade announced the Skype call would begin in ten minutes.

Matt recaptured Geena's hand before they started toward Rosie and Herb's office. "I hope this works."

"I have a good feeling about it. It's your brothers, after all, and they only want the best for you."

"Good point." He took a deep breath and they walked down the hall.

She'd never peeked into the office, but she doubted it looked this way normally, with the computer connected to a large flat-screen and chairs grouped in two rows in front of it. Matt continued to hold her hand and Cade positioned them both front and center, with Rosie and Herb on one side, and Damon and Phil on the other.

"We're not key players," Damon said. "We don't need to be in front."

"Yeah, you do." Cade gestured to Sophie. "Everyone wants to see the baby. Before we address the problem, we need to let them go nuts over your kid." Then he turned to Geena. "I can introduce you first, though, since you're the guest—"

"Not necessary." She laughed. "It's an old Hollywood saying—never work with animals or kids. They'll upstage you every time. Let Sophie have her moment."

Cade nodded. "Good call. Has Matt briefed you on the folks we'll be talking to?"

"I know Finn's the Seattle brewer and Chelsea's the marketing guru he's in love with, and she likes to use interesting colors in her hair. But I have no info on the other couple you mentioned."

Matt glanced at the digital time on the screen. "We have a couple of minutes. I'll fill you in." He quickly told her about Ty Slater, his foster brother with the photographic memory who'd become a successful lawyer in Cheyenne, and Ty's wife, Whitney, a talented barista who managed a local coffee shop.

"It's time," Cade said. "Here's our agenda." He passed out sheets of paper to everyone.

"Agenda?" Damon laughed. "Seriously?"

"Seriously, bro. We need to stay on track. We'll have Sophie time for five minutes and then I'll ask Matt to introduce Geena and explain the situation. After that we'll throw it open for brainstorming."

"He gets this drill sergeant attitude from working with teenagers all day," Lexi said. "I've learned that once he's in this mode, it's best to just go along."

"I'm happy to." Geena was quickly becoming a Cade Gallagher fan. Obviously he'd taken on a leadership role and seemed to have a talent for it. He'd been right about providing some Sophie time. She was the first child born to a member of the brotherhood and she'd always occupy a place of honor because of that. She'd also have a passel of adoring uncles. The thought made Geena smile.

Sophie acted as if she already knew that she was a lucky girl. While everyone exclaimed over how cute she was and how big she'd grown, she waved her arms and bounced on Damon's lap as if welcoming the spotlight.

True to his word, Cade broke in on the baby party after five minutes to announce that they had to get on with the agenda. He took some more flak for his dedication to a timetable, but he stuck to his guns.

Matt introduced Geena and gave a brief overview of the PR issue they were working with. "Basically, what I'm looking for is a way to combat the negative publicity without creating a tabloid nightmare for anyone else, especially Mom and Dad."

Ty's wife, Whitney, a blonde with classic features, was the first to speak. "Like everybody here, I've been following the news about you ever since you got the part. I think it's wonderful that you landed it and I hate this for you, even though we don't really know each other."

"Thanks, Whitney. Rosie's told me so much about you, I feel like I know you."

"Same here." She smiled. "But I have a question. In all the stuff I've read or seen, no one's mentioned that you were a foster kid or that you lived in Wyoming, let alone at Thunder Mountain. Was that on purpose?"

Geena's breath caught. Apparently Whitney wasn't part of the inner circle and didn't realize that was a loaded question.

Matt wasted no time in answering her. "Yes, ma'am, it was definitely on purpose. I figured it was nobody's business. I didn't even tell Geena. And now I really can't bring it up even if I wanted to. Fans will think it's a bid for sympathy."

"I cherish my privacy, too." Ty put his arm around his wife. "Whitney will testify to that. But when I ended up on the academy's promo calendar two years ago, my story was out there for all to see. That made me *really* uncomfortable. But since then a lot of foster kids have told me they were inspired because I overcame the odds."

"Same here," Damon said. "I was asked to give a talk at the high school on that very subject. I had a couple of emails after that from kids who said they weren't going to think of themselves as victims anymore."

Matt nodded. "I can understand why talking to you would help them. I'll admit I never considered that angle. I will from now on."

"But you're right about bringing the info to light now." Chelsea tucked her hair, streaked with various shades of green, behind her ears. "So, Geena, what are your thoughts? I'm sure you've been thinking about how to fix things."

"I have."

Chelsea's expression grew animated. "Great! Whatcha got?"

Geena hesitated. Was there any point in laying out a plan that Matt would hate? But, judging from her conversation with Cade earlier today, everyone else might go for it. She could be pitting him against his family.

"This is a brainstorming session." From his position in the second row, Cade reached over and laid a hand on her shoulder. "We need to hear all the ideas."

She turned to Matt. "You won't care for it."

His gaze was steady. "Like Cade said, anything goes in a brainstorming session."

Technically that was true, but he could consider her suggestion a betrayal, especially if the others jumped on board and he became the one dissenting voice.

Matt knew exactly why he'd agreed to this Skype session. Cade had invoked the Thunder Mountain Brotherhood code. In high school Matt had stood by his brothers whenever some guy with spaghetti for brains decided to make fun of the foster boys who lived at Thunder Mountain. Apparently their loyalty to each other bothered certain types of people, mostly bullies.

Now Matt was the one being threatened by a bully and his brothers were here to support him and make sure he didn't back down. He appreciated their support, but he trembled to think what kind of scheme Geena had dreamed up. She'd forewarned him that he wouldn't like it and so chances were good he'd hate it.

But he couldn't ask Geena to withhold her idea. Ultimately she couldn't force it on him, anyway. He was still the client.

"Okay, here goes." Geena sat up a little straighter. "What if Thunder Mountain Academy makes a promotional video during this break between semesters, and the story we put out is that Matt flew here specifically so he could be in it?"

Matt groaned. "That's—"

"Brilliant!" Chelsea said. "I love it! Instead of looking as if you ran away to dodge bad publicity, we show that leaving LA had nothing to do with that."

"That's the idea." Geena gripped his hand tighter.

"Matt, this could really work." Chelsea's expression was animated. "Fans will love that you're donating time to promote your family's enterprise. Make the video tomorrow and finish it by sundown. The video is released along with press about it, providing great publicity for the academy and wholesome PR for you. It's genius."

"Except making that video with me in it will destroy Mom and Dad's privacy." Letting go of Geena's hand for the first time since they'd sat down, Matt turned to them. "This place is special. You don't want reporters knocking on your door, asking invasive questions. You don't want—"

"Son." Rosie put her hand on his arm and looked into his eyes. "I'm not sure where you got this notion that privacy is important to us. We used to have up to twelve boys at a time living on this ranch, but after we retired we had more privacy than you could shake a stick at. We *hated* it."

"Yeah, we did," said Herb. "We've never worried about opening our home to others. When we ran a foster care facility we had to have the premises inspected regularly. After we got a reputation in the state for our work with kids, we were featured several times on TV."

"You were? I don't remember that."

"They interviewed us when you were all in school. Identifying any of you would have been an invasion of privacy because you were underage." Herb's voice gentled. "But now that we're running the academy, we're actively seeking publicity, so making a video is a great idea. But you don't have to be in it if that makes you uncomfortable."

"But would you even want my name attached to the academy with all the negative stuff that's been said about me this week?"

Rosie squeezed his hand. "We're not worried about

that. But we'd never want to exploit your fame for our benefit. That's not—"

"Wait. You're worried about *using me*?"

She nodded.

"We've all worried about that," Damon said. "Lots of times when people get famous their relatives take advantage. That's not who we are."

Sophie picked that moment to start fussing and Damon stood. "Sorry, everybody. I think Sophie's done with this Skype thing."

"Yep, it's dinnertime for her." Phil got up, too. "Hate to run. Great seeing you guys!"

Everyone on the screen called out goodbyes, and the baby was distracted by that and stopped fussing long enough for Damon and Phil to make a more leisurely exit. They'd all be seeing each other in August for Cade and Lexi's wedding, and while that event was being discussed, Matt had a chance to sort through what he'd just been told. Gradually the truth sank in, and as it did, he felt lower than a snake's belly.

He hadn't been protecting his family. He'd been protecting himself and his vision of retreating from the craziness of LA to the idyllic privacy of his home at Thunder Mountain. Talk about selfish.

If he'd been thinking about his folks instead of himself, he would have realized that the academy was a business like any other. Geena had tried to tell him he could help out when she'd mentioned the girls who'd stayed in the cabin they'd been cleaning earlier. He hadn't listened.

Oh, his motives had seemed so noble, but now they looked totally self-serving. He needed to get over himself and concentrate on being an asset to his parents' business. Teenagers liked movie stars. He'd idolized his share when he'd been that age. He hadn't cared if they got in a little trouble now and then. It made them human.

But he hadn't been willing to admit how much he could contribute to the cause because he'd been focused on his need for privacy. And why was that? A cold chill ran down his spine as the answer came to him. His mother. He could hide from her in LA, no problem. Not here.

His gut told him she wasn't that far away. She'd probably stayed in Wyoming all these years, where she knew the public assistance programs inside out and the cost of living was reasonable. If he made the video tomorrow and left town before it was released, he likely wouldn't have to deal with her.

But Rosie and Herb might. They could handle her, of course, but they shouldn't have to. She'd been nasty fifteen years ago and he doubted she'd changed. According to what he'd learned about her personality type, she was probably worse.

"Matt."

He turned to look at Geena. "It's okay." He hated seeing the anxiety in her green eyes, especially knowing he'd been the one who'd caused her to worry. "I'll do the video. Even more important, I want to."

She sighed and her shoulders relaxed. "Okay. That's good."

"But just so you know, my birth mother could see the video and contact the ranch looking for me. I'll alert Rosie and Herb."

"I'm sure they'll run interference for you."

"That's just it. I don't want them to. I'll stay an extra two days after the video goes live to give her plenty of time to make the call. If she does, I'll take it and invite her to the ranch."

Chapter Sixteen

Geena had no time to respond to that startling announcement because Sophie grew restless again and Damon and Phil left for real. That turned everyone's attention back to Matt and the prospect of a video being made within the next twenty-four hours.

"I'm absolutely doing it," he said. "Assuming it's even possible to get something like that together in a hurry."

"We mostly need a videographer." Geena turned in her seat to look at Cade, Lexi, Molly and Ben. "Any ideas?"

"Yes." Molly fairly crackled with energy. "One of the instructors at the community college, Drew Martinelli, would be perfect if she hasn't left on vacation yet." She pulled her phone out of her purse. "I'll text her now."

Lexi jumped on the idea. "This is serendipity. Cade and I need someone to video our wedding, so if she works out for this, maybe we could hire her for August."

"She'd be great." Molly typed quickly. "I just hope she's still in town."

"We need to have a potential script," Chelsea said from the screen. "Finn has to head back to O'Roarke's but I can stay on the call if you need my help."

"Yes, please." Geena turned to give her a quick smile.

"Whitney and I have to sign off, too," Ty said. "We're having dinner with her folks. But if you need anything, holler, and text or email us when it's up."

"Will do." Cade glanced at the screen. "Thanks for being here, both of you. See you in August. Lexi and I are expecting a really big present."

Ty laughed. "We're getting you a very expensive kitchen gadget, bro, now that you're such a gourmet cook."

"Can't wait." Cade grinned. "Hey, thanks for being here." Cade walked over to the computer. "So, it's Chelsea and Geena on this project so far. Who else is volunteering to work out a script?"

"I will," Rosie said.

"I'll help, too," Lexi said. "I've commissioned a few videos of my riding clinics, so I know a little about the process."

Geena decided somebody needed to take charge of the project and she was the logical one. "If we have Chelsea, Rosie, Lexi and me, that should be enough."

"And me," Matt said. "I've had some experience with scripts."

She gazed at him. "Yes, you have, and thanks for the offer."

"It's the least I can do."

His smile tugged at her heart, but now wasn't the time for a private conversation about how he was handling this turn of events.

"There's Drew." Molly grabbed her phone and glanced at the incoming text. "She's available all day tomorrow."

"Excellent." Geena took that as a positive sign that the video was meant to be. "I know this is a lot to ask, but if she can show up before dawn, she'll get some amazing footage."

"Let me see what she says." Molly typed in the request and waited. "Yes! In fact, she'd thought of that herself. She'll be here before five tomorrow morning."

"Good. Thank you, Molly. That's huge."

"Call if you need anything else." Molly left with Ben.

"Looks as if you have everything under control," Cade said. "I leave the project in your capable hands." He glanced at Lexi. "See you at home."

"You will. Fabulous job, cowboy."

"Thanks." He touched the brim of his hat and left with Herb.

"Okay, then," Chelsea said. "Where do we start?"

Geena knew where that should be. She just didn't think the man sitting beside her would go for it. "The video will publicize the academy, but let's get real. Matt's our biggest draw. We should start the video with him." She glanced in his direction. "Does that work for you?"

He met her gaze with surprising calmness. "Yes, it does. I should probably narrate the thing. Since we have the videographer committed to arriving before dawn, the script should begin with an exterior shot as the sun's coming up. Then pan to the barn, tight focus on the barn door and head inside to where I'm doing something."

"Something manly," Chelsea said, as computer keys clicked. "Like pitching clean hay into a stall. Keep talking. I'm writing all this down."

"Are the horses out or in?" Lexi moved up to the front row and sat next to Geena.

"Out in the pasture," Geena said. "More dramatic.

It would be great if we could get them to race around a little."

"I have an idea." Matt leaned forward as if he actually might be enjoying the process. "Put Cade out with the horses. Have him grab a handful of mane and swing up bareback on Hematite. That's always a crowd pleaser. Once he gets Hematite moving, Linus will follow and the others might, too."

"I can just picture it." Rosie's face glowed. "It'll be wonderful. Oh, I know what else we need in this video! We could use some roof repair on Cabin Three. Let's get Damon up there and film him doing it."

"Nice." Chelsea kept typing. "Stetson, snug T-shirt, jeans and a tool belt. Damon rocks that look."

"Before we go any further, I want to say something else." Rosie looked around at the group. "Phil deserves to be up on that roof as much as Damon. Lexi, you have every right to ride bareback along with Cade. I don't mean to be sexist, but—"

"The video needs to be about the brotherhood," Lexi said. "I figured that out right away. We know what we want to accomplish and putting great-looking cowboys in each shot is the way to go."

Geena nodded. "It is. We'll want a scene with Rosie and Herb, but other than that, it's all about the Thunder Mountain Brotherhood." Geena glanced over at Matt. "Are you comfortable talking about that connection?"

"You bet. Until Ty mentioned it, I never considered that our story might help other foster kids. And I should have. I wish that I'd—"

"Don't be too hard on yourself," Geena said. "We've all known celebrities who milked their tragic past to get attention. You didn't want to be that person."

He gave her a distracted smile. "Thanks."

"That's what will be so great about this video," Chelsea said. "We have a talented actor narrating it. I predict this thing will go viral in no time."

"Hallelujah!" Rosie threw both hands in the air. "I've always wanted a viral video!"

"Me, too." Chelsea said. "We need to nail down the rest of the scenes so we can turn Matt and Geena loose on the dialogue. I figure you two are the movie people, so you're the logical ones to handle it."

Matt nodded. "No problem."

After everyone agreed on the order of scenes, Chelsea emailed her notes to Geena and signed off.

Lexi glanced at Geena and Matt. "I'll leave you to it. Writing dialogue is so not my area."

"Not mine, either," Rosie said. "I'll rustle up your dinner and bring it in here so you can keep working."

After Rosie walked out the door, Geena gazed at Matt. She didn't have the words to express her admiration or her frustration. The two emotions were hopelessly tangled up in her mind, so instead of saying anything, she grabbed him and kissed him with enough force to knock off his hat.

He obviously wasn't expecting it and he froze.

Lifting her mouth a fraction of an inch, she took a quick breath. "Steam up my glasses, damn it. You know you want to."

With a groan, he pulled her close and his mouth came down on hers.

Oh, yes. She surrendered completely to the pleasure of kissing Matt. This was what he should be doing instead of worrying about whether he was the right guy for her. How could he doubt it when these moments of shared passion were so amazing?

Breathing unevenly, he pulled back. "We have to stop."

"I know. Rosie will—"

"Be here any minute." And he recaptured her mouth.

So sweet. So hot. She couldn't imagine living without his kiss.

He lifted his head again. "Enough." Blowing out a breath, he released her and stood. "I told myself I wouldn't do this."

"You didn't. I did." She gulped for air. "Not your fault."

"I could have said no." He located his hat on the floor and picked it up.

She smiled as she took off her glasses and polished them on her shirt. "I don't think so. I'm irresistible."

"Yes, ma'am, you sure as hell are." He ran his fingers through his hair and took a deep breath. "Before Rosie comes back, I need to clarify something I said earlier. Although I'm staying a couple more days, I don't expect you to."

"If you're staying, I'm staying."

He shook his head. "Let me put it another way. I'd rather you didn't."

Wow, that hurt. She was prepared to stick by him during a difficult time and he wanted her gone. She struggled to regain her composure. "Assuming your birth mother actually shows up, I won't be shocked by her, if that's what you're worried about. I have a fair idea of what to expect."

"How can you, when I don't? She was pretty messed up the last time I saw her. If she decides to come here, there's no telling what she'll be like. You don't need to experience that."

"What if—" She paused to clear her throat. "What if I want to?"

"Geena, I'm asking you to head back to LA." He put on his hat and tugged down the brim. "Please."

"Why?"

His voice was tight. "Maybe I should let you stay so you can see where I came from."

She clutched her denim-clad knees to keep her hands from shaking. "I know where you came from and it doesn't matter. No, I take that back. It does matter. Knowing your background makes me admire you that much more."

"Admire me? You've got to be kidding."

"Of course I admire you! You could have let your past define you. Instead, you set an ambitious goal and achieved it."

"All because my past *does* define me. Haven't you been paying attention? I'm as selfish as my mother!"

She gasped. "You are not! How can you say such a thing?"

"Look at the evidence." His bitter tone sent a chill through her. "I insisted that Rosie and Herb needed privacy when I really wanted privacy for *me*. I rejected your idea that I could help publicize the academy because it would louse up my precious retreat plans. It's always been about my needs, not theirs."

She had trouble breathing, but she forced the words out as best she could. "Matt, it happens to everyone. We think we're doing something noble and it turns out our motives were self-serving. But you figured it out and now you're doing the right thing."

"Or maybe I see a way to save my own hide and I'm taking it."

"No! You see a way to set everything right. You benefit and the academy benefits. It's a win–win!"

"Even if it turns out that way, and I hope it does,

that doesn't change anything. I clearly have the ability to block out everything except what I want. I lived with that woman for twelve years. I've kidded myself that I escaped who and what she was, but—"

"I guarantee that you have."

His gaze was shuttered. Not completely closed, yet, but it wouldn't take much for the wall to come up. "I wish I could believe that, but I can't."

"Then why wait for your mother? What's in it for you? If she does come here, I doubt it will be pleasant. You could leave before the video release and lock her out of your life forever. You could surround yourself with enough security that she'd never get through."

He looked as if he wanted to pace but the room was cluttered with furniture. He turned a chair backward and straddled it so he was facing her. "Once again, selfish motives. I told myself I had to stay and protect Rosie and Herb from having to deal with her, but that's not the real reason."

"Why can't it be one of the reasons? I'm sure they'd appreciate having you here if she comes calling."

"They probably would, but my main reason for staying has nothing to do with them. I want to find out if there's any trace of regret for what she did. But more than that, I need to know if I'll look at her and see myself."

"There's bound to be some resemblance, Matt. She gave birth to you."

"That's not what I mean."

"I know. I've done the same with my mother. I like to think I've taken after my father." Then she wished she hadn't said it. Matt couldn't use that strategy.

"Doesn't apply." His expression gave nothing away. The wall had come up.

"Dinner's served!" Rosie came bustling in with Herb

right behind her. Both were carrying trays. Matt jumped up immediately to help and Geena followed suit.

As they cleared a place on the desk to set the plates of food and bottles of O'Roarke's Pale Ale, Rosie's and Herb's forced cheer suggested that they'd heard at least part of the argument. The concern in Rosie's eyes as she glanced at Matt confirmed it.

Geena considered asking them to stay so they could bring the issue out in the open. But she might make the situation worse and she was a guest who'd been here less than forty-eight hours. Forcing an intervention seemed disrespectful.

After they left, she looked at Matt. "Are you going to be able to work on dialogue with me?"

"Yes. It needs to be done."

Of course he'd be able to do it. He was a professional. So was she. "I'll get my computer."

Chapter Seventeen

Matt knew he was behaving like a jerk and yet he couldn't stop himself, which was proof that he wasn't the guy for Geena. It was now clear as a bell to him, so he wished she'd accept it, too. The sooner she left town, the better, but everyone would expect her to stay until the video was finished and she would insist on it out of professional pride.

That meant she couldn't leave until the day after tomorrow, because of limited flights out of Sheridan. Which left a hell of a lot of hours to endure, especially when every time he looked at her he longed to pull her into his arms and kiss those full lips. More proof that he was a selfish bastard.

She reappeared with her laptop and he fought the urge to take it out of her hands and apologize for every terrible thing he'd said. He'd told her to leave when he desperately needed her to stay. He'd said they were wrong for each other when every time he held her it felt so right he wanted to shout for joy.

But that was his selfish side talking, the part he'd inherited from his screwed-up, narcissistic mother. For Geena's sake, he couldn't listen to that voice. He had to continue to push her away until she finally got the message.

They plunged into the dialogue project like the pros they were. They didn't eat much but they drank all the beer. In Matt's current frame of mind, another couple of bottles would have been welcome. But he wasn't going back to the kitchen to get them. Rosie would waylay him, for sure. He'd seen the look on her face when she'd brought the food. She knew something wasn't right.

Writing the dialogue under these circumstances was a tough slog, but he and Geena pulled it off. She emailed the finished product to Drew, who'd use it to plan the sequence of shots.

At last she closed her laptop and stood. "That does it."

He got to his feet, too. "Yes, ma'am, it does."

Irritation flashed in her green eyes. "If you're such a heinous person, why bother with the gentlemanly behavior?"

"Maybe it gets me what I want."

Her jaw tightened. "Are you implying that you used that *yes, ma'am* routine to get me out of my clothes?"

He could tell she was tired and pushed to the limit. The more obnoxious he was, the quicker she'd dump his sorry ass. "It worked, didn't it?"

She slapped him so hard it brought tears to his eyes. Good. He deserved it.

"This is not who you are." Her voice was choked with fury. "If you were really that rotten, Rosie and Herb wouldn't love you."

"They see what they want to see."

She growled in frustration and started out of the room. "I'll be back for the dishes. I'm sure Rosie and Herb have gone to bed by now and we need to clean up our mess."

"Don't worry about the dishes. I'll take care of them."

"Okay. Great." She paused in the doorway and turned around. "Feel free to sleep in your room tonight. My door will be locked, so no temptation there."

"Thanks for the thought, but I'll sleep in the barn again."

"Why do that? You and I are so done."

"That's not what your eyes say." He'd keep it up until she hated him.

"I don't give a damn what my eyes say. My mouth says we are *done*, cowboy. I'm locking my door."

"In that case, I probably should warn you there's something else I learned from my worthless mother."

"What?"

"I can pick locks."

"Then I should warn you of something I learned from my mother."

"Oh?"

"How to deliver a well-placed knee to the groin."

In spite of everything, that made him smile, but he ducked his head so she wouldn't see. Dear God, how he loved her. Then he went very still as the insight played in a slow motion loop in his head. *He loved her?* Well, yeah, of course he did. Otherwise he wouldn't be so determined to sabotage any feelings she'd developed for him.

He kept his head down until he heard her huff of anger and her retreating footsteps. Hiding his smile was about maintaining a consistent message. Hiding his love was about survival.

* * *

Anger fueled an adrenaline rush that carried Geena through her bedtime routine as she took a shower, and washed and dried her hair. Then she lay in the dark, eyes open, and prayed for him to come through the door. She hadn't locked it, had never intended to. Not that they would make love in this room, not with Rosie and Herb sleeping nearby.

But if he'd come to her and taken back all those mean things he'd said, they could escape to the barn and put things right between them. She longed to rewind the clock to this morning when he'd been so wild for her he'd risked being discovered by Lexi and Cade, or this afternoon when they'd made sweet love on a cool patch of green grass.

This evening, with the help of his folks, and his brothers and their wives, they'd created a potential solution to his PR disaster, but at what cost? He'd begun to doubt himself before the Skype call, and the revelations from that phone meeting had left him shattered. Another person might reluctantly acknowledge their self-serving behavior and vow to do better. Not Matt. He was drowning in the shame of thinking he was just like his mother.

She thought of her own mother, who had, in fact, taught her the knee-to-groin move. Although Geena liked to believe she took after her late father, she had many of her mother's traits, including fierce determination, which could easily become stubbornness.

Her mom had force-marched her through years of performance training, which had taught her self-respect and discipline. Her mom had been absent a lot, but she'd never completely abandoned the field. Geena had become self-reliant out of necessity, but that wasn't a bad quality.

Without the upbringing her mother had provided, she might not have had the guts to follow Matt to Sheridan. She definitely wouldn't have had the discipline to knock out a video script despite the tension that had ricocheted around the room the entire time. And the person she'd become would not lie staring at the ceiling until dawn, either.

Climbing out of bed, she put on her glasses. Then she located the boots Rosie had loaned her and the flashlight tucked in the bedside table drawer in case of a power outage. Once again she'd play the role of uninvited guest. He might turn her away. In fact, he probably would. But she had to try.

Rosie and Herb hadn't bothered to lock up, so she was able to slip out easily while carrying her boots and flashlight. Locked doors seemed to be a rarity in the country, which made her earlier comment to Matt all the more ludicrous. She wasn't sure her bedroom door even had a lock.

Cool air greeted her as she stepped out on the porch and sat in one of the Adirondack chairs to put on her boots. The ranch looked different at night, a little bit alien with only the dusk-to-dawn lights illuminating the circular drive and the barn several yards away. She descended the steps. The crunch of her boots on the gravel drive seemed unnaturally loud in the stillness. When a cricket chirped in the bushes beside the porch she jumped.

Placing a hand over her racing heart, she paused to take several deep breaths. She could do this. The barn wasn't that far away. She started out, putting her feet down carefully so her boots on the gravel wouldn't sound so much like somebody chewing potato chips.

No one was out here, so it might not matter, but she didn't want to attract attention from…anything. Belatedly she remembered that Wyoming was filled with wildlife. She'd heard that making a lot of noise would frighten animals away, but she wasn't sure that was true of really big creatures like bears.

Okay, now she was scaring herself. Time to calm the heck down. Once she'd passed outside the glow of the first yard light, she lifted her head to look at the stars. *Oh, my.* They covered the navy-blue sky like spilled sugar. She'd never seen so many.

Then she heard something. Glancing wildly around, she saw a shadow near the barn door. A pretty big shadow, like a bear on its hind legs would make. She tried to yell but only managed a tiny squeak. She was so stupid to come outside by herself! And now a bear would eat her and she'd never get to tell Matt that she—

"Geena?" Matt stepped into the light hanging over the barn as his long strides quickly eliminated the distance between them. "What in God's name are you doing out here?"

"I—I…wh-what are *you* doing out h-here?" Her teeth chattered as relief washed through her, leaving her weak and trembling. "I thought y-you were a b-bear!"

"Ah, Geena." He gathered her close and rested his cheek on the top of her head as he rocked her gently back and forth. "What am I going to do with you?"

"Is th-that a rhetorical question or d-do you want an answer? Because I c-can give you some ideas if you n-need any." She held on to his solid warmth and gradually the quivery feeling subsided.

His body started to shake and eventually she realized he was laughing. He'd muffled the sound in her hair, which was probably a good idea because maybe a bear really was lurking nearby. She'd seen grizzlies on

TV. Two people, even one built like Matt, were no match for a grizzly.

Even so, she felt a thousand percent safer in his arms than she had walking through the dark alone.

Finally he cleared his throat and gazed down at her. "What sort of ideas would you like to offer me?"

"Could we discuss this in the barn? I'm worried about bears."

"There aren't any bears around."

"How do you know?"

"The horses would get agitated."

"Oh. Well, good, but I'd still like to have this conversation inside, if you don't mind."

"Of course I mind." But as he said it, he drew her closer, which revealed that a certain significant part of him didn't mind at all. "I came down here to get away from you, and then you show up in your Captain America shirt and your boots, and you must have washed your hair because it smells amazing."

"I did wash it." She began to quiver for a different reason altogether. "And I admit I did that for you. I thought maybe you'd come to my room and we could...talk."

"Talk. Right." He rubbed her back, moving gradually lower until he cupped her bottom and pulled her in tight. "I thought you were planning to lock your door."

Her body warmed as his fingers flexed, creating an arousing massage. "Does it even have a lock?"

"No." And he started laughing again. "We'd better head for the barn before this gets any hotter and we wake up the folks. In the summer they like to sleep with their windows open." Looping an arm around her shoulders, he guided her toward the big double doors. "I should be walking you back to the house, but I can't seem to make myself do that."

"I'm glad. I really…the way we left things was…"

"It was awful. That's why I was outside, just looking up at the stars and thinking. I kept wondering if I should go back to the house and at least apologize, but then I knew you'd be in bed wearing that sleep shirt and the inevitable would happen."

"It wouldn't have."

"You would have rejected me?"

"No, I would have insisted we come down here, away from the house."

He looked at her and smiled. "You knock me out, you know that?"

"Yes, because you knock me out, too, which is why—"

"Nothing's changed. We'll go into the barn and make love because I can't stand not to, but after that…"

"I have an idea. Let's not think about what happens after that."

He took a deep breath. "Good thinking." He ushered her into the dim interior, lit only by small lights along the aisle between the stalls. "Wait here." He ducked into a room just inside the barn door.

She breathed in the scent of hay, horses and oiled leather while she listened to various snorts and soft groans, the clunk of a hoof against a floorboard and the rustle of straw. She loved being here because this was Matt's territory, one he could share with her if only he would. The possibility of that didn't seem very high at the moment.

But she'd suggested to him that they should forget about both the past and future, and concentrate on the present. Good advice. She ought to take it.

He reappeared, a blanket under his arm. "This way." Grasping her hand, he led her down the wooden aisle to an empty stall.

The door was open, and now that her eyes had adjusted, she could make out mounds of straw inside. "Is this where you slept last night?"

"Yes, ma'am." He unfolded the blanket and laid it out on the straw.

"Can you do something with these?" She handed her glasses to him.

"We'll hook them over the stall door latch." He made sure they were secure, draping his hat over them. "That should do it." He turned to her, his hands on his hips. Then he sighed. "You know what? This is nuts. I'm taking you back to the house. Making love again will only—"

"Don't you dare back out now, cowboy." Launching herself at him, she nearly knocked him over.

He staggered when he caught her but he managed to keep them upright. "Geena, come on. This is crazy."

"Shut up and kiss me." She grabbed him around the neck and pulled his head down. If she could get him in a lip-lock, he'd be toast.

"It's a mistake."

"We're doing it anyway."

He groaned. "Looks like it." And when his mouth found hers, there was no doubt. He kissed her with the hunger of a man barely in control. He broke away only long enough to pull the sleep shirt over her head and toss it down. Then he lowered her to the blanket and began tasting every inch of her.

Gasping, she writhed on the blanket. "My…boots."

"I'm leaving 'em." He kissed his way from her breasts to her navel. "I've never made love to a woman wearing boots." He planted soft kisses along her trembling thighs. "I'm guessing you've never made love to a man while wearing them, either."

She moaned. "Good guess."

"I'm all wrong for you." He blew gently on her damp curls. "But I'm selfish enough to want you to remember me." And he settled into the most intimate kiss of all.

She'd remember him, all right, whether she kept the boots on or took them off. A woman didn't easily forget a man who gave her more pleasure than she'd ever dreamed possible. Her climax arrived with such force that she pressed the back of her hand to her mouth to keep from yelling.

After bestowing a few more tender kisses in strategic places, he moved away and began stripping off his clothes. As she lay on the soft blanket, sprawled in reckless abandon, she wished they had more light because he was the most beautiful man she'd ever seen and this might be the last...no, she wouldn't think about that. Worrying about the future robbed her of precious time with him tonight.

Her body hummed with anticipation. Before long they'd once again experience that magic connection and they'd share the joy of...wait a minute. He hadn't expected her to walk down here. "Matt, do you have a condom?"

"Yes, ma'am." His breathing was a little ragged.

"How could you, when you weren't expecting me?"

"Pure luck." Foil crinkled. "I left the rest of the box hidden in the tack room this morning. After our conversation today, I didn't figure I'd have a use for them." He lowered himself to the blanket, propped himself on his outstretched arms and settled between her thighs. "You changed my mind." His face was in shadow as he leaned down and brushed his mouth over hers.

"I'm encouraged that I can do that." She ran her hands up his muscular chest and savored the tactile thrill of springy hair beneath her palms.

"Don't be encouraged. It's temporary." He nibbled on her lower lip.

"Oh, Matt, I wish—"

"You're thinking about the future. You told me not to."

"I know."

"Don't think, just…feel." He slid in smoothly, effortlessly.

Sighing, she lifted her hips to bring him closer. "Like that?"

Muttering a soft oath, he held very still. "Yes, ma'am."

"It does work."

"What?" His voice sounded strained.

"Those cowboy manners." She explored the manly terrain of his broad shoulders. "To get me naked."

"That was a stupid thing to say. I didn't mean it."

"I know." She stroked lower and pushed her fingertips into his impressive back muscles.

He sucked in a breath. "I wanted you to be mad at me."

"I was, but I'm sorry I slapped you."

"I deserved it." He feathered a kiss over her lips. "But right this second, I have a problem."

"What?"

"I desperately want to start moving, but I don't have much control. I'm liable to get a little crazy. Can you handle that?"

Her heartbeat kicked into high gear. "Uh-huh."

"Then hang on."

He wasn't kidding. It was the wildest few minutes of her life, and the most thrilling, too. His intensity triggered an orgasm before she expected it, but he kept going, urging her on as he stroked faster, and faster yet.

"Again." He changed the angle and she gasped, on the brink of a second climax.

He bore down and she came. Jaw clenched, he stifled

a deep groan as he surrendered to his own release. He shuddered in the grip of his orgasm then he slowly lowered his body and allowed it to rest lightly against hers.

She stroked his sweaty back. "Relax," she crooned. "Let go."

At last he did, nestling his body against hers. The tension slowly drained away and she thought he might be asleep, or at least dozing.

She might never have a better chance to say what was in her heart. "I love you," she murmured softly.

He didn't stir. He probably was asleep, and that was okay. She'd needed to say it and now she had.

Chapter Eighteen

After Geena drifted off to sleep, Matt eased away from her, took care of the condom and set the alarm on his phone. Then he gathered her into his arms and held her as he savored the words she'd spoken. He'd never forget that she'd said them, even though he wouldn't be building dreams based on her words of love.

She might believe what she'd said, but she'd glossed over his failings because she was generous that way. Incredible sex had a way of affecting a person's judgment. It certainly had affected his. Until the Skype call he'd thought he might have a future with her.

But he could see the situation clearly now, even if she couldn't. He was still too mired in his toxic past to be with anyone, and letting her go was the most loving gesture he could make. Maybe someday she'd understand that he'd helped her avoid a gigantic mistake.

Exhaustion claimed them both and they slept until the

alarm woke them at four. He threw on his clothes as fast as he could, but she still had to wait for him. She stood there quietly, obviously half asleep. Arms around each other, they made their way back to the house. They pulled off their boots before slipping inside and he walked her to her room.

"You'd better not come in," she murmured.

So true. The chilly morning air had swept away his grogginess and he'd become very aware that he had a half-naked Geena beside him. "I won't." Silently lowering his boots to the floor, he pushed back his hat and cupped her face in both hands. "Thank you." Before she could say anything, he kissed her gently, angling his head so he didn't bump her glasses. He kept his passion in check as he released her.

A night-light shining in the hall bathroom revealed that he'd fogged her lenses, anyway, probably for the last time. He wanted nothing more than to follow her into that room and confess the love that made him ache in ways he'd never thought he could ache. Instead, he picked up his boots and walked away.

At his door, he glanced back to discover that she hadn't moved. She stood exactly as he'd left her and he memorized how she looked in her Captain America sleep shirt because he'd never see her wearing it again. Slowly she raised her hand in farewell. He touched the brim of his hat. Then she turned, walked into her room and closed the door.

He knew then that she'd accepted his decision that they should end it. And why wouldn't she? *Thank you* wasn't exactly a declaration of undying love. More like good manners, and he certainly had those in spades. Her trip to the barn had been her Hail Mary pass, a final attempt to break him down.

No doubt she thought she'd failed, but she'd succeeded beyond her wildest dreams. He loved her with every ounce of his being. And she would never know.

More than once during the shooting of the video that morning, Geena mentally thanked her mother for teaching her the value of discipline and self-reliance. Inheriting some of her mother's stubbornness hadn't hurt anything, either. Although she'd notified everyone except Matt that she planned to leave the ranch after the video was uploaded, she wouldn't get on a plane yet. Not until she knew he was okay.

Fortunately Drew Martinelli was a crackerjack videographer. During the filming Geena learned that the slim brunette had been a hockey star in high school because she could anticipate where the puck would be. That skill gave her a unique advantage as a videographer because she was always ahead of the action instead of following it.

Her dynamic images should accomplish exactly what Geena had hoped for, great PR for Matt and more visibility for Thunder Mountain Academy. Before the afternoon was over, Lexi and Cade had hired Drew to film their wedding. Damon and Phil had debated whether to get a professional video of Sophie at the crawling stage or wait until she was walking. They'd ended up choosing to do both and Rosie had immediately put in an order for copies.

Drew did her edits in Rosie and Herb's office to make sure the final cut met with everyone's approval. That created a standing-room-only situation by the time she'd finished and uploaded the video to the internet.

Later that night, Rosie had champagne and glasses ready for a celebratory toast. As the good cheer flowed around her, Geena soaked it up and reminded herself that, when it came to Matt, it wasn't over until it was over. Scanning the crowded room, she discovered he was working his way toward her.

When he finally made it, she touched her flute to his. "Good job." Taking a sip from her glass, she dared to look him straight in the eye for the first time since they'd started this long day. The depth of emotion she found there took her breath away. That was love, damn it, even if he'd never said so.

He continued to hold her gaze as he took a quick swallow and lowered his glass. "I couldn't have done it without you."

She managed a smile. "True."

"And it was generous of you to offer to be here if my mother shows up. Instead of being appreciative I was rude. I'm sorry."

"Apology accepted."

"But the thing is..." He paused. "I really do need to handle it by myself."

"Which is why my overnight bag is packed and ready to go."

"Does Rosie know you're about to leave?"

"Everybody does." Rosie had insisted she keep the outfit she was wearing and the boots. She'd been offered a place to stay tonight at both Damon and Phil's house and Molly and Ben's. She'd been touched but had politely declined and chosen a hotel in Sheridan, instead. She wasn't feeling her usual social self right now.

He gave her a long look. "Are you okay?"

"Yes." She was more okay now that he'd allowed her to see how much he cared. For a man who was used to disguising his true feelings, that was huge. "Are you?"

"I wouldn't say that. If my birth mom's been following my career online, she's probably seen the video by now and will jump on the opportunity." He took another swallow of his champagne. "Waiting to find out is…"

"Hell?"

"Pretty much."

Geena noticed Rosie walking toward them. "The wait might be over. Here comes Rosie and she looks as if she just bit into something nasty."

Matt sucked in a breath and set down his champagne flute. "Hey, Mom."

"Mindy's on the line. You can take the call in the kitchen." Rosie's cheeks were flushed and her eyes glittered with anger. "I was polite because you asked me to be, but it was one of the hardest things I've ever done."

"Thank you." Matt gathered her close. "Love you, Mom."

"Love you, too, son."

When he released her, he looked over at Geena. "You aren't going to leave right this minute, are you?"

"I'll wait until you get back."

"Thanks." Giving the brim of his hat a decisive tug, he left the room.

His foster mom gazed after him. "Inviting that woman here may be exactly what he needs to do, but I don't have to like it."

"You certainly don't."

"When are you flying out?" Rosie glanced up at her. "In all the confusion I can't remember if you told me."

"I didn't because I'm not flying out tomorrow."

"Oh?"

"I'll be staying in town for a couple more days. I won't tell him, but if at some point you think he might want to know…"

"Got it." Rosie sighed. "That boy is crazy about you."

"That's what gives me hope. And I'm crazy about him, which is why I'm not going anywhere just yet."

Approval shone in Rosie's eyes. "I knew I liked you."

"Same here, Rosie. I'll never forget how you—wow, that was quick. He's coming back already." Her heart ached as she watched him cross the room, his back ram-rod straight as if preparing himself to face a firing squad.

All light and warmth had left his expression. He'd locked his emotions away, and when he reached them he spoke with a chilling lack of inflection. "She'll be here in the morning."

Matt didn't sleep much that night. He chose the barn again, which wouldn't make sense to anyone but him. Being there sharpened the pain of Geena's absence, but it also brought him comfort because she'd confessed her love while lying with him on this bed of straw. Saying goodbye to her had been really tough.

Wide-eyed, he waited for dawn and considered the various strategies he'd planned for dealing with his mother. So much depended on her behavior when she ar-rived. When the sky lightened to the color of rich cream, he saddled Navarre, left a note tacked to Navarre's stall and rode over to his ranch. He could have asked her to meet him there instead of polluting Thunder Mountain with her presence, but instinct had warned him not to let her know about this place.

Tying Navarre to the railing again, he walked over to the grassy spot where he and Geena had made love. The grass was wet with dew and the crushed blades had mostly recovered. Even so, he imagined he could see the outline of her beautiful, naked body as she'd welcomed him into her warm embrace.

Her hairpins glinted in the soft light. He gathered them

up and shoved them into his pocket. He'd decide later if returning them would be insensitive. Probably.

Next he climbed the porch steps and unlocked the front door. Two days ago he'd come through this door to the sound of Geena practicing a tap-dance routine in the master bedroom so she could perform for Rosie. Between the Skype call and working on the video, that hadn't happened. She'd never had her riding lesson with Lexi, either.

As he roamed the empty house remembering how they'd discussed the improvements Damon and Phil could help him make, he came to a decision. He would keep this ranch because Geena believed in his ability to make a home here. Maybe someday he'd accomplish that and be the man she thought he was.

His dad and Cade were in the middle of feeding when he came back to Thunder Mountain, so he gave Navarre a quick rubdown before taking him inside for his grain and flake of hay. The ride had soothed him and he was able to return the cheerful greetings sent his way as he pitched in to do his share.

He made a quick call to Ty down in Cheyenne before breakfast. There was a legal issue concerning his mother that he needed clarified before he saw her, and Ty was able to give him a quick answer.

Being with his family helped calm him even more. He ate a little and participated in the breakfast-table conversation. Lexi had brought Ringo down to see him and Ringo had graciously agreed to sit in his lap and keep two strips of bacon from going to waste. A purring cat turned out to be a terrific stress reducer. Nobody mentioned his mother's visit.

But later, after he'd showered and shaved and gone to

wait for her on the porch, Rosie came out, although she didn't sit down.

Immediately he stood. Rosie had taught him never to remain seated when a lady was standing.

She gazed at him, sympathy in her blue eyes and compassion in every line of her plump body. "Do you want to invite her in? I just need to know if we should clear out of the living room."

"Mom, I don't want her here at all, so I'm definitely not inviting her in. At one time I thought about meeting her in town, but a public place didn't seem right. I don't know what she'll be like or what she'll do."

"I know you don't, son. Just remember we're here if you need backup for any reason."

"Thanks, Mom." He gave her a tight hug. "Love you."

"Love you, too." She patted his cheek. "You'll be fine." Then she went back inside.

He didn't feel fine. He wished he'd taken up whittling so he'd have something to do with his hands, although in the shape he was in he'd likely maim himself with the knife.

The sound of a vehicle coming down the ranch road sent his pulse into the red zone. The engine sputtered and coughed as if it might not last long enough to make the journey. Eventually a dented pickup with a faded blue paint job pulled up in front of the ranch house.

Matt got to his feet as the passenger door opened and an overweight woman with dull brown hair slowly climbed down. He didn't recognize her. Maybe his mother was driving the truck and this was a friend.

Then the woman took off her sunglasses and peered at him. "Matty? Is that you?"

His mother's voice. A chill swept over him even though it was a warm day. "Yes, ma'am." He came down the steps toward her but stopped before he was within touching distance and shoved his hands in his pockets.

He'd wondered if he'd have the urge to hug her. Nope. He might as well be meeting a complete stranger. The person he remembered had been proud of her figure and her glossy black hair. She'd been in her midthirties then, so now she'd be around fifty, but she looked much older.

Her face was puffy, which made her eyes seem smaller. They'd been dulled by age and whatever drugs she'd ingested over the years. She'd piled on the makeup, though, which only made her look worse. "*Yes, ma'am*, is it?" Her comment was delivered with an unbecoming sneer. "Who taught you *that*?"

"My mother."

"The hell I did! You were raised to be a tough smart-ass! None of this *yes, ma'am* and *no, ma'am* crap." She looked around, her avid gaze taking in the ranch house and the barn. "Looks like you had it pretty good here, though."

"Yes, ma'am." He felt a twinge of pity. She really was pathetic.

"Oh, cut it out, Matty. I'm not impressed. You and me, we're poor white trash, so don't go putting on airs. You said on the phone that you had something to discuss with me."

"I do."

"You implied that it involves money and I hope it does. I'm between a rock and a hard place and since you have plenty, I figure you can give your poor mother a—"

"It does involve money." Not only was she pathetic, she was greedy. He might have made some self-centered decisions recently, but he'd never been greedy. He'd never expected a handout, either, and yet she obviously felt entitled to one.

"Okay, now we're talkin'."

Had she turned out to be different, he would have adjusted his plan, but after this brief exchange he knew what needed to be done. She'd given him life and he would permanently settle that debt. He was about to buy his freedom. "I'm prepared to give you a lump sum with a condition attached."

She licked her red lips. "How much?"

He named a figure that made her eyes widen. "But, like I said, there's a condition."

She shrugged. "I don't care."

"I never want to hear from you again." As he said it, he felt self-respect flowing back into his body.

"Matty!" Her mouth dropped open. "That's mean."

"No, it's drawing boundaries. It's self-preservation. It's realizing that I don't have to be defined by my past and I certainly don't have to stay in touch with you. That's my condition. Do you accept?"

"Sure." But her little smile said otherwise.

"It's important that you keep your word, because if you do try to contact me, I'll have you arrested for child abuse."

"That's a laugh. You can't—"

"Turns out I can. According to one of my foster brothers, an excellent lawyer by the way, there's no statute of limitations in Wyoming. So stay away from me or end up in jail. Your choice."

"You are a cold person, Matty."

"No, ma'am, I'm not. A cold person would want revenge. A cold person would have lured you here with the hint of giving you money and instead he'd have cops waiting with a warrant."

Her gaze shifted to the front door. "You don't have cops here, do you?"

"No. Give me your address and I'll send you a cashier's check."

"Hang on." She went back to the truck, said something to the driver and returned with a scrap of paper and a pen. She wrote the information down and handed him the paper. "I need to get going. Lenny's tired of waitin' on me."

"Under the circumstances you'd think he'd put up with the inconvenience."

She sidled close, bringing with her a whiff of cigarette smoke. "He won't be getting a dime. Once that check arrives, I'm leaving him. There's better out there than Lenny." She put on her sunglasses. "So long, Matty."

"So long." He couldn't bring himself to call her anything. Not Mom, for sure, but not Mindy, either. She was nothing to him.

For years she'd been a shadowy memory, a person who might have turned out to have some redeeming qualities, things he hadn't remembered. Not really. In a world full of amazing people like his foster family and Geena, why would he waste another second on someone he was only connected to by an accident of birth?

He watched her climb laboriously into the pickup. Then he continued to stand there as the truck wheezed and clattered around the drive and onto the ranch road. He kept listening until he couldn't hear it anymore. *Gone.* He sagged with relief.

On the heels of that emotion came a powerful surge of joy. He wasn't like her at all. Instead, he was a proud member of the Thunder Mountain Brotherhood and the lucky son of Rosie and Herb Padgett. If he hadn't completely messed things up with Geena, he might... no, that was getting ahead of himself. Anyway, because he'd asked her to leave, she'd be on a plane to Denver by now.

* * *

Heart thumping, Geena drove up to the ranch house and climbed out of the rental car. Rosie had sounded like an excited teenager on the phone.

She must have been watching for the car, because she hurried out onto the porch and down the steps. "I sent him to the barn to muck out stalls." She put a hand on her chest and took a quick breath. "He was driving us crazy."

"How?"

"Going on and on about what an idiot he'd been to insist you go back today. We had to agree. But of course he didn't know I'd already called you."

Geena smiled. "You could have told him I didn't leave."

"It's better if you appear and explain it to him. The shock of seeing you when he thinks you're gone might finally convince him that this is true love we're talking about."

Geena's throat tightened. "Yes, it is."

"Have you been online this morning?"

"Of course. I've been fielding requests for interviews from people eager to talk to Matt about Thunder Mountain. All the negative stuff is old news. We did it, Rosie."

"Mostly *you* did it. Now, get on down there before he takes a notion to come back to the house for some reason and ruins the dramatic moment."

"Okay." Geena figured that if Rosie had grown up in Hollywood she'd have become a director.

"I can guarantee you maybe thirty minutes of privacy. Herb's in the office doing paperwork and Cade's staying in his cabin until I give him the all clear. He mentioned calling one of his brothers about the caretaking job at Matt's ranch."

"So, Matt wants to keep it?"

"Honey, he wants it all, you included. After he sent that woman packing he was a changed man. The realization that he's nothing like her was exactly what he needed, but he had to see her to believe it. Now, go on so you can make a grand entrance."

Geena gave her a quick hug. "Thanks, Rosie."

"You're welcome. It's what I do."

Yes, it certainly was, Geena thought as she walked down to the barn wearing the boots Rosie had given her. Her pants and blouse were clothes she'd brought from LA, but at least she was making this trek in Wyoming-worthy boots. On her way she glanced over at the pasture to admire the horses grazing in it.

After such a short time, the ranch felt like home. But Matt's ranch would feel that way, too, once Damon and Phil made some changes and the place had furniture and a couple of horses in the barn. She yearned to be part of creating that ambience.

Matt had never had a place of his own, but then, neither had she. She'd postponed buying anything in the city and maybe this was why. She envisioned a no-maintenance rental in LA with plenty of room for two. When she was ready to kick back and relax, she belonged on a ranch in Wyoming. With Matt.

Rosie had assured her that he felt the same, but that didn't stop the butterflies from swarming in her stomach as she walked inside the cool interior of the barn. The rhythmic sound of straw being shoveled into a wheelbarrow directed her to a stall near the back of the barn.

Although her boot heels clicked on the wooden aisle, he kept shoveling so he probably hadn't heard her. The wheelbarrow nearly blocked the aisle next to the stall where he was working, but she managed to maneuver around it so she could look in.

He'd pulled off his white T-shirt and tossed it over the open stall door. His back and chest glistened with sweat as his impressive muscles flexed with each movement of the shovel. She almost hated to interrupt him.

Almost. She waited for the brief moment of silence between dumping one load into the wheelbarrow and scooping up another. "Matt."

He wheeled toward her and stood there clutching the shovel. "Geena?"

"I didn't leave today."

He swallowed. "Obviously."

"I didn't leave because I love you."

For one long moment he stared at her. Then he chucked the shovel in the straw and closed the distance between them. But when he was about two feet away he came to an abrupt halt. "I'm sweaty."

"I don't care. Hold me, Matt! Kiss me and tell me you love me as much as I love you, because if you don't, then—"

"I do!" He swept her into his arms. "I love you, Geena." He held her gaze. "I didn't think I had the right, but now everything's different in my mind. That woman is out of my head and out of my life. Which leaves room for us."

"I love the sound of that word. *Us.*"

"Good, because you'll be hearing it a lot." He smiled down at her. "You stayed. I told you to leave but you stayed. How great is that?"

"Yeah, well, when you love someone, you stick around."

"I sure hope so, because I want you to stick around forever, pretty lady. I want you to make love to me in the grass and practice tap dancing in our bedroom."

"*Our* bedroom?"

"I thought of it that way from the minute we walked in."

"Me, too." She looked into blue eyes shining with love. "Now fog up my glasses, cowboy."

Epilogue

Zeke Rafferty hadn't counted on tearing a rotator cuff. Disability insurance was a pricey proposition, so he hadn't taken out a policy. The surgery had wiped out his savings and now he had weeks, maybe even months, before he could go back to trick roping.

So when his foster brother Cade Gallagher called with a job offer that he could do with one arm out of commission, he thanked his lucky stars. "I can absolutely take care of Matt's ranch for a few months," he said. "But I have to be honest with you, bro. I plan to go back to roping as soon as my shoulder heals. If he's looking for a permanent caretaker, I can't in all good conscience take the job."

"Here's how I see it, Zeke. When I heard that you were laid up, I—"

"How did you hear about it, anyway? That's a mystery to me."

"You were in Cheyenne when it happened, right?"

"I was."

"And while you were recovering from surgery you went into Rangeland Roasters for a cup of coffee."

"Several times. They have an excellent brew. Okay, I get it. I talked to Whitney. She's real friendly, which is perfect for someone managing a coffee shop. I've been so busy on the rodeo circuit I haven't kept up. Didn't know ol' Ty was married."

"Luckily Whitney mentioned you to Ty, who called Rosie, who gave me your number. When the planets align like that, I figure you should take the job and we'll worry about finding a replacement later. Besides, if you move back for a few months, you can come to my wedding in August. I would have sent you an invitation but I didn't have an address."

"You and Lexi?"

"Me and Lexi."

Zeke smiled at the pride in Cade's voice when he said that. "Congratulations. You two were always meant to be together."

"Fortunately she finally saw that, too. So, can I tell Matt you're on board? That'll be one less thing he has to deal with."

"By all means, tell him I'm on board. And also tell him I always knew that scandal nonsense was bogus. The Thunder Mountain Brotherhood doesn't pull crap like that."

"Indeed we don't. Listen, I just realized I have no authority to offer you a salary, so who knows what Matt will pay you. He's a straight shooter, though, so it'll be a fair wage."

"Don't worry about it. A free place to stay and a little

money for food is all I'll need. I'm obliged, Cade. I didn't know how I'd navigate the next few months."

"Yeah, and that reminds me that we shouldn't have had to find this out by the back door. You should have contacted Rosie and Herb right away when you ran into a spot of trouble."

"I feel like they did enough when we were there." Zeke exhaled. "I'm not the kind of guy who goes running back home to—"

"Hey, we're the brotherhood, remember? We stick together and we look out for our own."

"That's…that's good to hear. Really good. See you soon, bro." Zeke disconnected the call. He'd been a lone wolf all his life, even while he was a foster kid at Thunder Mountain. He'd vowed that once he was capable of living on his own, he'd make sure he never needed anybody.

But the torn rotator cuff had punched a big hole in that plan. For the time being, he'd take the job offered to him and be grateful, even if it chafed that he'd been brought so low that he required help. In the future he'd plan better so that wouldn't happen again.

* * * * *

HOLLYWOOD BABY AFFAIR

ANNA DePALO

For DeLilah & Bob,
thanks for the support & encouragement

One

Actress and Stuntman Lovefest! More Than Movie Pyrotechnics on Display.

The gossip website headline ran through Chiara Feran's head when it shouldn't have.

She clung to Stunt Stud's well-muscled shoulders, four stories up, wind blowing and helicopter blades whipping in the background—trying to act as if her life depended on it when the truth was that only her career did. After all, a gossip site had just written that she and Mr. Stunt Double were an item, and right now she needed the press distracted from her estranged father, a Vegas-loving card-sharp threatening to cause a controversy of his own.

She tossed her head to keep the hair out of her face. She'd learned Stunt Stud's first name was Rick when they'd rehearsed, but she thought *insufferable* was a better word for him. He had remarkable green eyes…and he looked at her as if she were a spoiled diva who needed the kid-glove treatment.

I don't want you to ruin your manicure.

Thanks for your concern, but there's a manicurist on set.

They'd had a few brief exchanges over the course of filming that had made her blood boil. If the world only knew… True, his magnetism was enough to rival that of the biggest movie stars, so she wondered why he was content with stunt work, but then again, his ego didn't need any further boosting. And the rumors were that he wasn't who he seemed to be and that he had a shadowy, secretive past.

There was even a hint that he was fabulously wealthy. Given his ego, she wouldn't be surprised if he'd put out the rumors himself. He was a macho stuntman ready to save a damsel in distress, but Chiara could save herself, thank you. She'd learned long ago not to depend on any man.

She opened her mouth, but instead of an existential scream, her next line came out. "Zain, we're going to die!"

"I'm not dropping you," he growled in reply.

Chiara knew his voice would be substituted later with her costar's by the studio's editing department. She took perverse satisfaction in calling him by her costar's character name. And since Rick was pretending to be her costar, and her costar himself was just acting, she was two steps removed from reality.

And one long fall away from sudden death.

Even though both she and Rick had invisible harnesses, accidents could and did happen on movie sets. As if on cue, more explosions sounded around them.

As soon as this scene was over, she was heading to her trailer for coffee and maybe even a talk with Odele—

"Cut!" the director yelled through a bullhorn.

Chiara sagged with relief.

Rick barely loosened his grip as they were lowered to the ground.

She was bone-tired in the middle of a twelve-hour day on set. She didn't dwell on the other type of tired right now—an existential weariness that made it hard to care about anything in her life. Fortunately filming on this movie was due to wrap soon.

Action flicks bored her, but they paid the mortgage and more. And Odele, her manager, never stopped reminding her that they also kept her in the public eye. Her Q score would stay high, and it would keep those lucrative endorsement deals flowing. This film was no exception on both counts. *Pegasus Pride* was about a mission to stop the bad guys from blowing up the United Nations and other key government buildings.

As soon as her feet hit the ground, she ignored a frisson of awareness and stepped away from Rick.

His dark hair was mussed, and his jeans clung low on his hips, a dirty vest concealing his tee. Still, he managed to project the authority of a master of the universe, calm and implacable but ready for action.

She didn't like her reaction to him. He made her self-conscious about being a woman. Yes, he was all hard-packed muscle and latent strength. Yes, he was undoubtedly in top physical shape with washboard abs. But he was arrogant and annoying and, like most men, not to be trusted.

She refused to be intimidated. It was laughable really—after all, *her* bank account must dwarf his.

"Okay?" Rick asked.

His voice was as deep and rich as the hot chocolate she wished she had right now—damn him. It was a surprisingly damp and cold early April day on Novatus Studio's lot in Los Angeles. "Of course. Why wouldn't I be?" Dozens of people milled around them on the movie set. "All in a day's work, right?"

His jaw firmed. "This one is asking for more than usual."

"Excuse me?"

He looked at her quizzically. "Have you spoken to your manager recently? Odele?"

"No, why?"

His gaze moved to her trailer. "You may want to give it a go."

Uh-oh.

He fished his cell phone out of his pocket and showed her the screen.

It took a moment to focus on the newspaper website's headline, but once she did, her eyes widened. Chiara Feran and Her Stuntman Get Cozy. Is It More Than High Altitudes That Have Their Hearts Racing?

Oh...crap. Another online tabloid had apparently picked up the original gossip site's story, and worse, now Rick was aware of it, too. Heat rushed to her cheeks. He wasn't *her* stuntman. He wasn't her anything. Suddenly she wondered whether she should have sent that first story into internet oblivion when she'd had the chance by denying it. But she'd been too relieved they were focusing on a made-up relationship rather than the real pesky issue—her father.

At Rick's amused look, she said abruptly, "I'll talk to Odele."

He lifted her chin and stroked her jaw with his thumb—as if he had all the right in the world. "If you

want me, there's no need for extreme measures like plant-
ing stories in the press. Why not try the direct approach?"

She swatted his hand away and held on to her temper.
"I'm sure there's been a mistake. Is that direct enough
for you?"

He laughed at her with his eyes, and said with lazy
self-assurance, "Get back to me."

As if. In addition to her deadbeat father making news,
she had to contend with burgeoning rumors of a relationship with the last stuntman on earth she'd ever walk the
red carpet with.

She turned her back on Rick and marched off. The
man sent a red mist into the edges of her vision, and
it had nothing to do with lust. She clenched her hands,
heart pounding. Her jeans and torn tee were skintight—
requisite attire for an action movie damsel in distress—
and she was aware she was giving Rick a good view as
she stomped away.

At her trailer, she banged through the door. She immediately spotted Odele sitting at a small table. The older
woman lifted her head and gave Chiara a mild look from
behind red glasses, her gray bob catching the light. If
Chiara had learned anything during her years with her
manager, it was that Odele was unflappable.

Stopping, Chiara touched her forehead. "I took pain
medication for my headache an hour ago, and he's still
here."

"Man problems have defied pharmacology for decades, honey," Odele replied in her throaty, raspy voice.

Chiara blurted out the gossip about her and Rick, and
the stuntman's reaction. "He thinks he's God's gift to
actresses!"

"You need a boyfriend," Odele responded cryptically.

For a moment, Chiara had trouble processing the

words. Her mind, going sixty miles an hour, hit the brakes. "What?"

She was one of those actresses who got paid to be photographed sporting a certain brand of handbag or shoes. She glanced around her trailer at the gleaming wood and marble countertops. She had more than she could possibly want. She didn't desire anything, especially a boyfriend.

True, she hadn't had a date in a long time. It didn't mean she couldn't get one. She just didn't want the hassle. Boyfriends were work…and men were trouble.

"We need to retain a boyfriend for you," Odele rephrased.

Chiara gave a dismissive laugh. "I can think of many things I need, but a boyfriend isn't one of them. I need a new stylist now that Emery has gone off to start her own accessories line. I need a new tube of toothpaste for my bathroom. And I really need a vacation once this film wraps." She shook her head. "But a boyfriend? No."

"You're America's sweetheart. Everyone wants to see you happy," her manager pointed out.

"You mean they want to see me making steady progress toward marriage and children."

Odele nodded.

"Life is rarely that neat." She should know.

Odele gave a big sigh. "Well, we don't deal in reality, do we, honey? Our currency in Hollywood is the stardust of dreams."

Chiara resisted rolling her eyes. She *really* needed a vacation.

"That's why a little relationship is just what you need to get your name back out there in a positive way."

"And how am I supposed to get said relationship?"

Odele snapped her fingers. "Easy. I have just the man."

"Who?"

"A stuntman, and you've already met him."

A horrifying thought entered Chiara's head, and she narrowed her eyes. "You put out the rumor that Rick and I are getting cozy."

OMG. She'd gone to Odele with the rumor because she expected her manager to stamp out a budding media firestorm. Instead, she'd discovered Odele was an arsonist…with poor taste in men.

Odele nodded. "Damn straight I did. We need a distraction from stories about your father."

Chiara stepped forward. "Odele, how could you? And with—" she stabbed her finger in the direction of the door "—him of all people."

Odele remained placid.

Chiara narrowed her eyes again. "Has he said anything about your little scheme?"

"He hasn't objected."

No wonder Rick had seemed almost…intimate a few minutes ago. He'd been approached by Odele to be her supposed love interest. Chiara took a deep breath to steady herself and temper her reaction. "He's not my type."

"He's any woman's type, honey. Arm candy."

"There's nothing sweet about him, believe me." He was obnoxious, irritating and objectionable in every way.

"He might not be sugar, but he'll look edible to many of your female fans."

Chiara threw up her hands. It was one thing not to contradict a specious story online, it was another to start pretending it was *true*. And now she'd discovered that said story had been concocted by none other than her own manager. "Oh, c'mon, Odele. You really expect me to stage a relationship for the press?"

Odele arched a brow. "Why not? Your competition is making sex tapes for the media."

"I'm aiming for the Academy Awards, not the Razzies."

"It's no different from being set up on a date or two by a friend."

"Except you're my manager and we both know there's an ulterior motive."

"There's always an ulterior motive. Money. Sex. You name it."

"Is this necessary? My competition has survived extramarital affairs, DUIs and nasty custody disputes with their halos intact."

"Only because of quick thinking and fancy footwork on the part of their manager or publicist. And believe me, honey, my doctor keeps advising me to keep my stress level to a minimum. It's not good for the blood pressure."

"You need to get out of Hollywood."

"And you need a man. A stuntman."

"Never." And especially not *him*. Somehow he'd gotten his own trailer even though he wasn't one of the leads on this film. He also visited the exercise trailer, complete with built-in gym and weightlifting equipment. Not that she'd used it herself, but his access to it hadn't escaped her notice.

Odele pulled out her cell phone and read from the screen: "Chiara Feran's Father in Illegal Betting Scandal: 'My Daughter Has Cut Me Off.'"

Oh…double damn. Chiara was familiar with yesterday's headline. It was like a bad dream that she kept waking up to. It was also why she'd been temporarily—in a moment of insanity—grateful for the ridiculous story about her budding romance. "The only reason I've kept him out of my life for the past two decades is because he's a lying, cheating snake! Now I'm responsible not only for my own image, but for what a sperm donor does?"

As far as she was concerned, the donation of sperm was Michael Feran's principal contribution to the person she was today. Even the surname that they shared wasn't authentic. It had been changed at Ellis Island three generations back from the Italian *Ferano* to the Anglicized *Feran*.

"We need to promote a wholesome image," Odele intoned solemnly.

"I could throttle him!"

Rick Serenghetti made it his business to be all business. But he couldn't take his gaze off Chiara Feran. Her limpid brown eyes, smooth skin contrasting with dark brows and raven hair made her a dead ringer for Snow White.

A guy could easily be turned into a blithering fool in the presence of such physical perfection. Her face was faultlessly symmetrical. Her topaz eyes called to a man to lose himself in their depths, and her pink bow mouth begged to be kissed. And then came the part of her appearance where the threshold was crossed from fairy tale to his fantasy: she had a fabulous body that marked her as red-hot.

They were in the middle of filming on the Novatus Studio set. Today was sunny and mild, more typical weather for LA than they'd had yesterday, when he'd last spoken to Chiara. With any luck, current conditions were a bellwether for how filming on the movie would end—quickly and painlessly. Then he could relax, because on a film set he was always pumped up for his next action scene. In a lucky break for everyone involved, scenes were again being shot on Novatus Studio's lot in downtown LA, instead of in nearby Griffith Park.

Still, filming wasn't over until the last scene was done.

He stood off to the side, watching Chiara and the action on camera. The film crew surrounded him, along with everyone else who made a movie happen: assistants, extras, costume designers, special effects people and, of course, the stunts department—*him*.

He knew more about Chiara Feran than she'd ever guess—or that she'd like him to know. No Oscar yet, but the press loved to talk about her. Surprisingly scandal-free for Hollywood...except for the cardsharp father.

Too bad Rick and Chiara rubbed each other like two sheets of sandpaper—because she had guts. He had to respect that about her. She wasn't like her male costar who—if the tabloids were to be believed—was fond of getting four-hundred-dollar haircuts.

At the same time, Chiara was all woman. He remembered the feel of her curves during the helicopter stunt they'd done yesterday. She'd been soft and stimulating. And now the media had tagged him and Chiara as a couple.

"I want to talk to you."

Rick turned to see Chiara's manager. In the first days of filming, he'd spotted the older woman on set. She was hard to overlook. Her raspy, no-nonsense voice and distinctive ruby-framed glasses made her ripe for caricature. One of the crew had confirmed for him that she was Odele Wittnauer, Chiara's manager.

Odele looked to be in her early sixties and not fighting it—which made her stand out in Hollywood. Her helmet hair was salt-and-pepper with an ironclad curve under the chin.

Rick adopted a pleasant smile. He and Odele had exchanged a word or two, but this was the first time she'd had a request. "What can I do for you?"

"I've got a proposal."

He checked his surprise, and joked, "Odele, I didn't think you had it in you."

He had been propositioned by plenty of women, but he'd never had the word *proposal* issue from the mouth of a Madeleine Albright look-alike before.

"Not that type of proposition. I want you to be in a relationship with Chiara Feran."

Rick rubbed his jaw. He hadn't seen that one coming. And then he put two and two together, and a light went off. "You were the one who planted that story about me and Chiara."

"Yup," Odele responded without a trace of guilt or remorse. "The press beast had to be fed. And more important, we needed a distraction from another story about Chiara's father."

"The gambler."

"The deadbeat."

"You're ruthless." He said it with reluctant admiration.

"There's chemistry between you," Odele responded, switching gears.

"Fireworks are more like it."

Chiara's manager brightened. "The press will eat it up. The stuntman and the beauty pageant winner."

So Chiara had won a contest or two—he shouldn't have been surprised. She had the looks to make men weak, including *him*, somewhat to his chagrin. Still, Odele made them sound like a couple on a C-rated reality show: *Blind Date Engagements*. "I've seen the media chew up and spit out people right and left. No, thanks."

"It'll raise your profile in this town."

"I like my privacy."

"I'll pay you well."

"I don't need the money."

"Well," Odele drawled, lowering her eyes, "maybe I can appeal to your sense of stuntman chivalry then."

"What do you mean?"

Odele looked up. "You see, Chiara has this teeny-weeny problem of an overly enthusiastic fan."

"A stalker?"

"Too early to tell, but the guy did try to scale the fence at her house once."

"He knows where she lives?" Rick asked in disbelief.

"We live in the internet age, dear. Privacy is dead."

He had some shred left but he wasn't going to go into details. Even Superman's alter ego, Clark Kent, was entitled to a few secrets.

"Don't mention the too-eager fan to her, though. She doesn't like to talk about it."

Rick narrowed his eyes. "Does Chiara Feran know you approached me?"

"She thinks I already have."

All right then.

He surmised that Odele and Chiara had had their talk. And apparently Chiara had changed tactics and decided to turn the situation to her advantage. She was willing to tolerate him…for the sake of her career at least. He shouldn't have been surprised. He'd already had one bad experience with a publicity-hungry actress, and then he'd been one of the casualties.

Still, they were in the middle of the second act, and he'd missed the opening. But suddenly things had gotten a lot more interesting.

Odele's eyes gleamed as if she sensed victory—or at least a chink in his armor. Turning away, she said, "Let me know when you're ready to talk."

As Rick watched Chiara's manager leave, he knew there was a brooding expression on his face. Odele had presented him with a quandary. As a rule, he didn't get involved with actresses—ever since his one bad episode—but he had his gallant side. On top of it, Chiara was the talent on his latest film—one in which he had a big stake.

As if on cue, his cell phone vibrated. Fishing it out of his pocket, Rick recognized the number on-screen as that of his business partner—one of the guys who fronted the company, per Rick's preference to be behind the scenes.

"Hey, Pete, what's going on?"

Rick listened to Pete's summary of the meeting that morning with an indie director looking for funding. He liked what he heard, but he needed to know more. "Email me their proposal. I'm inclined to fund up to five million, but I want more details."

Five million dollars was pocket change in his world.

"You're the boss," Pete responded cheerfully.

Yup, he was…though no one on set knew he was the producer of *Pegasus Pride*. He liked his privacy and kept his communications mostly to a need-to-know basis.

Right. Rick spotted Chiara in the distance. No doubt she was heading to film her next scene. *There* was someone who treated him more like the hired help than the boss.

Complications and delays on a film were common, and Rick had a feeling Chiara was about to become his biggest complication to date…

Two

"Hey."

It was exactly the sort of greeting she expected from a sweaty and earthy he-man—or rather, stuntman.

Chiara's pulse picked up. *Ugh.* She hadn't expected to have this reaction around him. She was a professional—a classically trained actress before she'd been diverted by Hollywood.

Sure, she'd been Miss Rhode Island, and a runner-up in the Miss America pageant. But then the Yale School of Drama had beckoned. And she'd never been a Hollywood blonde. The media most often compared her to Camilla Belle because they shared a raven-haired, chestnut-eyed look.

Anyway, with her ebony hair, she'd need to have her roots touched up every other day if she tried to become a blonde. As far as she was concerned, she spent enough time in the primping chair.

She figured He-Stuntman had gotten his education in the School of Hard Knocks. Maybe a broken bone or two. Certainly plenty of bumps and bruises.

Rick stopped in front of her. No one was around. They were near the actors' trailers, far away from the main action. Luckily she hadn't run into him after her talk with Odele two days ago. Instead, she'd managed to avoid him until now.

Dusk was gathering, but she still had a clear view of him.

He was in a ripped tee, jeans and body paint meant to seem like grease and dirt, while she was wearing a damsel-in-distress/sidekick look—basically a feminine version of Rick's attire but her clothes were extratight and torn to show cleavage. And from the quick perusal he gave her, she could tell the bare skin hadn't escaped his notice.

"So you need a boyfriend," he said without preamble.

She itched to rub the smug smile off his face. "I don't need anything. This would be a completely optional but mutually advantageous arrangement."

And right after this conversation, she was going to have another serious talk with her manager. What had Odele signed her up for?

"You need me."

She burned. He'd made it sound like *you want me.*

"I've been asked to play many roles, but never a stud."

"Don't get too excited."

He grinned. "Don't worry, I won't. I have a thing for the doe-eyed, dark-haired look, but since Camilla Belle isn't available, you'll do."

The flames of temper licked her, not least because he was clued in as to her Hollywood doppelgänger. "So you'll settle?"

"I don't know. Let's kiss and find out."

"If the cameras were rolling, it would be time for a slap right now," she muttered.

He caught her wrist and tugged her closer.

"This isn't a movie, and you're no actor!" she objected.

"Great, because I intend to kiss you for real. Let's see if we can be convincing for when the paparazzi and public are watching." He raised his free hand to thread his fingers through her hair and move it away from her face. "Your long dark hair is driving me crazy."

"It's the Brazilian-Italian heritage," she snapped back, "and I bet you say the same thing to all your leading ladies."

"No," he answered bemusedly, "some of them are blondes."

And then his mouth was on hers. If he'd been forceful, she'd have had a chance, but his lips settled on hers with soft, tantalizing pressure. He smelled of smoke from the special effects, and when his tongue slipped inside her mouth, she discovered the taste of mint, too.

She'd been kissed many times—on-screen and off—but she found herself tumbling into this one with shocking speed. The kiss was smooth, leisurely…masterful but understated. Rick could double for any A-list actor in a love scene. He touched his tongue to hers, and the shock and unexpectedness of it had her opening to him. As an unwritten rule, actors on-screen did not French kiss, so she was already in uncharted territory. The hard plane of his chest brushed against her, and her nipples tightened.

Think, Chiara. Remember why you don't like him.

She allowed herself one more second, and then she tore her mouth away and stepped back. For a fleeting moment she felt a puff of steam over his audacity. "All right, the screen test is over."

Rick curved his lips. "How did I do?"

"I don't even know your last name," she responded, sidestepping the question.

"I'll answer to anything. 'Honey,' 'baby,' 'sugar.'" He shrugged. "I'm easy."

"Clearly." This guy could charm his way into any woman's bed. "Still, I'd prefer your real one for when the police ask me to describe the suspect."

He grinned. "It's Rick Serenghetti. But 'darling' would add the appropriate air of mystery for the paparazzi."

Serenghetti. She knew an Italian surname when she heard one. "My last name was originally Ferano. You know, Italian."

His smile widened. "I'd never have guessed, Snow White."

"They used to call me Snow White, but I drifted," she quipped. "Not suitable for the role."

"No problem. I'm not Prince Charming. I'm just his body double."

She wanted to scream. "This is never going to work."

"That's why you're an actress." He looked curious. "And, Odele mentioned, a beauty contestant. Win any titles?"

She made a sour face. "Yes. Miss Congeniality."

He burst out laughing. "I won't ask what your talent was."

"Ventriloquism. I made my dummy sing."

"'Some Day My Prince Will Come'?"

"Nothing from *Snow White*! I was also Miss Rhode Island, but obviously that was on the state level." She'd gone on to be a finalist in Miss America, which was where she'd earned her title of Miss Congeniality.

"Rhode Island is the smallest state. Still, the competition must have been fierce."

"Are you mocking me?" She searched his face, but he looked solemn.

"Who, me? I never mock women I'm trying to score with."

"Wow, you're direct. You don't even like me."

"What's *like* got to do with it?"

"You have no shame." When it came to sex, she was used to men wanting to bed anyone in sight. This was Hollywood, after all.

"Is it working?"

"Nothing will work, except Odele convincing me this is a good idea."

Rick frowned. "You mean she hasn't already?"

It took Chiara a moment to realize he wasn't joking. "Please. She may have persuaded you to go along with her crazy scheme, but not me."

"I only went along with it because I thought you'd said yes."

Chiara watched Rick's dawning expression, which mimicked her own. "I believed you'd agreed."

"Stuntmen are made of sterner stuff." He threw her attitude right back at her.

Chiara realized they'd both been tricked by Odele into believing the other had agreed to her plan. Rick had dared to kiss her because he thought she'd already signed up for her manager's plot. "What are we going to do?"

Rick shrugged. "About the gathering media frenzy? We're already bickering like an old married couple. We're perfect."

Chiara's eyes widened. "You can't tell me you're seriously considering this? Anyway, we're supposed to act like new lovebirds, not a cantankerous old married couple."

"If we're already arguing, it'll make our relationship seem deeper than it is."

"Skip the honeymoon phase?" she asked rhetorically. "What's in this for you?"

He shrugged. "Have some fun." He looked at her lingeringly. "Satisfy my fetish for Snow White."

Chiara tingled, her breasts feeling heavy. "Oh, yeah, right…"

"So what's your take?"

"This is the worst storyline to come out of Hollywood."

For the second time in recent days, Chiara banged open the door of her trailer and marched in. "I can't pretend to be in a relationship with Rick Serenghetti. End of story."

Odele looked up from her magazine. She sat on a cushioned built-in bench along one wall. "What's wrong with him?"

He was too big, too macho, too everything—most of all, *annoying*. She still sizzled from their kiss minutes ago, and she didn't do vulnerability where men were concerned. But she sidestepped the issue. "It's the pretending part that I have trouble with."

"You're an actress."

"Context is everything. I like to confine my acting to the screen." Otherwise, she'd be in danger of losing herself. If she was always pretending, who was she? "You know I value integrity."

"It's overrated. Besides, this is Tinseltown."

Chiara placed her hands on her hips. "You misled me and Rick into thinking the other one had already agreed to this crazy scheme."

Odele shrugged. "You were already open to the idea.

That's the only reason it even mattered to you whether he was already on board with the plan."

Chiara felt heat rise to her face, and schooled her expression. "I'm not signing up for anything!"

Her conversation with Rick had had no satisfactory ending. It had sent her scuttling, somewhat humiliatingly, back to her manager. Chiara eyed the shower stall visible through the open bathroom door at the end of the trailer. If only she could rinse off the tabloid headlines just as easily.

"Fine," Odele responded with sudden and suspicious docility, putting aside her magazine. "We'll have to come up with another strategy to distract the press from your father and amp up your career."

"Sounds like a plan to me."

"Great, it's settled. Now…can you gain twenty pounds?" Odele asked.

Chiara sighed. Out of the frying pan and into the fire. "I'd rather not. Why?"

She'd gained fifteen for a film role two years ago in *Alibis & Lies*—in which she'd played a convicted white-collar criminal who witnesses a murder once she's released from jail and thinks her husband is framing her. To gain the weight, she'd indulged her love for pasta, creamy sauces and pastries—but she'd had to work for months with a trainer to shed the pounds afterward. In the meantime, she'd worn sunglasses and baggy clothes and had lain low in order to avoid an unflattering shot by the paparazzi. And she'd been disappointed not to get a Golden Globe nomination.

She wondered what movie project Odele had in mind these days… Usually her talent agent at Creative Artists sent projects her way, but Odele kept her ear to the ground, too.

"Last time I was heavier on-screen, I got a lot of back-lash." Some fans thought she'd gained too much weight, some too little. She could never please everyone.

"It's not a film," Odele said. "It's a weight-loss com-mercial."

Chiara's jaw dropped. "But I'm not overweight!"

Odele's eyes gleamed. "You could be."

Chiara threw her hands up. "Odele, you're ruthless."

"It's what makes me good at what I do. Slender You is looking for a new celebrity weight-loss spokesper-son. The goodwill with fans alone is worth the pounds, but Slender You is willing to pay millions to the right person. If you land this contract, your DBI score will go up, and you'll be more likely to land other endorse-ment deals."

"No." Her manager was all about Q scores and DBIs and any other rating that claimed to measure a celeb-rity's appeal to the public. "Next you'll be suggesting a reality show."

Odele shook her head. "No, I only recommend it to clients who haven't had a big acting job in at least five years. That's not you, sweetie."

For which Chiara would be forever grateful. She was having a hard enough time being the star of her own life without adding the artifice of a reality show to it.

"How about writing a book?" Odele asked, tilting her head.

"On what?"

"Anything! We'll let your ghostwriter decide."

"No, thanks. If I have a ghost, I won't really be writ-ing, will I?" Chiara responded tartly.

"You're too honest for your own good, you know." Odele sighed, and then suddenly brightened. "What about a fragrance?"

"I thought Dior just picked a new face for the brand."

"They did. I'm talking about developing your own scent. Very lucrative these days."

"You mean like Elizabeth Taylor's White Diamonds?"

"Right, right." Odele warmed up. "We could call it Chiara. Or, wait, wait, Chiara Lucida! The name suggests a bright star."

"How much is an Oscar worth?" Chiara joked, because her idea of becoming a big star involved winning a golden statuette.

"Of course, an Academy Award has value, but we want to monetize all income streams, sweetie. We want to grow and protect your brand."

Chiara sighed, leaning against the walnut-paneled built-in cabinet behind her. There'd been a time when movie stars were just, well, movie stars. Now everyone was *a brand*. "There's nothing wrong with my brand."

"Yes, of course." Odele paused for a beat. "Well, except for the teeny-weeny problem of your father popping up in the headlines from time to time."

"Right." How could she forget? How could anyone fail to remember when the tabloids followed the story breathlessly?

"How about a lifestyle brand like Gwyneth Paltrow or Jessica Alba has?" Odele offered.

"Maybe when I win an Academy Award or I have kids." Both Alba and Paltrow had had children when they'd started their companies.

At the thought of kids, Chiara had an uncomfortable feeling in the pit of her stomach. She was thirty-two. She had an expiration date in Hollywood *and* a ticking clock for getting pregnant without spending thousands of dollars for chancy medical intervention. Unfortunately the two trains were on a collision course. If she was going to avert disaster, she needed to have a well-established career—er, Oscar—before she caved in to the public clamor for her to get a happily-ever-after with marriage and children.

Of course, she wanted kids. It was the husband or boyfriend part that she had a problem with. Michael Feran hadn't set a sterling example for his only child. At least she thought she was his only child.

Ugh. Her family—or what remained of it—was so complicated. It wouldn't even qualify as a Lifetime movie because there was no happy ending.

Still, the thought of a child of her own brought a pang. She'd have someone to love unconditionally, and who would love and need her in return. She'd avoid the mistakes that her parents had made. And she'd have something real—pure love—to hold on to in the maelstrom of celebrity.

"So," Odele said pleasantly, "your other options aren't too appealing. Let me know when you're ready to consider dating Rick Serenghetti."

Chiara stared at her manager. She had the sneaking suspicion that Odele had known all along where their conversation was heading. In all probability, her manager had been set on showing her the error of her ways and her earlier agreeableness had just been a feint. "You're a shark, Odele."

Odele chuckled. "I know. It's why I'm good at what I do."

Chiara resisted throwing up her hands. Some actresses confided in their personal assistants or stylists. She had Odele.

"So what's got you down?"

Rick figured he needed to work on his acting skills

if even Jordan was asking that question. "I don't know what you're talking about."

They were sitting in his kitchen, and he'd just handed his brother a cold beer from the fridge. He grabbed opportunities with his family whenever he could since he spent much of his time on the opposite coast from everyone else. Fortunately, since his current movie was being filmed on a Novatus Studio lot and nearby locations around LA, he was able to get to his place at least on weekends—even if home these days was a one-bedroom rental in West Hollywood.

"Mom asked me to check on you." Jordan shifted his weight on the kitchen barstool.

"She always asks you to check on me whenever we're in the same city. But don't assume the reconnaissance runs one way. She wants me to keep an eye on you, too."

"My life hasn't been that interesting lately."

Jordan was in town because his team, the New England Razors, was playing the Los Angeles Kings at the Staples Center. He was the star center player for the team. The youngest Serenghetti brother also had movie star looks, and hardly ever let an opportunity pass without remarking that their parents had attained perfection the third time around.

Rick followed hockey—family loyalty and all—but he wasn't passionate about it like Jordan and their older brother, Cole, who'd also had a career with the Razors until it had ended in injury. Rick had been a wrestler in high school, not a hockey team captain like his brothers.

The result was that he had a reputation as the family maverick. And hey, who was he to argue? Still, he wasn't intentionally contrary—though Chiara might want to argue the point.

An image of Chiara Feran sprung to mind. He'd been

willing to tease her about playing a couple, especially when he'd thought Chiara was going along with the idea. After all, it was nice, safe, *pretend*—not like really getting involved with an actress. And it was fun to ruffle Chiara's feathers.

If he was being a little more serious, he'd also acknowledge that as a producer, he had a vested interest in the star of his latest film maintaining a positive public image despite her problematic family members—not to mention staying *safe* if she really had a would-be stalker.

Still, being a *pretend boyfriend* and *secret bodyguard*, if Odele had her way, was asking a lot. Did he have enough to overcome his scruples about getting involved with a celebrity? Hell, even he wasn't sure. He'd been burned once by an aspiring starlet, and he'd learned his lesson—never stand between an actress and a camera.

For a long time, he'd counted actors, directors and other movie people among his friends. Hal Moldado, a lighting technician, had been one of those buddies. Then one day, Rick had run into Isabel Lanier, Hal's latest girlfriend. She'd followed him out of a cafe and surprised him with a kiss—captured in a selfie that she'd managed to take with her cell phone and promptly posted to her social media accounts. Unsurprisingly it had spelled the end of his friendship with Hal. Later he'd conclude that Isabel had just been trying to make Hal jealous and stay in the news herself as an actress.

The saving grace had been that the media had never found out—or cared—about the name of Isabel's mystery man in those photos. It had been enough that Isabel looked as if she were cheating on Hal, so Rick had been able to dodge the media frenzy.

Ever since, though, as far as he was concerned, starlets were only interested in tending their public image.

And up to now Chiara had fit the bill well—even if she hadn't yet agreed to her manager's latest scheme. After all, there was a reason that Chiara had partnered with someone like Odele. She knew her celebrity was important, and she needed someone to curate it.

But Odele had increased the stakes by referring to a possible stalker… It complicated his calculations about whether to get involved. He should just convince Chiara to get additional security—like any sane person would. Not that *sanity* ranked high on the list of characteristics he associated with fame-hungry actresses.

Jordan tilted his head. "Woman in your thoughts?"

Rick brought his attention back to the present. "Anyone ever tell you that you have a sixth sense where the other sex is concerned?"

His younger brother smiled enigmatically. "Sera would agree with you. Marisa's cousin is driving me crazy."

Their brother Cole had recently married the love of his life, Marisa Danieli. The two had had a falling-out in high school but had reconnected. Marisa's relatives were now an extension by marriage of the Serenghetti clan—including Marisa's younger cousin Sera.

Apparently that didn't sit well with Jordan.

"I'm surprised," Rick remarked. "You can usually charm any woman if you set your mind to it."

"She won't even serve me at the Puck & Shoot."

"Is she still moonlighting as a waitress there?" Rick had had his share of drinks at Welsdale's local sports bar.

"Off and on."

He clasped his brother's shoulder. "So your legendary prowess with women has fallen short. Cheer up, it was bound to happen sometime."

"Your support is overwhelming," Jordan replied drily.

Rick laughed. "I just wish Cole were here to appreciate this."

"For the record, I haven't been trying to score with Sera. She's practically family. But she actively dislikes me, and I can't figure out why."

"Why does it matter? It won't be the first time a family member has had it in for you." Jordan had come in for his share of ribbing and roughing up by his two older siblings. "What's to get worked up about?"

"I'm not worked up," Jordan grumbled. "Anyway, let's get back to you and the woman problems."

Rick cracked a careless smile. "Unlike you, I don't have any."

"Women or problems?"

"Both together."

Jordan eyed him. "The press is suggesting you have the former, and you look as if you've got the latter."

"Oh, yeah?"

"Who's the starlet on your latest film?"

"Chiara Feran."

His brother nodded. "She's hot."

"She's off-limits."

Jordan raised his eyebrows. "To me?"

"To anyone."

"Proprietary already?"

"Where did you get this ridiculous story?"

"Hey, I read."

"Much to Mom's belated joy."

Jordan flashed the famous pearly whites. His good looks had gotten him many modeling gigs, including more than one underwear ad. "*Gossipmonger* reported you two have been getting cozy, and the story has been picked up by other websites."

"You know better than to believe everything you

read." If the gossip had reached Jordan, then it was spreading wider and faster than Rick had thought. Still, he figured he shouldn't have been surprised, considering Chiara's celebrity.

"Yup. But is it true?"

Frankly, Rick was starting not to know what was true anymore, and it was troubling. "Nothing's happened."

Except one kiss. She'd tasted of peaches—fruity and heady and delicious. He'd gotten an immediate image of the two of them heating up the sheets, his trailer or hers. She challenged him, and something told him she'd be far from boring in bed, too. Chiara was full of fire, and he warmed up immediately around her. The trouble was he might also get burned.

Jordan studied him. "So nothing's happened yet…"

Rick adopted a bland expression. "Unlike you, I don't see women as an opportunity."

"Only your female stars."

"I'm done with that." Isabel had been the star of Rick's movie when they'd been snapped together. The fact that they'd both been working on the film—he as a stuntman and secretly as a producer, and she as an actress—had lent an air of truth to the rumors.

Jordan looked thoughtful. "Right."

Rick checked his watch because he was through trying to convince his brother—or himself. In a quarter of an hour, they needed to head to dinner at Ink, one of the neighborhood's trendy restaurants. "Just finish your damn beer."

"Whatever you say, movie star," Jordan responded, seemingly content to back off.

They both took a swill of their beers.

"So, the new digs treating you well?" his brother asked after a moment.

The apartment had come furnished, so there wasn't a hint of his personality here, but it served its purpose. "The house is nearly done. I'll be moving in a few weeks."

Jordan saluted him with his beer bottle. "Here's to moving up in the world in a big way." His brother grinned. "Invite me to visit when the new manse is done."

"Don't worry. I'll tell the majordomo not to throw you out," Rick replied drily.

Jordan laughed. "I'm a babe magnet. You'll want me around."

Privately, Rick acknowledged his brother might have a point. These days, the only woman he was linked to was Chiara Feran, and it wasn't even real.

Three

For two days, Rick didn't encounter Chiara. She and Adrian Collins, the male lead, were busy filming, so today Rick was hitting the gym trailer and working off restless energy.

So far, there'd been no denial or affirmation in the press that he and Chiara were a couple. As a news story, they were stuck in limbo—a holding pattern that kept him antsy and out of sorts. He wondered what Chiara's camp was up to, and then shrugged. He wasn't going to call attention to himself by issuing a denial—not that the press cared about his opinion because for all they knew, he was just a stuntman. They were after Chiara.

After exiting the gym trailer, Rick made his way across the film set. He automatically tensed as he neared Chiara's trailer. Snow White was a tart-tongued irritant these days—

He rounded a corner and spotted a man struggling with the knob on Chiara's door.

The balding guy with a paunch was muttering to himself and jiggling the door hard.

Frowning, Rick moved toward him. This section of the set was otherwise deserted.

"Hey," he called, "what are you doing?"

The guy looked up nervously.

All Rick's instincts told him this wasn't a good situation. "What are you doing?"

"I'm a friend of Chiara's."

"Does she know you're here?"

"I've been trying to see her." This time there was a note of whininess.

"This is a closed set. Do you have ID?" Rick didn't recall seeing this guy before. He was within a few feet of the other man now. The guy stood on the top step leading to the door of the trailer. Rick could see perspiration had formed on the man's brow. Was this the creepy fan Odele had referred to?

Rick went with his gut. "I'm her new boyfriend."

The other guy frowned. "That's impossible."

Now that he was closer, Rick could see the other man was definitely not the glamorous or debonair celebrity type that he would expect an actress like Chiara to date.

In the next second, the guy barreled down the trailer's steps and shoved past him.

Rick staggered but grasped the trailer's flimsy metal bannister to keep himself upright.

As Chiara's alleged friend made a run for it, Rick instinctively took off after him.

The man plowed past a crew member, who careened back against a piece of lighting equipment. Then two extras jumped aside, creating a path for the chase.

The guy headed toward the front gate of the studio lot, where Rick knew security would stop him. Rick could only guess how the intruder had gotten onto the lot. Had he hidden in the back of a catering truck, as paparazzi had been known to do?

Gaining on Chiara's admirer, Rick put on a final burst of speed and tackled the guy. As they both went down, Rick saw in his peripheral vision that they'd attracted the security guards' attention at the front gate.

The man struggled in his grasp, jabbing Rick with his elbow. "Get off me! I'll sue you for assault."

Rick twisted the man's arm behind his back, holding him down. "Not before you get written up for trespassing. Where's your pass?"

"I'm Chiara's fiancé," the guy howled.

Rick glanced up to see that two security guards had caught up to them. "I found this guy trying to break into Chiara Feran's trailer."

"Call Chiara," her alleged fiancé puffed. "She'll know."

"Chiara Feran doesn't have a fiancé," Rick bit back.

Someone nearby had started filming with his cell phone. *Great.*

"We're together. We're meant to be together!"

Nut job. Rick was in great physical shape due to his stunt work, so he wasn't out of breath, but Mr. Fiancé was no teddy bear, either; he continued to put up a struggle.

Suddenly the trespasser wheezed. "I can't br-breathe! Get off me. I have asthma."

Great. Rick eased back and let one of the security guards take over while the other spoke into his radio.

Things happened slowly but methodically after that. Police were summoned by the studio's security, and Chiara's special fan—who'd given his name as Todd Jeffers—was led away. Eventually Rick was questioned by a police officer. Chiara materialized soon after and was similarly prodded for details by the officer's partner.

Before the police left, Rick gleaned that Chiara's overly enthusiastic fan would be charged with criminal trespass, disorderly conduct and harassment. *Well, that's something.* But by the time Rick had finished talking about the incident to Dan, the director, Chiara had holed up in her trailer.

Rick eyed Chiara's door, twisted his mouth in a grim line and made his way to the trailer for some answers.

He didn't bother knocking—chances were better for a snowstorm in LA right now than for her rolling out the red carpet for him—and simply marched inside.

He came up short when he found Chiara sitting at a cozy little table, a script in front of her.

She was memorizing her lines? He expected her to be rattled, upset...

He looked around. The trailer was a double-decker, and with walnut paneling, it was swankier than his own digs, which were done in a gray monochrome and had no upper level.

When his gaze came back to rest on Chiara, she tilted her head, and said, "People weren't sure when you tackled him whether it was a stunt, or if you were rehearsing a scene from the movie."

"You're welcome." Leaning against a counter, he folded his arms, like a cop getting ready for an interrogation. He wanted answers only she could provide, and after getting into a fight with her admirer, he was going to get them. "Luckily you weren't in your trailer when he got here."

"I was rehearsing. We're shooting a difficult scene."

Rick figured that helped explain why she was sitting with a script in front of her, though he imagined her concentration was shot.

"I can only imagine the press coverage that today will

get." A horrified look crossed her face, and she closed her eyes on a shudder.

So she wasn't as unaffected as she seemed. In fact, Rick had already dealt with suppressing the video of him tackling Jeffers. The person who'd been taping had turned out to be a visiting relative of one of the film crew. But even if those images didn't become public or weren't sold to the tabloids, the media would get wind of what happened from the police report and show up for Jeffers's court hearing. Then, of course, Jeffers himself might choose to make a public statement…

"Hey, at least it'll take attention away from your father's latest losses at the gambling tables." He wondered if Chiara appreciated just how close she'd come to danger. It had been dumb luck that her overly enthusiastic fan hadn't found her earlier.

She opened her eyes and raised her head. "Yes, how can I forget about my father? How can anyone?"

"So you have a stalker." He kept his tone mild, belying the emotions coursing through him. *Damn it.* Chiara was slender and a lightweight despite her mouth and bravado. His blood boiled just thinking of some jerk threatening her.

"Many celebrities have overly enthusiastic fans." She waved her hand, and Rick could practically see her walls going up. "But my property has a security gate and cameras."

Rick narrowed his eyes. "Have you dealt with this Todd Jeffers guy before? What kind of unstoppable fan is he? The sort who writes you pretty letters or the type who pens twisted ones?"

She shrugged. "He tried to scale my property fence once, but he was spotted by a landscaper and shooed away even before he got within view of the security cameras. I haven't heard from him in the months since."

So today's guy was the same person who'd shown up at Chiara's house once, and yeah, she wasn't understanding the risk... Still, Rick strove for patience. "How do you know it was Jeffers at your house that day?"

She hesitated. "He wrote to me afterward to say he'd tried to see me."

"He wrote to you about an attempted criminal trespass?" Rick let his tone drip disbelief. "Have you gotten a temporary restraining order?"

Chiara sighed. "No. He's never been a physical threat, just a pest."

"Just because he *only* tried to jump the fence doesn't mean that's what he'll settle for doing in the future. There's often an escalation with these nut jobs once they figure out that plan A isn't working."

Chiara raised her chin. "He's probably a lonely, starstruck guy. Plenty of fans are."

"Probably? I don't deal in probabilities. Your run-of-the-mill serial killer often starts out torturing animals before moving to the big time. As I said, escalation."

"Like A-list stars starting out in B movies?" she asked snippily.

"Right," he said, his voice tight even as he ignored her flippant attitude. "Listen, Snow White, there are villains out there aside from the Evil Queen."

Rick raked his fingers through his hair. He could understand why this guy was besotted with Chiara. Unfortunately Chiara herself wasn't appreciating the gravity of the problem. They were like two trains on parallel tracks. "You've got a stalker. It's time you acquired a boyfriend. Me."

He'd been mulling things over, his mind in overdrive

ever since he'd tackled Jeffers. If he pretended to be Chiara's boyfriend, he could stick close and keep an eye on her. Maybe once this guy realized Chiara had a supposedly real boyfriend, he'd back off. Odele may have been onto a good idea.

Chiara opened and closed her mouth. "You're not in the protection business."

"I'm appointing myself right now. Besides, I've got the right background. I used to do security." He'd worked as a guard at an office building during his college days and beyond in order to earn extra cash. He'd been a good bouncer, too. His parents had instilled the value of hard work in their children even though they'd been well-off.

Chiara slid off her seat and stood. In the confined space, she was within touching distance. "You can't unilaterally decide to be my protector." She spluttered as if searching for words. "I won't agree to it."

"You could solve two problems at once. The bad press from your father, and the issue of your stalker and needing security. Don't quibble."

"I'll get a restraining order."

He took a step forward. "Damn straight, you will."

"So I don't need you."

"You need physical protection, too, unless you have seven dwarves hanging around, because a court order is just a piece of paper." He didn't want to think about how many news stories there'd been concerning an order of protection being violated—and someone getting hurt or killed.

She looked mutinous. "I'll hire professional security."

"It still won't solve the problem of your father and distracting the press."

Chiara threw up her hands.

"Don't worry. I'll always be a step behind you, like a good prince consort—I mean, bodyguard."

"Hilarious."

"I'll make sure to hold an umbrella open for you in the rain," he added solemnly.

"What's in this for you?"

"Let's just say I have a vested interest in the star of my next blockbuster staying safe until the end of filming. Everyone working on this movie wants to see it finished so they can get paid."

"I thought so. Well, my answer is still no."

He'd given her the wrong answer, and she'd responded in kind. "Do you just act contrary, or is this your best side?"

"How can you say that about the damsel in distress you helped save from a helicopter?" she asked sweetly.

"Exactly."

They were practically nose-to-nose, except because she stood several inches shorter than his six-foot frame, it was more like nose-to-chin. But then she raised her face to a stubborn angle, and he abandoned his good intentions about keeping himself in check during this conversation.

Hell, here goes nothing.

He tugged her forward and captured her mouth. It was just as good as before, damn it. There was a little zap of electricity because they were differently charged, and then he was kissing her in earnest, opening that luscious mouth and deepening the kiss.

She smelled faintly of honeysuckle, just like Snow White ought to. He caressed her cheek with the back of his hand. She was petal-soft, and he was getting hard.

After what felt like an eternity, she pushed him away.

Her chest rose and fell, and he was breathing deeply with arousal.

She touched her fingers to her lips and then shot fire at him with her eyes. "That's twice."

"Are we getting better? We've got to be convincing if we're going to pull this off."

"We're not practicing scenes, but if we were, try this response on for size." She stretched out her arm and pointed to the door of the trailer, giving him his marching orders.

It was a proverbial slap in the face, but Chiara was wrong if she thought he was backing down. "Let me know when our next scene is scheduled for filming. It might be time to throw a plate or break something. For real, not pretend."

After this parting shot, he turned and headed to the door, almost laughing as he heard her bang something behind him.

"She doesn't want to get extra security." Rick ran his hand through his hair. "She's stubborn."

"Hmm." Odele nodded. "And I'm her manager, so I don't know this?"

"And reckless, too." They were sitting in Novatus Studio's commissary having coffee before lunchtime. Rick had asked to meet and had told Odele not to mention it to Chiara. "How long has this guy Todd been hanging around thinking he's her special friend?" *Or fiancé.*

Odele shrugged. "Several months. I had staff look at Chiara's fan mail after he showed up at her house. He'd sent an email or two, and my assistant says he's cropped up on social media, too. Then he started a fan club and wanted autographed photos."

"And now he's moved on to believing he's her fiancé."

Odele sighed. "Some people buy into the Hollywood celebrity stuff a little too much."

Right. Rick leaned back in his chair. "Besides trying

to scale the fence at Chiara's house, has he made any other moves?"

"Not until yesterday. At least not that I know of." Odele took a sip from her cup. "I've already instructed Chiara's attorney to go for a restraining order."

"You and I both know it's only a piece of paper, but she doesn't want to consider additional physical security. Not even if I appoint myself." Rick didn't hide the frustration in his voice. Damn it. Who was he kidding? Chiara would resist, especially if it was him.

"So you're considering my idea of being a pretend boyfriend? You need to move in."

Rick shook his head in exasperation because Odele was a bulldozer. "If she doesn't want a fake relationship and won't tolerate a bodyguard, she definitely won't have someone living in her house."

If he and Chiara lived under one roof, they'd drive each other crazy. He'd alternate between wanting to shake some sense into her and take her to bed. And she'd… Well, she'd just rage at him and deny any sparks of a simmering attraction.

It was a recipe for disaster…or a Hollywood movie.

Odele gave him a mild look. "It's all a matter of how it's presented to her. If you're going to distract the press as her new boyfriend, the story will play even bigger in the media if you move in. There'll be more opportunities for the two of you to be photographed together."

"*Pretend* boyfriend." Everyone needed to be clear on the fake part, including and particularly *him*, if he was going to get involved with another actress.

Odele inclined her head. "Leave convincing her to me. I won't say anything more about having you function as a bodyguard. But believe me, the press attention surrounding her father is really upsetting her."

In Rick's opinion, Chiara should be spending more time worrying about her stalker than about her estranged father. Still... "Tell me about Michael Feran."

Odele set aside her coffee cup. "There's not much to say. Chiara's parents divorced when she was young. Chiara and her mother were in Rhode Island until Hollywood beckoned. Her mother died a few years ago. She developed sepsis after an illness. It was a shock for everyone."

"But her father continues to make waves."

"Last year, he accepted money from a third-rate weekly to dish about Chiara."

Rick cursed.

Odele shot him a perceptive look from behind her red glasses. "Yes, Chiara felt betrayed."

So Chiara's was far from a fairy-tale upbringing. No wonder she was prickly around him, and no doubt distrustful of men.

"Take it from me. Be the good boyfriend that she needs and keep an eye on her. Just don't bring up the bodyguard part to her."

"A pretend boyfriend." *Pretend* being the operative word there. He wasn't sure if he was reminding himself or Odele, though.

"Right."

Right.

Chiara took Ruby out of her box and perched her on her knee. The dummy wore a sequined gown, and her hair and face were worthy of a Vegas showgirl.

Chiara sat at the writing desk occupying one corner of her master bedroom. There'd been a break in filming for the weekend, and she was happy to retreat to her sanctuary. She needed time away. First her father, then Rick and finally a stalker had frayed her nerves.

Still, even though it was a beautiful and sunny Saturday afternoon, and she should have been in a great mood, she…*wasn't*. She was irritable and restless and anxious. She'd been having trouble memorizing her lines ever since the attempted break-in at her trailer. *Pegasus Pride* was an action flick, so the script wasn't heavy, but there was still dialogue that she had to be able to say without prompting.

Frustrated, she'd finally resorted to using Ruby to help her relax. She hadn't taken the dummy out in months, but ventriloquism kept her in touch with her former life—and at moments like these, let her deal with her present concerns.

Chiara searched the dummy's face. "What am I going to do?"

Ruby tilted her head.

"I must be out of my mind to be talking to a dummy by myself."

"You're not alone if you're having a chat with someone," Ruby responded in her singsong voice. "I just help you figure things out, sugar."

"I thought that's what Odele is for."

Ruby waved her hand. "You already know where Odele stands. She's on the hunk's side, and frankly, I don't know why you aren't, too." Ruby tossed her hair—because rolling her eyes was out of the question. "He's delicious."

"Annoying. You're reading too much gossip."

"I have to, it's about you," the dummy chirped. "Anyway, it's time you let someone under your skin, and back into your bed. And Rick…that body, that face, that kiss. Need I say more?"

"You are saucy and naughty, Ruby."

"And you wish you could be. Let your hair down, sugar."

Chiara's gaze fell to the laptop at her elbow. "I have too many responsibilities...and plenty of problems."

The headline on the computer screen spoke for itself: Chiara Feran's Father Thrown Out of Casino.

Maybe now that he couldn't gamble because he'd been caught counting cards, Michael Feran would stay out of trouble. But Chiara knew that was wishful thinking.

The public thought she had an enviable life—helped by Odele's relentless image craftsmanship. But the truth...

She'd never thought of herself as a beauty queen, for one. Oh, sure, she'd been blessed with good genes—a nice face and a fast metabolism that meant it wasn't impossible to adhere to Hollywood standards of beauty. But she also considered herself an outsider. She'd been raised by an immigrant mother, grown up enduring cold New England winters and would have still been doing theater but for a quirk of fate and Odele risking taking her on as a client.

She liked her privacy, her best friend was a smart-mouthed talent manager ripe for caricature and her sidekick was a doll made of wood. Obviously Todd Jeffers was crazier than she gave him credit for if he couldn't pick a better-credentialed starlet to stalk. And now she had a rumored *boyfriend*—a muscle-bound stuntman who looked as if he could enter a triathlon.

She'd already ignored a text from Odele about the latest headline, but Chiara knew her manager was right— they needed a distraction *fast*...

Her lawyers were due in court in the coming days to get a temporary restraining order—so there'd be more unwanted press attention because of her unpleasant fan.

Still, Rick Serenghetti? *Argh*.

Her cell phone buzzed again, a telltale ringtone, and this time Chiara knew she couldn't ignore it. With an apologetic look, she propped Ruby on a chair and took the call. "Hello, Odele."

"Enjoying your time off?"

"Define *enjoy*. I'm memorizing my lines." Among other things. She cast Ruby a hush-hush look.

"Rick needs to move in if we're going to make this fake relationship work. It'll help believability."

"No." The refusal fell from her lips without thought. Rick in her house? They'd throttle each other...if they weren't jumping into bed. And the contradiction of trying to make a *fake* relationship *work* was apparently lost on her manager.

Odele sighed. "We need to move quickly. I'm going to tell my assistant to break the story on social media accounts so we can control the initial message. I took an amateur shot with my cell phone of you and Rick seemingly engaged in an intimate conversation on the Novatus Studio lot."

"Of course you did."

"It looks great. Really like the two of you having a tête-à-tête," Odele added, warming to her subject and ignoring the sarcasm.

"Did it also look as if I was going to kick him in the shins?"

"And I've already set up a print interview for the two of you with a trusted reporter," Odele went on as if she hadn't heard.

"I'm not looking for a protector. And have you even done a background check on Rick Serenghetti? Maybe he's the one I need safeguarding from!"

Rick was dangerous to her tranquility, but she didn't care to delve into the reasons why. He had a way of looking at her with a lazy, sultry gleam that she found…annoying—yes, definitely annoying.

She'd done a quick search online for him—*only* for the purpose of satisfying herself that he didn't have a criminal record, she told herself—and had come up with nothing. She supposed no news was good news.

"Who said anything about a bodyguard?" Odele said innocently. "This is to help everyone believe you two are an item."

So Rick had backed off the part about offering personal protection? Somehow she had her doubts. "He doesn't need to move in to do that. What ever happened to dating? We're going from zero to sixty."

"It's Hollywood. Pregnancies last five months, and babies arrive right after the wedding. Everything is fast here."

Chiara couldn't argue. Celebrities were well-known for trying to hide their pregnancies from the press until the second trimester or beyond.

"Do I need to resend you the latest headline about Michael Feran?" Odele asked.

"I've already read it. I should have taken a different surname when I started my career."

"Too late now, sweetie. Besides, the media would have found him anyway, and he'd still be giving you trouble."

"Yes, but it would have made the connection between us seem less close."

"Well, time to distance yourself by cozying up to a hot stuntman."

"I know I'm going to regret this," Chiara muttered.

"I'll arrange for him to move in at the end of the week," Odele responded brightly.

"The guest bedroom, Odele!"

Four

Rick roared up on his motorcycle.

Since he was in temporary digs, and most of his stuff was in storage, he didn't have much to bring to Chiara's house in the affluent Brentwood neighborhood. Instead, he'd had a taxi deposit his suitcases and duffel bags at the foot of Chiara's front steps shortly before his arrival midafternoon.

Looking up, he eyed the house. It was a modest size by Tinseltown standards. Three bedrooms and three baths, according to the write-up on a celebrity gossip site. Reminiscent of an English cottage, it had white stucco walls, an arched doorway and a pitched roof with cross-gables and a prominent chimney. Lush gardening added to the atmosphere of a place that might be featured in *Architectural Digest*.

He'd taken Odele's advice and planned to say nothing about being a bodyguard. As far as Chiara was concerned, he was here only as a pretend live-in boyfriend. He had no idea, however, how Odele had convinced Chiara to let him move in.

By the time he'd taken off his helmet, Chiara was standing on the front steps.

"Of course you'd ride a motorcycle," she commented.

He gave an insouciant smile.

"I thought it was an earthquake."

"I rock your world, huh?"

"Please."

He looked at her house. "Nice digs. I should have guessed a typical English-style cottage for you, Snow. But where's the thatched roof?"

"Wrong century," she responded. "Where do you call home?"

He gave a lopsided grin. "Technically a small apartment in West Hollywood, but my heart is always where there's a beautiful woman."

"I thought so."

He couldn't tell what she meant by her response. Still, he couldn't resist provoking her further. "Shouldn't we kiss for the benefit of the paparazzi and their long-range lenses?"

"There are no photographers," she scoffed.

"How do you know? One could be hiding in the bushes."

She eyed his suitcases. "I'll put you in the guest bedroom."

"Relegated to the couch already," he joked. "Are you going to do a media interview about our first lovers' spat?"

The temperature between them rose ten degrees, and even the planted geraniums perked up—they apparently liked a good show as much as anybody.

"Hilarious," Chiara shot back, "but it's a perfectly fine bed, not a couch."

"And you won't be in it."

She cast him a sweeping look. "Use your imagination. A make-believe relationship means pretend sex. But something tells me you have no problem with letting your dreams run wild."

"Will you still awaken me with a kiss, Snow White?"

She huffed. "You're hopeless. I don't do fairy tales, modern or otherwise."

"That's obvious."

"Don't act as if you're disappointed. Your forte is action flicks, not romantic comedies."

"Then why do I feel as if I'm trapped in a romance?" he murmured.

"Go blow something up and make yourself feel better."

"It's not that type of itch that I need to scratch."

She huffed and then turned toward her front door. "I'll have you checked for fleas then."

Rick stifled a grin. This was going to be one interesting stay.

After he got settled in the guest bedroom, he found Chiara in the large country-style kitchen. Warm beige cabinets and butcher-block countertops added to the warm atmosphere. Sniffing the air, he said, "Something smells delicious."

She glanced up from a saucepan on the range, edible enough herself to be a food advertiser's dream. "Surprised?"

"That you cook? Gratified."

"Dinner is beef Stroganoff."

"Now I'm surprised. You're an actress who eats."

"Portion control is everything."

"Can cook. I'll check that little detail off my list."

She cast him a sidelong look, her cloud of dark hair falling in tantalizing waves over one shoulder. "What list?"

"The one that Odele gave me. A little quiz for the both of us…so we can get acquainted. Be believable as a couple."

Chiara frowned, and then muttered, "Odele leaves nothing to chance. Next thing, she'll have us convincing the immigration service that we're not in a sham marriage for a residency card."

"Because you need one…being from the Land of Fairy Tales?" He almost got a smile out of her with that.

"What do you—I mean, Odele—want to know?"

Rick consulted his cell phone. "What first attracted you to me?"

Chiara spluttered and then set down her stirring spoon with a *clack*. "This is never going to work."

"Come on, there must be something that you can tell the reporters."

She looked flustered. "Does she ask you the same question about me?"

He lowered his eyelids. "What do you think?"

As the question hung there, Rick's mind skipped back to their stunts…the rehearsals…every single moment, in fact, that he'd become aware of her close by. The air had vibrated with sexual energy.

Chiara wet her lips. "I'll take that as a 'Yes, she did ask.'"

Rick gave her a seductive smile. "When you showed up for the rehearsal of our first stunt, I knew I was in trouble. You were beautiful and smart and had guts." He shrugged. "My fantasy woman. The perfect match."

Chiara blinked.

After a pause, he asked, "Sound good enough for an interview answer?"

She seemed to give herself a mental shake, and then pursed her lips. "Perfect."

He focused on her mouth. *Kissable, definitely.* "Great."

She slapped the lid on the saucepan and made for the kitchen door. "Things are simmering. Dinner will be ready in thirty minutes."

"It'll give you time to think of your own answer to Odele's question," he called after her, and could swear she muttered something under her breath.

But when she was gone, Rick acknowledged that much as he enjoyed teasing Chiara, the joke was on him. Because she was his dream woman. If only she wasn't also a publicity-hungry actress…

Through dinner, he and Chiara trod lightly around each other. The beef Stroganoff was delicious, and he helped clean up—a little surprised she didn't keep a full-time housekeeper even if she traveled a lot. Afterward, she excused herself and retreated to her room, announcing that she had to memorize her lines.

Left to his own devices, he took a quick tour of the house and grounds, familiarizing himself with its security…and possible vulnerability to intruders. Then, with nothing more to do, he headed to bed.

Passing Chiara's door, he could see a light beneath, and shook off thoughts of what she wore to bed and how her hair would look around her bare shoulders above a counterpane… Still, in the guest bedroom, he found himself punching his pillow multiple times before he drifted off to sleep.

"Rick?"

He opened his eyes and saw Chiara's shadowy silhouette in his bedroom doorway. His lips curved. Apparently she'd had a hard time sleeping, too.

She walked toward him, and he made no attempt to disguise his arousal—he'd been thinking about her. Her short slip with spaghetti straps hid little, her nipples jutting against the fabric. She had a fantastic figure. High breasts and an indented waist…softly curved hips. His fingers itched to touch her.

Instead, he propped himself on the pillows behind him.

She sat down on the side of the bed, and her hand brushed his erection.

He saw no prickliness—just need…for him.

"What can I do for you?" His voice came out as a rasp.

Chiara's eyes glowed in the dim light afforded by the moon. "I think you know."

She leaned closer. Her lips brushed his and her pretty breasts tantalized his bare chest.

He cupped the back of her head and brought her closer so he could deepen the kiss. His tongue swept inside her mouth, tangling and dueling with hers.

She moaned and sank against him, breaking the kiss just long enough to say, "Love me."

He needed no further invitation. He pulled her down onto the mattress next to him and covered her body with his.

She responded with the lack of inhibition that he'd hoped for, arching toward him and opening in invitation, her arms encircling his neck as she met the ardor of his kiss.

His only thought was to get even closer…to sink into her welcoming warmth and find oblivion.

It would be sweet release from the restless need that had been consuming him…

Rick awoke with a start. He couldn't tell what had jerked him from his fantasy, but the room was empty, and he was alone in his bed.

He was also frustrated and aroused.

He groaned. *Yup.* It was going to be torture acting as if he were Chiara's boyfriend and hiding the fact that he was her protector.

The next morning, Chiara was up early for the drive to Novatus Studio. She donned jeans and a knit top. No use prettying up since she'd be sitting in a makeup chair at work soon enough. In fact, it was so early, she figured she might be able to get in a few minutes to study today's lines of dialogue before the drive to the lot.

Concentrate, that's what she had to do. But she hadn't slept well. In bed last night, she'd stared up at the ceiling, very aware of Rick's presence in her house.

What attracted her to him?

He was the epitome of rough manliness—cool, tough and exuding sex appeal. His green eyes were fascinatingly multihued, and even the hard, sculpted plains of his face invited detailed study by touch and, yes, taste.

A woman could feel safe and sheltered in his arms.

And there was the problem. She'd learned a long time ago not to rely on any man. Starting with her father, who'd disappeared from her life at a young age, and had become a gambling addict and reprobate.

She didn't hear a sound from Rick's room, so she tiptoed downstairs with script in hand.

When she reached the kitchen, she was taken aback to spot him sitting outside on the veranda, gazing at the sunrise, dressed in black denim jeans and a maroon tee. He looked peaceful and relaxed, so far from the constant motion and barely leashed energy that she was used to from him.

As if sensing her presence, he turned and met her gaze.

Rising, he gave a jaunty salute with the mug in his hand and said, "Good morning."

"I didn't hear you," she blurted as he entered through the French doors.

"We stuntmen can be stealthy."

She lowered her lashes and swept him with a surreptitious look. His jeans hugged lean hips and outlined muscular legs. The tee covered a flat chest and biceps that were defined but not brawny. He had the physique and face for a movie screen, except there was nothing manicured about him. Rick had a rough male aura instead of polish.

She looked at the cup in his hands. "I didn't even smell the brew."

"It's not coffee. It's a vitamin power drink."

Ugh. "For your superhero strength."

"Of course." He gave her a wicked smile. "Helps with the stamina. Sleep well?"

"For sure. And you?" She refused to give an inch, treating him with cool civility, even if that smile made her body tighten.

"Naturally."

The truth was she'd lain awake and tossed around for close to two hours. She wondered how she was going to maintain this charade…especially since Rick was adept at provoking her. And she refused…*refused*…to dwell on his kiss.

"Nice story about your father in the news. I had time to catch up on the headlines while I waited for you to come down, Sleeping Beauty."

Damn it. She should have gotten up even earlier. "My father?"

"Yeah, you know, the guy who shares a last name with you."

"That's all we have in common," she muttered.

"Nice story about the card counting recently."

"Maybe he'll stay out of trouble now that he's been barred from his favorite haunts." Casinos were Michael Feran's drug of choice.

"Is that what you're hoping?"

"Why are we discussing this?"

He shrugged. "I figured we should talk about the reason we're together." A smile teased his lips. "It seems logical."

So he wanted an extension of yesterday's get-to-know-you? *No, thanks.* Not that last night's question had haunted her sleep or anything. "We're not together."

"It's what the tabloids think that matters."

Argh.

"So Michael Feran is a sensitive topic."

Chiara walked to the kitchen cabinets. "Only in as much as he's a liar, gambler and cheat."

"Hmm…must be hard to share the same surname."

She got a glass and poured herself some water from the fridge's water filter.

"Eight glasses a day?"

She glanced at him. "What do you think? It's good for the complexion."

"You're very disciplined."

She took a sip. "I have to be."

"Because your father isn't?"

"I don't define myself relative to him."

Rick's lips twitched. "Okay, so you're not your father."

"Of course."

"How old were you when he walked out?"

She put down the glass. "Nearly five. But even when he was there, he wasn't really. He disappeared for stretches. Some of it was spent touring as a sax player with a band. Then he moved out for good a few days before my fifth birthday."

"Must have been rough."

"Not really. The party went on without him." She remembered the pink heart piñata. Her first major role was putting on a smile for the photos when it was just her and her mother.

"Did he ever try coming back?"

"There were a few flyovers until I became a teenager."

"Brief?"

"Very." Either her parents would argue, or Michael Feran would quickly move on to his next big thing.

"Right." Rick looked as if he'd drawn his own conclusions.

"Why are we talking about this?" she asked again, her voice sharp.

"I need to get the story straight so I'm not contradicting you when I speak."

"Well, there's nothing to tell."

"That's not what the press thinks."

Yup, he had her there. Which was the crux of her problem. Straightening her shoulders, she grabbed her car keys from the kitchen counter. On second thought, she could have breakfast at the studio—there was always food around. "Well, I'm off. See you on set."

"I'm coming with you," Rick responded casually. "Or rather, you're coming with me."

She stopped and faced him. "Excuse me?"

"My car or yours?"

"Do you have an endless supply of pickup lines?"

"Do you want to find out?"

"No!"

"That's what I thought you'd say." He took a sip from

his mug. "How can we be two lovebirds if we don't arrive together?"

"We're trying to be discreet at work."

"But not for the press."

"Anyway, you own a motorcycle."

"Look outside. I had my car deposited here early this morning by a concierge service."

Rats. He'd been up even earlier than she'd thought. She tossed him a suspicious look and then walked over to peer out the French doors. She spotted a Range Rover in the drive. "Lovely."

"I think so."

She glanced back at Rick with suspicion, but he just returned a bland look. Another of his sexual innuendoes? Because it was impossible to tell what he'd been referring to—her or the car.

Then she sighed. She had to pick her battles, and it was clear the drive to the office was not one worth fighting over.

Rick walked toward her, pausing to glance at a script that she'd left on the counter yesterday. "It's early. Want me to quiz you on your lines?"

"No!" Not least because there was a scene were the leads got flirty.

Rick raised an eyebrow and then shrugged. "Suit yourself but the offer stands. Anytime."

Yup, he was an anytime, anywhere kind of guy.

"What else are we supposed to do while we're shacked up together?" he asked, his eyes laughing at her.

She raised an eyebrow. "Go to work?"

Within the hour, she and Rick pulled up to the gate to Novatus Studio in his car.

Rick rolled down his window in order to give his identification to security, and with a sixth sense, Chiara turned her head and spotted a hovering figure nearby. The flash of a paparazzi camera was familiar.

"Odele," she muttered, facing forward again.

There was a good chance that her manager had tipped off a photographer so someone could snap her and Rick arriving *together* at the studio. Odele was determined to give this story her personal spin.

Rick gave an amused look. "She thinks of everything."

Rick tried to be on his best behavior, but having some fun was oh-so-tempting…

The Living Room on the first floor of The Peninsula Beverly Hills was nothing if not a den for power brokers, so he supposed it was perfect for a print interview over afternoon tea with *WE Magazine*—which wanted the dishy scoop on Chiara's new relationship.

Rick eyed the sumptuous repast set out on the coffee table before them: finger sandwiches, scones and an assortment of petite pastries. Arranged by Odele, of course, the afternoon tea in The Living Room was worthy of a queen. Of course, all of it went untouched.

This wasn't about food, but business. *Showtime in Hollywood.*

When he and Chiara had arrived at Novatus Studio that morning, Odele had surprised them with the news that she'd arranged a friendly press interview for them later the same day. Chiara was already scheduled to have the cover of the next issue of *WE Magazine* in order to promote the upcoming release of *Pegasus Pride*, but Odele had deftly arranged for it to become a joint interview about her new relationship. He and Chiara had left work early, because Odele had already spoken to Dan, the director, about their appointment. Dan had been happy to oblige if it meant more positive ink ahead of the release of the film—everyone was banking on it opening big at the box office.

Rick had to hand it to Chiara's manager—she wasted no time. But he knew what Odele was thinking—better to get ahead of the gossip by getting your own version of the story out there before anyone else's. So he'd gone along with the whole deal.

Too bad Chiara herself didn't want him here. But Odele had insisted, arguing his presence would make the relationship more believable. As Odele had put it, *Readers inhale romance. Touch each other a lot.* To which Chiara had responded, *Odele, I'm not making out in public for the benefit of gawkers.*

Now, at his sudden grin at the recollection, Chiara shot him a repressive look. She'd already told him she saw his role here as a yes-man supporting player. He figured he could bridge the gap between stuntman and Prince Charming easily enough, but if Chiara thought he'd toady to a gossip columnist, she had another think coming. He stretched and then settled one arm on the back of the sofa—because he knew it would drive Chiara crazy.

The couch was in a cozy and semiprivate corner. The interviewer, Melody Banyon—who looked to be in her late forties and was a dead ringer for Mindy Kaling—leaned forward in her armchair. "So was it love at first sight?"

From the corner of his eye, Rick noticed Chiara's elbow inching toward him, ready to jab in case he made a flippant comment. But then Chiara just smiled at him before purring, "Well, I don't usually notice the stuntmen on my movie sets…"

Rick glanced at the interviewer and a corner of his mouth lifted. "You could say Chiara's manager played matchmaker. She thought we'd be perfect for each other."

Chiara's eyes widened, but then she tossed him a grateful look. "Yes, Odele is always looking out for my best interests…"

Melody gave a satisfied smile. "Great, just great." Repositioning the voice recorder on the table before them, she looked back and forth between her interview subjects. "And I understand you two just moved in together?"

"Yup," Rick spoke up, unable to resist. "Like yesterday." It was also roughly when their whole "relationship" had started.

Chiara shot him a quelling look, and he tossed back an innocent one. He moved his arm off the sofa, gave her shoulder a squeeze, and then leaned in and nuzzled her temple for a quick kiss.

"Mmm," Melody said, as if tasting a delicious story, "you two move fast."

Rick relaxed against the sofa again, and responded sardonically, "You don't know the half of it."

He knew he risked Chiara's wrath, and he was surprised to find himself relishing the challenge of sparring with her again. No doubt about it—they set sparks off in each other. And it would probably carry over to the bedroom.

He glanced at Chiara's profile. She was a beautiful woman. Winged brows, pink bow lips, thick, rich chocolate hair and a figure that was hourglass without being voluptuous. She was also talented and tough enough to play a kick-ass action movie heroine and do her own stunts. He had to respect that—all the while being attracted as hell—even though he knew celebrity actresses like her couldn't be trusted.

They were duplicitous—they had to be for the press. *Like right now.*

Chiara seemed chummy with Melody—as if they

were friends, or at least acquaintances from way back. Melody asked a few questions about *Pegasus Pride*, and Chiara answered, while Rick threw in a few sentences at the end.

He wasn't the star attraction here, and there was no use pretending otherwise. Sure, he had a lot riding on this film—money and otherwise—but he wouldn't be why this movie succeeded, or not, at the box office. Chiara was the public face of *Pegasus Pride*.

After a few minutes, Melody changed the subject, mentioning the upcoming Ring of Hope Gala to Benefit Children's Charities, for which half of Hollywood turned out. "So give me the scoop, Chiara." Her voice dipped conspiratorially. "What will you be wearing?"

"I haven't decided yet. There are two dresses…"

"Give me the details on both!" Melody said, her face avid with anticipation.

Rick suppressed a grunt. As far as he was concerned, a dress was a dress. He didn't care what it was made out of—whether a pride of lions had to be sacrificed for the embellishment, or the designer used recycled garbage bags. His youngest sibling might be an up-and-comer in the fashion business, but it was all the same to Rick—or as his sister liked to say, *Bless your style-deaf soul.*

"There's a one-shoulder pale blue column dress from Elie Saab. The other gown is a red chiffon—"

"Oh, I love both! Don't you, Rick?"

If it wasn't for Chiara's significant look, Rick would have answered that *naked* was his first preference. Chiara had a body that invited fantasies even, or especially, if she was aiming verbal barbs at him.

He settled back. "I don't know…isn't pale blue the color for Cinderella?"

Chiara turned to him and smiled, even as her eyes shot a warning. "Wrong fairy tale."

When Melody just appeared confused, Chiara cleared her throat. "Well, keep your eyes open on the night of the gala to find out which dress I go with."

The reporter pressed Stop on her recorder. "So when am I going to see you again, Chiara? Girls' night sometime at Marmont? Paparazzi snapped Leo there just last week."

Rick raised his eyebrows. From the lack of a ring, Rick deduced Melody was divorced, widowed or had never married. "You ladies do go for the chills and thrills."

Chateau Marmont was a trendy celebrity haunt. Some booked one of the hotel rooms for privacy, and others just went to party and be seen. But he preferred his thrills a little more real than a Leonardo DiCaprio sighting.

"I'd love to, Melody," Chiara said, "but can I take a rain check? This movie is wearing me out—" she looked down demurely "—when Rick isn't."

Yup, strong acting chops.

Melody laughed. "Of course. I understand."

When Melody excused herself a moment later in order to freshen up, Rick regarded the woman who'd been driving him crazy. "So…I wear you out?"

Chiara flushed. "Don't look at me that way."

"Mmm. The image of us and a bed is sort of stuck in my mind."

Chiara shifted, and her skirt rode up her leg.

He focused on her calves. She had spectacular legs. He'd seen them encased in skintight denim on set, and in a barely there miniskirt in a photo that had circulated online. He imagined those legs wrapped around him as he lost himself inside her…

On a whim, he reached out and took her hand, and caressed the back of it with his thumb.

"What are you doing?"

Was it his imagination or did her voice sound a little uneven?

"Move closer," he murmured. "There's a photographer watching us from across the room."

Her eyes held his. "What? Where?"

"Don't look." Then he leaned in, his gaze lowering.

Chiara parted her lips on an indrawn breath.

Rick touched his mouth to hers.

When Chiara made a sound at the back of her throat, he deepened the kiss. He stroked and teased, wanting more from her, craving more and not caring where they were. When she opened for him, he fanned the flames of their passion, cupping her face with his hand as she leaned closer.

When her breast brushed his arm, he tensed and stopped himself from bringing his hand up to cup the soft mound in public. He wanted to crash through her barriers, making his head spin with the speed of it.

As if sensing someone approaching, Chiara pulled back and muttered, "We have to stop."

Rick spotted Melody walking back from across the room, a big grin on her face. Obviously the reporter had seen the kiss. Odele would be pleased. "Not if we're going to pretend to be a couple."

When the reporter drew near, she teased, "Did I say you two are fast? Now, that moment would have provided some photo op for the magazine!"

Rick settled back and forced a grin for the reporter's benefit. "We'd be happy to give a repeat performance."

"No, we wouldn't," Chiara interjected, but then she smiled for Melody's benefit. "I'll make sure you get plenty of good pictures for the cover story at the photo shoot tomorrow."

"Of course," Melody said politely, maintaining her perkiness as she sat down to gather her things.

Rick hadn't gotten an invitation to the photo shoot—which was just as well. They were boring and went on for hours. Apparently, though, even Odele had drawn the line at a cozy tableau of him and Chiara with their arms around each other.

"Do you have a cover line yet for this article, Melody?" Chiara asked, her face suddenly turning droll. "Or has Odele already suggested one?"

Rick knew from his experience with movie promotions that the cover line was the front cover text that accompanied a magazine article: *From Tears to Triumph, I'm Lucky to Be Alive*, or even the vague but trustworthy standby, *My Turn to Talk*.

"No," Melody said, "Odele hasn't offered anything."

"How about 'Chiara Feran—True Love at Last'?" he offered drily.

Melody brightened. "I love it. What about you, Chiara?"

Chiara looked as if she was ready to kick him out of this interview, and Rick suppressed a laugh.

Oh, yeah, this was going to be a roller coaster of a relationship. *Make-believe* relationship.

Five

Soon after she and Rick arrived at her house—a place that she used to consider her haven and sanctuary until Rick moved in—she decided to escape to the exercise room to let off steam. Every once in a while, the urge to do the right thing and work out for the sake of her career kicked in, so she changed into a sports bra and stretchy pedal pusher exercise pants.

It had been a long day, and she'd risen early only to find Rick in her kitchen. At the studio, she'd gotten prepped in her makeup chair and then shot a few scenes. Afterward, she'd still had to be *on*, public persona in place, for the interview with Melody. It hadn't helped that the whole time she'd been aware of Rick lounging beside her—his big, hard body making the sofa seem tiny and crowded.

He'd enjoyed toying with her, too, during the interview. She'd been on pins and needles the whole time, wondering whether he'd say the wrong thing and Melody would see through their charade.

Except the kiss at the end had been all too real. She'd tasted his need and his slow-burn desire underneath the playfulness, and she'd responded to it.

I have to be more careful.

And on that thought, she entered the exercise room and came to a dead halt.

Apparently Rick had had the same idea about burning off steam. And in a sleeveless cutoff tee, it was clear he was in phenomenal shape.

She'd seen her share of beautiful people in Hollywood. But Rick was…impressive. He had washboard abs, a sprinkling of hair on his chest and muscles so defined they looked as if they could have been sculpted by a Renaissance master.

She shouldn't be once-overing him. She was still annoyed with his behavior in front of Melody that afternoon.

Rick looked up and gave her a careless lopsided smile. "Enjoying the view?"

A wave of embarrassment heated her face. "Nothing I haven't seen before."

"Yeah, but I'm not airbrushed."

And there was the problem in a nutshell.

"Need an exercise buddy?"

Oh, no. They were so not going to do this together. "I don't need you to act as my workout instructor. I've been doing fine on my own."

"Yeah," he drawled, "I can tell."

She gave him a quelling look and walked toward the weight bench.

He followed her and then scanned the weights. He

lifted one of the lighter ones as if it were a feather and placed it on the bar.

She put her hands on her hips. "What do you think you're doing?"

"Helping you out, but not as much as I'd like."

"You're already doing more than I want, so let's call it a draw and say we're splitting the difference."

He quirked his lips. "Just trying to get you to release that pent-up energy and frustration."

She narrowed her eyes and then lay back on the bench as he fixed the weight on the other side. Unfortunately she hadn't anticipated how much he seemed to be looming over her from this angle.

She flexed and then grasped the barbell. Before she could do more, however, Rick adjusted her grip.

"I started with sixty pounds," he said, stepping back. "That's about right for a woman your size."

Chiara wondered how much he lifted. He'd hoisted her with amazing agility and ease during their stunts...

Then she turned her attention back to the weights, took a breath and began lifting. Once, twice... Rick faded into the background as she brought the same attention to the task as she did to acting.

"Slow and smooth," he said after a few minutes. "Slow and smooth... That's right."

Damn it. Chiara's rhythm hitched as she brought the weight back up again and then down. She refused to look at Rick. He was either a master at sexual innuendo or set on unintentionally making her lose her mind.

She gritted her teeth and lifted the weight a few more times. After what seemed like an eternity, during which she refused to show any weakness, Rick caught the barbell and placed it on the nearby rack.

Chiara concentrated on slowing her breathing, but her chest still rose and fell from the exertion.

Rick leaned over her, bracing himself with one hand on the metal leg of the weight bench. "Nice work."

They weren't touching but he was a hair's breadth away—so close that she could get lost in the gold-shot green of his eyes. Her mind wandered back to their last kiss…

He quirked his lips as if he knew what she was thinking. "Want to indulge again?"

She pretended not to understand his meaning. "No, thanks. I'm dieting. You know Hollywood actresses. We're always trying to shed a few pounds."

Rick's eyes crinkled. "Seems more like fasting to me."

Damn him. As a celebrity, it wasn't as if she could just get online, or even on an app, and hook up with someone. There was her public image to consider, as Odele never stopped reminding her, and she didn't want to be exploited for someone else's gain. As a result, she'd had far fewer romantic partners than the press liked to imagine. These days, a lot of men were intimidated by her status. But not Rick. He was just a lone stuntman, but he had enough ego for an entire football team.

Still, need hummed within her, and her skin shivered with awareness. What was it with this man? He had a talent for getting under her defenses, and together they were combustible.

"Have I been doing it right?" His eyes laughed at her.

"What?"

"The kissing."

If the response he stirred in her was any indication, then…yeah. She tingled right now—wanting him closer against her better judgment. "All wrong."

"Then we need to practice." His lips curved in a sultry smile. "For the photographers and their cameras."

She'd walked into that one. "There isn't one here right now."

"Then we'll need to make this real instead of make-believe," he muttered as he focused on her mouth. "You have the fullest, most kissable lips."

Chiara inhaled a quick little breath. It was heady being the focus of Rick's attention. He brought the same intensity to kissing as he did to his stunts.

But instead of immediately touching his mouth to hers this time, he surprised her by smoothing a hand down her side.

She shivered, and her nipples puckered, pushing against her sports bra. She itched to explore him the way he was doing to her. She raised her hand to push him away, but instead it settled on his chest, where she felt the strong, steady beat of his heart.

"That's right," he encouraged. "Touch me. Make me feel."

She parted her lips, and this time he did settle his mouth on hers. She felt a little zing, and was surrounded by his unique male scent.

His chest pressed down on the pillow of her breasts, but he didn't give her all his weight, which was still braced on his arms.

Wrapped in his intoxicating closeness, she felt him everywhere, even on the parts of her body that weren't touching his.

His hand cupped her between her thighs, where her tight spandex shorts were the only barrier between her heat and his. He stroked her with his thumb, again and again, until she tore her mouth from his and gasped with need.

She grasped his wrist, but it was too late. Her body splintered, spasming with completion and yet unfulfilled desire.

When she looked up, she was caught by his glittering gaze. She was vulnerable and exposed, more so even than when they'd been hanging from a helicopter and his embrace had been a haven.

She could tell he wanted her, but he was holding himself in check, his breathing heavy.

Sanity slowly returned. This was so wrong.

"Let me up," she said huskily.

He straightened, and then tugged on her hand to help her up.

"I don't want this," she said, standing and knowing the last thing she needed was to feel this way—especially when wrong felt...right.

"Sometimes what we think we should want is beside the point."

She wanted to argue, but for once, she didn't know what to say.

"I'm going to take a cold shower," he said with a rueful smile, and then turned.

She half expected a teasing addition—*Want to join me?*

But he said nothing further, and somehow she found his seriousness more troubling than his playfulness.

Bed & Breakfast in Brentwood. Chiara Feran and Her Stuntman Seen Moving in Together.

Chiara stalked back to her trailer along a dirt path, her scene complete. Filming had moved for today from the Novatus Studio lot to nearby Griffith Park.

The blog *Celebrity Dish* had scooped *WE Magazine* and run a relationship story about her and Rick. Melody should still be happy about her exclusive interview, but it hadn't taken long for the gossip to start making the rounds...

Chiara attributed her bad mood to lack of coffee... and a certain stuntman.

Yesterday afternoon, they'd had a near tryst on her weight bench. There was no telling what he was capable of if he stayed in her house much longer.

She'd shown up at work at six in the morning intent on avoiding Rick, and had sat in the makeup chair. It was now ten, and there was still no sign of him. After their encounter in the exercise room, she'd heard him shower and leave her house. He still hadn't returned when she'd gone to bed hours later.

Perhaps he'd met and hooked up with a woman. Not that it was her business. Even if it meant he'd gone straight from her arms to those of another... *Damn it*.

At least *Pegasus Pride* would wrap soon. They were in the last days of filming. The scenes that she'd been in with Rick acting as a body double for her costar Adrian had been thankfully few.

Head down, she turned a corner...and collided with a solid male chest.

The air rushed out of her, and then she gasped.

But before she could wonder whether her favorite fan had made a surprise appearance again, strong arms steadied her, and she looked up into Rick's green eyes.

"You."

"For two people who are roommates, we hardly ever run into each other," he said in an ironic tone.

Chiara blinked. His hands were still cupping her upper arms, the wall of his chest a mere hair's breadth away. The heat emanated from him like a palpable thing.

"It's a big house and an even larger movie location."

She sounded breathless and chalked it up to having the air nearly knocked out of her.

He was irritating but also impossible to ignore—and she'd been throwing her best acting skills at the problem.

"Miss me?" he teased drily. "I thought we were supposed to be joined at the hip these days."

How could she answer that one? After he'd left last night, she'd succumbed to a restless night's sleep. He'd left her satisfied and bereft at the same time. Sure, she'd gotten release, but they'd missed out on the ultimate joining, and hours later, her body had craved it. At least he wasn't openly chastising her for her artful dodge that morning.

He stepped closer and eased her chin up, his gaze focused on her lips. "I missed you."

"The mouth that can't stop telling you off?"

He gave her a crooked smile. "We'd be good in bed. There's too much combustible energy between us. Admit it."

"Can't you tell good acting when you see it?"

"That was no act. If that wasn't an orgasm last night, I'll stand naked under the Hollywood sign over there." With a nod of his head, he indicated the iconic landmark in the distance.

"We are acting. This is fake. We're on a movie set!"

"Yup," he drawled and glanced around, "and I don't see any cameras rolling right now. Just because we're playing to the media doesn't mean we can't have fun along the way."

She didn't do *fun*. She left that to her dice-rolling father, who'd run away from responsibility—a wife, a child, a home...

"Oh, I like it!"

Chiara turned and spotted Odele.

"Did I interrupt something? Or let me rephrase that one—I hope I was interrupting something!"

"He needs to go," Chiara retorted.

Odele looked from her to Rick and back. "What went wrong? It's only been—" she checked her watch "—two days."

"A lover's spat," Rick joked. "We can't keep our hands off each other."

Odele's eyes gleamed behind her red glasses. "You can't quit now. The press is reporting Chiara's father was tossed out of a Vegas casino."

Rick quirked a brow at Chiara.

"On top of it," Odele went on, "there's a big fundraiser tomorrow night, and I managed to secure a ticket for Chiara's date."

"And let's not forget *WE* just got the exclusive interview that *we* are an item," Rick continued drolly.

Chiara faced her nemesis. "You are impossible."

"Just acting the part."

"You're giving an Oscar-worthy performance in a B movie."

"I believe in doing my best," Rick intoned solemnly. "My mother raised me right."

She wanted to claim his *best* wasn't good enough, but the truth was he'd been…impressive so far. "This isn't working."

"You don't want me?" He adopted a wounded expression, but his eyes laughed at her.

Grr. "I'm stuck with you!"

"Then why don't you make the most of it?" His voice was smooth as massage lotion. "Who knows? We might even have fun together."

The last thing she needed was his hands on her again.

"*Fun* is not the word that comes to mind. This is crazy. Are we nuts?"

"You know the answer to that question. I hang from helicopters for a living—"

"Clearly the altitude has addled your mind."

"—and you are an actress and celebrity."

"*Fame* is a dirty word in your book?"

Rick shrugged. "I'm camera-shy. Call it middle-child syndrome. I leave the high-profile celebrity stuff to my older and younger brothers."

She frowned. "You're an agoraphobic stuntman?"

He bit back a laugh. "Not quite, but putting on the glitz isn't my thing."

"Odele just mentioned we have a big fund-raiser to attend tomorrow night," she countered. "And since you signed up for the boyfriend gig, you'll need to put on a tux."

"Trust me, you'll like me better naked."

Chiara felt her cheeks heat, and on top of that, her manager was tracking everything like a talent agent on the scent of a movie deal.

She narrowed her eyes at Rick. "Oh? Is that the usual attire for reclusive stuntmen?"

He gave a lazy smile. "If we live together much longer, you'll find out."

She hated his casual self-assurance. And what was worse, he was probably right…

Chiara gave her manager a what-have-you-gotten-me-into look, but Odele returned it with a beatific one of her own.

"I came to tell you that you're needed. Dan wants to reshoot a scene," Odele said.

Chiara wasn't normally enthusiastic about retakes, but right now she thought of it as a lucky break…

* * *

Hours later, during some downtime in his schedule, Rick sat in a chair outside the gym trailer, his legs propped on a nearby bench. He consulted his cell phone to make sure he was caught up on work.

Often his emails were mundane matters sent by a business partner, but today, lucky him, he had something more salacious to chew over. All courtesy of *Celebrity Dish*—and a specific actress who'd occupied way more of his thoughts than he cared to admit.

After his encounter with Chiara in her exercise room yesterday afternoon, he'd done the only thing that he could do in the face of frustration and lack of consummation: he'd taken a cold shower and then sat alone at a nearby sports bar to have dinner.

Still, now that the story had progressed in the media to him and Chiara shacking up, Rick knew he'd better tackle his family. In the next moment, his cell phone buzzed, and Rick noted it was Jordan before answering the call.

"Wow, you move fast," his brother said without preamble. "One day you're denying there's anything going on, the next you're moving in together."

"Hilarious."

"Mom asked. Has she rung you yet?"

"Nope." Camilla Serenghetti was probably vacillating between worry and being ecstatic that her middle son might have gotten into a serious relationship—preferably one heading toward marriage and children.

"She's concerned some temptress has worked her wiles on you, and not just on the big screen, either. I told her that you're not innocent and naive enough to resist a beautiful woman."

"Finger-pointing never got you anywhere, Jordan."

"Except for some scratches and bruises from you and Cole in retribution. But don't worry, I bounced back."

"Clearly," Rick responded drily.

"Mom is talking about coming to the West Coast to tape an episode of her cooking show. You know, do something different and expand the audience, and if I'm not mistaken—" his brother's voice dripped dry humor "—she wants to check up on you."

No, no and no. The last thing he needed was for his mother to add a sideshow to the ongoing drama with Chiara—though Camilla Serenghetti would no doubt easily become best buds with Odele. Two peas in a pod. Or as the Italians liked to say, *due gocce d'acqua*—like two drops of water. *In a pot of boiling pasta water.* Still, the thought gave him an idea…

"Mom can't come here."

"She's worried about the show. The station is under new management and she wants to make a good impression."

"Fine. I'll go to her."

The idea was brilliant. If he delivered Chiara Feran to his mother's show, he'd drive up ratings for a program that was only in local syndication. And it would add steam in the press to his and Chiara's supposed relationship. All while getting Chiara out of her house in LA and away from her crazy fan.

It was fantastic…clever…an idea worthy of Odele.

Rick suppressed a smile. Chiara's manager would love it.

"You're serious?" his brother asked.

"Yup." If he was going to engage in this charade, he was going to be all in.

With that in mind, he ended his call with Jordan and went looking for his favorite actress.

Things had slowed down on set because Adrian Collins didn't like some of his lines and had holed up in his trailer with a red pen. Rick would have gotten involved and gone to read the riot act to the male lead, but he didn't like to blow his cover. Not even Dan knew how much he had invested in this movie.

Besides, Adrian's antics were mild in comparison to other off-camera drama he'd witnessed on movie sets—stars kicking each other, hurling curses and insults, and throwing tantrums worthy of a two-year-old while breaking props. Yet another reason he hadn't gotten involved with mercurial actresses…until now.

As luck would have it, he soon caught up with Chiara some distance from the parked movie trailers. She was walking back alone, picking her way along a dusty path, apparently having finished filming another scene.

Maybe it was unfulfilled sexual desire, maybe it was the picture she presented, but his senses got overloaded seeing her again. Since this morning, she'd changed into business attire because her scenes called for her to have escaped from a federal office building. She was wearing a pencil skirt paired with sky-high black pumps and a white shirt open to show a bit a cleavage. The effect was sexy in an understated way.

He liked the way the light caught in her dark halo of hair—which was just the right length for him to run his fingers through in the throes of passion. His body tightened.

He wasn't one to be overcome by lust—particularly where actresses were concerned—but Chiara was just the package to press his buttons. He hadn't been kidding when he'd said she was his type. His brothers would say he was attracted to women who were a study in contrasts: dark hair against a palate of smooth skin; humor and pas-

sion; light and hidden depths… On top of it all, Chiara
was blessed with a great figure, which was emphasized
at the moment by a come-hither outfit made for the big
screen…and male fantasies.

He, on the other hand, was in his usual stunt clothes
for this movie: a ripped tee, makeup meant to resemble
dirt smeared on his abs, an ammo belt across his chest
and another one slug low on his hips with an unloaded
gun. He felt…uncivilized.

And the setting was appropriate. They were at the
bottom of a canyon, surrounded by mountain roads
and not far from actual caves. Only the presence of the
Hollywood sign spoiled the effect of unspoiled nature.

Still, he tried for some semblance of polite conversation when they came abreast of each other. Thanks
to Jordan, he had a brilliant idea—one that should deal
with multiple problems at once. "I have a favor to ask."

She looked at him warily. "Which is?"

He cleared his throat. "I'd like you to appear on my
mother's cooking show."

Her jaw went slack. "What?"

He shrugged. "If you appear on her show, it'll feed the
rumors that we're involved. Isn't that what you want?"

"Your mother has a cooking show?"

He nodded. "It's on local TV in Boston and a few
other markets, and it films not far from my hometown
of Welsdale in western Massachusetts. *Flavors of Italy
with Camilla Serenghetti.*"

Chiara's lips twitched. "So you're not the Serenghetti
closest to fame? I'm shocked."

"Not by a long shot," he returned sardonically. "Not
only is Mom ahead of me, but my brothers and sister
are, too."

Chiara looked curious. "Really?"

He nodded. "You don't watch hockey."

"Should I?"

"My kid brother plays for the New England Razors, and my older brother used to."

She seemed as if she was trying to pull up a recollection.

"Jordan and Cole Serenghetti," he supplied.

"And your sister is…?"

"The youngest, but determined not to be left behind." He cracked a grin. "She's a big feminist."

"Naturally. With three older brothers, I imagine she had to be."

"She had a badass left kick in karate, but these days she's rechanneled the anger into a fashion design business."

Chiara's eyes widened. "Ooh, I like it already it."

So did he… Why hadn't he dreamed it up before? He had an opening with Chiara that he'd been too blind to see till now. "Mia would love it if you wore one of her creations."

"I thought I was helping your mother."

"Both." He toasted his brilliance. "You can wear Mia's designs on the cooking show."

Chiara threw up her hands. "You've thought of everything!"

Rick narrowed his eyes. "Not everything. I still need to figure out what to do about your overenthusiastic fan and your Vegas-loving father. Give me time."

Number three on his list was getting her into bed, but he wasn't going to mention that. He didn't examine his motives closely, except he was nursing one sad case of sexual frustration since their truncated tryst on her weight bench late yesterday. He tucked his fingers into his pockets to resist the urge to touch her…

He cleared his throat. "It would mean a lot to her if you made an appearance as a guest. The show is doing well. The name recently changed from *Flavors of Italy* to *Flavors of Italy with Camilla Serenghetti*. But the station is under new management, and Mom wants to make a good impression."

"Of course," Chiara deadpanned. "It's a slow climb up the ladder of fame. I can relate."

"Mom's is more of a short stepladder."

"What happens when your mother and I land on the cover of *WE Magazine* together?" Chiara quipped. "Will you be able to deal with being caught between two famous women?"

"I'll cross that bridge when I come to it," Rick replied drolly. "And knowing Mom, she'll want to be on the magazine with the both of us, like a hovering fairy godmother."

"She sounds like a character."

"You don't know the half of it."

"This is serious," she remarked drily. "You're bringing me home to meet Mama."

"In a sense," he said noncommittally—because what he wanted to do was bring her home to bed. "She'd be even more impressed if you'd starred in an Italian telenovela."

"A soap opera?" Chiara responded. "Actually I was a guest on a couple of episodes of *Sotto Il Sole*."

Rick's eyebrows rose.

"It was before I became known in the States," she added. "My character wound up in a coma and was taken off life support."

"They didn't like your acting?"

"No, they just needed more melodrama. My character was an American so it didn't matter if I spoke Italian well."

"Still, my mother will eat it up." He flashed a grin. "No pun intended."

In fact, Rick suspected his mother would love everything about Chiara Feran. Their relationship "breakup," which inevitably loomed on the horizon, would disappoint his mother more than a recipe that didn't work out. He'd have to fake bodily injury and blame the rupture with Chiara on the distance created by their two careers...

"What about filming?" Chiara asked with a frown.

"We're in the last few days. Then Dan will move to editing. I can arrange with Odele for us to fly to Boston once you're done with your scenes. Mom's taping can wait till then." He didn't add he still had to broach the subject with his mother, but she'd no doubt be thrilled to move heaven and earth with her producers in order to fit a star of Chiara's caliber into the schedule.

"Where will we stay?" Chiara pressed.

Rick could tell she was debating her options, but the wavering was a good sign. He shrugged, deciding to seem nonchalant in order to soothe any doubts she had.

"I've got an apartment in Welsdale."

"Oh?"

"It has a guest bedroom." Still, he hoped to entice her into making their relationship in the bedroom more real—purely for the sake of their romantic believability in front of the press, of course.

"Naturally."

"Don't worry, though," he said, making his tone gently mocking. "There'll be enough luxuries for an A-list celeb."

Chiara narrowed her eyes. "You think I can't rough it?"

He let his silence speak for him.

"As a matter of fact, I was born and raised in Rhode Island. I'm used to New England winters."

"Of course, Miss Rhode Island should visit her old stomping grounds."

"I was an undergraduate at Brown."

"Rubbing shoulders with other celebrity kids?"

"Financial aid. Where did you get your stunt degree?"

He quirked his lips. "Boston College. It's a family tradition."

"Now you've surprised me. I expected the school of hard knocks… So, what have you told your family about us?"

He shrugged. "They read *WE Magazine*." He flashed a smile. "They know I have the goods."

Chiara rolled her eyes. "In other words, they think we really are an item?"

"My ego wouldn't have it any other way."

"I'm not surprised."

Rick heard a noise, and then felt a telltale little jolt, followed by a gentle rocking.

Chiara's eyes widened.

"Did you feel that?"

She nodded.

Earthquakes were common in Southern California, but only a few were strong enough to be felt. "We may have sensed it because we're at the bottom of a canyon." Rick looked around, and then back at her with a wry smile. "I'm surprised you didn't fling yourself into my arms."

"We actresses are made of sterner stuff," she said, tossing his words from days ago back at him.

He stifled a laugh. "We made the ground move."

"It was a truck rumbling by!"

"My motorcycle sounds like an earthquake, but an earthquake is just…a truck rumbling by?" he teased.

"Well, it's not us making the ground move, much as you have faith in your superpowers!"

Rick laughed and then glanced around again. "This earthquake didn't seem like a strong one, but you might want to rethink your position on my rocking your world."

"Your ego wouldn't have it any other way?" she asked archly.

"Exactly. Good follow-up, you're learning." He glanced down at her impractical footwear. "Need a hand…or a lift?"

She raised her chin. "No, thanks."

He doubted she'd thank him if he said she looked adorable. "You know, if you left one of those shoes behind…"

"A frog would find it?"

"Some of us are princes in disguise—isn't that how the story goes?"

"Well, this princess is saving herself," she said as she walked past him, head held high, "and not kissing any more frogs!"

Six

The Armani suit was fine, but Rick drew the line at a manicure. He did his own nails, thanks.

In his opinion, premieres and award ceremonies were an evil to be endured, which was another reason he liked his low-profile, low-key existence. Tonight at least was for a good cause—the Ring of Hope Gala to Benefit Children's Charities.

The fund-raiser also explained why Chiara's spacious den was a hub of activity on a Saturday afternoon. The room was usually a quiet oasis, with long windows, beige upholstery and dark wood furniture. Not now, however.

Chiara sat in the makeup chair. Someone was doing her hair, and another person was applying polish to her nails, and all the while Chiara was chatting with Odele. A fashion designer's intern had dropped off two gowns earlier, and at some point, Chiara would slip into one of them, assisted by plenty of double-sided tape and other tricks of the Hollywood magic trade.

Rick figured this amounted to multitasking. Something women were renowned for, and men like him apparently were terrible at—when the reality was probably that men just preferred to do their own nails.

Suddenly Odele frowned at Chiara. "Have you gone through your normal skincare regimen?"

"Yes."

Rick almost laughed. For him, a regimen meant a grueling workout at the gym to get ready for stunts on his next film. It didn't apply to fluffy skincare pampering.

Odele rolled her eyes. "I imagine you raided the kitchen cabinets for sugar and coconut oil, and threw in some yogurt for one of your crazy DIY beauty treatments."

From her chair, Chiara arched her eyebrows, which had been newly plucked. "Of course."

Rick studied those finely arched brows. He hadn't known there was such a thing as threading, and especially not applied to eyebrows. He was a Martian on planet Venus here. Still, he could understand that for an actress like Chiara, whose face was part of her trade, the right look was everything. Subtle changes or enhancements could impact her ability to express emotional nuances.

His gaze moved to Chiara's mouth. Their interlude in the exercise room still weighed on him. She'd been so damn responsive. If she hadn't put a stop to things, he would have taken her right there on the weight bench. In fact, it had been all he could do to keep a cool head the past few days. If it hadn't been for work on the movie set and coming back exhausted after a fourteen-hour day...

Odele sighed. "You're the bane of my existence,

Chiara. You could be the face of a cosmetics and skin-care line. You're throwing away millions."

"My homemade concoctions work fine," Chiara responded.

"You make your own products?" Rick asked bemusedly.

Chiara shrugged. "I started when I was a teenager and didn't have a dime to my name, and I saw no reason to give it up. I use natural items like avocado."

"Me, too," Rick joked. "But I eat them as part of my strength-training routine."

Chiara peered at him. "I could test the green stuff on your face. You might benefit."

Rick made a mock gesture warding her off. "No, thanks. I'm best friends with my soap."

"Not everyone is blessed with your creamy complexion, Chiara," Odele put in. "Have a little sympathy for the rest of us who could use expensive professional help."

The hairstylist and manicurist stepped away, and Chiara stood, still wrapped in her white terry robe. "Well, time to get dressed."

Rick smiled. "Don't let me stop you."

Odele steamed toward him like a little tugboat pulling Chiara's ship to safe harbor. "We'll call you when we need you."

He shrugged. "More or less explains my role."

Without waiting for further encouragement, he stepped out of the room. For the next half hour, he made somewhat good use of his time by checking his cell phone and catching up on business. Finally, Odele opened the door and motioned him into the den again.

Rick stepped back into the room…and froze, swallowing hard.

Chiara was wearing a one-shoulder gown with a short

train. The slit went all the way up one thigh, and the deep red fabric complemented her complexion. She had the ethereal quality of, well, a fairy-tale princess naturally.

"I can't decide which gown," she said.

"The one you're wearing looks good to me."

He knew what the big minefields were, of course. *Do I look fat in this dress?* The automatic answer was *no*. Maybe even *hell, no*. Still, he was ill-equipped for the bombshell that was Chiara Feran—sex poured into a gown.

"You look spectacular," he managed.

She beamed. "I'm wearing a Brazilian designer. I have a platform, and I want to use it."

He knew what *he* wanted.

He'd like nothing better than to swing Chiara into his arms and head for the bedroom. He wasn't particular about *where* frankly, but he didn't want to scandalize her entourage. And if Odele was tipped off, she would be on the phone with Melody Banyon of *WE Magazine* in no time to report his and Chiara's relationship had become serious—never mind that it was make-believe.

Still, the evening was young, and Chiara's manager wouldn't be here at its close…

Flashbulbs went off around them in dizzying bursts of light. The paparazzi were out in full force for this red-carpet event. Chiara gave her practiced smile, crossed one leg in front of the other and tilted her head, giving the photographers her best side.

Her one-shoulder silk organza gown had a deep slit revealing her leg to the upper thigh. It was a beautiful but safe choice for an awards show. Invisible tape ensured everything stayed in place and she didn't have a wardrobe malfunction. Her hair was loose, and her jewelry was limited to chandelier earrings and a diamond bracelet.

The Ring of Hope Gala to Benefit Children's Charities was being held at The Beverly Hilton Hotel. The hotel's sixteen-thousand-foot International Ballroom could seat hundreds—and did for the Golden Globe Awards and other big Hollywood events. Soon she and Rick would be inside, along with dozens of other actors and celebrities.

Rick's hand was at the small of her back—a warm, possessive imprint. It was for the benefit of the cameras, of course, but the reason didn't matter. He made her aware of her femininity. She'd never been so attuned to a man before.

Despite the presence of plenty of well-known actors tonight, Chiara saw women casting Rick lingering looks full of curiosity and interest. He had a blatant sex appeal that was all unpolished male...

Chiara put a break on her wayward thoughts—aware there were dozens of eyes upon them. Not only were bulbs constantly flashing, but the press kept calling out to them.

"Chiara, look this way!"

"Who's the new guy, Chiara?"

"Can you tell us about your gown?"

"Who's the mystery man?"

Chiara curved her lips and called back, "We met on the set of *Pegasus Pride*."

"Is it true he's a stuntman?"

She cast Rick a sidelong look, and he returned it with a lingering one of his own. She could almost believe he was enraptured for real...

"I don't know," she murmured, searching Rick's face. "Do you know some stunts, honey?"

"Not for the red carpet," he said, smiling back. "Maybe I should practice."

Ha. In her opinion, he was doing just fine with his *publicity stunt* for the red carpet. He was *too* believable in the role of boyfriend.

She knew what the headlines would say, of course. *Chiara Feran Makes Debut with New Man.* She and Rick had given their interview to *WE Magazine*, but every media outlet wanted their own story.

Chiara smiled for another few moments. Then she linked hands with Rick and moved out of the spotlight so the next prey—uh, *celebrity*—could take her place. She knew how these things worked.

She and Rick walked into the Hilton, where sanity prevailed in contrast to the paparazzi and fans outside. They followed the crowd toward the International Ballroom. Fortunately she didn't cross paths with anyone she knew well. She wasn't sure if she was up for further discussion of her ultimate accessory—namely, Rick.

When they reached their table, she sighed with relief. *So far, so good.*

"Rick, sugar!"

Chiara turned and spotted an actress she wasn't well-acquainted with but whose name she'd come across more than a few times. *Isabel Lanier.*

She'd never heard Rick's name said in the same breath as *sugar* before. In her opinion, *spice* was more appropriate.

"Wow, I haven't seen you in ages!" Isabel said—and though she addressed Rick, she directed her crystalline blue gaze to Chiara. "And you're one half of an item, too, I hear."

"Isabel, this is—"

"Chiara Feran," Chiara finished for him.

She assessed the other woman. Isabel Lanier had a reputation in Hollywood, and there wasn't enough Botox in LA to make it pretty. She'd slept with directors to land supporting roles. She'd broken up a costar's marriage by having an affair with him during filming. And she'd been named in a lawsuit involving back rent on a house in the Hollywood Hills.

Isabel looked her over in turn, and then, directing her gaze to Rick, murmured, "I'm so glad you've moved on, sugar, and to another actress, too. No bad feelings, hmm?"

Rick seemed to tense, but then Chiara wondered whether she was imagining it.

Isabel fluttered her mascara-heavy eyelashes. "I'd love to talk to you about—"

"Isabel, it was a surprise running into you. Glad you're well."

The dismissal on Rick's part was polite but unmistakable.

Chiara wondered about his past tie to Isabel. It gave her a bad feeling—though, of course, not jealousy. What had Rick been thinking? Isabel? *Really?* The woman's reputation followed her like a trail of discarded clothing in a tacky Vegas hotel room.

Isabel gave them a searching look, and then nodded as if reaching a conclusion. "It's time I got back to my date."

"Hal?" Rick inquired sardonically.

Isabel tossed her head, her smile too bright. "Oh, sugar, you know better." She flashed her hand and a ring caught the light. "But this time, I did find one who is for keeps."

"Congratulations."

The smile stayed on Isabel's lips but her eyes were sharp. "Thank you."

When the other woman moved off, Chiara turned to Rick. "Should I ask?"

"Will you be able to stop yourself?"

"Do you date all your leading ladies?"

"In Isabel's case, it was more her trying to hook up with me. Misguidedly, as it turned out."

Chiara raised her eyebrows.

"Isabel is the reason that I don't get involved with starlets. They're trouble."

"Men are trouble."

"Finally, a topic that we agree on," he quipped. "The opposite sex is trouble."

Chiara shrugged. "Isabel Lanier seems an odd choice for you."

Chiara definitely wasn't jealous. The irony wasn't lost on her, though. Usually her dates were the ones having to contend with overeager male admirers. Now the shoe was on the other foot—sort of.

"Possessive?" Rick asked, lips quirking, as if he'd read her mind.

"Don't be silly," Chiara retorted.

"It's not like you to get territorial, but I like it."

"So what is the connection between you and Isabel Lanier?" she tried again.

Rick regarded her for a moment. "Isabel made a play for me in front of some photographers. Unfortunately her boyfriend at the time was also a good friend of mine. End of friendship."

"Why would she do that?"

Rick gave her a penetrating look. "Fame, public image, to make Hal jealous. You know, all the likely ulterior motives."

She didn't want to dwell on their own ulterior motives right now.

"Shall we sit down?" Rick asked.

She felt compelled to go on. "If you were more high profile, the organizers here would have made sure your path didn't cross Isabel's, and that you were seated on opposite sides of the ballroom."

"Fortunately I'm not. High profile, that is."

"But I am." Chiara made a mental note to put the word out that she and Isabel should be kept apart—at least until her "relationship" with Rick came to an end.

Rick pulled out a chair for her, and she sat down. As Rick turned to acknowledge a waiter, Isabel fished the cell phone out of her clutch and typed a quick text to Odele. No time like the present to make sure a viper stayed in her tank, she thought, her mind traveling back to Isabel.

After that, the evening passed quickly and painlessly. The master of ceremonies was a well-known comedian, and he drew regular laughs from the crowd, who dined on butterfly salmon pâté with caviar and peppered chateaubriand with port wine glacé.

Before long, Chiara found herself heading home with Rick. She'd never had a live-in significant other, and in the past, it had been easy enough to say goodbye at the end of a date. Not this time, however. *Awkward.*

When they entered the hushed silence of her foyer, she faced Rick. She reminded herself that she held the cards here. She was the celebrity. This was *her* house. And he, for all intents and purposes, was *her* employee, thanks to Odele.

Still, it was of little help when faced with Rick's overwhelming masculinity.

He was tall and broad, and all evening she'd been ignoring how he filled out his tux. Should she be surprised he even owned one?

Rick quirked his lips. "I guess this is the part where I kiss you good-night—" he glanced past her to the stairs "—except I'm staying here." His gaze came back to hers, and he looked at her with a slow deliberateness.

All of a sudden, she was searching for air. They hadn't been this close since their encounter in the exercise room, and she'd vowed it was an experience that would never, ever be repeated.

But the memory of how easily he'd aroused her—her body tightening and then finding blessed release—played havoc with her senses and scruples right now.

He bent his head, and said in a low voice, "It would aid in believability."

There was no need for him to elaborate. If he kissed her…if he excited her…if they became lovers…

Yes…no. She mentally shook her head.

He looked down at her gown, and she felt his gaze everywhere—on her breasts, her hips and lower…

"Do you need help with that dress?" he muttered, his eyes half-lidded. "There's no Odele here, no designer's assistant or fashion stylist."

Didn't she know it. They were alone, and the quiet of the night and the empty house surrounded them. The only illumination was the dim light that she'd left on in the foyer.

Chiara cleared her throat. "You did well tonight for an agoraphobic stuntman."

"Isn't this the time in the movie for a love scene?" he teased.

She tried gamely for her typical maneuver. She did *outrage* really well. "This isn't a movie and we're not—"

"Actors," he finished for her. "I know."

He took her hand and drew her near. Another smile

teased his lips. "That's what's going to make this so great. No pretending."

She swallowed. "I don't know how not to pretend."

The brutal honesty escaped her before she could help herself.

"Just feel. Go with your instincts."

"Like method acting?"

"Like real life." He settled his hands and massaged her shoulders. "Relax. We stuntmen are not so bad."

"Are you the baddest of the bunch?" she asked, her voice husky.

His smile widened. "Want to find out if I'm the Big Bad Wolf?"

"Sorry, wrong fairy tale again."

She could feel the heat and energy coming off him even though only his hands touched her. She was attuned to *everything* about him. As an actress, she was trained to observe the slightest facial sign, the subtlest inflection of voice, the intention behind a touch. But with Rick, she quivered with sensation approaching a sixth sense.

Slowly he raised her chin, and her gaze met his.

They'd been working up to this moment ever since the exercise room, and she saw in his eyes that he knew it, too.

He searched her face and then, focusing on her mouth, he brushed her lips with his.

She parted for him on an indrawn sigh, touched her tongue to his and twined her arms around his neck. She needed this, too, she admitted, and for tonight at least she couldn't think of a reason to deny herself.

He settled his hands on her waist, and she felt the press of his arousal. He deepened the kiss, and she met him, not holding back. Her evening clutch slipped from her limp hand and hit the ground with a small *thump*.

He broke the kiss, only to trail his mouth, whisper-soft, across her jaw and to her temple.

"Rick…"

"Chiara."

"I…"

"This isn't the time to start one of your arguments."

"About what?"

"About anything."

He nuzzled the side of her neck, and she angled her head to afford him better access. She fastened her hands on his biceps in order to anchor herself, and the hard muscle under her fingers reminded her that he was built… and right now primed to mate with her.

Chiara felt that last realization to her core, even as Rick's lips sent delicious shivers down her spine.

One of his hands shifted lower and settled on her exposed thigh. She felt the caress of his slightly callused fingers.

He kissed the shell of her ear, and then whispered, "Your dress has been giving me a thrill all evening."

"Oh?" she managed.

"The slit is so high…playing peekaboo all the way up…making me wonder whether this time I'll get a glimpse…"

She gave a throaty laugh. "I'm not commando. I don't take those kinds of risks."

His hand moved lower, slid under the slit and covered her. "Oh, yeah? But I want you to go on all kinds of adventures with me. Let me show you, baby…"

Chiara's eyes closed and her head fell back as Rick's finger slipped inside her and the pad of his thumb brushed her in a wicked dance. Her lips parted. *Oh, my.* They hadn't even made it past the inside of her front door and all she wanted to do was strip for him and let him take her against the hard wall of the foyer, pounding into her until she wept with the pure ecstasy of it, her legs wrapped around him and holding him close.

"Ah, Chiara." His voice sounded rough with arousal as he nipped and nibbled along her jaw. "So hot. There's nothing cold about you."

His words wrapped around her like a warm caress. She'd worked all her life to get her walls up and, most of all, be independent and succeed. But with Rick, her defenses came crashing down, and in their place rushed in powerful need.

Rick snaked his free hand beneath the one-shoulder bodice of her gown and cupped her breast. He kneaded her soft flesh and she peaked for him.

A moan escaped her.

"I should have stuck around earlier tonight so I'd know how you got into this gown, and how to get you out," he muttered.

A laugh caught in her throat, but then the buzz of a cell phone interrupted the mood like the beam of car headlights slicing through the night.

It took a few moments for Chiara to clear her head and get oriented. And then she flushed. She and Rick had gone from zero to sixty in minutes, and any longer...

As her phone continued to buzz from the inside of her clutch on the floor, she pulled away from Rick, and he dropped his hands and stepped back.

"You don't have to answer it," he said roughly.

"It's Odele. I can tell from the ringtone." She started to bend down, but Rick was faster and retrieved the clutch for her.

"You don't have to answer it," Rick commented, his voice edged with frustration.

Flustered and still aroused, Chiara gathered her scattered thoughts. "She's used to having her calls answered. I—I've got to take this. I've...got to go."

"Of course." His expression was sardonic, knowing, and he raked his hand through his hair. "I'm guessing it's time for another cold shower."

Turning away from Rick to regain her composure, she hit the answer button. "Odele, hello?"

"Hello, sweetie. How are you? Did you have a fine evening?"

"Yes, of course," she answered as she hurried up the stairs. "What can I do for you, Odele?"

"I'm responding to your request, hon."

For a moment, Chiara was confused, but then she remembered her text to Odele earlier in the evening.

"From what I could see on TV, you and Mr. Stuntman were doing an excellent job at your first public appearance together. But then I got your message about keeping you and Isabel Lanier separated at future social events. Did something happen that I'm not aware of?"

Chiara didn't know whether to be relieved or frustrated. If not for Odele's untimely—or rather, timely—call, she'd have been moments away from inviting Rick to follow her to the bedroom. A mistake that she would have regretted.

"Not that I don't have sympathy," Odele went on in her trademark raspy voice. "Isabel Lanier reeks of tacky perfume, and her manager is worse."

Chiara smiled weakly. Leave it to Odele to be competitive with even Isabel's snarky manager.

"So, honey, are you going to tell me what the story is, or make me guess? I have my sources, you know."

Chiara lowered her voice even as she reached the privacy of her bedroom and flipped on the light. "Rick and Isabel were involved at one point."

"Really?" The word was a long, drawn-out drawl.

"Well, not really." Chiara dropped her clutch on the vanity table. "She sort of threw herself at him in a publicity stunt and that was the end of his friendship with her then boyfriend."

"Damn it, I knew her manager was cunning."

"It takes one to know one, Odele."

"Okay, all right," her manager responded grumpily. "Now that I've got the details, I'll put the word out about Isabel and file away the information for any future events that I book you for."

"You're a doll, Odele."

"Oh, stop," her manager rasped. "I'm a barracuda in a town infested with sharks."

When she ended the call with Odele, Chiara sighed. The conversation had let sanity back in. She couldn't get involved with Rick. Sweet heaven, she didn't even like him. She *couldn't* like him.

Too bad she was having an increasingly hard time remembering why.

Seven

Welsdale was a quaint New England town with brick buildings dotting the main streets and colorful homes lining the back roads.

Chiara could hardly believe she was here except that Odele had, of course, loved Rick's idea for an appearance on his mother's cooking show. Before Chiara had caught her breath, she and Rick had been on an early flight from Los Angeles to Boston.

She supposed it was just as well. Ever since the Ring of Hope Gala last weekend, she'd done her best to keep Rick at arm's length. Only a long couple of days on set had saved her. She'd collapsed into bed, exhausted, late at night.

From the airport, where Rick had a car in long-term parking, they drove to Welsdale and then, after no more than twenty minutes on oak-lined roads, to a stunning home on the outskirts of town. Rick had mentioned that his parents were hosting a small party at their house.

The elder Serenghettis lived in a Mediterranean-style mansion with a red-tile roof and white walls. Set amidst beautiful landscaping, the house greeted visitors with a stone fountain at the center of a circular drive.

Chiara didn't know what she had expected, except perhaps a humbler abode. Clearly she'd been wrong in her assumptions. Rick came from an established family and a comfortable background, unlike her.

When they stepped inside, Rick stretched out his arms and joked, "Welcome to the Serenghetti family reunion."

Chiara blinked. "They're all here?"

"We like to support Mom."

Oh, sweet heaven. She wasn't prepared for this. The gathering was larger than she'd expected, and it seemed that assorted Serenghettis were sprinkled among the crowd.

There'd be no Feran family reunion, of course. Or if there were, it would be at a Las Vegas gaming table, where she'd be settling her father's debts.

People were standing around chatting in the family room and adjacent living room, and she noticed in particular how two of the men were as attractive as Rick. It appeared the Serenghetti men came in one variety only: drop-dead gorgeous.

"Come on," Rick said, cupping her elbow. "I'll introduce you."

As they approached, one of the two men glanced at them and then came forward. "Ah, the prodigal son returning to the fold…"

"Stuff it, Jordan." Rick's tone was good-natured—as if he was used to being ribbed.

Jordan appeared unabashed and gave Chiara an openly curious look. "Well, this time you've outdone yourself. Mom will be pleased. But how you managed to convince a beautiful actress that you've got the goods, I'll never know." He held out his hand. "Hi, I'm Jordan Serenghetti, Rick's better-looking brother."

"Which one of us was a body double for *People*'s Sexiest Man Alive?" Rick retorted mildly.

"Which one is featured in an underwear ad on a billboard in Times Square?" Jordan returned.

"Nice to meet you," Chiara jumped in with a light laugh. "I've been putting up with his humor—" she indicated Rick "—for days. Now I see it's a family trait."

"Yes, but I'm younger than Rick and our older brother, Cole, so I like to say our parents achieved perfection only the third time around."

When Rick raised his eyebrows, Chiara laughed again. It was good to see Rick getting back some of his own.

Rick's gaze went to the arched entrance to the family room, and Chiara spotted an attractive woman with honey-blond hair caught in a ponytail, a nice figure showcased in tights and a short-sleeved athletic shirt. Unlike many women in Hollywood, she seemed unaware of her beauty, sporting a fresh-faced natural look with little makeup.

"Your nemesis is here," Rick murmured.

Jordan followed his brother's gaze. "Heaven help us."

At Chiara's inquiring look, Rick elaborated. "Serafina is related to us by marriage. She's Cole's wife's cousin. She also happens to be the one woman under the sun Jordan can't charm."

Jordan wore an unguarded look that said he was attracted like a bee to nectar—and befuddled by the feeling. Chiara hid a smile. She suspected that like her, Jordan lived in a world with plenty of artifice—big-time sports likely resembled Hollywood that way—and Serafina was a breath of fresh air.

Serafina was something different, and Jordan appeared at a loss as to how to deal with her. Relative? Friend? Lover? Maybe he couldn't make up his mind—and it wasn't only his choice to make, either.

"Excuse me," Jordan announced. "Fun just walked in."

"Jordan," Rick said warningly.

"What?" his brother responded as he stepped away.

"Just make sure that while you're getting a rise out of our newest in-law, you don't come in for a pounding yourself."

Jordan flashed a quick grin. "I'm counting on it."

Chiara watched Serafina's eyes narrow as she noticed Jordan step toward her. It seemed as if Jordan wasn't the only one who was aware of someone else's every move...

Then Chiara quashed a sudden self-deprecatory grimace. She couldn't judge Serafina. She herself was attuned to Rick's every gesture.

At that moment, the other attractive man Chiara had spotted earlier approached.

"Hi, I'm Cole Serenghetti," he said, holding out his hand.

"Chiara Feran," she responded, shaking hands.

She could tell on a moment's acquaintance that Cole was the serious brother.

Unlike Jordan and Rick, Cole's eyes were more hazel than green. Still, the family resemblance was strong. But Chiara noticed that Cole sported a scar on his cheek.

A beautiful woman walked up to them, and Cole put his arm around her. She had the most translucent brown eyes that Chiara had ever seen, and masses of brown hair that fell in waves and curls past her shoulders.

"This is my wife, Marisa," Cole said, looking affectionately at the woman beside him. "Sweet pea, I'm sure you've heard of Chiara Feran."

"I loved your movie *Three Nights in Paris*," Marisa gushed, "and I follow you online."

Chiara smiled. "It's good to meet you. So you like romantic comedies?"

"I adore them." Marisa threw a teasing look at her husband. "Though it's hard to get Cole here to watch them with me."

"Ouch." Cole adopted a mock-wounded expression. "Hey, I'm just showing family loyalty to Rick for his adventure flicks."

"A great excuse," Marisa parried before turning back to Chiara. "You aren't filming a romantic comedy now, are you?"

Chiara sighed. "Unfortunately no." Unless she counted the banter that she had going on with Rick offscreen. "Blame Hollywood. Action movies bring in the big bucks at the box office."

Marisa made a sympathetic sound.

"You're a woman after my own heart," Chiara said.

"I've had my tenth grade students watch you in the film adaptation of *Another Song at Dawn*," Marisa added enthusiastically. "I've taught here in Welsdale."

Chiara warmed to the other woman. "I'm so glad. That's the nicest compliment—"

"Anyone's ever paid you?" Rick finished for her.

Cole cast Rick a droll look. "Quite the romantic boyfriend, aren't you?"

Chiara flushed. "I meant the best professional praise."

Cole and his wife just laughed.

"Cole's gotten better with sharing warm thoughts since we've gotten married," Marisa added, throwing a playful look at her husband, "but I'm still not finding little heart drawings in my lunchbox."

Chiara envied Cole and Marisa's obvious connection.

In contrast, she and Rick pushed each other's buttons. Then she reminded herself there was no *her and Rick*. They had a fake relationship for the benefit of the press.

When Cole and Marisa excused themselves, another woman approached, and Chiara again saw a resemblance to Rick.

"Chiara, this is my younger sister, Mia," Rick said.

Mia was slender and lovely, with arresting almond-shaped green eyes. She could have qualified as a model or actress herself.

"I wish I could say Rick has told me a lot about you," Mia quipped, "but I'd be lying."

"Family," Rick muttered. "Who needs enemies?"

Mia tossed her brother a droll look that made Chiara smile.

"Rick mentioned you're a designer," Chiara said.

"He did?"

"I'd love to see some of your creations."

"I'm based in New York."

"Do you have something that Chiara could toss on for an appearance on Mom's cooking show?" Rick prompted.

When Mia rolled her eyes, Chiara held back a grin.

"Leave it to my brother to give me the professional opportunity of a lifetime, and no fair warning."

"Hey," Rick said, holding up his hands, "I did tell you to bring a trunk of stuff to show a friend of mine."

"Yeah, but you didn't say who!"

"Don't you read any of the celebrity glossies or supermarket tabloids?" Rick countered. "I'm dating one of the hottest actresses around."

Chiara felt a wave of heat at the word *hottest*.

"How am I supposed to know what's true and what isn't?" Mia responded. "It's a good thing I know my way around a needle and thread for a little nip and tuck if necessary."

"I'm not that thin," Chiara chimed in.

"Yeah, she has the appetite of a lumberjack," Rick agreed jokingly. "I should know. I've carried her out of exploding buildings and onto a helicopter with one hand."

"Hilarious, Rick," Mia said. "Next you'll be telling us that you have real superpowers."

Rick arched an eyebrow. "Ask Chiara."

Chiara flushed again. The last thing she wanted to do was discuss Rick's prowess—sexual or otherwise—with his siblings.

When Chiara didn't immediately reply, Mia laughed. "I guess you got your answer, Rick."

An older woman came bustling over, clapping her hands. "*Cari, scusatemi.* I'm sorry, I was speaking on the phone with my producers."

Rick's face lightened. "Don't worry, Mom. We're all good here. Just introducing Chiara to everybody."

Rick's mother clasped her hands together. "I'm Camilla. *Benvenuti.*"

"Thank you for the welcome, Mrs. Serenghetti," Chiara said.

"Camilla, please. You are doing me a huge *favore.*"

"She mixes Italian and English like they're flour and water," Rick said in a low voice. "Interrupt at your own risk."

"Now, Chiara—what a lovely name! You are Italian and Brazilian, no?"

She nodded her head.

"You are a celebrity, yes? And beautiful, too, no?"

"Um…"

"*Basta, così.*" Camilla nodded her head approvingly.

"It is enough. You are doing me a huge *favore*. Anything else will be extra filling in the cannoli, no?"

"Mrs. Serenghetti—"

"Camilla, please. Do you want me to demonstrate a recipe to you on the show, or—" Camilla brightened hopefully "—you have one to share?"

"Actually I do." Chiara had been thinking about the show on the plane ride. She didn't want to disappoint. It had nothing to do with Rick, but rather her own high standards and integrity, she told herself. "I used to visit relatives in Brazil when I was growing up. Italian food is very popular there."

Camilla beamed.

"Brazilian barbecue—" Chiara began.

"Churrascaria, sì."

"—is well-known, but we also have *galeteria*. It's chicken and usually an all-you-can-eat pasta and salad. So I would like to make a pasta dish that sounds Italian, but was really popularized by the Italian immigrant community in Brazil. *Cappelletti alla romanesca.*"

"Perfetto." Camilla nodded approvingly.

Mia linked arms with her mother. "Excuse us while I get Mom's opinion on how to finish the tagliatelle salad."

When his female relatives had departed, Rick turned to Chiara with a bemused expression. "I'm impressed. Have you actually made this dish before?"

"Please." Chiara gave him a long-suffering look. "Do I look Brazilian and Italian to you?"

"Yes, but—"

"Trust me." The words were out of her mouth before she could stop them.

"Isn't that my line?" he mocked.

She felt the heat rise in her cheeks and turned away.

"Rick!"

Chiara spotted an older version of Rick coming toward them.

"Brace yourself," Rick murmured. "You have yet to meet the most colorful member of the family. Serg Serenghetti."

Oh, dear.

"So the prodigal son has returned."

"Wrong script, Dad," Rick quipped. "This is *The Son Also Rises.*"

Serg Serenghetti fastened his eyes on Chiara. "What do you see in this guy?"

Chiara gave a weak smile.

"How do you know about us?" Rick retorted, addressing his father.

"I read *WE Magazine*," Serg grumbled. "Same as everyone else. Your mother leaves copies lying around." Serg lowered his brows. "And with my recovery, I have plenty of time to surf the internet for news about my wayward children."

Rick looked at Chiara and jerked a finger in his father's direction. "Do you believe he knows about surfing? He's keeping up with those teenagers that make action flicks such blockbusters at the box office."

As Rick poked fun at his father, his tone was laced with affection.

Serg grumbled again. "I've known a lot about a lot for a lot longer than you've been around, but all I get is guff from the young pups."

Rick pulled out a chair, and Serg sank into it.

"He's still recovering from a stroke," Rick murmured for her benefit.

Oh. Chiara felt a tug at her heartstrings. Beneath the bluster, the affection between father and son sounded loud and clear. In contrast, her relationship with her father was a distant echo.

Chiara realized that with the Serenghettis, she was in for something new and different from her own experience. And as she settled into a conversation with Serg, she realized that might not be such a bad thing—except for the fact that meeting his family made Rick even more likable and attractive, and she was already in danger of succumbing to him…

Rick couldn't believe his eyes, but then he should have known Chiara would be a natural in front of the cameras—even on Camilla Serenghetti's cooking show.

He was also tense. He wanted this episode to boost ratings for his mother, but he had little idea about Chiara's cooking skills, let alone how they'd play out on television. And he also wanted Chiara and his mother to get along.

So far so good.

"The reason I'm not wearing an apron," Chiara said brightly into the camera, "is because this outfit is too scrumptious to cover up." She gestured at her V-neck berry-colored top with clever draping, the cream trousers underneath barely visible above the kitchen counter. "It's courtesy of Camilla's daughter, Mia Serenghetti, whose clothes are mouth-watering."

Camilla laughed, and because she sat next to him in the audience, Rick could tell his sister looked amused.

"I guess Camilla is not the only talented one in the family."

"*Grazie tanto*, Chiara *bellissima*," his mother said.

"*Prego.*" Chiara acknowledged the thanks and then dumped prosciutto in a blender before smiling at the studio audience. "I sometimes prefer an electronic device to hand-chopping. Goes faster, too."

As she scanned the buttons on the blender, Rick realized something was wrong and started to rise from his front-row seat.

Chiara pressed a button, and prosciutto pieces started flying everywhere.

Chiara yelped, and Camilla covered her mouth with her hands. The audience exploded in shocked laughter.

Rick stared, and then sank back into his seat.

Chiara quickly pressed another button to turn off the blender, and then she and Camilla stared at each other... before dissolving into peals of laughter.

"Oops." Chiara looked into the camera and shrugged, a teasing smile on her face. "Next time I'll remember to put the top on the blender first. But first let's get this cleaned up."

Moments later, after help from behind-the-scenes staff, Chiara raised a wineglass, and she and Camilla toasted each other.

Rick watched, fascinated by the interplay between the two women. Looking around him, he realized everyone else was entertained, as well.

After that, Chiara proceeded to prepare the cappelletti recipe without another hitch. She chopped more prosciutto, by hand this time, and added it to a shallow pan containing peas, mushrooms and a light cream sauce. With a saucy look, she added a touch of *vino* from the open wine bottle, and said with a wink, "Do try this at home, but not too much."

His mother laughed, and then both she and Chiara took more sips from their wineglasses.

Rick couldn't imagine what they were both thinking, but when Chiara motioned for his father, Serg, to join them from the audience, Rick knew things were only going to get more interesting. His father was a character, but this was the first time Serg had been so public since his stroke.

Rick made to help his father out of his seat, but Serg just batted his hand away.

"Bah!" Serg said, doing a comical rendition of a grumpy old man even though he had the grin of an eager fan.

"I hear Camilla's husband, Serg, knows his way around wine," Chiara announced. "Perhaps he can suggest a vintage to pair with my dish."

"I'd be happy to," Serg replied as he climbed the two steps to the stage. "It's not every day that my son brings home a beautiful actress."

Rick suppressed an embarrassed groan. His and Chiara's pretend relationship had just gotten a major advertising boost from his father. Odele would be overjoyed.

When Serg reached the stage, he sampled the cappelletti dish from a plate Camilla handed to him. After taking a moment to savor, he declared, "Bianco di Custoza, Verdicchio or Pinot Bianco."

Chiara beamed. "Thank you so much for the wine suggestions, Serg."

Serg winked at the audience. "You know I'm Italian, so I suggest Italian wines. I like them on the dry side, but you can pair this dish with a lighter Chardonnay if you like."

Getting the signal from a producer offscreen, Camilla addressed the camera in order to wrap up the show. "*All prossima volta.* Till next time, *buon appetito.*"

As the show's support staff approached to remove Camilla's and Chiara's mics, Serg returned to his seat.

"Good job, Dad," Rick remarked with a smile. "I didn't know you had it in you."

He was still trying to process Chiara's interaction with

his parents on camera. It was like she'd known them forever, it had been so natural.

"Bah!" Serg said, though his expression again belied his grumpiness. "Don't be jealous I was the one called on stage by a beautiful woman. You've got to work it, Rick."

"And a star is born," Rick replied with dry humor to his sister, who gave a knowing smile.

"Do you want my autograph?" Serg chortled, picking up his sweater from his seat as Mia moved to help him.

Rick stepped off to the side, and when Chiara approached, minutes later, he remarked, "That was quite a scene-stealing performance."

"It's why I'm an in-demand actress."

She looked sexy in Mia's designs, and he liked her even more for lending her celebrity to help his family.

"So it was all planned?"

"Planned? Like reading lines?" She shook her head. "No. More like improv and stand-up comedy."

"It worked."

"I hope the show's ratings reflect it." She shrugged. "Viewers want drama and action. Or maybe I just think that because I've been doing too many adventure movies."

"Hey—" he chucked her under the chin "—that's how you met a hunky stuntman who's given you a new lease on life in the press."

"Oh, yes, the media." She made a disgruntled sound that he didn't expect. "Of course, I have to attend to my public persona."

He tucked his hands in his denim pockets—because the urge to comfort and, even more, get closer to her, was overwhelming. "So who is the real Chiara Feran? Odele mentioned a few details about your childhood and parents."

She sighed, and there was a flash of pain. "My mother was in some ways a typical stage mother, but in other ways, she wasn't. She had thwarted dreams of being a star, so she was ambitious for me."

"Things didn't work out for her?"

"Well, she had some modest success in Brazil, so she went to Hollywood. But the Portuguese accent didn't help when it came to acting roles. Who knows what would have happened if she'd stayed in South America."

Curious, Rick asked, "Your mother didn't want more kids?"

Chiara sobered. "No. Her marriage broke up, and I was enough for her to handle as a single parent living far from her family in Brazil. Plus, I was her spitting image in many ways, so she already had a Mini-Me. She died a few years ago, and I still miss her a lot. I have mixed feelings about my childhood, but I loved her with my whole heart. She did the best she could in raising me."

Rick was starting to understand—a lot. Chiara's upbringing couldn't have been more different from his own. While he'd been tossing around a football in the backyard with his siblings, she was probably being prepped and groomed for a chance to appear in a national commercial or catalog.

"Your mother should think of doing a food blog," Chiara commented, changing the subject. "She needs to think of branching out and building the Camilla Serenghetti food empire."

"Empire?" he repeated in a sardonic tone. Because while it was one thing for his mother to have a local cooking show, it was another for her to be an empress in the making. Still... "She'll like the way you think, and appreciate the pointers on building a brand."

"Of course. That's what we're about in Hollywood.

Building a brand." Chiara looked around. "You, on the other hand, are about wholesomeness, surprisingly enough. Or at least your family is. You come from a nice little town in Massachusetts that's ages away from the Sunset Strip."

"You grew up in Rhode Island, not far from here. You're not so different."

Chiara shook her head. "I'm all about performing these days. The show must go on."

"Whatever the cost?" Rick probed.

Chiara nodded. "Even if the show is a sham."

"And yet, I think of you as real and vital," Rick replied, stepping closer. "And my physical reaction to you definitely is."

She gave a nervous laugh and shook her head. "You must be mistaken. I'm Snow White, remember? A make-believe character."

Rick's lips twitched. He wasn't sure when they had gotten so mixed up. Suddenly *she* was insisting she was a make-believe character, and *he* was arguing the opposite.

One thing was for sure: he was more determined than ever to finish exploring their very real attraction. He'd kept his distance since they'd left Los Angeles, but he wanted her with a need that was getting hard to ignore.

In the now nearly empty television studio, Chiara stood to one side, waiting for assorted Serenghettis to depart. Rick was speaking to his mother and one of her producers, no doubt making sure everything was in order with respect to today's guest appearance.

Chiara was glad for the respite. Minutes ago, her conversation with Rick had devolved into a far more intimate and personal exchange than she'd been prepared for. What had she been thinking?

She'd revealed more about her background and her mother than she'd intended. And then she hadn't been able to keep out the wistfulness when contrasting her circumstances with Rick's own family. *Wholesome. Warm. Loving.* She felt relaxed here, in the embrace of the Serenghettis and away from her problems—the limelight, her father, her would-be stalker…

Still, she'd dodged the very real emotional and sexual currents between her and Rick by making light of the matter. *The show must go on.* She doubted Rick would be satisfied with that response, however. Awareness skated over her skin as she remembered the gleam in his eyes followed by his words: *I think of you as real and vital. And my physical reaction to you definitely is.*

Her resolve to keep him at a distance was weakening, aided by her very real yearning for what he'd had—still had—in comparison: a tight-knit family who cared about each other.

As if on cue, Rick's sister appeared, her face wreathed in a wide smile. "Thank you for the on-air plug, Chiara. You are the perfect model to bring out the best in my designs."

Chiara smiled back and then touched the other woman's arm. "Don't mention it."

"I've never dressed someone so high profile before. You have a great sense of style."

"I owe a lot to my former stylist Emery. But she went off to start her own accessories line, so I'm open to new ideas." Chiara's eyes widened, as an idea struck. "I should connect the both of you. Emery would be a natural complement to your clothing line."

Mia gave a look of wry amusement. "I can see it now—'ME by Mia Emery… Not Your Mom's Everyday.'"

"Perfect." So this was what it might be like to have a sister. Chiara let the wistful feeling wash over her again.

Mia tilted her head. "Rick isn't the only maverick in the family, though he likes to think so. I've abandoned the family construction business and run off to New York to follow the bright lights of fashion."

"You make *maverick* sound like a bad thing. It's not so terrible."

"Not so wicked, you mean?" Mia gave a sly grin. "So Rick's worked his charm on you then?"

Chiara's face warmed. Was it *charm*—or something more? Just a short time ago, she'd have called Rick the least charming man she knew, but somehow her feelings had been changing. Now with his family, she was even more…charmed.

Mia leaned in conspiratorially. "You're beautiful, smart and famous. How did you and Rick wind up together?"

"We…um…" Somehow she couldn't bring herself to lie to Rick's sister, so she finished lamely, "Don't believe everything you read in the press."

What could she say? *We're not really a couple. It's a big fat lie.* Even if she was having increasing trouble remembering that, especially surrounded by the Serenghettis.

"I see," Mia responded, and then nodded as if satisfied. "Well, you two bounce off each other in a charming way. It's as if Rick has met his match."

Even if that were true, it meant one of them was going down for the count…

"You're someone who can't be impressed by his money," Mia added.

What? Chiara mentally shrugged, and said carefully, "I'm not sure how much money Rick has."

Mia laughed. "Neither am I, but after making a killing with his hedge fund, he's got enough to play with."

Hedge fund? Chiara felt her head swim. Rick was a gritty rolling stone of a stuntman as far as she knew. If he had millions, what was he doing…?

"He's a stuntman," she blurted. "He jumps off buildings, leaps from moving cars…" *And embraces actresses while hanging from a helicopter.*

"And takes big risks with money by betting things are going up or down in value." Mia shrugged. "Same thing."

Chiara froze. Mia made it seem as if Rick was a risk taker—which wasn't far from her gambling father. She'd never seen the similarity, and now she was in a very public relationship with Rick. She needed therapy…and not the kind provided by pretending to talk with a wooden dummy, either. *Sorry, Ruby.*

But even more shockingly, Rick wasn't merely a stuntman, he was—

"*Pegasus Pride* is his baby right now," his sister said.

Chiara blew out a breath and tried to keep her voice steady. "He's got money invested in the film?"

Mia nodded. "You didn't know?"

Nope. Otherwise she'd never have spent her time insulting the boss—the producer of her current film—who could have had her fired any day.

Mia gave a choked laugh. "That's just like Rick. He always wants to keep a low profile." Her eyes suddenly danced. "We're still talking about his favorite childhood Halloween costume. You know, he just tossed a brown paper bag over his head and made cutouts for eyes."

"And the school play?" Chiara nearly squeaked.

"Stage crew, or he'd play the tree, of course."

"Well, he's graduated to leaping from speeding motorcycles and hanging from airplanes," Chiara replied drily. *And tricking unwary actresses.*

She glanced over at Rick. Why hadn't he told her? She'd thought...they'd... Chiara nearly closed her eyes on a groan.

She *really* needed to talk to him. But not around his family. No, she'd have to wait for the right moment...

Eight

Chiara somehow managed to keep her silence until they were at Rick's place.

At least now she understood why he might be checking his phone all the time. He was a behind-the-scenes Hollywood power player who liked to keep his name out of the press. And perhaps he needed to keep track of his substantial financial investments, too.

When they arrived at his condo, she was impressed all over again. But at least now she was prepared for what she found, unlike when they'd first arrived in Welsdale. The airy space had the stamp of muted luxury: exposed brick, rich leathers, recessed lighting and electronics hidden behind sliding panels of artwork. Nearly floor-to-ceiling windows made the most of the apartment's perch on the top floor of a block of high-priced condos, and Welsdale's evening lights twinkled outside.

How was it possible she'd been in the dark? She'd researched Rick again online after her conversation with Mia, and nothing had come up. He was good at covering his tracks. Except she was on his trail, thanks to his sister.

She sauntered into the muted light of the living room ahead of Rick. He was dressed in slacks and an open-collar navy shirt. A five o'clock shadow made him look even sexier.

Chiara smoothed her hands down the front of her pants. Then, taking a deep breath, she pinned Rick with a steady gaze. "You didn't tell me you're the producer of *Pegasus Pride* as well as doing its stunt work."

When he didn't react, she didn't know whether to stamp her foot or applaud his acting skills.

"Surprise."

"Now is not the time for humor, Serenghetti."

"When is?" He continued to look relaxed.

She placed her hands on her hips. "You misled me."

"You didn't ask. Anyway, does it matter?"

"I never date the boss," she huffed. "I don't want the reputation of being the actress who slept her way to the top."

On the long list of what he'd done wrong, it was one of the lesser of his transgressions, but she was nearly speechless and didn't even know where to begin.

Rick, though, had the poor grace to smile. "Does it help to know I'm only the behind-the-scenes guy? I'm an investor in Blooming Star Productions."

"Why don't you get your mother a cameo in a movie then? She could play herself. A cook with a local television show trying to make it big."

"God help us."

Chiara narrowed her eyes. "And where did you get the money to be the financial backer for a film production company?"

She'd heard it from Mia—and hadn't quite believed it—so she wanted confirmation from the source himself.

He shrugged. "I worked on Wall Street after Boston College and created a hedge fund."

She felt light-headed when he told her this, just as she had at the television studio. How much money were they talking about? Millions? Billions?

As if reading her mind, he said, "I've made a few best-of lists, but I left New York before joining the billionaires' club."

She figured he had serious bank dwarfing that of a run-of-the-mill actress. "It's unheard of to be both a producer and a stuntman!"

"They're not as different as you think. Both involve calculated risks. One with money, the other physically."

His words echoed Mia's earlier. What was this, a Serenghetti press release? Or did Rick and his siblings just think alike?

She should have been able to read the signs and put them together. They were all there. The expensive car. The apartments on two coasts.

He shrugged again. "I'm a maverick."

"You said you lived in a rental in West Hollywood!"

"Until the house is finished. It's under construction."

"And where is this house?" she asked suspiciously.

"Beverly Hills."

But of course. "Brentwood must seem…quaint to you."

There were plenty of celebrities in her section of LA but it was a little more low-key than the brand-name neighborhoods where tourists flocked—Beverly Hills, Bel Air…

Rick's lips twitched. "Brentwood has its charms, particularly if there's a thatched English cottage…and fairy-tale princess involved."

"She's the kick-ass modern variety," she sniffed—because she should be verbally demolishing him right now for letting her believe he was just an *aw-shucks* stuntman living for the next thrill and its accompanying paycheck.

"Don't I know it." His eyes laughed at her.

"Why would you give up New York, the financial industry and your own hedge fund to go out West to Hollywood?"

He smiled a little, still unflappable. "New challenges. Hollywood is not that different from Wall Street. The studios take major gambles with movies. Different rules, but the same game. And it's still about trusting your instincts and making money—or not."

"Well, it all makes sense now—" sarcasm crept into her tone "—except for the part where you led me to believe you were a regular Joe."

"Is this our first argument?"

She nearly snorted. "Or our hundredth."

He sauntered closer. "Would it have made a difference if you'd known?"

"You could have hired a stable of bodyguards for me with your bank!"

"Ah," he drawled, "but then I wouldn't have had the pleasure of…your company."

"The joy of sparring with me, you mean? And living in a humble cottage instead of a castle in Beverly Hills?"

He burst out laughing. "I'm paying you enough to live in more than a humble cottage."

"But are you paying me enough to put up with you?"

He gave a sultry smile and reached for her. "I don't know. Let's find out."

She should be mad at him. She *was* angry with him. Still, it didn't matter. The truth was she'd been lured in by the seductive cozy family life of the Serenghettis. She yearned for it. They were miles removed from her existence in Southern California, and the distance wasn't just a matter of geography.

When Rick's lips met hers, Chiara was transported, winging through the clouds as if they were performing another one of their stunts. Exhilaration ran through her, the feeling humming alongside one of safety, family… and coming home.

He molded her to him with his hand on her back, making her feel his need—his desire. She rested her hands on his shoulders, and then, caving, slid her arms around his neck, bringing his head closer.

Rick lifted his head slightly, and muttered against her mouth, "We need props."

She gave a choked laugh. "This is not a film scene."

Rick raised his eyebrows. "You're an actress who's not into role-playing?"

"I like to keep it real. Well, except for this pretending about being a couple that Odele has me doing!"

"Believe me, this is as real and raw as it's going to get."

Awareness shivered through her. "Okay, what if I'm a chilly A-list actress and you're…the help who is intent on seducing me?"

"There's nothing cold about you, Snow," he said, tilting up her chin. "Well, except for maybe your nickname."

"But you're here to melt me?"

He flashed his teeth. "I'm trying."

It had been safer to pretend he was the help. Just the movie stuntman. Or the make-believe boyfriend. Not a man whose wealth dwarfed hers. One who had no use for her money or her fame and celebrity. One who'd put himself on the line to protect her—just because.

She didn't know what to do with a man like that. She'd

spent years living as if she didn't need any man. Because she could provide for herself, thanks. But with Rick, she was at a disadvantage. He'd come to her defense against a stalker, and now it turned out he was her boss. She didn't have the upper hand. He didn't need her for anything, either.

Well, except for sex. He clearly wanted her *badly*.

And what was wrong with making herself feel feminine and powerful for an interlude? After all, it wasn't as if she was giving up something. Except she risked falling for him.

The pent-up desire that she'd been feeling these weeks and refusing to acknowledge slipped from its shackles. Rick drove her crazy, and it was a thin line between being irritated and jumping his bones. Giving in meant easing some of the frustration, and suddenly nothing else mattered.

Seeming to read the assent in her eyes, Rick slowly took off her clothes, tossing the pieces aside one by one onto nearby furniture and peeling away her defenses to find what was in no way artifice. Then he shed some of his own clothes until they were both down to underwear.

She shivered as the cool air hit her.

"Let me warm you up," he muttered.

She wanted to say he already had, and that that was the problem. She was melting, her defenses flowing away like so much ice under a hot sun.

Chiara stepped out of the clothes pooled at her feet. Clad in just a lacy black bra and the barest slip of underwear, she had no mask. But if she felt nervous, the naked appreciation stamped on Rick's face put an end to it. She straightened her shoulders, and the resulting movement thrust her breasts forward, their peaks jutting against their thin covering.

Rick's face glowed with appreciation, and then he muttered what he wanted to do with her, his prominent arousal testimony to his words. Waves of heat washed over her, and she sucked in a breath.

He stepped forward, and when the backs of her legs hit the sofa, she let herself fall backward, bracing herself with one hand on a pillow. Rick followed, bent and took one of her nipples in his mouth through her bra, fabric and all, suckling her gently.

Chiara gasped, a strangled sound caught in her throat, and need shuddered through her. Her head fell back when he pushed aside her bra and transferred his attention to her other breast. She was awash in sensation, the universe popping with a kaleidoscope of color.

Rick knelt, pulled her to the end of the sofa arm so that her legs straddled it, and then pushed aside her underwear to use his mouth to love her some more. Cries of pleasure were ripped from her throat…and she felt herself splintering—until she bucked against him with her release.

Afterward, Rick straightened and shed his underwear like a man possessed. Watching him, Chiara stood up and did the same, her remaining garments melting away.

Rick suddenly cursed. "Damn it. Protection is still packed in my suitcase."

"I'm on contraception," she said throatily, dizzy with want.

His gaze caught with hers. "I want you to know I've gotten a clean bill from my doctor. I would never put you at risk."

She licked her lips. "Same goes for me."

They looked at each other for a moment, neither moving, savoring this moment.

And then Chiara held her hand out to him. "We're not going to make it to the bed, are we?"

He gave her a lopsided smile. "Stuntmen can do it everywhere."

Chiara followed his gaze to the nearby long leather ottoman, which doubled as a coffee table. *Oh.* As she bent to sit on it, Rick followed her down, giving her a long, sweet, lingering kiss.

When she embraced him, he entered her in one fluid movement, rocking her to her core. Joined to him, Chiara gave herself up to sensation, following the pace that Rick set.

When she felt Rick tighten, nearing his climax, she ran her hands over his ripped arms and bit back a moan.

"Let me hear you," Rick said as the air grew thick with their deep breathing.

"Rick, oh…now."

And just like that, as he thrust deep, Chiara felt herself coming apart again, dazed with her release.

Rick gave a hoarse shout and buried himself in her, collapsing into her embrace.

Chiara had never felt so at one with someone…exposed and yet secure.

As she walked by, Chiara glanced in her hallway mirror and resisted the urge to pinch herself. She looked happy…relaxed…and yes, sexually satisfied. Filming was over, so the main item on her agenda today was reading a script for a role that she was considering.

Ever since she and Rick had returned to LA from Welsdale two days ago, she'd been in a lovely cocoon. She flushed just thinking about what they'd done yesterday. Foreplay on the weight bench, but the exercise mat and even the jump rope had come in handy…

Walking into the den, she plopped herself on the couch, feet dangling off one end. She began reading the script on her tablet. Moments later, Rick walked in.

After an extraordinary bout of sex this morning, he'd gone out to run errands and she hadn't seen him in the two hours since. He looked just as yummy as earlier, however. They were both dressed in sweats, but somehow, he managed to make his look sexy rather than casual. He hadn't bothered shaving this morning, and she'd come to like the shadow darkening his jaw. Contrasting with his wonderful multihued eyes, it lent him an air of quiet magnetism...

Rick nodded toward the device in her hand. "Have you checked the news yet?"

"No, should I? I just sat down." She belatedly realized he looked more serious than usual.

Rick folded his arms and leaned against the entryway. "Well, the good news is your temporary restraining order came through, so your bad fan can be arrested for getting too close."

"Great." She hadn't given much thought to Todd Jeffers in the past several days, though now that she was back home and he knew her address, she supposed she did feel an undercurrent of more stress. She asked cautiously, "What's the bad news?"

"Your father has gotten himself arrested."

Chiara leaned her head back against the pillows and closed her eyes briefly. "In Sin City? What could he have possibly done? The police turn a blind eye to practically every vice imaginable there. Even prostitution is legal in parts of Nevada, for heaven's sake."

"Apparently he argued about a parking ticket."

"Sounds just like him. Responsibility has never been his strong suit."

"You have to deal with the daddy problem."

"I've never called him *Daddy*," she scoffed, straightening. "Sperm donor, maybe. Daddy, no."

"Whatever the name, you'll keep having the same pesky PR problems if you don't address the issue. And your next big movie might not come with a stuntman willing to double as the star's boyfriend."

"Hilarious." Still, she felt a pull on her heartstrings at the reminder that their arrangement was temporary and fake.

Rick dropped his arms and sauntered into the room. "We may have had some success in distracting the press from your father recently, but you need to turn around and face the issue."

"I don't run from anything," she scoffed again.

"Right. You're a daredevil. Guess who gave you the risk-taking gene?"

She shrugged off a sudden bad feeling as she got up. "I don't know what you're talking about."

Rick's gaze was penetrating. "What do you think gambling is? It's a high from taking risks. There's a rush from the brain's rewards system. You like risks, your father likes risks. Different species of risk, but same family."

She had *nothing* in common with her father. How dare Rick make that connection? Even worse, it was one she hadn't seen coming. So she was in a profession with big highs and lows… So she did some of her own stunts…

Rick folded his arms again. "The funny thing is the only situation where you won't take a chance is arranging a meeting with Michael Feran."

"I don't have anything to say to him."

Rick tossed her a disbelieving look. "Of course you do. You have a lifetime's worth of questions to grill and cross-examine him with," he said pleasantly, "but let's just stick with the issue at hand, which is getting him to stop attracting bad press."

She jutted her chin forward. "And how do you propose I do that?"

"I've got some ideas…ones that might appeal to his own self-interest."

"Oh? And since when have you turned into a psychologist?"

Rick braced his hands on his hips. "People management is part of the job description for a Hollywood producer. And stunt work is about getting your mind ready to conquer fear about what could happen to your body. Mind over body."

"Thanks for the tip."

"I also found your Las Vegas showgirl ventriloquist's dummy on the chair where you left her. She had plenty of insights about you," he joked, "but mostly she was content to just sit there and listen."

"She's trashy."

Rick choked on a laugh. "Great. She'll be popular."

"You like them that way," she accused.

"I like you. The dummy is just the repository for the part of your personality that you're afraid you might have inherited from your father."

"Oh, joy."

Rick suddenly sobered. "Your father has a gambling problem, and I understand addiction. Hal went back to drinking too much after Isabel's antics sent him into a spiral."

"You never mentioned there were consequences from Isabel's media stunt." She caught herself at Rick's droll look at the mention of the word *stunt*. "Sorry, bad choice of words. I meant her diva moment for the press."

Rick dropped his hands and shrugged. "Hal is sober

these days after a stint in rehab. Or so I hear through the grapevine…since we don't socialize anymore."

Chiara was starting to understand more and more about Rick's wariness regarding the limelight, actresses and fame in general. An aspiring actress had not only cost him a friendship but had crushed someone he knew.

"I'll even offer my house for a meeting with your father," Rick went on. "Odele can contact Michael Feran and figure out the details, including flying him to Los Angeles. I'll pick up the tab."

She sighed before asking wryly, "So all I have to do is show up?"

"Affirmative."

"Your house isn't even finished!"

"There's landscaping and stuff still to be done, but it's habitable. And more important, it's neutral territory for a private meeting with your father." He raised his eyebrows.

"Is there anything you haven't thought of?" she demanded.

He gave her a lingering look. "There are still a few fantasies that I'm playing with…"

"You know, it's astonishing you come from such a nice family considering—"

"I'm an ego-driven macho stuntman who doesn't respect the rights of actresses to do their own daredevil acts and knows nothing about the uses of double-sided tape?"

"No, considering your dirty mind."

One side of his mouth lifted in a smile. "Well, that, too. I know plenty of uses for tape and blindfolds and silk ties."

Oh…wow.

Rick's eyes crinkled. "Stunts call for diverse props."

"I go propless."

Rick stepped closer and murmured, "Interesting. No need of any assistance?"

She tossed her hair back as sexual energy emanated off him in luscious waves that wrapped themselves around her. "Yes, I go it alone."

He reached out and took a strand of her hair in his fingers. "Might be more fun if it's two."

"Or three or more?" she queried. "What's your limit? A menagerie?"

He gave a soft laugh. "A couple is good. The number of times, on the other hand…limitless, I'd say."

Her breath started coming quick and shallow. *Oh.*

She swallowed and focused on the faint lines fanning out from the corners of his eyes, and the ones bracketing his mouth.

He lowered his head and then touched his lips to hers, and she sighed. He nudged her—once, twice, coaxing a response. *Open. Open.*

Chiara shivered and felt her breasts peak even though only their lips were touching. She leaned in, falling into something that she knew was bottomless…still relatively unknown…and exciting.

Rick deepened the kiss and raked his fingers through her hair, his hand anchoring at the back of her head. They moved restlessly, unable to get enough of each other.

Then Chiara followed Rick's lead as they stripped off their clothes hurriedly, desperate for skin-on-skin contact. When they were down to underwear, he stopped her.

She drank him in from beneath lowered lashes. He was hot and male and vital. There was the ripped midriff, muscular arms, taut legs…the erection pushing against his boxers. Suddenly she needed to catch her breath.

He lowered the straps of her lacy bra and peeled the garment away from her, and then swallowed. "Chiara."

"Make love to me, Rick."

It was all the invitation that he needed. He kissed her with unrestrained passion, pulling her close as her arms wrapped around his neck. And she responded with a hunger of her own, the feel of his arousal against her fueling her passion.

When she broke away, she pushed down her panties and he did the same with his boxers. And then they were tumbling onto the sofa, reaching for each other in a tangle of limbs and desperate passion.

She grasped Rick's erection and began a pumping motion designed to stoke his passion and hers. He was warm, pulsating male—rigid with his need for her.

He tore her mouth from hers and expelled a breath. "Chiara, we've got to slow down or this is going to be over—"

"Before the director yells cut?" she purred. "There is no director, Stunt Stud."

He gave a strangled laugh. "Stunt Stud?"

"It's the name I came up with when I was objectifying you."

"I was going to say to slow down or this will be finished before you're satisfied."

"Worried I won't be able to keep up with you?" In response, she led his hand to her moist heat, already ready for him.

He stilled, and in the next moment, he was pushing her back against the pillows. Then he sheathed himself in one long stroke that had them both groaning.

As Rick hit her core, she arched her back, taking him in.

She followed his lead and the rhythm he set…building and building until she hit her climax in one husky cry.

"Chiara." In the moment after Rick called her name, he groaned, stiffened and then spilled inside her.

He slumped against her, and she cradled him.

Contentment rolled through her—a feeling that had been too elusive in her life until now...

Nine

When they pulled up in Rick's Range Rover to the nearly completed house, Chiara sucked in a breath. *Wow.*

Nervousness about the upcoming meeting with her father, who was scheduled to arrive within the hour, was replaced by happy surprise.

Rick's home wasn't a house but a castle. It was all gray stone and stunning turrets. She loved it.

She was so entranced that Rick had already come around and opened the car door for her before she thought to get out. She could see there was plenty of landscaping yet to be done, but still the effect from the outside was stunning.

"Want to take a look?" Rick teased as she got out. "I'm sure you've seen plenty of impressive homes belonging to famous people."

None shaped like a castle. She looked at the mansion, and then glanced at Rick. "I'm impressed. You have the castle…were you looking for your fairy-tale princess?"

Rick's lips curved. "Only you can answer that, Snow."

He put his hand at her elbow. "Come on, let's look inside. It's done except for minor details, and is sparsely furnished."

Rick's house—*castle*—made her home look like a small and cute cottage.

Chiara gasped when they entered the foyer. She'd seen this house in her mind's eye.

The double-height entry was airy and sunny but also warm and inviting. Done in light colors, it belied the imposing exterior. A curving staircase led to the upper levels, and various open doorways offered glimpses of other parts of the house.

She followed Rick in a circuit of the ground floor. A warm, country-style kitchen with beige cabinetry and a large island connected to a spacious dining room. An immense living room was bifurcated by a two-way fireplace and was made cozy by coffered ceilings in a warm mahogany wood. A library, den, two bathrooms and a couple of storage rooms for staff rounded out most of the lower level. The only thing missing was furnishings for a family...

When they came full circle back to the entry, Chiara's gaze went to the staircase leading to the upper floors.

Rick adopted a teasing expression. "In case you are wondering, a home office with a built-in desk sits at the top of the principal turret. I haven't stashed a fairy-tale princess there."

"Rapunzel?" She tapped her chest. "Wrong fairy tale. I'm Snow, remember?"

Despite her joking, she felt comfortable here—too at home. It was almost enough to make her forget she was about to have one of the most significant meetings of her life.

She was an actress, she reminded herself sternly. She needed to adopt a persona—a shield—and get what she wanted out of this meeting.

As if reading her thoughts, Rick said, "You and your father can meet in the library. It has two club chairs and a coffee table at the moment."

"Okay." Why had she let Rick talk her into this? She knew he had a good point—dragons must be faced—but she wasn't relishing the chance to slay one of hers. She almost gave a nervous laugh at the thought of Rick cast as her knight in shining armor...

Except of course, she didn't believe in such knights or in Prince Charming—or in fairy tales, for that matter. Though she was having a hard time remembering that these days.

At the sound of a car pulling up, Rick said, "That must be him. I had a driver pick him up from the hotel where he stayed last night after his flight from Vegas."

"Oh, good," she managed, and then cleared her throat.

Rick looked at her searchingly, and then cupped her shoulders. "Are you okay?"

She gave him a blinding smile—one she usually reserved for the cameras. "Never better."

"Remember, you're in charge here. You hold the cards."

"Playing cards are what I intend to take out of his hands."

Rick lifted one side of his mouth. "Sorry, bad choice of words. I'll meet him outside and show him into the library."

"Of course." She'd dressed in a navy shirt dress— something she'd pulled out of the closet herself. Because even if Emery hadn't headed off to start her own fashion line, Chiara couldn't imagine asking a stylist about what to wear to a meeting with her estranged father. For some occasions in life, there was *no* fashion rule book.

Rick shoved his hands into his front pockets and nodded, the hair on his forearms revealed by rolled-up shirt-sleeves. "Back soon."

When Rick turned away, Chiara walked into the library. And then, because she couldn't think of what else to do, she faced the partially open doorway...and waited.

The sound of quiet voices reached her. Greetings were exchanged...and then moments later, she heard footsteps.

Someone stepped into the library, and she immediately recognized Michael Feran—*her father*.

Her heart beat a thick, steady rhythm. She hadn't expected to feel this nervous. She hated that she did. *He* was the one who should be tense. After all, he'd walked out on her.

She hadn't seen him in person in years, but the media had made sure she hadn't forgotten what he looked like. She wished she could dismiss him as a gaunt and lonely gambling addict wallowing in his misery, but he looked... good.

She silently cursed the Feran genes. They'd graced her with the looks and figure that had propelled her to the top in Hollywood, but they also hadn't skipped a generation with Michael Feran. His salt-and-pepper hair made him look distinguished—a candidate for the father role in any big studio blockbuster.

"Chiara." He smiled. "It's wonderful to see you."

She wished she could say the same. Under the circumstances, it was a forced meeting.

At her continued silence, he went on, "I'm glad you wanted to meet with me."

"Rick convinced me that I needed to have this face-to-face meeting."

Michael Feran smiled. "Yes, how is the stuntman?" So her father read the press about her. *Of course.*

"I met him when I came in. Is he a candidate for future son-in-law?"

Chiara was hit with a sudden realization that left her breathless. She was falling for Rick. She had fallen for him. But they'd never discussed making their fake relationship permanent… She pushed aside the thought that had come with staggering clarity because if she dealt with any more emotion right now, she'd overload.

Instead, she forced herself to focus on Michael Feran. "You're creating unwanted publicity."

"I see."

"Why did you talk to that tabloid about me last year?" It was an unforgivable transgression to add to his list of sins.

"Money would be the easy answer."

She waited.

He heaved a sigh. "The hard one is that I wanted your attention."

"Well, you got it." She folded her arms.

She wasn't going to offer him a seat, and she sure wasn't going to sit down herself, despite the fact that Rick had pointed out this room had comfortable chairs. Michael Feran had to understand this was a halfhearted welcome and not an olive branch.

His gray brows drew together. "I probably didn't go about it in the best way. Believe it or not, it was the only time I took money from a reporter."

"Because you needed to pay off your gambling debts," she guessed.

He looked aggrieved. "It was a mistake. One I don't intend to make again."

She was definitely going to see to it that he didn't spill the beans again.

"Usually I'm winning at the card tables. Enough to pay my bills."

"Naturally. It's what matters in life." She couldn't help the tone of heavy sarcasm in her voice. "But you're generating bad press."

"Chiara—"

"Do you have any idea what it meant for a little girl to wake up wondering if her father had bolted again?" she interrupted, even while she didn't know why she was being so forthright. Maybe it was because, without even realizing it, she'd waited years for this opportunity to confront him about his misdeeds. Just as Rick had suggested.

"Chiara, I know I hurt you." Her father paused. "That's why I stopped showing up after you turned five. I thought that not making a sudden appearance was better than hurting you by coming and going."

He made it seem as if he'd done her a favor. She remembered the betting games they'd played when she was young. *I bet I can throw this pebble farther. Race you to the tree, loser is a rotten egg.* Even then Michael Feran hadn't been able to resist a bet. "You left a wife, a child, a home…"

"You don't know what it's like to walk away from a family—"

"I never would."

"—but you get to reinvent yourself with every film role."

"It's acting." First Rick, now her father. Was there no man in her life who could understand she was just pretending? She *liked* acting.

"You can become someone different, follow your dreams…"

Of course, but… She was so *not* going to feel sorry for him.

Michael sobered. "I can't turn back the clock."

She took a deep breath and addressed the elephant in the room. "Why did you leave that first time?"

She'd never asked because posing the question might be interpreted to mean she cared what the answer was. And she'd spent years making sure she didn't care—ignoring Michael Feran, leading her glamorous life and making sure her image stayed polished. Except he kept putting a dent in it.

Her father looked at her for a long moment, and then heaved another sigh. "I was an ambitious musician and I had dreams to follow, or so I thought."

She could relate to the career and the ambition part. Wasn't that what she'd spent her life pursuing? She loved acting…getting to know a character…and, yes, even getting immersed in a role. Except had she ever gotten to know herself—before Rick convinced her to stop and deal with her problems?

"I had some moderate success. We were the opening act for top singers. But I never broke through in the way you have." There was a note of pride in Michael Feran's voice, before he went on, "You're more successful than I was. Maybe…you always wanted to prove you could be more successful."

Again, she was floored by his observation. Had her drive to succeed been motivated by her need to outperform him—the absentee father? She'd never looked at it that way, but in any case she wasn't about to admit anything, so she said aloud, "You don't know me."

Michael Feran's face turned grave. "I don't. I don't know you, but I'd like to."

"As you said, we can't do a rewind."

"No, no, we can't." His face was grave, sad.

"You'd have to clean up your act if we're going to be any sort of family."

Where had that offer come from? But the minute the words were out of her mouth, her father perked up. *Her father.* Looking at his face, the resemblance was undeniable. She saw herself in the texture of his dark hair sprinkled with gray, in the shape of his face...in the slant of his aquiline nose.

Okay, she did feel sorry for him. He'd done very little for her since she was born, but he'd done even less for himself. Maybe it was for the best he hadn't been in her life. She'd been protected from the gambling...drifting... *Ugh.* It sounded just like life in Tinseltown, except she was committed to clean living even if she was based in Hollywood.

"I'd like to try," he said.

"Well, you're going to do more than try this time, you're going to succeed. You're checking into rehab for your gambling addiction." She felt...powerful...in control...*relieved*. She'd been the helpless kid who'd watched him walk away, not knowing when her father would be back, if ever. But this time, she was calling the shots.

She set down her terms. "I'm prepared to offer you a deal. You get into a facility to help with your problem and agree to stop making headlines. In return, I'll cover your living expenses. The deal will be in writing, and you'll sign."

She had Rick to thank for that bit of inspiration. After their last sexual encounter, they'd sat in her garden and watched the sun set. He'd revealed himself to be more than a lover. He'd shown himself to be a partner and skilled negotiator who'd helped her come up with a plan for this meeting.

"And if I relapse?" There was a hint of vulnerability in her father's eyes that she hadn't expected.

"Then back to rehab you go…for as long as it takes."

He relaxed into a smile. "That's a gamble I'm willing to take."

"Because you have no choice."

"Because I want to improve if that means having a relationship with you, Chiara." As if he sensed she might argue, he continued in a rush, "It's too late for me to help raise you, but I hope we…can be family."

Family. Wasn't that what she'd yearned for when she'd been around the Serenghettis? And now here was her *father* offering the ties that bind. Choked up by emotion, she cleared her throat. "Fine, it's a role I'm willing to take on, but I'm putting you on notice, I expect an Oscar-worthy performance from you as a family member getting a second chance."

An unguarded look of hope crossed her father's face before he responded gruffly, "I have faith that the acting gene runs in the family."

Trouble for Chiara Feran and Her New Man? Sources Close to the Couple Admit That Blending Two Careers Is Causing Stress.

Chiara looked up from her cell phone screen and at Odele's expectant gaze. Her manager was clearly waiting to hear what Chiara thought about the web site that she'd told her to pull up.

They were sitting sipping coffee in the Novatus Studio commissary. Chiara had met Rick here earlier, where postproduction work had begun on *Pegasus Pride*. As an actress, she wasn't involved in picture and sound editing, but since Rick was a producer on this film, she'd tagged along when he'd said he was interested in checking in with Dan to see how things were going. Afterward, she'd made her way to the commissary to wait for Odele, so they could discuss business.

"Well, what do you think?" Odele asked in her raspy voice, nodding to the cell phone still clutched in Chiara's hand.

"You fed this story to *Gossipmonger*?"

Odele nodded. "I needed a way to hint at a possible end to your dalliance with Rick now that your father is going to rehab, while still keeping you in the public eye."

"I'm still wrapping my head around the fact that you didn't know Rick was a wealthy producer!"

Her manager shrugged. "He's a wily one, I'll admit. I thought I knew everyone in this town, but I guess I can be forgiven for not being acquainted with every silent investor in a film production company. Once you told me about the pile that he built in Beverly Hills, I realized I should have had him on my radar, though, I'll give you that."

"We don't need to rush to bring the ax down on the Chiara-Rick story, do we?" Chiara set down her phone, her heart heavy.

Odele was right. She no longer had to worry about her father making bad headlines, and she had Rick to thank for helping to engineer the resolution to that situation. It also meant she no longer *needed* Rick. Wasn't the entire purpose of their fake relationship to divert attention from her father's negative publicity?

Odele gave her a keen look. "No rush…but planning ahead wouldn't hurt, sweetie. Drop a few suggestions in the press that all might not be happily-ever-after. So when the story does end, it won't seem abrupt and it'll be a soft blow."

For whom? Chiara stifled the question even though she couldn't tell if Odele was referring to the hit to her or to her public image. Did it matter? The two were intertwined. She and Rick weren't a *relationship*, after all, but a *story*.

Chiara worried her bottom lip with her teeth. "Has Rick seen this headline?"

Odele adjusted her glasses. "Of course. I ran into him earlier when you'd momentarily left his side. He knows the script. He's known it from the beginning."

Chiara blanched and glanced down at her coffee cup. So he had seen it, and judging from Odele's expression, it hadn't ruffled him. He knew the bargain they'd struck.

Chiara squared her shoulders, seeing with clarity the road ahead—the path that had been there from the beginning. If she made the first move for a clean break, it didn't even have to damage Rick's reputation. She was familiar with how these things worked. A face-saving explanation would be issued. She could even see the headline: *Snow White and Prince Charming Go Their Separate Ways.*

She was doing Rick a favor. He'd never wanted to be tied to an actress…a *celebrity*. He could take his bow and retreat behind the curtain to his nice quiet life—on his large estate in LA. She was being fair.

But the two of them definitely needed to talk. *Soon. Right now.* Before she fell apart…or at least deeper into the warm cocoon of their relationship, where it was *her love* and his…*what*? He'd never come close to saying he loved her. Her heart squeezed and she blinked against a sudden swell of emotion.

She was a highly rated actress—she could do this.

She had sudden flashes from interludes in his arms.

They'd been wonderful…but there'd been no promise of forever, and tomorrow started today. The next chapter.

Chiara looked at her watch. Rick was supposed to meet her here when he was done. And now she had more than enough to say to him…

She forced herself to continue her conversation with Odele, but twenty minutes later when her manager left to make her next meeting, Chiara was relieved…and then nervous as she waited for Rick to show up.

After a quarter of an hour, he walked in, looking casual…relaxed…happy. And as attractive as ever in gray pants and a white shirt.

Chiara swallowed when he gave her a quick peck on the lips.

He sat down across from her at the small table and then lounged back in his chair.

"How did your meeting with Dan end?" she asked brightly.

"Fine. The editor showed up and we discussed plans for the rough cut." He cracked a grin. "Dan's grateful to you for not needing many retakes and keeping us on schedule. Everything's looking great, and with any luck, the box office receipts will reflect it."

They talked about the postproduction work for a few more minutes. Then when the conversation reached a lull, she jumped in and said, "So you must be relieved." He looked at her quizzically, and she shrugged. "Odele's latest planted story in the press."

"I don't give a damn about Odele's PR moves."

His words surprised her, but then hadn't he always been anti-publicity?

"Okay, but we need to talk—" she wet her lips "—because the reason we got together as a couple no longer exists."

She willed him to…what? Get down on bended knee and pledge his eternal love? She'd said all along that she didn't believe in fairy tales.

She smiled tentatively. "Thank you for helping me resolve the impasse with my father. He loves your idea of the two of us partnering to combat his gambling addiction." Her expression turned wry. "Odele likes it, too, of course. She thinks it would be a good way to turn a negative story into a positive one. I could even take it on as a charitable cause."

Rick inclined his head but looked guarded. "Okay, yeah."

"But now that the problem with my father is gone," she said, taking a deep breath, "we no longer have to continue this farce."

Had she really said *farce*? She'd meant to say…

Rick's expression hardened. "Right."

"You disagree?"

He leaned in. "You're still that little girl who is afraid of being abandoned—of someone walking out on her again."

"Please, I know where you're going with this is, and it's not true." It wasn't abandonment she was scared of. She was a grown woman who feared she'd have her heart broken. *Her heart was broken*—because she was in love with Rick and he steered clear of actresses.

Still, wasn't his keen perception what she liked about him? Loved? Yes, *loved*—in addition to his humor, intelligence and daring. They were qualities that appealed to different sides of her personality, even if they made her uncomfortable and yes, infuriated her sometimes.

"What about your overeager admirer?" Rick demanded.

"That's my problem to deal with."

"And mine."

She furrowed her brow. "What do you mean?"

"I mean my role here wasn't solely to play boyfriend but to make sure you stayed safe."

Her eyes narrowed. "Odele hired you?"

"She didn't need to hire me. Do you know how much money I have invested in *Pegasus Pride*? Keeping the main talent safe was inducement enough."

She felt his words like a blow to the chest. All those lingering touches, kisses, and his motivation had been... "You lied to me."

"Not really. You knew I was primarily a fake boyfriend."

"And secondarily a rat."

He raised his eyebrows. "You're offended because I may have had ulterior motives, too, in this game of ours?"

Yes, it had been a game. She was the fool for forgetting that. "I'm annoyed for not being told the whole truth. At least I was clear about my motivations."

"Yes, and you're determined not to rely on any man, aren't you?"

"Was Odele in on this?" she countered.

He shrugged. "We might have had a conversation about how it was in everyone's interest for me to keep an eye on you."

"Everyone's interest but mine," she said bitterly.

Rick set his jaw. "It was in your best interest, too, though you're too pigheaded to admit it."

Her heart constricted. Had he meant those things he'd whispered in the heat of passion—or had she run into the biggest actor of all? Even now, the urge to touch him was almost irresistible.

How had this conversation gotten very serious and very bad so fast? She'd wanted to talk about their charade and give him an out that she hoped he *wouldn't* take. Instead, she was left deflated and wondering whether she'd ever understood him.

Still, she rallied and lifted her chin. "You should be glad I'm setting you free. We never talked about forever, and you don't like fame. You don't want to be dating an actress, even if it's pretend." Two could play at this game. If he was going to cast her as another high-maintenance starlet, albeit one with an aversion to vulnerability where men were concerned, then she could portray him as camera-shy and hung up on celebrity.

He firmed his jaw but took a while to answer. "You're right. Fame isn't my thing." He raked a hand through his hair. "I should have learned that lesson with Isabel."

Chiara held back a wince. In some ways, she understood. The last thing some stars' egos could handle was to be cast in someone else's shade. There were A-list celebrities who refused to date other A-list celebrities for that very reason. Still, it rankled. She was not some random fame-seeker. If she couldn't fall in love with a celebrity, and an anonymous civilian would be put off her fame, who was left? Did she have to settle for a brief interlude with a stuntman with hidden layers? Was that all there was for her?

She lifted her chin, willing it to hold firm. "It's probably best if you moved out at this point. We could do with some space." Then she decided to echo Odele. "It'll plant the seeds for when our breakup is announced."

Rick's expression tightened. "Can't forget to spin it for the press, right?"

Ten

Chiara looked in her bathroom mirror. It had been a month since her breakup with Rick. A sad, depressing but uneventful month...*until now.*

She looked down at the stick in her hand. There was no mistaking the two telltale lines. Two lines that were about to change her life. She was pregnant.

The irony wasn't lost on her. She'd been wrestling with how to combine a career with her desire to start a family. Now the decision had been made for her.

As she disposed of the stick in the bathroom's waste-paper basket, she thought back to the last time she and Rick had been intimate—and her mind whirled.

She'd recently discovered that she'd expelled her contraceptive ring. It had probably gotten dislodged during rigorous sex, and then gone down the toilet afterward without her knowing it. Preoccupied with her breakup with Rick, she hadn't dwelled too much on it. But now...

Chiara looked at herself in the bathroom mirror as she washed her hands. She didn't look any different—*yet*.

She'd spent years trying not to be pregnant. She had a career to tend.

But while it wasn't the best of circumstances, it wasn't the worst, either. *A baby.* She was in her early thirties, financially independent, and had an established career. She'd always wanted a child, and in fact had started worrying that she couldn't see how it was going to happen. It had finally come to pass, but in a way she hadn't planned or foreseen. She'd been drawn to the Serenghettis, and now she was pregnant with an addition to the family. If things had been different—if Rick had loved her—she'd have been overjoyed right now instead of shadowed with worry. Still, she let giddiness seep through her. *A baby.*

She walked into her bedroom and sat on the bed, taking a calming breath. Then she picked up the phone receiver, toyed with it and replaced it. She had to tell Rick, of course…but she just needed time to process the information herself first. This wasn't avoidance or procrastination. At least that's what she kept telling herself…

She got up, paced, went downstairs to poke around in her fridge and then came upstairs again to stare at her phone.

When she couldn't stand it any longer, she called Odele and spilled all to her manager.

Odele was surprisingly equanimous at the news.

"Don't you know this means I'll be too pregnant to take on another action movie?" Chiara demanded, because she knew career suicide was at the top of Odele's list of sins.

"You wanted to stop doing them anyway."

Chiara lowered her shoulders. "Yes, you're right."

"What was Rick's reaction?"

"I haven't told him yet. I've been working up to that part."

There was a long pause on the line as Odele processed this information. "Well, good luck, honey. And remember, it's best to eat the frog."

"We fairy-tale types are supposed to kiss them, not eat them," Chiara joked weakly. "But okay, I get your point about doing the hard stuff first and getting it over with."

"Exactly."

"I just…" She took a deep breath. "I'm not sure I'm prepared to make that call to Rick." *Just yet.*

"I'm always here to help."

"Thanks, Odele."

The next day, Chiara wasn't feeling calm exactly, but she'd come down from her crazy tumult of emotions. She ventured out to her doctor's office for a consultation, having gotten herself an early appointment after there was a cancellation.

She didn't go into detail with the staff on the phone. She knew how juicy a piece of gossip a pregnant actress was, and medical staff had been known for leaks despite confidentiality laws. Out of an abundance of caution, she wore sunglasses and a scarf when she showed up for her appointment—because the paparazzi also knew that staking out the offices of doctors to the stars was a great way to get a scoop, or at least a tantalizing photo.

Dr. Phyllia Tribbling confirmed she was pregnant and assured her that everything was fine. She told her to come back when she was a few weeks further along.

Chiara found she was calmer after the doctor's visit, no doubt due to the obstetrician's soothing manner.

She spent the rest of the day researching pregnancy

online. She didn't dare visit a bookstore—and certainly not a baby store—because of the risk of being spotted by the press. Instead, she stayed home and took a nap. She should have read the signs in her unusual weariness lately, but pregnancy had been the last thing on her mind.

When she woke late in the day, she checked herself for any sign of morning sickness, but didn't feel a twinge. With the all-clear, she fixed herself a salad and a glass of water. Walking into the den, she sat on the sofa and placed the food on a coffee table.

After a few bites, she scrolled through the day's news on her phone.

When she came across a headline about herself, it took her a moment to process it, but then she nearly collapsed against the cushions.

Chiara Feran Is Pregnant!

She scanned the article and reread it, and then with shaking fingers, called her manager.

"Odele," she gasped. "How did *Gossipmonger* get this info?"

"They probably saw you exiting the doctor's office, sweetie," Odele said calmly. "You know, paparazzi like to stalk the offices of celebrity gynecologists and obstetricians."

"I just got back! Not even the gossip sites operate that fast." Chiara shook her head, even though her manager wasn't there to see it. "I should have worn a wig."

"I don't think that would have done the trick," Odele said drily. "Now, not getting knocked up to begin with, that would have done it."

Chiara's eyes narrowed. "You didn't feed them this story, did you?"

"No."

"But did you slip someone a tip to watch the doctor's office?" Chiara pressed.

"You have a suspicious mind."

"Did you?"

"I might have mentioned Dr. Tribbling has seen a lot of business lately."

"Odele, how could you!"

"Why don't you call Mr. Stuntman and let him know he isn't shooting blanks?" Odele answered sweetly.

"Why?" Chiara was close to wailing. She'd done it enough times on-screen to know when she was nearing the top of the emotional roller coaster.

"Better to squelch the rumor fast that you've broken up with Rick. Otherwise we'll be putting out fires for months. The press loves a story about a spurned pregnant woman going it alone."

Chiara took a breath. "Rick and I are broken up. Period."

"Not as far as the press is concerned. They're going to love stringing your two names together in real and virtual ink."

"And that's the only thing that matters, right?"

"No…it isn't." Odele sighed, softening. "Why don't you talk to him? Then reality and public perception can be aligned."

Chiara steeled herself and took a deep gulping breath. "Odele, you're fired."

They were words she'd never thought she'd say, but she'd had enough of manipulation…of public scrutiny… of Hollywood…and yes, of one stuntman in particular.

"Sweetie, you're overwrought, and it can't be good for the baby. Take time to think about it."

"Goodbye, Odele."

Yes, she'd calm down…right after she burst into tears.

* * *

Rick spit out his morning coffee. The hot liquid hit the oatmeal bowl like so many chocolate chips dotting cookie batter.

He prided himself on being unflappable. A cool head and calm nerves were a must in stunt work, particularly when something unexpected happened. But as with everything concerning Chiara, levelheadedness walked out the door with his better judgment.

He looked around his West Hollywood rental, still his home since Chiara had canceled his roommate privileges and his Beverly Hills place wasn't finished. The rain hitting the windows suited his mood. Or rather, it fit the rest of his life, which stretched out in a dull gray line in front of him. He got the same adrenaline rush from being with Chiara as he did from stunts, which probably explained the colorlessness of his days since their breakup.

Except now... *Chiara was pregnant.*

Rick was seized by turns with elation and shock. A baby. His and Chiara's. He was going to be a father.

Of course he wanted kids. He'd just never given much thought to how it would happen. He was thirty-three and at some point he'd be too old for stunt work. Sometime between now and then, his life would transition to something different. He figured he'd meet a woman, get married and have kids. Except along the way, he'd never foreseen a fake relationship with a maddening starlet who would then turn up pregnant.

Suddenly someday was now...and it wasn't supposed to happen this way—knocking up an actress tethered to fame when they weren't even married, living together or talking about forever.

Chiara infuriated and amused him by turns, the combustible passion between them feeding on itself. They were good together. Hell, he'd thought things had been heading to…something. But never mind. She'd made it clear he'd served his purpose and now there was no role for him in her life.

Now, though, whether she liked it or not, he had a place. She was pregnant.

He wondered whether this announcement was a public relations ploy, and then dismissed the idea. Chiara had too much integrity. He knew that much even though they were no longer a couple.

Still, she hadn't had the decency to tell him, and his family would be reading the news online and in print, just like everyone else. Her handlers hadn't yet sent out a second volley in this juicy story, but already he was looking like a jerk. *He just broke up with her, and now his ex-girlfriend has announced she's pregnant.* That's what everyone would think. *Maybe he left her because there was a surprise baby.*

There was one thing to do—and he wasn't waiting for an invitation. He still had the passcode to Chiara's front gate, unless she'd changed it.

Rick got his wallet, keys and phone, and then made a line for the door. He'd woken up this morning moody and out of sorts—more or less par for the course for him since his breakup with Chiara, but that was even before realizing he'd been served up as delicious gossipy dish for his neighbors to consume along with their morning coffee.

He cursed. "Moody" had just given way to "flaming-hot pissed off."

He made record time on the way to Chiara's house, adrenaline pumping in his veins. He knew from experience working on stunts that he was operating on a full head of steam. He needed to force himself to take a breath, slow down, collect his thoughts… *Hell.*

A baby. And she hadn't told him.

When he got to Chiara's front gate, rationality returned enough for him to pause a moment and call her from his cell. The last thing he needed was for Chiara to assume her surprise visitor was her stalker.

"It's Rick, and I'm coming in," he announced when she picked up, and then hit the end button without waiting for a response.

When he got to the house, the front door was unlocked and he let himself in.

He found Chiara in the kitchen, dressed in an oversize sweater and leggings, a mug in one hand.

His gaze went to her midriff, before traveling back to her face. Not that she would be showing yet—but she did look weary, as if she hadn't slept well. He resisted the urge to stride over and wrap her in his arms.

"I assume you unlocked the door for me when I called from the gate and that you don't have a standing invitation for your overeager fan to walk in." It was a mild reproach, much less than he wanted to say.

She set the mug down. "What do you think?"

"You're *pregnant*." The last word reverberated through the room like the sound of a brass bell.

Chiara blanched.

"I found out the news with the rest of the world."

"I didn't have time to call you first." She wrung her hands. "The story broke so fast."

"You could have called me when the pregnancy test came back positive."

She hugged her midriff with her arms. "I wanted to be sure. I only went to the doctor yesterday."

"How did this happen?" he asked bluntly.

She raised her eyebrows. "I think you know."

"Right." *Mind-blowing sex.*

"My contraceptive ring accidentally fell out, and I didn't notice. I didn't give it much thought when I realized what happened." She shrugged. "I've always wanted kids. I guess it's happening sooner than I anticipated."

A very real sense of relief washed over him at her words. She wanted this baby, but birth control failure had led to very real consequences for the both of them. "You're going to announce we're still together."

She blinked. "Why?"

"Why? Because I don't want to look like a first-class jerk in front of the world, that's why."

"That your reason?" She appeared bewildered and a flash of hurt crossed her face.

"Aren't you the one who has been all about public image until now?" he tossed back. "Maybe this pregnancy is another PR stunt."

She dropped her arms, her expression turning shocked and offended. *"What?"*

"Are you saying Odele didn't plant the story in *Gossipmonger*?"

"I didn't know anything about it!"

He let another wave of satisfaction wash over him before he turned all-business. "Anyway, it doesn't matter. We're going to start acting and pretending like we never have before—the happy couple expecting a bundle of joy."

She lifted her chin. "I don't need your help."

He knew Chiara had the resources, but that was beside the point. "Sweetheart," he drawled, making the endearment sound ironic, "whether you want it or not, you've got it."

"Or?"

"Odele will be needing medication to deal with the ugly media firestorm."

"And will a wedding in Vegas follow?" she asked sarcastically. "I'll need to put Odele on retainer again."

"Whatever works."

She threw up her hands. "It's ridiculous. How long do you plan for this to go on?"

Until he figured out his next steps. He was buying himself time. "Until I don't look like a loser who abandoned his girlfriend the minute she turned up pregnant."

Rick paced in the nearly empty library of his multi-million-dollar new home. Raking his fingers through his hair, he stared out the French doors at the blazing sunshine bathing his new property in light. He'd just met with a landscaper and walked over the grounds. This morning, his appointment had been uppermost in his mind...until he'd checked the news.

Still, what was it all for? He'd bought and renovated this house as a keen investor...but now it felt insignificant. Because what really mattered in his life was half a city away. *Pregnant. With his baby.*

His gaze settled on the two upholstered armchairs. He'd brokered a cease-fire and even a rapprochement between Chiara and her father, but he couldn't figure out how to dig himself out of a hole—except by muscling in on Chiara earlier and ordering her to get back together until he figured things out. But then what?

His cell phone buzzed, and he fished it out of his pocket.

"Rick." Camilla Serenghetti's voice sounded loud and clear.

Rick hadn't even bothered to look at who was calling. He hadn't had a chance to figure out what to say to his family, but it was showtime.

"I read I'm going to be a grandma, but I know it can't be true. My son would have told me such happy news."

Of course.

"I told Paula at the hairdresser, 'No, no, don't listen to *Gossipmonger*. I know the truth.'" Pause. "Right?"

Rick raked a hand through his hair. "I just found out myself, Mom."

His mother muttered something in Italian. "So it is true? *Congratulazioni*. I can't believe it. First Cole has a surprise wedding. Now you have a surprise baby."

"You still have Jordan and Mia to count on." His remaining siblings might go a more traditional route.

"No, no. I'm happy...*happy* about the baby." His mother sounded emotional. "But no more surprises. *Basta*—enough, okay?"

"I'd like nothing better," he muttered, because he'd gotten the shock of his life today.

When he got off the phone, he texted his siblings.

The gossip is true, hang tight.

He knew he had to deal with stamping out questions— or at least holding them off—until he figured things out. Before he could put away his cell, though, his phone rang again.

"Rick."

"What can I do for you?" Rick recognized the voice, and under the circumstances, Chiara's father was the last person he wanted to have a conversation with. Michael Feran had his number from when he'd helped broker the meeting with Chiara, but he'd never expected the older man to use it.

"This is an odd request."

"Spit it out." The words came out more harshly than Rick intended, but it had already been a hell of a day.

Michael Feran cleared his throat. "I can't get in touch with Chiara."

Great. "What did you do, Michael?"

"Nothing. I called her at eleven, when we'd agreed to talk."

Rick knew Chiara had opted to periodically touch base with her father now that she was paying his bills.

"No one answered."

"I was heading out, and I'm not far from her house. I'll swing by." He didn't examine his motives. Michael Feran had given him another excuse to see Chiara, and maybe this time they could have a more satisfactory meeting—one that didn't end with her turning away and him walking out.

Besides, she was pregnant. His gut tightened. She could really be in trouble.

"Good." An edge of relief sounded in the older man's voice. "And I understand congratulations are in order."

"To you, too."

"Thank you. I just got an invite to be a father again. I didn't expect being a *grandfather* to be part of the bargain. At least not so soon."

"I'm sure," Rick replied curtly. "But one thing at a time. I'll go check on the mother-to-be now."

After ending the call, Rick made for the front door. For the second time that day, he found himself racing to Chiara's house, adrenaline thrumming through his veins.

She was fine. She had to be fine. She was probably dealing with pregnancy symptoms and in no mood to talk to her father. In the meantime, he might have another opportunity to set things to rights between them.

Marry me. The words popped into his head without thought, but of course they were the right ones. Right, natural…logical.

Exiting his house, he got behind the wheel of his Range Rover for the drive to Brentwood. Fortunately, traffic was light, and he reached Chiara's house faster than he expected.

When he reached her front gate, he tried calling her again. And when she didn't answer, he stabbed in the security code, jaw tightening.

Moments later, he pulled up in front of Chiara's house and saw her car parked there. His gut clenched. *Why isn't she answering her phone?*

Noticing the patio door open at the side of the house, he strode toward it…and then froze for a second when he realized there was broken glass on the ground.

Stepping inside the house, he could sense someone was there. Then he saw a man reflected in a mirror down the hall. The intruder crouched and ducked into the next room.

Rick's blood pumped as he raced forward. Damn it, he'd be lucky if this was an ordinary street burglar. But the brief glimpse he'd caught said this guy resembled Chiara's stalker.

Chiara came out of the marble bath in her bedroom suite and then walked into the dressing room. She pulled underwear and exercise clothes from a dresser and slipped into them.

In order to help her relax, she'd just taken a shower— and intended to take another after her workout. Her doctor had cleared her for moderate exercise in her first trimester.

After her argument with Rick earlier, she'd been torn

between wanting to cry and to wail in frustration. Her life had been a series of detours and blind turns lately...

She went downstairs to her home gym, and then glanced out the window at the overcast day. It suited her mood. Even the weather seemed ready to shed some tears...

Suddenly she spotted a hunched figure darting across the lawn. Frowning, she moved closer to the window. She wasn't expecting anyone. She had a regular cleaning service, and a landscaper who came once a week, but she didn't employ a live-in caretaker. There was no reason to, since she was often away on a movie set herself. Still, thanks to her fame, and now a sometime stalker, she had high fences, video cameras, an alarm system and a front gate with a security code. Even if she no longer had a bodyguard...

How had he gotten in?

As Chiara watched, the intruder slipped around the side of the house and out of view. Moments later, she heard a crash and froze. She ran over to the exercise room door and locked it.

Spinning around, she realized how vulnerable she was. Her workout clothes didn't have pockets, and she'd left her cell phone upstairs. She'd also never put a landline extension in this room, because there'd seemingly been no need to. The gym was on the first floor and faced a steep embankment outside. While it would be hard for someone to get in, it also meant she was trapped.

She heard the distant noise of someone moving around in the house. Her best bet was to stay quiet. She hoped whoever it was wouldn't look in here—at least not immediately. In the meantime, she had to figure out what to do... If the intruder wandered upstairs, perhaps she could make a dash for freedom and quietly call 911.

She heard the sound of a car on the gravel drive and almost sobbed with relief. Whoever it was must have known the security code at the front gate. Her heart jumped to her throat. *Rick?*

He didn't know about the intruder. He could be hurt, or worse, killed. She had to warn him.

Only a minute later, voices—angry and male—sounded in the house, but the confrontation was too indistinct for her to make out what was said.

"Chiara, if you're here, don't move!" Rick's voice came to her from the rear of the house.

She heard a scuffle. Something crashed as the combatants seemed to be fighting their way across the first floor.

Ignoring Rick's order, she wrenched open the door to the exercise room and dashed out in the direction of the noise. The sight that confronted her in the den made her heart leap to her throat all over again. Rick was pummeling Todd Jeffers, and while Rick appeared to have the upper hand, his opponent wasn't giving up the fight.

She looked around for a way to help and found herself reaching for a small marble sculpture that her interior decorator had positioned on a side table.

Grabbing it, she approached the two men. As her stalker staggered and then righted himself, she brought the sculpture down on the back of his head with a resounding thud.

Jeffers staggered again and fell to his knees, and Rick landed a knee jab under his chin. Her stalker sprawled backward, and then lay motionless.

Rick finally looked up at her. He was breathing heavily, and there was fire in his eyes. "Damn it, Chiara, I told you not to come out!"

As scared as she was, she had her own temper to deal

with. "You're welcome." Then she looked at the figure at their feet. "Sweet heaven, did I kill him?"

"Heaven is unlikely the place he'll be," Rick snarled.

"So I killed him?" she squeaked.

Rick bent to examine Jeffers and then shook his head. "No, but he's passed out cold."

She leaped for the phone even though what she wanted to do was throw up from sudden nausea. "I have to call 911."

"Do you have any rope or something else we can tie him up with?" Rick asked. "He's unconscious but we don't know for how long."

With shaky fingers, she handed him the receiver. While Rick called the police, she ran to get some twine she kept for wrapping presents. Her uninvited guest needed to be hog-tied, not decorated with a pretty bow, but it was all she had.

As she passed through the house, she noticed some picture frames had been repositioned—as if her stalker had stopped to admire them—and some of her clothes had been moved. Chiara shuddered. Likely Jeffers's obsession with her stuff had bought her time—time enough to stay hidden in the gym until Rick arrived.

Eleven

Chiara sat in her den attempting to get her bearings. Todd Jeffers was on his way to prison, not least because he'd violated a restraining order by scaling her fence, taking advantage of the fact that her alarm system had been off and she'd been ignoring the video cameras. Breaking and entering, trespassing… Thanks to Rick, the police would throw the book at him.

While Rick walked the remaining police to the door, she called Odele. She needed someone who would deal with the inevitable press attention. And even though she'd uttered the words *you're fired*, she and Odele were like family—and there was nothing like a brush with danger and violence to mend fences. She filled in her manager on what had happened, and Odele announced she would drive right over—both to get the fuller story, and perhaps because she sensed Chiara needed a shoulder to lean on.

Because Rick wasn't offering one—he continued to look mad as hell.

She knew she was lucky Rick had shown up at the right moment. She'd been in the shower when her father had attempted to reach her, and because he was worried she hadn't picked up, he'd called Rick. Michael Feran had done nothing for her...until today, when he may have saved her life. The ground beneath her had shifted, and there hadn't even been a major seismological event in LA. Forgetting about her scheduled call with her father had been a lucky break because minutes later she'd had an intruder in her house.

When Rick walked back in, Chiara hugged her arms tight across her chest as she sat on her couch.

He looked like a man on a short leash. The expression on his face was one she'd never seen before—not even in the middle of a difficult stunt. He was furious, and she wondered how much of it was directed at her.

"Thanks," she managed in a small voice.

"Damn it, Chiara!" Rick ran his hand through his hair. "What the hell? I told you to get extra security."

"You were it. I didn't have time to replace you...yet."

"You didn't have time? There's been a court order in place for weeks!"

She stood up. "Sarcastic stuntmen willing to moonlight as bodyguard and pretend boyfriend are hard to come by."

"Well, you almost gained an unwelcome husband!" Rick braced his hands at his sides. "According to the police, your Romeo had picked a wedding date and drafted a marriage announcement before he showed up today."

Chiara felt the hairs on the back of her neck rise. As a celebrity, she'd gotten some overzealous adulation in the past, but this was beyond creepy. "Don't lecture me."

She was frustrated, overwhelmed and tired—nearly shaking with shock and fear. She needed comfort but Rick was scolding her. It was all too much.

Rick crouched beside her. "We need to resolve this."

She raised her chin. "My stalker is behind bars. So that's another reason I don't need you anymore, I guess."

Except she did. She loved him. But he'd offered nothing in return, and she couldn't stay in a relationship based on an illusion. She'd learned this much from Tinseltown: she didn't want make-believe. She didn't want a relationship made for the press, and the false image of a happy couple expecting their first child. She wanted true love.

Rick stood up, a closed look on his face. He thrust his hands in his pockets. "Right, you don't need me. You'll never need any man. Got it. Your father may be back in your life, but you always stand on your own."

She said nothing. In her mind, though, she willed him to give her the speech that she really wanted. *I love you. I can't live without you. I need you.*

He braced his hands on his sides. "We're stuck playing out this drama, the two of us. The press junket for *Pegasus Pride* is coming up, and we don't want to be the story instead of the movie. I'll move back in with you here until my house is ready. We'll do promo for the movie and then nest until the baby arrives. All the while, we're back to Chiara and Rick, the happy expectant couple, as far as the press is concerned."

She lifted her chin again. "Got it."

The only thing that saved her from saying more was Odele breezing in the front door and descending like a mother hen.

"Oh, honey," her manager exclaimed.

Chiara looked at her miserably and then eyed Rick.

"I'm glad you're here because Rick was just leaving to pack. He's moving back in with me."

"I'll be back soon."

She'd dreamed about their getting back together, but it wasn't supposed to happen like this.

Rick looked around his West Hollywood rental, debating what to pack next. The movers could do the rest.

Chiara's stalker may have been arrested, but the threat to Rick's own sanity remained very real. He'd always prided himself on being Mr. Cool and Unflappable—with nerves of steel in the face of every stunt. But there was nothing cool about his relationship with Chiara.

"So the first Serenghetti grandbaby, and it was a surprise." Jordan shook his head as he taped a box together. "Mom must be beside herself."

His brother happened to be in town for another personal appearance, so he'd come over to help Rick pack. Together, they were surrounded by boxes in the small living room.

"Last I heard, she was trying three new recipes." Rick knew cooking was stress relief for his mother.

Damn it, he wished the news had broken another way. Yet, if Chiara was to be believed, it wasn't her doing that the cat was out of the bag.

Jordan shook his head. "Of course Mom is cooking. First Cole throws an unexpected wedding, now you hit her with a surprise grandchild. She's probably trying to figure out what went wrong with her parenting recipe—was she missing an ingredient?"

"Hilarious," Rick remarked drily. "She's got two more kids she can hang her hopes on."

Jordan held up his hands as if warding off a bad omen. "You mean, she has Mia to help her out."

Rick shrugged. "Whatever."

His brother looked around. "You know we could just throw this stuff in a van ourselves instead of using movers."

"Yeah, but I've got more pressing problems at the moment."

Jordan cocked his head. "Oh, yeah, daddy duty. But that doesn't start for another…?"

"Seven months or more," Rick replied shortly.

Chiara had gotten pregnant in Welsdale or soon after. There'd been plenty of opportunities. Once the floodgates had opened, they hadn't been able to keep their hands off each other.

"You know, I was debating what housewarming gift to get you. Now I'm thinking you need one of those dolls they use in parenting classes…to practice diapering and stuff."

"Thanks for the vote of confidence."

"Well, you and Chiara are definitely in the express lane of relationships," Jordan remarked.

"The relationship was a media and publicity stunt."

Jordan's face registered his surprise. "Wow, the work of a stuntman never ends. I'm impressed by your range."

"Put a lid on it, Jordan."

His brother flashed a grin. "Still, a publicity stunt… but Chiara winds up pregnant? How do you explain that one?"

"I was also supposed to protect her from her stalker friend. That was the real part."

Jordan picked up his beer and toasted him with it. "Well, you did do that. I suppose one thing led to another?"

"Yeah, but it could have gone better." The nut job had

already been in Chiara's house when he'd arrived. As for the relationship part...

"Or worse."

Rick's hand curled at his side. Damn it. Why hadn't Chiara listened to him and taken more precautions? Because she was hardheaded.

Jordan shook his head. "I can't believe I had to get the news from *Gossipmonger*."

"Believe it. Chiara's team has a contact there."

"Still, I figured I'd hear it from you. I thought the brotherly bond counted for something," Jordan said in a bemused tone.

"You didn't need to know it was a publicity stunt."

His brother shrugged. "It seemed real enough to me. So what are you going to do?"

"For the moment, I'm moving back in with her. What does it look like I'm doing?"

Jordan nodded, his expression blank. "So you're muscling back into her life. Do you know an approach besides caveman-style?"

"Since when are you a relationship expert?"

"This calls for a grand gesture."

Rick nearly snorted. "She's practically announced she doesn't need a knight on a horse."

Jordan shrugged. "She doesn't need you, you don't need her, but you want each other. Maybe that's what you have to show her." His brother's lips quirked. "You know, upend the fairy tale. Show up on a horse and tell her that she needs to save you."

Rick frowned. "From what?"

Jordan grinned. "Yourself. You've been bad-tempered and cranky."

"So says the Serenghetti family philosopher who only does shallow relationships."

Jordan placed his hand over his heart. "My guru powers only work with others."

Rick threw a towel at his brother, who caught it deftly. "Get packing."

Still, he had to admit Jordan had given him some ideas.

"You look like a miserable pregnant lady," Odele remarked.

"My best role yet." Chiara felt like a mess...or rather, her life was one. Ironically the situation with her father was the only part she'd straightened out.

After yesterday's drama, Odele had stayed over, feeling Chiara needed someone in the house with her. And Chiara was thankful for the support. She'd let herself cry just once...

Chiara toyed with her lunch of salmon and fresh fruit. Outside the breakfast nook, the sun shone bright, so unlike yesterday. Her mood should have picked up, too, but instead she'd been worried about spending the next months with Rick in her house—falling apart with need, so unlike her independent self.

"I hate to see you make a mistake," Odele remarked from across the table.

Was that regret in her manager's voice? "You sound wistful."

"I'm speaking from experience. There was one who got away. Don't let that be your situation."

"Oh, Odele."

"Don't *Odele* me," her manager said in her raspy voice. "These days there's a fifty-three-year-old editor at one of those supermarket rags who is just waiting for a date with yours truly."

Chiara managed a small laugh. "Now, that's more like it."

Odele's eyes gleamed. "He's too young for me."

"At fiftysomething? It's about time someone snatched him out of the cradle."

"I'll think about it…but this conversation isn't about me, honey. It's about you."

Chiara sighed. "So how am I supposed to avoid making a mistake? Or are you going to tell me?"

"I've got an idea. You and Rick are meant to be together. I've thought so for a long time." She shook her head. "That's why—"

"This pregnancy is a sign from the heavens?"

"No, your moping expression is."

Chiara set down her fork. "I guess I'm not as good an actress as I thought."

"You're a great actress, and I've lined up Melody Banyon at *WE Magazine*. She can come here for an interview tomorrow." Her manager harrumphed. "My second attempt at making you and Rick see reason."

"Another of your schemes, Odele?" she said, and then joked, "Haven't we had enough of the press?"

"Trust me, you're going to like this plan better than my idea of lighting a fire under your stuntman with the pregnancy news, but it's up to you what you want to say."

When Odele explained what she had in mind, Chiara nodded and then added her own twist…

By the next morning, Chiara was both nervous and excited. She felt as if she was jumping off a cliff—in fact, it was not so different from doing a movie stunt.

Sitting in a chair in her den facing Melody Banyon, she smoothed her hands down the legs of her slacks. It was

almost a replay of her last interview with the reporter...
except Rick wasn't here.

"Are you pregnant?"

There it was. She was about to give her confirmation
to the world. "Yes, I am."

"Congratulations."

"I'm still in my first trimester."

"And how are you feeling?"

Chiara sucked in a shaky breath. "Good. A little
queasy but that's normal."

Melody tilted her head and waited.

"Even though this pregnancy was unexpected," she
went on, "I've always wanted children. And, you know,
I've learned you can't plan everything in life."

"You were dating a stuntman working on one of your
movies. Rick Serenghetti?"

"Yes. Rick did me an enormous favor. It started as a
PR stunt. Rick was supposed to pose as my boyfriend to
distract the press from stories about my father and his
gambling. I know celebrities aren't supposed to admit
to doing things for publicity, but I want to clear the air."

This was *so* hard. But she had to do it. Odele had convinced her to talk honestly about her feelings for Rick,
but Chiara had thought it was important to come clean
publicly about the whole charade. Risky, but important.

"You say *started*..."

"Even though I didn't know it, Rick signed up for
our make-believe because he also wanted to protect me
from a stalker. It was a threat that I wasn't taking seriously enough."

"But Todd Jeffers is now charged with serious crimes.
Are you relieved?"

"Yes, of course. And I'm so grateful to Rick for tackling Jeffers when he broke into my house."

"And how is your father doing?"

"Great. We met, and he agreed to go into rehab for his addiction. I'm proud of him." She had Rick to thank there, too.

Melody leaned forward. "So with your father addressing his addiction, and your stalker behind bars, you and Rick are…?"

Chiara gave a nervous laugh. "Somewhere along the way, I fell in love with Rick. I love him."

Melody leaned forward and shut off her voice recorder. "Perfect."

Chiara blew a breath. "You think so?"

The reporter gave her a sympathetic look. "I know so. A headline will appear on the *WE Magazine* site in a few hours, and then we'll go to press with the print edition for the end of the week."

Hours. That's all she had before Rick and the world would know what lay in her heart.

Best to keep occupied. She still needed to put in motion the last part of the plan, which she'd suggested to Odele.

Rick nearly fell out of his seat. *I love him.*

He'd followed the news link to *WE Magazine* in Odele's text and got a sucker punch.

Looking around his now nearly bare and sparsely furnished rental, he felt the swoosh of air that he normally associated with a high-altitude stunt.

His cell phone rang, and it was Melody Banyon from *WE Magazine.*

"Do you have a public comment on Chiara Feran's interview with us? She confirmed her pregnancy."

Yes. No. I don't know. "I won't ask how you got my number."

"I think you know the answer," Melody replied, amusement in her voice.

Odele, of course.

And then with sudden clarity, he realized going for broke was the thing to do. His concerns about privacy, getting manipulated by the press, or even publicity-hungry actresses, flew out the window. He didn't have time to think about whether this was another of Odele's PR moves. He was done with charades, make-believe and pretend.

"Anything you'd like to say for the record?" Melody prompted again.

"Yes. My feelings for Chiara were real from the beginning. There was no pretending on my part."

"And the baby news?"

Yeah, wow. Somehow tomorrow was today…but he couldn't be more elated with every passing day. "It may not have been planned, but I'm happy about it."

"Are you Prince Charming?"

He laughed ruefully. "I've enjoyed my privacy up until now. And I've liked keeping my aliases under wraps, but things are becoming public knowledge."

Melody cleared her throat. "Okay, off the record now… I wouldn't let Chiara get away if I were you. She's scared, but I've seen you two together. You belong together."

"And here I thought Chiara and I had done a good snow job convincing you that we really were a couple."

"Not as good a snow job as you two have done on each other," Melody replied.

Yeah. And suddenly he knew he had to follow through on the idea that Jordan had given him…

"Give me until tomorrow before you publish my comment, Melody. I want Chiara to be the first to know."

"Of course!" the reporter responded with a smile in her voice.

Rick barely heard her. His mind was already buzzing with ideas for props for his next stunt.

Chiara was tense. Controlling one's image was paramount in Hollywood, and she'd just blown her cover. *I love him...* And the entire world knew. There was nowhere to hide.

She wrung her hands as she stared out her kitchen window. *WE Magazine* had published parts of her interview online late yesterday. It had been hours...and still no word from Rick.

He could humiliate her. He could issue a stunning rejection that handed her heart back to her.

Picking up the phone, she made a lifeline call to her manager.

"Oh, Odele, what have you gotten me into?" she moaned.

"Have you looked at social media?"

"Are you kidding? It's the last thing I can bring myself to peek at."

"Well, you should. The confirmation of your pregnancy has taken the internet by storm, of course."

"Great," she said weakly.

"Yup, but the viral storm is turning in your favor, sweetie. People are applauding your honesty."

"About being a fraud?"

"You were honest about the phoniness of celebrity culture."

Chiara closed her eyes. She'd gone viral as a recovering liar...and people loved it. "I'm afraid to leave the house."

"You weren't scared when you had a stalker, but now you are?"

Of course she was. She hadn't heard from Rick. The ax could still fall.

Then a distant sound reached her, and she frowned. "Hold on, Odele."

It sounded like hoof beats. *Impossible.*

She peeked out the window. A rider on a white horse was coming up the drive.

The *clomp* of hooves sounded louder as horse and rider came closer. It couldn't be…but her heart knew it was. "Odele… I've got to go."

"What's the matter, honey?" Chiara could practically hear the frown in her manager's voice. "Do I need to send the police?"

"Um, that won't be necessary. I think I'm being rescued…"

"What…?"

"It's Rick on a white horse…bye."

"Well, I'll be damned. And he didn't even give me a heads-up so I could send a photographer to snap the moment."

"We'll do the scene over for you."

"Great, because romances are my favorite."

"I'd never have known from the way you've pushed me to do action flicks—"

"And you met a hunky stuntman in the process."

"Odele, I have to go!"

Her manager laughed. "Good luck, honey."

Rushing to the front door, Chiara took a moment to glance at herself in the hall mirror. Her eyes were bright, but she wished she could have looked more polished than she did in stretch pants and a T-shirt. Still, at least these clothes continued to fit her.

She took a deep breath and opened the door, stepping outside.

Rick stopped his horse in front of her, a smile playing at his lips.

Chiara placed her hands on her hips. "You got a horse through my front gate...really?"

"I still have the code. You've got to change it if you don't want to keep having unexpected visitors."

She nodded at the animal that he sat astride, her insides buzzing. "And you rode him along canyon roads to my house?"

"Hey, I'm a stuntman."

She met his gaze head-on. "And this is one of your stunts?"

"Jordan told me to get on a horse. Before I could do it or go with the backup plan of coming by with a wood boyfriend for Ruby, you had your interview with *WE Magazine*," he said, not answering her directly. "But I thought I'd...accommodate you anyway."

She tilted her head. "Accommodate how?"

He swung down, all lithe physique, and then pulled her into his arms and kissed her.

She leaned into him, kissing him back.

When they broke apart, he said, "I love you."

She blinked back sudden emotion, and joked, "You should if you rode a horse here."

"It took me a while to recognize it, but then you were put in danger by Jeffers." His face blazed with emotion. "Damn it, Chiara, I could have lost you."

She nodded, swallowing against the lump in her throat.

"I let my experience with Isabel color my perspective even though it was becoming increasingly obvious you couldn't be more different."

She gave a watery smile. "Well, you can be forgiven

for that one. Thanks to Odele, I was using you to manipulate the press, too."

"In the beginning, yeah. But you had guts and determination. Plus more and more layers that I wanted to uncover even though I kept trying to pigeonhole you as just another evil starlet."

"Who, me? Snow White?" she said playfully.

He cracked a smile and then gave her another quick kiss.

She braced her hands on his chest. "Thank you for tackling Jeffers…twice. I didn't take the risk seriously enough because I wasn't going to let you tell me what to do. But you helped me save my father from himself." When he started to say something, she placed a finger on his lips to stop him. "Thank you for coming into my life and dealing with all the craziness of fame. I was so afraid of being vulnerable and getting hurt."

He grasped her wrist and kissed her hand.

"I love you. I was falling in love with you and it scared me to feel so much," she finished.

"We're getting married."

She gave an emotional laugh—happiness bubbling out of her. "Before or after the baby is born?"

"Before. Vegas, even. Your father can give you away."

"He doesn't want to give me away. He just got me back! And I can't be an actress eloping to Vegas. It's too clichéd," she protested.

"You're a pregnant Hollywood actress who'll be a few months along at the wedding. You're already a cliché." He winked. "We'll leave people guessing about whether we're taking our stunt to the extreme by actually getting married."

"So our love isn't real?"

"Snow, if my feelings were any more real, they'd be jumping around like the Seven Dwarves."

"Funny, Serenghetti."

And then he proceeded to show her just how real they were…

Epilogue

Two months later...

Chiara mingled with other Serenghettis who'd gathered for Serg's sixty-seventh birthday barbecue on a hot August afternoon in Welsdale. She was still getting used to these family get-togethers. They were a world apart from her past experiences with her own family. Serg and Camilla's home brimmed with animated voices and laughter.

Still, her relationship with her father had come a long way. Her father was in rehab, but he'd already announced he'd like to become an addiction counselor. And Odele had been and continued to be like a second mother. She'd already started shopping for baby clothes. And now, of course, Chiara had the Serenghettis, as well.

"The food is delicious," Marisa announced as she stepped onto the patio bathed in late-afternoon sun. "I feel even more like an overstuffed piñata."

Chiara smiled at her sister-in-law. "Now, there's a metaphor for being pregnant I haven't heard before."

In a nice surprise, shortly after her own pregnancy had gone public, Cole and Marisa had quietly announced they were expecting, too. Her sister-in-law was only a month further along. Naturally, Chiara thought, there'd be another female Serenghetti to take this journey with.

Marisa sighed. "I know what a chicken cordon bleu feels like."

"A ham?" Jordan asked, having overheard.

His sister-in-law shot him a droll look. "Funny."

"Just don't have a surprise birth," Jordan teased. "Mom wants a chance to plan for a big event for once."

Chiara bit back another smile, and then looked down at her plain platinum wedding band and large canary diamond solitaire engagement ring. She and Rick had had a quick wedding in Las Vegas with just immediate family present. It had been small, intimate and private, just like they'd wanted. There'd been no press, though they'd given Melody an exclusive after the fact.

Now as Marisa and Jordan stepped away, Rick came up and settled his hands on her shoulders, kneading them gently. Chiara nearly purred with contentment.

"How are you feeling?" Rick asked in a low voice.

"Like my next role should be as a pregnant stuntwoman," she responded.

"You'd be great. I've got just the vehicle."

"I feel like a starlet who has slept her way to the top with the studio boss."

He chuckled. "Snow, we're partners now."

At home and at the office. She and Rick were starting their own production company. He'd vowed to support her career in any way he could, and that included helping her find appropriate acting roles. For her part, she wanted to respect Rick's preference to not be in the glare of celebrity. She'd done interviews herself, but he'd insisted that as her prince, he needed and wanted to be her escort to public events.

Just then, Serafina, Marisa's cousin, stepped onto the patio and then frowned as she spotted Jordan.

"Uh-oh," Rick said in a low voice for Chiara's ears only. "Trouble."

As if on cue, Jordan gave a lazy grin, and then sauntered toward Serafina with a gleam in his eye.

Chiara smiled. "Only the best kind for those two." Then turning, she snuggled against Rick as he draped an arm around her shoulders. "Don't you agree?"

Her husband winked and gave her a kiss. "Definitely. You're the best trouble I ever had, Snow. And then love had walked in for us."

* * * * *

THE MYSTERIOUS
ITALIAN HOUSEGUEST

SCARLET WILSON

CHAPTER ONE

PORTIA CLOSED THE door behind her and breathed out as the car puttered off into the distance. Finally, peace perfect peace.

Somewhere, on the other side of the house, she could hear the chirrup of birds. After three days of being constantly surrounded by people and chatter it was music to her ears.

She leaned back against the cool wall, tempted to just slide down it.

Her sister Miranda's wedding was over. She could stop smiling. She could stop fending off the intrusive questions from her sisters. Miranda had looked radiant, lost in the pink cloud of love and drifting off somewhere that seemed a million miles out of Portia's reach.

She was the oldest sister—wasn't she supposed to get married first?

The tightness that had gripped her chest since she'd got here eased just a little.

The last wedding guest had left. Miranda was off on her honeymoon, Posy had gone back to work, and Immi had returned to her job in the family business. Finally, Portia could have some quiet.

It wasn't that she didn't love her sisters. Of course she did. It was just that being around them was so...busy.

They all talked at once, and over the top of each other. And what she really needed right now was a chance to take stock, to weigh up what to do next.

Her discarded mobile phone lay on one of the gilded tables in the large entrance hall almost mocking her.

L'Isola dei Fiori had patchy mobile coverage. Villa Rosa had an old phone line that didn't currently work, and no Internet.

She didn't need emails. She didn't need a phone signal.

The last conversation on the phone had turned her work life upside down.

'What have you brought us in the last four weeks, Portia? The award ceremony was weeks ago. Your red carpet interviews are yesterday's news. You're supposed to be an investigative reporter. This is Hollywood. And at twenty-seven your time is almost up. Bring me a headline story in the next four weeks or you're history.'

She'd felt numb. Studying investigative journalism at university had been a dream come true. Finding a job in Fleet Street had been much harder. When she'd decided to hitch around the US with a friend for a few weeks she'd no idea how her life would turn out. One random conversation in a small café in Los Angeles had led to a temporary job at a TV station as a runner. When one of the producers had found out what she'd studied he'd asked her to pull some material together for their entertainment gossip show. Portia was smart and Portia was beautiful. Two months later she'd still been there and when the TV host had been involved in an auto accident on the way to the studio, she'd filled in with less than an hour's notice. The audience had loved her. Social media had exploded. The gorgeous brunette with tumbling curls, dark eyes, plummy English accent and sense of humour had attracted more viewers. Within a year the show had been a hit. All for a job that Portia had landed due to a complete fluke.

Five years on she'd broken more Hollywood stories than any of her rivals. The truth was, she'd been a little ruthless at first. She'd had a natural tendency to sniff out a story at fifty paces and her boss had quickly pushed her for more and more headlines. At first, she'd enjoyed it. She'd interviewed film stars past and present with aplomb. And while she'd charmed them with her smile, she hadn't lost her investigative edge. For the last five years she'd happily exposed liars, cheats and corruption in Hollywood. But as time had marched on the colours around her had muted a little. She was becoming jaded. She'd lost the fire that had once burned in her belly. Hollywood seemed to be a cycle, with only the faces changing while the stories sounded the same. And her boss was pushing and pushing her for more scandal-led headlines—the kind that had started to make her stomach flip over.

The thing was, she did have two major stories she could break. But the conscience she'd developed wouldn't let her. One, about an elderly well-respected actor who was gay. As far as she was aware, virtually no one knew. And no matter how much the information spun around in her brain—and even though she knew it would make headlines around the world—she really didn't feel the urge to 'out' him. The second story, about a major actress who was secretly crippled by depression, would also make headlines. This woman was known for her sense of humour and smile. But it was all completely fake. The thing was, Portia knew why. Her daughter was very sick. And it was a story that she didn't think she should break either.

It played on her mind. Unless she could find another story in the next few weeks she would have to find a whole new career. And what kind of story could she find on L'Isola dei Fiori? A place with a tiny population and barely any mobile phone signal.

It might be time to take another look at that book she'd been writing for the last three years. Anything would be better than feeling like this.

A gentle sea breeze blew through the hallway. The back French doors must be open.

Space. That was one of the marvels of this place.

Portia wandered through to her favourite room of the house. The ceiling curved into a dome and the washes of blue, mauve and pink—even though faded—made it seem as though a magical sunset were taking place right above your head. If she closed her eyes she could remember this house in its prime. It had belonged to Sofia, her sister Posy's godmother. Sofia had been a famous model and, a number of years ago, the then Prince's mistress. If Portia could turn back the clock she'd love to interview Sofia. When she was a child it had all just seemed so normal. A godmother who lived in a huge house on a mystery island, sweeping up and down the grand staircase in a whole array of glittering gowns like some forgotten starlet.

If she closed her eyes she could remember most of the movie stars, rock stars and models of the nineties that had filled the rooms in this house. If she could really turn back the clock she would pay more attention to some of the conversations and liaisons she could vaguely remember hearing and witnessing.

Coming to L'Isola dei Fiori had always been such an adventure. The flight to Italy and then the journey over on the ferry had always seemed like part of a children's story complete with the image of the pale pink Villa Rosa sitting on the headland.

But Villa Rosa wasn't quite as magnificent as it had remained in her head. The pale pink stucco had cracked and faded. The exotic flowers in the gardens had been surrounded by weeds. Part of the scullery roof had fallen in and been mended by Miranda's new husband, Cleve, along with some of the ancient electrics in the house. It seemed that in years gone by each room had only required one plug point.

Portia ran her hand along the wall. Some of the plaster was crumbling. There was a crack running up the wall towards the top of the dome, bisecting part of the beautiful paintwork. The whole place was more than tired. Parts of it were downright neglected.

Even though Posy had inherited it from Sofia, all the sisters felt an element of responsibility. They'd all enjoyed holidays here as children. Sofia had been the ultimate hostess. Sipping cocktails and treating the girls like adults instead of children. There had been no fixed bedtimes. No explicit rules. As long as the girls were respectful and well-mannered Sofia had seemed to be entirely happy.

Villa Rosa conjured up memories of lazy days with beautiful sunrises and sunsets, long hours on the private beach and by the hot spring pool, the many legends about the craggy rock arch bisecting the beach, and a flurry of fun in a rainbow of satins, silks and sequins. Sofia had had the most spectacular designer wardrobe and she hadn't hesitated to let her mini charges play dress up.

Portia leaned against the wall and sighed. The ugly crack annoyed her. Doubtless it would require some specialist to repair it. Like most of this house. Why did it feel as if the house was reflecting her life right now?

She couldn't remember. Was Villa Rosa a listed building? Did they have listed buildings in L'Isola dei Fiori? Miranda and Cleve had done some emergency repairs on the house. There were a few liveable rooms. But the kitchen and bathrooms were antiquated and barely functioning. The dusty full attics would probably be an antique dealer's dream. But Portia knew nothing about things like that and was too wary to even attempt to help with a clean-up for fear she would throw something valuable away.

She breathed in deeply. The warm sea air was wafting through the house bringing with it the aroma of calla lilies, jasmine and a tang of citrus from the few trees along the wall of the garden. She sighed, walked through to the kitchen and retrieved a semi-chilled bottle of rosé wine from the sometimes functioning fridge, grabbing a glass and walking through the double doors to the glass-ceilinged conservatory. There was a sad air about it. A few of the delicate panes were missing or cracked. At some point Sofia had commissioned a specialist stained-glass maker to install some coloured panes in a whole variety of shades, randomly dotted throughout the conservatory. It meant that when the sun streamed in from a particular angle the conservatory was lit up like a rainbow, sending streams of colour dazzling around the space. The doors at the end of the conservatory opened out to the terrace and gardens, which led to the sheltered cove below with a bubbling hot spring. It really was like a little piece of paradise.

She settled on an old pale pink wooden rocker sitting on the terrace that creaked as she sat down. She smiled, holding her breath for a few seconds for fear the wood might split. But the rocker held as she poured her wine then rested her feet on the ledge in front.

The azure sea sparkled in front of her. The horizon completely and utterly empty. It was as if the whole rolling ocean had been made entirely for her viewing pleasure.

She closed her eyes for a second. There was something about this place. Something magical.

In her head she could see the glittering parties that Sofia had hosted. Full of film stars, models, producers, and Sofia's very own special Prince. Portia sipped her rosé wine, letting the dry fresh flavour with hints of cherry and orange zest fill her senses as she rocked back and forward in the chair.

If she could capture just one of those moments, and bring all the gossip twenty years into the future, she wouldn't need to worry about her job any more. Times had been different then. No instant social media. No mobile phones in every pocket or every bag.

She gave a little smile as she closed her eyes and continued to rock. A warm breeze swept over her, scented with jasmine and hugging around her like a comforting blanket. It was almost as if time had stood still at Villa Rosa.

And for Portia's purposes, that was just fine.

Javier finished nursing his last bottle of beer. He'd crossed over on the last evening ferry to L'Isola dei Fiori and, instead of heading straight to the house, he'd headed straight to the nearest bar.

L'Isola dei Fiori had been a favourite haunt of his mother's. Her friend Sofia's house had been a refuge for her when her manic behaviour had got out of control, she'd stopped eating and stopped taking her medication. His father had learned quickly not to try and intervene. Sofia's presence had been one of calmness and serenity. A fellow model, she'd understood the ingrained eating habits and learned behaviour that his mother just couldn't shake in later life. Even though she was always beautiful in Javier's eyes, as his mother had aged she hadn't taken kindly to losing modelling jobs. Each loss had seemed to spark more erratic behaviour and his film producer father had struggled to cope.

Javier had been too young to understand much. He'd just learned that when his father pulled out the large monogrammed case, it generally meant a visit to Aunt Sofia's. She'd never really been an aunt, but he'd thought of her in that way. Sofia's air of grace could never be forgotten. She hadn't walked—she'd glided. She'd talked to him as if he were an adult, not a child, with no imposed rules or regulations. Instead, Javier had been mainly allowed to amuse himself. Not always wise for a young boy.

But somewhere, in the back of his brain, he'd held fast the little element that this place was a sanctuary. Somewhere to find calmness. Somewhere to find peace. And that was what he needed right now. A place where the paparazzi weren't waiting around every corner. A place where he could nod at someone in the street without their frowning and wondering where they'd seen him before. A place where he could have a drink in a bar without someone whipping out their phone to take a selfie with him in the background.

He left his money on the bar and picked up his bag. He'd been here for at least three hours with minimal conversation. He liked that. The hours of travel had caught up with him. He patted the large iron key in his pocket. At some point over the years his mother had 'acquired' a key to Villa Rosa. It was odd. Neither of them had been back since Sofia's funeral a few years ago and he'd heard that the house, once in its prime, was now pretty run-down.

Maybe he could make himself useful while he kept his head below the parapet for a while. When he was a teenager his Uncle Vinnie—a veritable handyman— had taken him on many of his jobs. Anything to keep him from turning down the wrong track. At the age of thirteen, with a mother as a model and a father as a film producer, he'd probably already seen and heard a million things he shouldn't. After he'd almost dabbled with some drugs, his father had shipped him back to Italy and into his brother's care for the summer. Javier had learned how to plaster and how to glaze. It appeared that sanding and smoothing walls, and cutting panes of glass were therapeutic for a teenage boy. Not that he'd used any of those skills in Hollywood…

He walked out into the warm evening. Dusk was settling around him. The port was still busy with the boats silhouetted against a purple and blue darkening sky. If he were an artist he would be tempted to settle down with some paints, a canvas and easel. But Javier Russo had never been known for his painting skills.

Instead, his name normally adorned the front of Hollywood cinemas. His latest film had just been publicised by putting a forty-five-foot-high image of Javier next to the *D* on the Hollywood sign. He'd never live that one down.

But it seemed that Hollywood loved Italian film stars. In another year it was predicted he'd be one of Hollywood's highest earners—much to his agent's delight.

He'd just finished four back-to-back movies taking

him halfway around the world. Two action movies, one romantic comedy and one sci-fi. He'd ping-ponged between the Arabian Desert, the expanse of the Indian Ocean, the nearby island of Santorini, the Canadian Rockies and the streets of London. For some it sounded completely glamorous. In truth it was lonely and had taken him away from those that he loved. The family that he'd failed.

Now, he was exhausted. Pictures had emerged of him attending the funeral of a family friend looking tanned and muscular—just as well nothing could reveal how he was feeling, the way his insides had been curling and dying from the fact he hadn't been there to help.

Much to his agent's disgust he'd reneged on some immediate future arrangements. In another four weeks the cycle would start again with publicity and interviews for the first of those films. Right now he needed some space.

He smiled as he turned the corner to Villa Rosa. The long walk had done him some good. He stretched muscles that had been cramped on the flight over from Los Angeles and frowned at the cracks in a pale pink façade. This place was in bad need of repair. He wasn't entirely sure about the material. Maybe he could phone Uncle Vinnie for some advice?

He set his bag down and pulled the key from his pocket. With a wiggle, the key gave a satisfying turn in the lock. He pushed the door open not quite knowing what to expect.

Silence.

He frowned. Something was off. The house wasn't as musty as he'd expected. He walked slowly through the large main hall. It was clear someone must have been here. There were small signs of life.

Large dust covers had been pulled from the furniture in the painted room and heaped in one corner. He ran his finger along the plaster, snatching it back as a tiny piece of paint flaked to the ground. In the dim light his eyes caught the line snaking up the curve of the dome. He felt his frown deepen. It would take skill to mend a crack like that. Skill he wasn't sure he possessed.

He glanced around him. The air in here was fresh. There was a hint of something else. The rustling from outside sounded far too close. Windows were open in this house.

He strode through towards the back of the house. The conservatory had seen better days. A few of the small panels of glass were missing and others were cracked or damaged. Something crunched beneath his feet. He knelt down; a small fragment of red glass was under his shoe. He brushed it off as he heard a small cough.

His head shot back up, looking out across the terrace.

A woman.

Who on earth was here?

According to his mother this place had been deserted since Sofia had died. That was why it had fallen into the state it was in. He hadn't stood up yet. Wondering how to deal with the mysterious woman on the terrace.

Could she have broken in? Was she some tourist who had spotted the giant pale pink neglected house and decided she could squat here? He moved his head, squinting at the figure.

A brunette. In her twenties. Dressed in something short and red. He shifted uncomfortably. Whatever she was wearing, it seemed to have inched upwards as she lay in the rocking chair, sleeping with her legs stretched out and resting on the low wall. He could see a hint of black underneath. She moaned a little and shuffled in her seat, the hard wood beneath her obviously not as comfortable as she wanted. The chair rocked back and forth.

He straightened up, trying to get a better look. On the terrace was an empty glass and a bottle of wine. Was she drunk?

Maybe Sofia had a wine cellar that everyone had forgotten about and some light-fingered thief was now drinking her way through the contents?

Now, he was getting angry. He'd come here for some peace. Some tranquillity. The last thing he wanted was to have to call out the local *polizia*.

He strode out onto the terrace ready to tackle the intruder. But his footsteps faltered. He'd only really glimpsed her from sideways. Now he could see her clearly he was surprised.

Her hair tumbled around her face, chocolate at the roots, blonde-tipped courtesy of the sun—or a salon. Her dress was indeed almost around her hips revealing her well-shaped firm legs blessed with a light golden tan. Her chest went up and down lightly beneath the thin cotton of her dress that did little to hide her curves.

There was something vaguely familiar about her. Something he couldn't quite place.

His foot crunched on a stone on the terrace and her eyes flew open.

Before he even had a chance to speak she was on her feet, her eyes wide and her hands grabbing for the nearest item.

'*Mi scusi, non volevo spaventarti...*'

He'd automatically reverted to his native language but it did nothing to stop the wine glass being hurled in his direction and catching him squarely on his brow.

It shattered at his feet on the terrace as he took another step towards her.

This time she had the wine bottle, brandishing it like a weapon in front of her.

'Don't move, buster. Take another step and I'll… I'll…'

She glanced sideways. And he caught the wave of fear that had rolled over her.

But the comedy of the moment hadn't escaped him. He stepped forward and took the empty wine bottle firmly from her hands and smiled. 'You'll spring vault backwards past the hot spring and straight down to the beach and the lovers' arch?'

Her eyes widened even further. If it were possible they were the biggest brown eyes he'd ever seen. Like a dark whirlpool that could suck you right in.

Waves of confusion were sweeping over her face. The obvious change from Italian to English seemed to have caught her unawares. Her head flicked sideways to the lovers' arch. He could almost read her mind. Only someone who was familiar with this property would know about the hot spring and private beach beneath.

And there was still something vaguely familiar about her…

Her body was still stuck in the vaguely defensive stance. 'You know about Neptune's arch?'

The accent. That was what it was. And those eyes. The plummy accent had sounded strange when she'd shouted so quickly. A bit like a member of the British royal family yelling at him. He smiled again and set the bottle down on the terrace, folding his arms across his chest.

He was around ten inches taller than her. He didn't

want to intimidate her. She didn't look like the cat-burglar type.

He let out a laugh. 'I invented it.' Then shook his head, curiosity piqued even further. 'I didn't tell you it was called Neptune's arch.'

She jerked. As if she were getting used to his Italian accent speaking English to her.

Her gaze narrowed. Now, she looked angry. She planted her hands on her hips. 'Who on earth are you, and what are you doing in my house?'

'Your house?' He raised his eyebrows. 'Are you So-fia's goddaughter?'

She shook her head. 'Yes. Well…no.'

'Well, make up your mind. You either are, or you aren't.'

She gritted her teeth. 'No. Posy is Sofia's goddaugh-ter. She's my sister.' She frowned again. 'But who are you? And how do you know Sofia?'

The more she spoke, the more he felt the waves of familiarity sweeping across his skin. She wasn't an ac-tress. He knew every British actress that spoke as she did.

The hairs on his arms stood on end in the cool coastal breeze. Realisation was hitting home. Chances were this English siren was staying here. All hopes of hiding away on this island in peace and quiet were gen-tly floating away in the orange-scented air.

'Sofia was a good friend of my mother's. We stayed here often when I was a child and a teenager.'

She mirrored his position and folded her arms across her chest. 'Well, you're not a teenager now and Sofia's been dead for two years.'

'I was at her funeral. I never noticed you.' Even as he said the words he was struck by the realisation that he wasn't likely to forget a woman like this. She was downright beautiful. As beautiful as any one of his Hollywood leading ladies.

In fact, she was much more natural than most of them. No Botox. No obvious surgery. And skin that was clear and unblemished. If only the public knew just how much airbrushing went on in film studios.

It made him smile that she didn't remember him. Didn't recognise him.

But right as that thought crowded his brain, he saw the little flicker behind her eyes.

'What's your name? Who is your mother?' It wasn't a question, it was a demand.

Something sparked inside him. It had been a long time since someone had spoken to him like that. Being a Hollywood movie star meant he was usually surrounded by 'yes' people. Part of the point of coming here was to get away from all that. He just hadn't expected to reach the opposite end of the spectrum.

He sucked in a breath. 'You tell me yours, I'll tell you mine.'

Her beautiful face was marred by a deeper frown. He could sense she wasn't used to being lost for words. She drew herself up to her full height. She had bare feet and the top of her head was just above his shoulder. The perfect height for a leading woman.

'I'm Portia. Portia Marlowe.' She tossed her hair over her shoulder, glancing over at the azure sea, then rapidly sucked in a breath and spun around to face him as the recognition struck.

She pointed her finger. 'You're Javier Russo.' Her voice had gone up in pitch.

There it was. Anonymity gone in a flash. He sighed and walked over to the edge of the terrace. The beach looked inviting, even if it was a bit of a scramble to reach it. As a child he hadn't given it a moment's thought.

He almost laughed out loud at the thought of the film insurers' opinion on him staying in such a place. They'd want to wrap him in cotton wool. What on earth had his last action movie insured his legs for—ten million dollars?

The sun was dipping lower in the sky, sending dark orange streaks across the water. It was a beautiful sunset. He understood why she was sitting out there. But he still didn't know what she was really doing here. More importantly, was she staying?

She moved next to him. 'You're Javier Russo,' she repeated. Her voice was getting quicker. 'Javier Russo. Italian movie star.' She gave him a sideways glance. 'Thirty. Just finished filming a sci-fi film in the Arabian Desert, and last year the second highest paid action movie star.'

The hairs prickled at the back of his neck. He'd met hundreds of fans over the last few years. Some verging on the slightly obsessive. But he couldn't imagine he'd be so unlucky to end up staying with one of them on L'Isola dei Fiori.

'How on earth do you know that?' Something else flashed into his brain and he gave a half-smile. 'And what's with the look you gave me when you said I was thirty?'

'Is that your real age or your Hollywood age?' she shot back cheekily.

She waved her hand. 'Oh, come on, you know. Most Hollywood stars take a few years off their age. Some even more than ten.' There was the hint of a teasing smile on her face. She seemed to have regained her composure. 'But once you get up close and personal, you always know if it's an extension of the truth or not.'

He laughed out loud and turned back from the view to meet her head-on. There was a sparkle in her eyes. She'd obviously moved from the initial fear factor to the having-fun factor. She wasn't flirting. That didn't seem like her agenda. But she certainly seemed much more comfortable around him. And she wasn't tugging at her dress or hair. Often, once people recognised him, they frantically tried to get a glimpse of their own appearance, sometimes cursing out loud that they didn't look their best.

Portia didn't seem to care. Her simple red dress—which looked as if it came from any high-street store—stopped mid-thigh. The only remnant of make-up on her face was a hint of red stain on her lips.

He moved a little closer. 'So, what do you think?'

His chest was only a few inches from her nose. She looked a little surprised. She lifted her hand up and he wondered if she was going to push him away.

Her hand stayed in mid-air. 'Think about what?' Her voice had quietened and as she looked up at him the sun was in her eyes, making her squint a little.

It was as if a wall of silence fell around him. He was in a movie now. A glass panel had just slid around the two of them and cut out all the surrounding noise. No lapping waves. No breeze. No rustling leaves or tweeting birds.

All that was present was a girl in a red dress, with tiny freckles across the bridge of her nose and dark chocolate eyes. It was that tiny moment in time. A millisecond, when something reached into his chest and punched him square in the heart.

He'd met dozens of beautiful women. He'd dated

some of them. Had relationships with others. But he'd never felt the wow factor. That single moment when... zing.

And he couldn't fathom what had just happened. It was that single look. That single connection.

She licked her lips.

And the sci-fi glass portal disappeared, amplifying all the noise around him. He swayed a little.

'Do I think that you're really thirty?' She threw back her head and laughed. 'Well, if you are—you're the only film star who doesn't lie about their age.' She lifted one hand. 'And don't get me started on their diets, workout plans or relationships.'

The wind caught her dress, blowing it against her curves. He took a step backwards.

'How do you know all this stuff?' His curiosity was definitely piqued. He'd heard that Sofia had a goddaughter. But he didn't know anything about her—or the fact she had sisters. Now, this sister—Portia—seemed weirdly knowing about Hollywood's poorly kept secrets.

'Do you work in Hollywood? How come I've never met you?'

Something glanced across her face. Hurt?

'I have met you,' she answered quietly.

'Where?' He tried to rack his brains. Somehow if he'd met her before he assumed he'd remember.

Her tone had changed. He'd definitely annoyed her. 'I met you at the award ceremony. I interviewed you on the red carpet about the pirate movie.'

She didn't even call it by its name—even though it had made one and a half billion dollars at the box office and counting.

The award ceremony—the biggest in Hollywood. That had been March. And reporters had lined the red carpet in their hundreds all hoping for a sound bite from a film star. Trying to remember anyone in amongst that rabble would be nigh on impossible.

It was as if someone had just dumped the biggest bucket of ice in the world over his head. He stepped back. 'You work for a newspaper?'

A reporter. Just what he needed.

The plague of the earth. At least that was what his mother used to call them. They'd harassed her to death when she'd been unwell. He had clear childhood memories of their home in Italy surrounded by people holding cameras and brandishing microphones, while his mother wept in her bedroom.

He'd learned early on to tell them nothing. Not a tiny little thing. Anything that was said could be twisted and turned into a headline full of lies the next day. Nothing had affected his mother's moods more than the press.

As a Hollywood star he couldn't possibly avoid them. But he could manage them.

And he always had. Two-minute press junkets. Any longer interviews done in writing by his press officer, along with a legal declaration about misquotes.

All press were to be kept at a distance. Even the pretty ones.

No, *especially* the pretty ones.

Her eyes narrowed a little. 'No, I work for Entertainment Buzz TV. Have done for the last five years.' She held up her hand and counted off on her fingers. 'I interviewed you after your first appearance in the Slattery action movies. I've met you at probably half a dozen film premieres and I met you on the red carpet in March.'

He was surprised she was offended. Every TV reporter in the world knew what press junkets were like.

Each person was given an allotted time frame—usually around two minutes—along with a long list of questions they weren't allowed to ask. It was like speed dating—usually with a really boring outcome, because all the questions that were asked you'd already answered sixty times before.

He felt himself bristle. A reporter. Absolutely the last person he wanted to be around right now. Not when he wanted some privacy and some head space.

'Are you staying here?' He couldn't help the pointed way his words came out.

She blinked at the change of conversation and stuck her hands on her hips. The sea air swept across them both echoing the instant chill that had developed. 'It's my sister Posy's house. Where else would I be staying?'

'But this place is supposed to be deserted.' Frustration was building in his chest. He turned around and gestured at the fading building behind him. 'I mean, look at it. How long has your sister had it? She hasn't done any work at all. This place is falling apart at the seams.'

Portia's dark eyes gleamed. 'I think you'll find that this place has been like this for around the last fifteen years. When was the last time you were here, *exactly*? Sofia let things fall by the wayside. She didn't keep up the house maintenance. After her relationship with Crown Price Ludano ended, I'm not sure she had the means.' Portia glared at him. 'My other sister Miranda and her husband Cleve have made some temporary repairs to the roof and electrics. I was hoping to tidy up a bit while I was here. Posy is a ballerina. She doesn't have any spare funds right now, let alone enough money to carry out the extensive repairs that this place will need.' It was obvious she was on the defensive.

But so was he.

'Last I heard no one was staying here at all.' All the hairs on the back of his neck were standing on the offensive. Press. He had to get rid of her. How on earth could he sort things out with someone like her around?

'So you thought you would just break in?' she shot back.

He pulled the ancient large key from his pocket. 'I didn't break in. My mother has a key to Villa Rosa—she has done for years.'

'And that gives you the right to just appear here and let yourself in? My sister inherited this property. It's hers.' She placed her hand on her chest and raised her eyebrows. 'I know that I'm supposed to be here. But I'm quite sure you haven't asked her permission. Particularly when you don't even know her name.'

Javier was stunned. He wasn't used to people treating him like an unwanted guest. He certainly hadn't expected anyone to be here. He'd wanted the place to himself. But it was clear that wasn't going to happen.

It was too late now to go anywhere else. The last ferry to the mainland had left hours ago. There weren't any hotels nearby.

If Ms Portia Marlowe wanted to toss him out to the kerb, movie star or not, he was in trouble.

It was time to use the old Italian charm. He'd won awards for his acting. He might not mean a single word of it, but that didn't matter right now. He needed a bed for the night and could sort the rest of this out in the morning.

He smiled. He already suspected she might have had a few drinks. Maybe it was time to play on the situation.

He put his hand to his forehead and gave it a rub, throwing in a little sway for good measure. He wasn't an actor for nothing. 'Yeow!' He squeezed his eyes shut, then opened them, giving his head a shake.

She frowned. 'What's wrong?'

He gestured to the glass on the terrace. 'I didn't notice at first. But that glass packed a bit of a punch.' He shot her a smile and shook his head again. 'I'm fine. Just dizzy for a second.'

For the briefest moment her eyes narrowed, almost as if she suspected she was being played. But then, guilt must have swamped her. She moved forward and pointed towards the rocking chair behind them. 'Do you want to sit down? Will I get you some water?'

He gave a nod, and stepped backwards to the chair. It creaked as he lowered himself into the wooden frame and he prayed it wouldn't splinter and send him sprawling on the ground.

Peaceful quiet surrounded him.

From up here he could hear the lapping sea. Hear the rustling leaves. Hear the occasional chirrup of a bird. Tranquillity. This was what he'd come here for. This was what he'd hoped to find.

Aldo would have loved this place. He wished he'd had the chance to bring him. He would have adored the waves crashing into the cove. At one point Aldo had fancied himself as a surfer, but the sea had had other ideas. When they were young guys, every holiday Aldo had hired a surfboard and spent hour after hour wiping out. Most of the time they'd nearly drowned laughing. His fists clenched. Why had he never taken the opportunity to bring him to Sofia's? It spun around in his head, adding to the list of things he 'should' have done. Instead, time had just slipped away. Life had been too busy. There was always tomorrow.

Until there wasn't.

A fact he was going to have to learn to live with.

Too busy. Too busy filming. Too busy in meetings. Too busy to answer the phone to an old friend. He'd meant to call back that night. But after sixteen hours on set it had just slipped from his mind.

The next call he'd received had ripped his heart out.

That was why he'd come here. To find space. To find peace. For a reality check on the life he was living.

Instead, he'd found Portia Marlowe. A beautiful woman, but a Hollywood reporter. It was like a romance and a horror movie both at once. He would have to manage this situation carefully.

He closed his eyes and let the chair rock back and forth. Maybe she was due to go home in the next day or so? This might actually be okay. He only planned to stay here for a few weeks. Just enough time to give him some space. Some *alone* space.

There was a tinkling noise. Portia was on her knees sweeping the broken glass up with a dustpan and brush, her face a little pink. She caught his gaze and shrugged. 'I didn't know who you were. You caught me unawares.'

'So did you.'

The answer came out before he had time to alter it. She looked surprised. Her dark gaze locked with his. Against the backdrop of the now purple and pink sky Portia almost looked as if she were standing inside the painted drawing room. A cameraman would wait hours for a shot like this. But right now, Javier was the only person with this view. Portia blinked, breaking their gaze and picking up the bottle of water she had next to her feet. 'Here, it's not too cold. The fridge seems to be a temperamental teenager right now. Sometimes it works. Sometimes it doesn't bother.'

He nodded and took the lukewarm bottle of water,

his fingers brushing against hers. A film director would have added a little twinkle and sparkling stars to match the pulses that shot up his arm.

He pushed the feeling aside. Being attracted to Portia Marlowe wasn't an option. Not for a second. It couldn't go anywhere. He had enough to sort out without bringing a Hollywood reporter into the equation.

She leaned forward, the soft curves of her breasts only inches from his hand. Her thumb brushed his forehead. 'There's not even a mark. I should probably be relieved.' She gave a nervous laugh. 'Can you imagine the hoo-ha if I'd damaged the face of one of the world's most famous film stars?'

Her face paled and her hand gripped the edge of the rocker. His stomach sank. The enormity of her actions had just hit her—him too. A scar would have resulted in his agent and publicist probably having some kind of fit. In the space of a few seconds, he could see the headlines, the plastic-surgeon consultations, the juggling of schedules and the threatened lawsuits all from an action that hadn't really been intentional. It had been reactive. Not pre-planned. When he'd feigned feeling dizzy it had only been for his own ends. He didn't want to spend the night sleeping on the street when he'd come here uninvited. Now he felt like some kind of cad.

He breathed in slowly, inhaling some of her rose perfume. It was tantalising. Or maybe that was just Portia. He gave his head a quick shake, trying to realign his senses. 'I think maybe I just need to sleep. I've been travelling for a long time. I'm sure after a good night's sleep I'll feel fine.'

He let the words hang in the air. She opened her mouth to start to speak then closed it again. He could practically see the thoughts tumbling around in her brain. Her English sensibilities and good manners were obviously bubbling underneath the surface.

'I'm sure I can fix up a bed for you. One of the other bedrooms is almost cleaned. I did some laundry the other day.' There was hesitation in her voice.

Javier shot her his best smile. 'That's really kind of you. Thanks very much.'

He closed his eyes again as he heard her walk back into the house. He rocked back and forward in the chair. This was almost therapeutic.

And he needed that right now.

Because his time at Villa Rosa had just changed beyond all measure.

CHAPTER TWO

PORTIA LAY IN her bed wondering if the man in the next room was up yet.

Or maybe he'd died in the night of some hidden head injury she'd caused by throwing the wine glass?

She groaned and rolled onto her side. Sleep had been a stranger to her. She'd tossed and turned all night.

Somehow, Javier Russo had ended up sleeping in the room next to hers.

Talk about messing with her head.

She'd interviewed dozens of famous stars and met every personality trait. The smug. The bored. The sweetheart. The ignorant. The people pleaser. The desperate. And the person who appeared to be from another planet.

Javier had been charming in the way that only an Italian film star could be. But it was all an act. Last time she'd met him he'd been arrogant. He could barely even bother to say hello. He'd looked at her with those steely grey eyes as she'd asked a question and replied, 'Is that really the best you can do?' before walking away with a dismissive glance. It was obvious he hadn't thought she'd been important enough to speak to.

Stars being rude was nothing new to Portia. But it

had felt as though he was mocking her. And that had stung.

Most Hollywood stars at least pretended to like the press. Some tried to charm her. A few had even sent her gifts. One particularly sleazy older guy had slipped his hand a bit too low and earned himself a slap and he was *apparently* happily married. Five years in Hollywood had fast made her realise that everything was merely a façade. Hardly any of it was real—let alone the love stories.

The charm was all superficial. As for Javier Russo? Last time around he hadn't even feigned interest—she'd felt as welcome as something on the bottom of his shoe. It was only when his press officer had nudged him and whispered in his ear harshly that he'd tried to turn on the charm again—but with the next person in line.

And it had annoyed her beyond belief that as soon as he'd started to speak the rhythm of his words in that alluring tone had sent shivers down her spine.

That same voice that she'd heard last night.

She still wasn't entirely sure why he was there.

And that was pretty much the reason she couldn't sleep.

This was it. This was her chance. This was her chance for a story. Why on earth would Javier Russo be here? The man could probably afford to rent an entire hotel to himself. What on earth was he doing at Villa Rosa?

She tried to remember everything she'd ever heard about him. The truth was there was very little scandal around him. Yes, he was arrogant and sometimes aloof. But there were never on-set rumours about weird demands or keeping others waiting for hours. His star had definitely risen in the last few years and he'd been known to date a model, a pop star, and a few co-stars.

She hadn't realised his mother had been friends with Sofia. They'd both been models around the same time; it made sense that they'd moved in the same circles. Sofia had photograph album after photograph album in the attic above Portia's head. Doubtless she would find some memento of the women's past history together.

In the meantime she was trying to keep calm. She shifted uncomfortably in the bed. This could be the story that could save her career. Or it could be nothing. It could simply be about a film star that had just filmed back-to-back movies and was looking for some peace and quiet. It wasn't really that outrageous a thought. Apart from an occasional interest in the royal family, L'Isola dei Fiori wasn't exactly the most sought-out destination. The ferry boat from the mainland was the only way here. Tourism was low. This place was off the beaten track. That was partly why she was here too.

But maybe it was something else? Maybe there was much more to Javier Russo than anyone knew. Her stomach flipped a little. She was still annoyed at him being so dismissive at their last meeting—one that he didn't even remember. Maybe finding a story on Javier Russo would give her the boost she needed for her flagging career?

She pushed the horrible nagging feeling to the back of her head.

She'd only agreed to let him stay here one night. Maybe if there was a chance of a story she should reconsider?

There was a noise from downstairs. She frowned and swung her legs out of bed. It only took a few minutes to source where the noise was coming from.

Oh, Javier Russo was awake all right. He was so awake he was standing bare-chested in the painted drawing room. She rubbed her eyes. Maybe she hadn't woken up yet. Maybe this was all just some kind of weird dream. He was wearing a pair of blue jeans and black boots. And he was mixing something in a bucket, his actions allowing her to admire every chiselled muscle in his arms and abs. She was pretty sure her chin just bounced off the floor and came back up again. That smattering of dark curls across the chest then thickening and leading downwards… There should be a law against this kind of thing.

'What on earth are you doing?'

He looked up and smiled. 'Just making myself useful.'

There was quiet confidence in those words that actually made her smart. The painted room was her favourite in the whole house and she knew that Posy felt the same. Although they hadn't exactly spoken about it, she was sure that getting repairs done in a room like this was entirely outside all of her sisters' budgets.

He smeared some of the white plaster on a metal square he held in one hand. There were a number of different-sized trowels lined up on the floor, some brushes and a large open bag of plaster powder.

'Where on earth did you get all this?'

He smiled again. 'I borrowed the scooter parked in the garage and went to the local hardware store early this morning. If you know what you're looking for you can always find it.'

She shook her head as she eyed the bag of plaster. That had to be heavy. 'Where even is the hardware store? I didn't even know one existed.' She glanced at her watch. 'And when on earth did you go there?'

He shrugged. 'It's on the outskirts of Baia di Rose. Most tradesmen like to start their work early. They don't like to work in the heat of the day. The hardware store opened at six.'

He ran his hand along the wall and frowned, grabbing a piece of sandpaper and giving a gentle rub around the crack.

'What do you think you're doing? Don't touch that. You'll make it worse. This place is in a bad enough state without you deciding to play Mr Handyman.'

Javier sighed and shook his head. 'You act like I haven't done this before.'

'You haven't!'

He took a step closer and gave her a serious look. 'Don't you do your homework on the people you interview? I've said a number of times that I worked in the summers as a teenager with my Uncle Vinnie—the best handyman in the world.' He waved the piece of metal smeared with plaster. 'There are a number of jobs I can do around here in the next few weeks. Plastering was one of the things I was best at. I can repair the cracks and skim the walls in all the rooms. It will be a good foundation for any other decorating your sister has planned.' He waved his other hand. 'And the conservatory. I can replace the broken glass. Another of my specialities.'

Portia couldn't speak. She was astonished. She didn't like to be caught unawares. There were probably a million women the world over that would currently love to be in her position. A half-dressed Javier Russo offering to work as handyman. She blinked and put her fingers at the edge of her hip and gave herself a sharp pinch.

Yep. She was definitely here. She was definitely awake.

He'd just criticised her. He'd implied she wasn't good at her job. He'd implied she didn't do her homework. Oh, this guy was clearly going to drive her crazy. Half naked or not.

And she hated to admit it right now, but she *didn't* know that much background on Javier Russo. Annoyance swept through her. She wasn't going to let him get the better of her. There was a story here. She could practically smell it in the air between them.

She licked her lips. Her intention had been to throw him out today. But the thought of a story was making her reconsider. Maybe she wouldn't mention anything today at all.

She glanced downwards and realised she was standing in her pale blue wrap robe and slippers, her hair tied in a tangled knot on her head. Not entirely appropriate. She'd been so focused on what the noise was she hadn't really thought about her appearance.

She sucked in a deep breath and tried to take a reality check on what was happening. She knew exactly how to play this. She laughed out loud and held up one hand, putting the other on her hip.

Javier looked amused. Perfect. 'What is it?'

She kept laughing. 'Well, I'm just thinking, whatever that wine was that I drank last night—and I only had two glasses—I think I better hunt down the rest of it.'

Javier lifted his hand from the wall. 'Why?'

She clicked her fingers. 'Well, look what's happened. I drink two glasses of wine, Javier Russo, world-famous movie star—and I think I remember you were last year's Most Eligible Bachelor—has turned up half naked in my sister's dilapidated old villa, offering to be my handyman for the next few weeks. This isn't real. There's no way this is real.'

He nodded slowly, contemplating her words. Javier had that tiny little gleam in his eye. It was famous. Often caught in pictures and on camera in films. It made him look as if he were talking to only you, sharing a joke only with you.

And right now, he *was* talking only to her. There was a real possibility of story here.

'What will it take to convince you?'

Her breathing stopped. Second time Javier Russo had caught her unawares. What did that mean? Her mouth couldn't find the next set of words.

For the tiniest second the thought of a story vanished. Instead, in its place, was the muscular body and grey eyes of Javier Russo. All man, right in front of her.

It was almost as if he read her mind. He put the metal square on the floor next to the trowels and stepped closer. So close that his hand rested on her hip. Yes, it did. It really did.

If this were a film she would have spent around three hours in make-up achieving the 'natural' look. Unfortunately, her natural look was entirely natural. Her face scrubbed last night and a bit of her usual moisturiser smeared on her face. She always tied her hair up when she went to bed and it generally managed to tangle its way into an unruly mess.

He'd got close last night. But she'd gone from being a little foggy with the wine, to thinking there was an intruder, assaulting a movie star, then finding herself making up a bed for him.

No one would believe that interview.

All of a sudden she was closer than she'd ever expected to be with a movie star. Up close and personal. She could see every tiny line around his eyes. Laughter lines. No Botox. Every strand of his dark hair. The stubble on his jaw line. Her palm wanted to reach up and feel it. His white straight teeth and something hidden behind his grey eyes.

That was what stopped her in her tracks.

She recognised the signs. Hurt. Now she'd glimpsed it she could see it as clear as day.

He still hadn't told her why he was here. He hadn't answered many questions last night at all. Had he been dating? Was he here to mend his heart? Somehow, it didn't really seem to fit the bill.

Hurt. It confused her. What could hurt Mr Arrogant? The part of her conscience that had invaded her thoughts this morning crowded forward again.

She lifted both her hands and placed them on his bare chest. The heat against her palms sent tingles up her arms. It was completely forward. But it didn't feel that way. It felt natural. Honest. Her voice was barely a whisper. 'Javier, what are you running from?'

Beneath her palms his chest rose as he sucked in a breath. Silence. The TV host in her ached to fill it. More than three seconds of silence in front of the camera usually meant that something had gone wrong.

But her senses kicked in. The senses that were still functioning while she had her hands on the chest of a film star.

He licked his lips and she stifled her groan. He was looking at her, but it didn't feel as if he were really *seeing* her. He was thinking about something else.

She watched as the virtual shields came down behind his eyes. The tiny part of Javier Russo she'd been about to see instantly hidden again. 'I've been busy. Four films in eighteen months and a whole range of press junkets for this year's new releases. I just needed a bit of time out.'

She bit her bottom lip. It was plausible. But it wasn't the truth.

'You have enough money at your disposal to go to a hundred private islands. You'd have as much peace and quiet as you want. Plus, you'd actually have a place with a functioning kitchen and bathrooms.'

He gave the hint of a smile and shook his head. 'But it wouldn't be the same.'

Something had changed behind his eyes. *Now*, he was being honest.

'What do you mean?'

He glanced down at her hands and her fingers jerked self-consciously. She should really move them. And she would. Just not yet.

He held up his arms. 'I mean, this is the place I remember. Once I got here as a kid, Sofia always filled it with happy memories. And I've never been a lie-on-the-beach kind of guy. I like to be doing something. I like to be industrious. It relaxes me. Helps me sort out things in my head. This place is my idea of a holiday. I just wish I'd thought of it a couple of years ago.'

Her stomach gave a little flip. Her head was all over the place right now. She'd planned to spend the next few weeks deciding what to do about her career. But she didn't really need to be here. She could be back in Hollywood right now, trying to dig up the career-defining story of a lifetime. Instead, she'd decided to take some time to contemplate her next step.

Entertainment Buzz TV had been good for her. She had a steady income. A nice apartment. A good lifestyle. She'd met more famous people—good and bad—than anyone could possibly want to. But things were changing. Hollywood had lost its glitter—even when there were men like Javier around.

Her mouth was dry. There could be a story right at her fingertips—literally. His arrogance had annoyed her before. But did she really want to dig deep and let him expose himself and his secrets to her? Was that really the type of person that she was?

'I want to stay here, Portia. Not in some hotel. Do you think that could be possible?'

Portia. He didn't say her name. He practically sang it.

He didn't even remember her. Not that she expected him to—really. But she had met him and interviewed him before. And it was kind of insulting for a guy not to remember you—even in cut-throat Hollywood.

Her rational head understood. At a press junket he met hundreds of journalists and could never be expected to remember them all. On award night he'd spoken to just as many again on the red carpet. She wasn't any different from any other person who'd shoved a microphone in his face and tried to think of an original question.

But it still stung.

And now he wanted to stay with her. Javier Russo wanted to stay with *her*.

She lifted her hands from his chest. She needed all her senses to be working. And they were already piqued. A fresh, clean scent drifted up under her nose. She scrunched up her face a second and tried to shake it off. The last thing she needed to think about was fresh, clean Javier Russo.

He'd lied to her. No, not strictly true. He just hadn't been entirely truthful. Why on earth would moneybags Mr Russo want to hide out in Aunt Sofia's home? He really wanted to get away from things?

It could be a story. But Internet was scarce around here, nearly as rare as a mobile phone signal. It was part of the reason she'd thought it was a good place to hide out.

She could get all defensive, like some creature marking out their territory, and tell him he couldn't stay. But...she could also be clever. There was always a chance she could get to the bottom of Javier Russo's story. It might just be the thing to save her career.

And in the meantime, she would have some company, and some eye candy.

She sucked in a breath and tried to find the ruthless streak she'd once had. 'You really just want to stay here?'

He nodded.

'How long for?'

Javier ran his fingers through his dark hair as he took a little step to the side. 'Not long. Just a few weeks.'

She folded her arms across her chest. 'You honestly just expected to show up, stay here and then leave, didn't you?'

His face creased into a smile. 'Well, kind of.'

She put her hand on her chest. 'And I've thrown a spanner in the works for you?'

He frowned for a second, as if he wasn't quite sure of the expression. But then he nodded. 'I get it.'

'You do?'

She stepped back a little, trying to get her head on straight for the first time since yesterday. Maybe it had been the wine. Maybe it had been the magical setting. But last night had been a bit unreal.

She gave him a serious look. 'Let's give this some perspective. Last night some stranger appeared at the place I'm staying. Okay, so he might have had a key— and a history of sorts with the place. But I'd made arrangements with my sister—' she put her fingers in the air '—the owner, to stay here for the next few weeks. I don't plan on going anywhere.' She pretended not to see the fleeting disappointment that shot through his eyes. 'We *both* thought we would have this place to ourselves.' She nodded out to the back conservatory. 'Let's face it. There's lots to be done here. And if you're as handy as you say you are, then I might not have any objections to you staying. My skills involve tidying up. That might sound mediocre, but, believe me, I've checked all the rooms and the attic—there's a *lot* of tidying up to be done.' She looked around the room as the acid in her stomach gave a little burn. She was trying her absolute best to be up front. She could hardly tell Javier that finding out what he was hiding from might save her career. Hopefully, it would be a woman. But that made the acid burn even more.

A picture of nails scraping down a chalkboard flashed into her brain with the associated noise. If it was trouble with a co-star, a contract, an affair—any of the above—it might just be enough to give her some leeway with her job.

It would save her telling the other secrets that weren't really hers to share.

She held out her hands. 'In the end, my sister needs this place to be liveable. If you can help with that, fine.' She shook her head and gave him a knowing glance. 'I just want you to know, I don't mix business with pleasure. Never have. Never will.'

Javier looked amused; the little glint was back in his eye. She liked it when that was there. It lightened the mood. She'd spent the last five years harmlessly flirting in front of the camera; it was the unwritten rule of TV hosts. She'd dated people in Hollywood. But never anyone to do with work. Dating a popstar/film star/TV star was the ultimate no-no. Inevitably there would be a messy fallout and he would tell all his fellow performers not to be interviewed by her. Two of her associated press members had found themselves almost blacklisted around Hollywood when their short-term flings had ended.

Portia was far too clever to be that girl.

Javier was watching her carefully. His tools were now on the floor and he made a grab for a T-shirt that she'd missed sitting on top of a white dust sheet.

'Come with me.'

'What?'

She followed him through the house to the kitchen, conscious of the fact she still didn't have on any real clothes. The kitchen—though ancient—was almost in working order. Miranda had arranged electricity and gas. Thankfully the water was still running. Portia had bleached a few cupboards in the last few days and put a few supplies away. But that didn't explain the bag on the countertop.

Javier pulled out some eggs and some freshly baked bread. 'I think our new arrangement calls for a celebratory breakfast.'

'We've made a new arrangement?'

He gave her his trademark Hollywood smile. 'Sure we have. I'm staying. I'll work on the plaster and arrange to get some glass for the conservatory.' He pulled out a frying pan and turned on the gas. 'How do you like your eggs?'

Portia sat up on a stool next to the countertop. 'You cook? And where did you get the eggs and the bread?'

'I got them when I went to get the supplies this morning.' He gave her a wink. 'I was a bit worried that the only sustenance in this place was wine.' He cracked the eggs as her cheeks flushed. But he hadn't finished. 'That was, of course...' he opened the cupboard nearest him '...until I found the candy supply.'

He was teasing her—she knew it. 'What can I say? There are fruit trees in the garden. Wine, fruit and chocolate. What more does a woman need?'

'What more indeed?' The sultry Italian voice shot straight through her, the suggestion in it taking her by surprise.

'Hurry up,' he said. 'Scrambled or fried?'

She stared into the pan. 'Fried is fine. Cooked all the way through.'

He narrowed his gaze. 'Yolk broken?'

'Don't you dare.' She sighed. 'I've never got the hang of sunny side up, over easy, over medium in the States and I've lived there five years now.'

'Maybe it's time to move back?' The hairs prickled at the back of her neck. Gossip spread fast in Hollywood. Did he know her job was on the line?

She tried not to sound as defensive as she felt. She had to remember that Javier could be the ticket to keeping her job. 'If I'm moving back, I'll need to hire a cruise ship to bring my clothes back. And my shoes. The studio doesn't let me keep any of the clothes I wear. But, due to the effects of social media, as soon as pictures start appearing the designers usually send me anything they've seen me wear—along with a whole host of other things. They like the publicity—' she shrugged as she broke off a piece of the bread '—and I like the clothes.'

He tossed the eggs. 'You took the job for the clothes? I don't believe that. What did you do before you got the job?'

She walked over to the sink and filled up a pan with some water. She hadn't found a kettle, so the old-fashioned way would have to do. She set it on the gas hob next to where Javier was cooking. 'I studied investigative journalism at university. I was on holiday in the US, when I kind of lucked into the job. The rest—as they say—is history.' She gave his arm a nudge. 'A film star who makes his own food. Who would have thought it?'

He let out a laugh. 'What did you expect?'

She counted off on her fingers. 'Well, your last co-star on the action movie flew in his own personal chef, who ensured no meal was above three hundred calories. Your last female co-star was on that new-fangled diet where people only eat prawns and drink spring water.'

He rolled his eyes. 'No. You mean *chilled* spring water. We'll not talk about how the smell of prawns seemed to emanate from her pores.'

Portia laughed but kept going. 'Then, there was the comedian in the sci-fi film who was on the spinach, Brussels sprout and fried beans diet.'

Javier shuddered. 'Four hours. That's how long he was on the toilet in his trailer one day. I gave up waiting to film a scene and went for a beer.'

He turned around and pulled out plates from a cupboard. He'd found his way around this kitchen better than she had. Just how much time had Javier spent here?

'A beer? You eat *and* drink? Well, you're just a Hollywood novelty.'

Javier put the eggs down in front of her, then searched through a few more cupboards. 'Yes, I eat. I know the damage it causes when you don't eat. Sorry, can't find the salt and pepper. Eggs and bread it is.'

He sat down opposite her with his own plate. Her stomach clenched. That sentence had just been thrown in there with the rest. Was he referring to his mother, or fellow film stars? Not eating was something that made the hackles rise on the back of her neck. A few years ago her sister Immi had suffered from an eating disorder. But that was the thing about not eating. It didn't just affect one person—it affected the whole family. Even now, every time she saw Immi the first thing she did was check her cheekbones, shoulder bones and her silhouette. Anything that might show any hint of trouble again.

She pushed the thoughts from her head, licked her lips and tried to keep the conversation going. 'I'm a terrible hostess, aren't I? I promise, once that water starts boiling, I'll make the coffee.'

He gave her a nod and she kept talking. 'So, how have you managed to stay away from the Hollywood madness, then?'

He raised his eyebrows. 'You haven't met my mother, have you?'

She shook her head. 'What was her name again? She modelled with Sofia.'

He nodded. 'Anna Lucia. She's around ten years younger than Sofia and I was a late baby. An unexpected surprise.' He picked up his fork. 'My mother is surprisingly traditional. She's seen all the madness of Hollywood and London. The drink, the drugs, the diets and general craziness.' He gave a little shrug. 'She won't admit what ones she trialled, but she's had her own problems.'

There was a change in his tone. It was only slight, but Portia picked up on it straight away. 'What kind of problems?'

He looked at her thoughtfully for a moment—as if he was trying to decide how to answer. 'We came here when my mother was stressed due to work.' He paused for a second. 'It didn't help at times that she was hounded by the press. Trapped in her home by reporters and photographers camped outside the house.' There was an edge of resentment in his voice and she shifted uncomfortably in her chair. He looked around himself. 'This place was good for her too. It calmed her. Brought her the peace that she needed.'

Portia's skin prickled. The words sounded so simple but the expression on his face was anything but. Guilt was swamping her. It felt as if he could see inside her heart and soul and knew that she was one of those people. The story chasers.

It made her uncomfortable. Especially when she wanted to reach out and touch his cheek right now. To offer some shred of comfort. 'And you came with her?' was all she could say.

He licked his lips. 'Most of the time. My father worked away a lot. When he realised my mother was getting unwell he tended to pack us both up and send us to Sofia.' He gave a half-hearted smile. 'I even went to school for a while on L'Isola dei Fiori. If you can call it that.'

'What do you mean?'

Javier shifted in his chair. 'Sofia arranged for me to be schooled "with friends" as she put it.'

'And who were the friends?'

'Alessandro and Nico del Castro.'

Portia started to choke on her eggs. Had he really just said that out loud? 'You went to school with the Princes?'

Javier looked nonchalant about it. 'Only for a few months until my mother was better. Sofia didn't want me to fall behind at school so she arranged for the palace tutor to include me in the lessons.'

'You were friends with the Princes?'

A black shadow crossed his eyes as she realised her mistake at once. Sometimes her press brain asked the questions before she'd had time to edit them. 'Nico, not so much. He was younger. But Alessandro, yes. There was only a year between us.'

Portia gulped. Alessandro had died two years ago. He and Nico had been cousins, but Alessandro was an only child, meaning Nico was now the heir to the throne.

'That must have been hard.'

Javier met her gaze with his grey eyes. 'Yes, it was. We weren't as close as we'd been as children. Alessandro was quiet. He didn't like the spotlight. The bright lights of Hollywood didn't suit him. But he visited a few times.'

Portia nodded as the water in the pot started to bubble. She got up to make the coffee. 'That's quite a difference in childhood. One part with glamorous Sofia and the Princes, and one part handyman with your Uncle Vinnie.' Javier Russo would be a biographer's dream. Why hadn't he done that yet?

He made a strangled kind of noise. 'Don't kid yourself. Small boys aren't glamorous—we spent most of our time conjuring up trouble. And Uncle Vinnie? He was probably my blessing in disguise. He kept me on the straight and narrow. He taught me discipline.' He gave her a cheeky smile. 'Let's face it, there are a number of my co-stars who could probably benefit from some Uncle-Vinnie-style hard work.'

'Oh, I don't doubt it.' She spooned the coffee into the cups and poured the boiling water on top, taking care not to spill it.

'So what about you?' he asked as she pushed the cup towards him.

'What about me?'

She was surprised. Again he was catching her unawares. It was clear that part of the conversation had
come to an end. Javier Russo was good at hinting without giving too much away. She was almost sure she
could name each of the co-stars he'd been referring to
when he talked. And the part about his mother? She'd
just tucked it away somewhere. Probably alongside the
older male film star who hadn't come out, and the depressed female film star. Already it felt too personal,
too deep. The kind of stories she'd spent the last year
pretending she hadn't heard.

'How many sisters do you have?'

She mopped up some of her egg with the bread. Sisters.
The easiest topic in the world for her. She could talk about
her sisters for hours. 'There are four of us. I'm the oldest,
then there's the twins, Imogen and Miranda—she's the
one that just got married—and then there's Posy—real
name Rosalind—she's the ballerina.'

He paused for a second. 'The names—they're all
Shakespeare characters. Were your mother and father
fans?'

She nodded. 'They met at the Royal Shakespeare
Theatre in Stratford watching *Romeo and Juliet*. My
mother said it was fate. They took us there a few times
as kids.' She shook her head and laughed. 'Posy tried
to get up on the stage and dance at one point.'

'And she's the one that inherited the house?'

Portia nodded. 'Sofia was Posy's godmother. My
godmother wasn't quite so exotic. She was my aunt, my
dad's sister, and lived about two minutes away from us.'
She gave him a smile. 'Sofia was always much more
exciting.'

He nodded. 'Oh, I know she was. I saw some of

the parties.' He looked thoughtful. 'Your sister must be very disciplined if she's a ballerina. It's every bit as cut-throat as Hollywood.'

Portia pressed her lips together. 'To be honest, I think it could be worse. I'm not sure how happy Posy is. She's been in the corps de ballet for a while now.' Portia put her hand on her chest. 'Now, personally, I think Posy is the best dancer they have. But I might be a little biased.'

'Really?' Javier was sipping his coffee. He looked amused. 'What about the others?'

'Well, Miranda's a pilot. Cleve, her new husband, is a pilot too. Their wedding was just perfect. When they stood in the garden and said their vows it was gorgeous. I can honestly say I've never seen my sister so happy. It almost made me believe that true love might actually exist.' There was a little pang in her chest. She hated to feel envy. But the love and connection between Andie and Cleve had been crystal clear. 'And Imogen...' Portia paused for a second, trying to find the right words. 'She works at my dad's company, Marlowe Aviation. She's planning on getting married soon too.'

Javier looked at her curiously. 'Why did you say it that way?'

Portia sucked in a breath. 'What way?'

Javier put down his cup. 'You don't want her to get married.' He was looking at her curiously. Had she really been so obvious?

Portia thumped her own cup down on the counter-top with a little more venom than she meant to. 'That's not true.'

'Really?' He smiled as he picked up the plates and carried them to the sink. He completely ignored her outburst.

He kept talking. 'What I'm not sure about is whether

you think you should have got married first, or if you don't like the guy that Imogen is marrying.'

Portia was shocked. And Javier still had that look on his face—the one the world had fallen in love with, half joking, half serious. The expression that had drawn women in all over the world. But right now Portia wanted to dump her coffee over his head.

'That's a terrible thing to say. How dare you?' She tossed her coffee cup in the sink, trying to ignore the loud crack. Oops.

'Well, which one is it?'

Darn this man. He wasn't going to let it go. The words stuck somewhere in her throat. The truth was she'd never liked Immi's intended. She never had. She never would. There was just something about him she couldn't put her finger on.

But she'd also already had horrible irrational thoughts about being left on the shelf and pictured herself with grey hair—a sad old spinster, sitting on a rocking chair like the one on the terrace, watching her sisters' families playing all around her.

Irrational. She knew it. But that didn't mean it wasn't there.

Anger surged through her. 'None of your business.'

Javier gave a little jerk backwards at her words. His amused, playful glance left his face.

She turned and strode out to the terrace. By the time the cool sea breeze started blowing her hair across her face she could feel a little wave of panic.

She was supposed to try and keep Javier sweet. She was supposed to be looking for some insider gossip that could help her keep her job.

But already things weren't sitting comfortably with her. What was it about sharing a house with a Hollywood heartthrob to make you feel like the only reject in town?

She was trying to be cool. She was trying to be professional.

She was trying to be underhand.

Ugh.

Her interview style had always been forthright, if occasionally flirtatious. Trouble was, just being around Javier was unsettling.

Maybe it was those grey eyes, sincere one moment as if the world were on his shoulders, and smouldering the next, as if any second now he would just push her up against a wall and kiss her as he had done his co-star in the last movie she'd watched.

She was pretty sure that had been rated the hottest scene on film that year.

And now she was living it—if only in her head.

Pathetic really.

She sensed him walk up beside her, shoulder to shoulder.

She was watching the azure-blue sea—perfect on a sunny day with waves rising in little white peaks of froth and crashing onto the rocks below.

'I'm sorry, I didn't mean to get personal.'

She licked her lips and begged her brain to find some nice, rational thoughts.

'I didn't mean to get shirty.'

He turned towards her, his brow furrowed. 'Shirty?'

The joys of language. 'Snappy. Impatient.' She waved her hand as his brow started to unfurl. 'Generally just a bit badly behaved.'

He smiled and nodded. 'Ah, well, maybe we're both a bit badly behaved.'

He was trying to be nice—she knew it—but, boy, did this guy speak in double entendres.

He stretched his hands out towards the perfect sea. 'How about I finish some of the more delicate plasterwork and we have a picnic on the beach in a few hours? I miss swimming in the sea around here. I haven't done it in years. It would be nice to bring back some memories.'

She glanced sideways at him. He looked contemplative. Thoughtful. Maybe he would be able to share a little with her once they knew each other better.

She nodded. 'I can get started on some cleaning. I'm going to wash some of the dust sheets and clean some of the windows in the rooms. How about I meet you back here in a couple of hours?'

He nodded and gave her a smile.

She licked her lips as she watched him walk away. In theory it all sounded fine. But the image of Javier Russo all wet in a pair of trunks had suddenly made her mouth go very dry.

Very, very dry.

CHAPTER THREE

HE WASN'T QUITE sure what it was about her. But Portia Marlowe was proving to be a little unexpected.

Javier had never been someone to believe his own press. Every film set, every job he worked on he got to know people from the runners, to the catering staff, to the executives who liked to visit for around ten minutes.

The film-star tag was a whole different ball game. He played the game when he needed to. He did the interviews. He'd even been conveniently photographed on occasion. The sexy label made him laugh out loud. He was comfortable around women. Usually, he had no problems communicating with them.

But he always kept a distance. He always controlled what was going on. He'd seen what the press had done to his mother. In a way he blamed them for her bipolar disorder. Most of her life she'd kept it under control. But when the press had decided to harass her, the stress had exacerbated all her symptoms. The sleeplessness. The fatigue. Her coping mechanisms. Her moods. Her erratic behaviour, coupled with her irritability and her inability to complete tasks—sometimes even sentences.

He'd been determined to always keep his press under control—to only let them know what he wanted them to know. The truth was he always mistrusted the press.

Portia? She was a little different. His mother had once described an English counterpart as 'prickly'. Today, it seemed to fit the bill. Prickly Portia. He wasn't quite sure how old she was, but he'd surely hit a nerve with her in the kitchen today. He wasn't usually so clumsy around women. His mother would have been horrified by him. Sofia would probably have slapped him around the back of the head.

He was getting little flashes of memories about her. There was something achingly familiar about Portia that he couldn't quite put his finger on. Maybe it was the occasional way she said a word with her English accent that was pushing his buttons. He loved that accent. Not that he would tell her that.

He'd come here for some peace. He needed to figure out what came next in his life. From the second he'd got that phone call about Aldo he'd known that things would never be the same. He'd known that *he* would never be the same.

The biggest ache for him was the final diagnosis. Aldo was bipolar.

His friend had suffered from the same disease as his mother and Javier hadn't picked up on it. They hadn't spent a lot of time together in the last year. And Javier had been aware that Aldo had been low after the breakdown of his marriage. But that had seemed almost natural. Almost understandable. But Javier had missed the highs that Aldo had also displayed. The erratic behaviour. The despairing lows. Things that would have helped him put the pieces together to get Aldo the correct diagnosis and treatment before it was too late.

He'd already decided he wanted to do something specific for people with the same disorder. For families with loved ones who were suffering and didn't know how to help.

He just hadn't managed to decide the best way to do it.

This was his time out. His chance to gather his thoughts, arrange his finances and look at his calendar of work for the next year to take time to devote to this. Working on the house would have been therapeutic. He just hadn't expected the house to be filled by Portia Marlowe.

He sighed and walked through to the painted drawing room.

The plasterwork had to be done slowly. And once plaster was mixed it had to be used within a certain time frame. The long snaking crack across the dome had taken some gentle sanding and filling. He'd need to examine it again tomorrow. But now he picked up his wide range of trowels, hawk and scarifier to clean them before he used them again.

Upstairs he could hear the shower running. The dust must have got to places that he didn't even want to tease her about and by the time she came downstairs again he'd finished washing his tools.

Her hair was still damp, coiled around into a bun at the back of her head. She was obviously wearing a swimming costume but had a black sheer kaftan over the top and a pair of flip-flops on her feet.

He shook his head and pointed to them. 'Remember, we've got to get down that path to the beach. Do you have something else?'

She nodded. 'Oh, yeah, I hadn't even thought about that path. I have a pair of trainers I can wear.' She glanced over at him. 'Do you need to get ready?'

He glanced down at himself. A few blobs of plaster

had landed on his grey T-shirt and three-quarter-length khaki shorts. He held up his hands. 'I got an award last year for best-dressed male.' He shook his head. 'I have no idea how that happened. They obviously don't know me at all.'

Portia crossed the kitchen and picked up the rest of the bread. She opened the fridge and came out smiling, holding a bottle of water with a little condensation around the outside. 'Look, it's decided to work today. We can take the rest of the bread, the ham and I have some cheese too.'

Javier had reached the door to leave but ducked his head back around. 'What, no wine?'

Something flitted across her face. 'I suppose we could if you wanted.' She ducked back into the fridge. 'Yep, there's some white. We'll take that.'

A few minutes later he'd washed his face and changed his T-shirt. He'd neglected to bring swimming shorts, but the beach was private and he was sure his black jockey shorts were respectable enough.

Portia had a couple of towels over her arm as well as a bag with the food. They made their way down the path to the beach. The stone was crumbling in places, and the path a little steep. A few times Portia's hand landed on his back as they headed down the slope.

The white sand practically sparkled. Javier kicked off his trainers and almost let out a yelp. 'Wow. It's hot.'

Portia smiled as she kicked hers off too. 'Well, it is brilliant sunshine—what do you expect?'

He looked at her skin. Her English rose complexion had seemed to gain an LA tan. It was light golden brown but she still looked as if she could burn easily. 'Are you all right being out in this sun?'

She winked at him. 'Factor fifty. Haven't you heard? I live in LA. Sun is a crime against skin.'

He laughed. 'You mean you haven't tried one of the crazy remedies?' He tapped his face. 'To stop wrinkles and regain youthfulness.' She burst out laughing as he mimicked one of the other popular male film stars who'd just filmed a TV ad for moisturiser.

There was a glint in her eyes as she laid the towels down on the sand. 'Which one? The elephant's urine? The fungus? Or the sixty-day-old-egg recipe?'

He shuddered. 'Is that the latest fad?' He waved his hands. 'My last co-star paid over a thousand dollars for some fish-egg cream. The smell—' he shook his head and screwed up his face '—was so horrendous, none of the crew would venture near her trailer.'

Portia started laughing as she walked towards the waves. 'And you had to kiss her?'

This time Javier exaggerated the shudder. 'I would never speak badly of a co-star. Thankfully, by the time we were filming, the cream was washed off and her make-up was firmly in place.'

Portia let out a little yelp as she paddled at the edge of the sea. 'Yikes, it looks so inviting but it's bitter cold.'

Javier grinned as he strode into sea. It was a little colder than he expected but it was exactly what he needed. He started sloshing the cold sea water over his chest and back. He turned around as he was doing it, letting the waves gently lap up to his back.

'Come on,' he gestured to her. 'Get in.'

She shook her head and pulled up the hem of her black sheer kaftan. 'Oh, no. Not yet. Paddling is as good as it gets.'

He squinted at her as she stood in the sun.

She laughed as the waves lapped up her thighs. 'How

is it that as soon as you put a toe in the sea, it seems to try and drag you in further?'

His stomach clenched a little. Press. It was easy to forget that Portia was press.

But he couldn't forget it. He had to remember—at all times.

He had to be nice to her. If he wanted to stay here—he had to keep her onside. But he could still do that by keeping her at arm's length.

Today was only about being polite. The work might seem like a bonus for Portia, but for him it was therapeutic. He could think while he worked. He could make plans while he worked.

There was something about Portia. Maybe it was because she was press. But he could see it hidden behind her careful glances at him. She made his spider sense tingle, and that helped him remember she was the enemy. He got the impression there was more to Portia than met the eye.

He watched her as she took a few steps in, changed her mind and took a few steps back again. 'There should be a law against water this cold,' she muttered, her kaftan poised around her thighs. She took another few steps in, then shook her head. 'Nope. Not for me. Changed my mind.' She gestured towards the water. 'You swim. I'll watch. How about I promise to phone for help if I see you being eaten by a shark?'

She let her kaftan drop and waded out of the water to drop on one of the towels. She lay back and pulled her sunglasses down from her head.

'How are you going to do that with no phone signal?'

She waved her hand and sighed. 'Yeah. Not the best plan. Don't worry. I'll think of something.'

He shook his head and started swimming. He didn't

notice the cold as he stroked out towards the buoy. It was only around half a mile out from shore and he'd swum this distance many times over the years. He kicked hard and got into the rhythm. No phone signal. And no Internet around here—although there might be a chance of Internet in town. Maybe he didn't need to worry about Portia too much. He reached the buoy and started back to the shoreline. It was easy to get into the rhythm. And this was a much better workout than heading to a gym. One of his favourite workouts back home was swimming at the various beaches around Los Angeles and he was spoiled for choice.

It didn't take long to reach the shore again and he waded out and dropped down next to her, rolling onto his back.

They were right in the middle of the white sandy beach. The naturally formed arch curving over them and offering just the slightest shade.

'It's safe,' he said. 'No sharks. At least not the seafaring kind.'

She frowned at him but didn't question the statement.

'Lovers' arch,' he said. 'You know what they say about that.'

She rolled onto her side to face him and leaned her head on her hand. 'We didn't call it Lovers' arch. We called it Neptune's arch. That sounds much more exotic. Sofia called it that.'

He sighed and leaned a little closer. Close enough to cast a shadow on her face. 'I know. Don't tell anyone, but I actually preferred the Greek god Poseidon. His legend was much more interesting than the Roman god's.'

Portia looked over her shoulder and whispered, 'I think around these parts that might be considered treason.'

He put his hands behind his head as he looked up at

the arch. 'Why? L'Isola dei Fiori is neither Italian nor Greek. For all we know they have their own ancient legends here.' He looked over at her. 'Do you remember the legend?'

She nodded as she reached for the bag of food. 'Sure I do. Neptune had found a lover, a woman on L'Isola dei Fiori. When we were children we used to joke it was Sofia.'

Javier nodded. 'I could imagine that.'

Portia pulled out the bottle of wine and opened it. 'But Neptune's consort, Salacia, was furious and called the other gods of the Underworld.' Portia poured the white wine into glasses. 'The woman—I can't remember what her name was—was heartbroken when Neptune said he had to leave her or she would be killed. He blasted the cliff with his trident, creating the rock arch, and told her that whoever kissed under the arch would find their true love.'

She handed one of the glasses to Javier and he propped himself up a little. He actually liked teasing her. It seemed that some clichés were true. The English were more uptight than Italian women and Portia was no exception.

'And have you ever tried to find your true love?'

She took a sip of the semi-chilled wine. She pointed back to the terrace on the cliff above. 'As children we often spied on the beach at night. If you were here during any of Sofia's parties you must have known that, at some point, all paths led to the beach.' She rolled her eyes. 'I'm just glad there are no lights down here. I think we would have seen a whole lot more than we should have.'

He nodded in agreement. 'I saw a proposal under here once.'

'You did?' Now that had captured her attention. She sat upright on the towel. 'Who was it?'

He shook his head. 'It was nobody famous. A pair of locals.' He glanced around. 'There must be a secret way onto this beach that no one knows about. Sofia and my mother were on the terrace drinking champagne cocktails when we spotted the couple under the arch at sunset. The guy kissed her then dropped onto one knee and proposed. Sofia was so excited she shouted down and invited them up to the villa for some champagne.'

'Wow. Do you have any idea what happened to them?'

He grinned. 'I might have. Let's just say I know twenty years later they're still together and living in Baia di Rose.'

Portia gave a sigh and took another sip of wine. 'It's a beautiful story.' She tilted her head to one side as she looked around. 'I've always been surprised that no one has tried to snap this place up.'

'What do you mean?'

'I just mean that this whole place—L'Isola dei Fiori—it's beautiful. It's breathtaking. And yet it doesn't seem overrun by tourists.' She gestured towards the arch. 'It's even got its own legend. In any other place there would be a multimillion-pound resort built on this coast with weddings held at the arch at sunset every night. What with the headline-stealing King Ludano years ago I'm surprised that L'Isola dei Fiori didn't turn into the next Monaco or Cannes.'

Javier couldn't help but laugh. 'You old cynic. But I can tell you one reason why it didn't.'

She looked curious. 'Why?'

Javier took a drink of his wine. 'Simple. No cinema. Can't do film premieres without one.'

Portia looked around her as if she expected a cinema

to just appear out of the sand next to them. 'There isn't a cinema in Baia di Rose? Really?'

'Oh, there is now. But there wasn't then. Around fifteen years ago they converted one of the old theatres into a cinema—but all they really did was put a screen at the back of the stage. Up until that point the only place that had a cinema was the palace.'

'Really?' Portia sat up a little straighter. He tried not to smile. He should have guessed the reporter in her would suck up any snippet of information that could turn into a story.

'Yeah. Alessandro and I used to sneak in when the adults were watching movies. And not all of them were meant for children.' He tipped his head back. 'It was probably the thing that sparked my interest in film. Let me think, twenty years ago I can remember watching *The Rock*, *Jerry Maguire* and *Independence Day*.' He gave her a joking stare. 'And you have no idea how much I wanted to be a Borg in *Star Trek*.'

'Wow, was that really twenty years ago? It just seems like yesterday. We went to London to watch that at the cinema. Posy was mad. *The Nutcracker* was on at the National Theatre and she definitely didn't want to watch a sci-fi movie. I can remember the expression on her face as if it were yesterday.'

Her words struck a pang somewhere in his heart. She laughed as he topped up their wine glasses, and looked out at the perfect azure sea. In the distance there was one tiny white blip, a boat far out at sea. To all intents and purposes it almost felt as if they had the island to themselves. He picked up a handful of sand and let it run through his fingers.

Time. The one thing he'd discovered he didn't have enough of, until it was too late.

Aldo's suicide had been a bolt from the blue.

They'd been friends since childhood, grown up together, met girls together, got into trouble together. When Javier had started to have some success in acting, he'd flown Aldo out a few times to some of his locations. But over the years those times together had diminished.

Aldo had married. Then divorced. He'd lost weight and been quieter. On the times that he'd seen him, Javier had asked if he was well, if he needed anything. But his childhood friend was much too proud to talk— which had left him in tatters when he'd found out that the last person Aldo had called was him. What if he'd answered the phone? What if he'd managed to get a signal and called back later? Would it have made a difference? Would a conversation have been enough to make Aldo reconsider?

News of the suicide had left him reeling. Standing next to the graveside while Aldo's sister sobbed her heart out had torn him apart. He'd never forget the expressions on Aldo's parents' faces. Two broken people that could never be put back together again.

Javier's mother had insisted on coming too, but had turned up in an Italian grey silk suit, which had wilted and clung in the heavy rain. The weather had matched the mood of the people attending.

There were a few old school friends. But Javier hadn't been sure if they'd been there to pay their respects to their old friend, or to spy on the now famous one. It had left a bad taste in his mouth.

For weeks after the funeral Javier had been haunted at night. Going over every conversation, every email, wondering why he hadn't picked up on the hints that Aldo was unwell.

It had been seventeen months since they'd actually seen each other. Seventeen months. In a world of social media and live streaming that now seemed awful that he hadn't made more of an effort to stay in contact with his friend.

His simple excuse was he hadn't had time.

And his gut twisted at how truly pathetic that made him feel.

How many signs had he missed because he was moving on to the next film, attending an interview or press conference, or discussing deals with his agent? If he'd just stopped to ask Aldo the question—how are you doing? *Really asked.* Could he have made a difference for his friend? If he'd had a conversation with Aldo's family and heard about his behaviour would he have recognised the signs?

If he'd answered the phone that night and realised how down Aldo was—what would he have done?

The thought had played over and over in his head. He couldn't have left the film set. He'd been under contract and in the middle of the desert wasn't exactly easy to get away from. But he might have spoken to Aldo's sister—or tried to find him a doctor that could help him. A counsellor to talk to. Anything.

He'd never really spoken to anyone about this. Aldo's sister's tear-streaked face had been enough. 'You were the last call he made,' she'd said. 'What did he say to you? Did he give you any clue?'

His reply felt so worthless. 'I never got the call, Estelle. He just left me a message. I was away filming and by the time I came back…' He let his voice tail off. It was easier than letting her know how guilty he felt. Guilty that the message had said Aldo really needed someone to talk to. And his oldest friend had forgotten to call back.

He'd come here to reassess. Re-evaluate his life. Villa Rosa was his haven. His time out.

But from the moment that he'd got there, he'd got the distinct impression that it was Portia's haven too.

He studied her as she sipped her wine. Long dark curls with sun-tipped ends, light golden tan, long legs— mostly hidden—snub nose and—when she wanted to—a dazzling smile.

In lots of ways Portia Marlowe really was the perfect woman.

If only she had another job.

Not that he could even contemplate a relationship right now. In the last two years he'd only had time for a few dates, and none of them had made him want to plan ahead.

The press hadn't picked up on Aldo's suicide. He'd been relieved. The last thing Aldo's family needed was a reporter poking into their private business.

A few lines in a couple of online reports had mentioned Javier had flown to Italy for a funeral. But it had been the lead up to one of the biggest award ceremonies at the time and there had been a hundred other scandalous stories to fill all the papers and magazines.

Portia sighed and turned towards him. He leaned forward and topped up both of their glasses with wine, handing hers back to her, then turned to face her too.

For a moment time seemed to stand still. Both lying on their towels, facing each other with heads propped on their hands and white sand beneath their toes. The craggy rock arch had thrown a shadow over part of Portia. Her black kaftan had moved as she turned, revealing a long expanse of tanned leg. The rest of the thin material flickered in the breeze, hinting at all the curves underneath.

She looked at him with her big brown eyes and took a sip of her wine. 'I'm a musical girl. Which doesn't help in Hollywood these days when they don't make them any more.'

He smiled at the easy subject matter. Portia was wise enough not to pry, and to give him a little space.

'I always wanted to be one of the kids in *The Sound of Music*. I may even have longed for a pair of red shoes like Dorothy in *The Wizard of Oz*.' She moved her feet in the sand. 'If I click my heels three times I'll get back home.' She closed her eyes just for a second. 'You're not ready to go back home?'

'No. Of course not. This is a holiday.' Now he was curious. 'You said it was your sister's wedding last week—and you have a few weeks' holiday. How did you manage to get so much time off?'

It was a natural question. Everyone knew that in Hollywood unless you were constantly on the TV you were instantly forgotten. One of LA's late-night talk-show hosts refused to take holidays. His predecessor had taken holidays and by the time he'd come back from a round-the-world cruise he'd been replaced. Hollywood was definitely fickle and he was quite sure there would be another, equally beautiful and ambitious, woman snapping at Portia's heels.

'I was due holidays. My producer knew that. I've always filled in and covered emergencies for them.' She raised her eyebrows. 'I've even presented the weather a few times despite the fact I can't tell one cloud from another.'

He laughed. 'I can top that for jobs we're not qualified for.'

She gave an easy smile. 'How?'

'When I was a jobbing actor I was an extra on an old Western made-for-TV movie. I was supposed to just sit in the background of the bar, then walk past with horses a few times.'

'And?'

He gave her a wink. 'If you look in the credits you'll see my name under "Old Hag".'

Portia spluttered then choked on her wine. 'What?'

'Hey!' Javier flung up his hands. 'I got a line out of it. It was worth it.'

'What was the line?'

He wrinkled his face up and leaned close to her. Portia leaned in a little too, waiting for him to whisper. She was almost holding her breath, waiting to hear the line.

He couldn't resist. He took a deep breath, his lips close to her ear. 'It was…' he pulled back—just for effect '…"*Stop thief!*"' His voice echoed across the beach and cove.

She fell back, tipping her wine over the sand as laughter shook through his whole body.

She slapped his shoulder. 'You ratbag.'

He winked. 'I might not have been the star, but it got my name on the credits. And the make-up was spectacular—even my own mother didn't recognise me.'

She tilted her head to the side. 'Where is your mother these days?'

He felt himself bristle. It was a natural question. It was him that had mentioned her. 'She lives in Rome these days.' He picked up his wine glass that was wedged in the soft sand. 'Here, have mine.'

Her fingers brushed against his as she reached for the wine. 'Thank you, I will. I think you owe me for that.'

'How can I make it up to you? Do you want me to

sing to you? A duet? Break into a musical routine? I once made an attempt at the chimney-top dance from *Mary Poppins*.'

She rested back on her towel. 'Oh, I'd love to see that. I'd pay money to see that.' But she shook her head. 'Although I love musicals, Posy's the one with all the dance talent. As for my singing? I can clear a room with a few notes.'

'That good?'

She nodded. 'Oh, yeah.'

This was the first time in a long time he'd actually felt relaxed. Actually wanted to be in a woman's company. Maybe it was Villa Rosa? Maybe it was the fact he knew he could do manual labour for a few days and clear his head. Or maybe it was the sometimes prickly woman with the best accent and the biggest brown eyes he'd ever seen.

She gave a sigh as she looked out across the ocean. 'The view here is just amazing. I always thought my favourite place in the universe was the Griffith Park Observatory.'

'You like it up there?' He was surprised. It was a popular place in LA. He just hadn't thought of it as a place Portia would visit.

'The view across LA is amazing. And the view at night?' She held up her fingers, blew a puff of air into them and flicked them in the air. 'It's just mesmerising.'

He gazed across the azure sea. 'As good as this?'

'Hmm...' She contemplated for a second. 'I guess they could be equal.' She lay back and looked up at the arch. Her eyes took on a wicked twinkle. 'You do know that Sofia wanted to paint the arch pink—don't you?'

'What?' He sat bolt upright, then shook his head and started laughing. 'No way. No, she didn't.'

Portia gave a firm nod. 'Oh, yes, she did. It was one of her phases. She thought the arch would look better in pink. My grandmother nearly had a fit.'

He turned around to face her again. 'I guess it never came to anything.'

She took a drink of her wine. 'Thank goodness.' She squinted up at the arch. 'Can you imagine if this had been painted *pink*?' She gave a shudder.

He couldn't help but smile at her. Portia was nowhere near as prickly as he'd first thought. She might even be fun.

'How about I make dinner tonight?'

Her eyes shot up for a second. Then she gave him a knowing smile. 'Are we barbecuing?'

'Why?'

She grinned. 'Because I'm not sure how reliable the oven is. You can cook on the stove—I've made a few mean omelettes in the last week—but that's it.'

He shook his head. 'You've survived the last week on omelettes? Oh, no. Surely we can do better than that. There are a few restaurants in Baia di Rose—why don't we see if I can arrange a taxi and head to one of those?'

She bit her lip. It was almost as if she were contemplating saying no. When was the last time a woman had turned him down? He almost couldn't remember.

Getting out for dinner might do them some good. He needed to head into the village anyway to order some glass for the conservatory. Having dinner seemed like a plan.

It might also help him keep his guard up. Being in a house with one person made things very informal. It tempted him to forget that Portia was a reporter. Particularly when she was lying next to him on the sand looking like this.

Her hair was tied back with some kind of clasp, with a few loose strands blowing in the breeze around her face. If he leaned forward right now, he could brush that hair back with his fingertips and just touch his lips against hers...

He couldn't help it. He reached over and trailed the tip of his index finger down her nose. Her dark eyes widened and she licked her pink lips.

Something clenched around his heart like a fist. A conversation. Rearing up from the back of his memory out of nowhere. Aldo. Telling him about the first time he'd kissed Lissa. Telling him he'd known straight away that she was the girl he was going to marry. He'd never seen his friend so happy. He'd teased him for months about the devotion to his wife before they were married. Before it had all fallen apart.

Could he really have made a difference?

He pulled his finger back, trying to forget the softness of her skin beneath his touch. He didn't deserve this. He had no right to reach out to Portia—and find even a second of happiness—when Aldo couldn't do that same.

A whole host of memories flooded through him again. *Sleeping with the enemy.* It was only a figure of speech but that was what this equated to. What on earth was he thinking? Portia was press—and press should always be kept at a safe distance.

His movement was sudden and Portia bit her lip, confusion flooding her eyes. She pulled herself back out of his reach, gathering up the glasses and bag from the sand.

'It's getting too hot for me,' she said quickly, her voice wavering slightly. 'I think it's time for me to go back inside.'

He cringed. What was he thinking? One second he wanted to be in her company, the next he was thinking about what he'd lost. He was so conflicted right now.

Guilt overwhelmed him. It might not be rational. It might not be justified. But it was just where his head was.

No matter how much he wanted to he couldn't turn back the clock.

He couldn't go back and have that conversation with Aldo.

And until he made peace with himself and put the steps in motion to make a change—he certainly couldn't do anything else.

CHAPTER FOUR

PORTIA WALKED OUT of the room and he sucked in a breath.

She was wearing a belted pink dress that shimmered and black stiletto heels. Her hair was pulled back from her face and tied in a bun at the back of her head and she was wearing bright red lipstick.

He hadn't moved. It was as if a warm breeze had just enveloped his skin making every tiny hair stand on end. There was something achingly familiar about the way she looked.

'I've seen those clothes before. That dress—it's striking. Is it a US designer?' Maybe one of his co-stars had worn the same dress at a photo shoot.

She took a long time to answer. Her hand ran across the satin material of the dress. 'Maybe at the awards ceremony. This is the dress I wore for the red carpet interviews when we met. It's not designer. I found it in a vintage dress shop a few years ago. I threw it into my case when I came for my sister's wedding in case I needed something more formal to wear.'

Her posture had stiffened and she wasn't quite meeting his gaze.

The awards ceremony. He'd tried to smile and be sociable but inside he'd felt as if he were dying. One of his co-stars had muttered beneath her smile that he was being inexplicably rude.

His mouth felt dry. The night had passed in a blur to him. He couldn't remember a single part of it. He'd still been in shock. Still trying to get his head around what had happened.

Doubtless Portia had been one of the people he'd been rude to.

He licked his dry lips as his stomach coiled in a way it hadn't in a long time. He felt like a kid in a headmaster's office. 'Did we talk on the red carpet?'

The look she shot him told him just about everything he needed to know. She waved her hand dismissively and walked past him. 'I don't think you could call it that.'

He caught her by the shoulder, stopping her in her tracks. 'Portia, wait. I'm sorry.'

She spun around, fire dancing behind her eyes. 'Really?' The word was spoken like a challenge.

'I wasn't myself that night.'

She tilted her head. 'Oh? You weren't? The arrogant man I met that night wasn't you?'

He cringed. He should have known. Portia was prickly. It was clear he had offended her. 'I'm sorry.'

'You're sorry? For asking me if that was the best I could do?'

She was angry with him. That much was crystal clear. He shook his head. He couldn't even remember what he'd said. But he did recall feeling exasperated by the never-ending questions that night about the film, his co-star and his suit. It had all seemed so superficial—so unimportant.

She was facing him now and he put his hand back up

on her shoulder. He spoke softly. 'Please. I was upset. I couldn't concentrate on being at the ceremony.'

She frowned. 'What do you mean? That's the biggest night in any actor's career—whether you're nominated or not.'

She was right. He knew she was right. Connections made on awards ceremony night could lead to great things—if your head was in the game.

He could feel all the barriers he'd put up earlier start to crumble. He knew she was a reporter. He knew he should be cautious. 'I'd just lost a friend. I'd just come back from the funeral.' He didn't add any more. He didn't want to reveal any more about the situation.

'I didn't know that.' She seemed surprised.

He gave a wry smile. 'Not everything reaches the gossip columns.'

She met his gaze and leaned towards him a little. 'And not every story that I hear makes the news.'

She was right under his chin now. The light in the corridor was dim and her pupils had dilated, making her eyes even darker than normal. Her voice was breathy. As she stepped closer her jasmine scent wound its way around him. He could hear one of the old-fashioned clocks ticking in the distance, marking the passing of time.

It was a simple sentence. But he could see a whole host of other things on her face. Conflict. Learning. She was a reporter. This kind of thing was her job. But how many secrets did Portia know that she hadn't shared? He'd never even contemplated that before.

'Isn't it your job just to find the next story?'

They stood in the dim hall for a few seconds. He was conscious of her breathing, of the rise and fall of her chest under the pink shimmering material. His finger itched to reach out and touch her skin.

But he resisted. He couldn't do that. He didn't want to start something he couldn't continue.

It felt as if they stood there for a while. Neither moving. Both of them wondering what could come next.

She met his gaze. 'That depends on me. I'm not as hungry for a story as I used to be. I won't let myself be pushed in directions I don't want to go. Hollywood lost its gloss for me a long time ago. We have a saying in Britain that today's headlines are tomorrow's fish and chip paper. It's Hollywood. There will always be countless affairs and scandals. I don't worry about revealing cheaters. I don't worry about breaking news about who has got the next big role in a blockbuster movie. But even I have morals. There are some things I won't tell. Ever.'

He was kind of taken aback at the declaration. She'd obviously listened when he'd revealed his dislike of reporters earlier. He hadn't invited Portia for dinner tonight in the hope that something would happen between them. Just the opposite.

He'd hoped that in a formal environment it would be easier to remember who she was. Too bad they hadn't even reached the restaurant yet. Because she seemed to have turned all that on its head.

He couldn't help the attraction that was simmering beneath the surface. Right now he wasn't even sure he wanted to.

Portia licked her lips and took a step to the side. 'I think that was our taxi.' She smiled.

'It was? I didn't even hear it.'

He stepped back and put a smile on his face, making

a sweeping motion with his hand. 'Ms Marlowe, can I take you to dinner?'

He strode over to the main door and reached for the handle just as she did too.

Their hands brushed together again. Somewhere, in that last romantic movie he'd made, the film director had just cut to include multicoloured fireworks in the distance. He could practically hear them exploding next to his ear.

Portia pulled her hand back. 'Sorry.' He could almost see something change in her eyes. There was a glimmer of determination. Where had that come from?

He watched as she sucked in a breath and tilted her head towards him.

'About the awards. You were cheated. You should have been nominated yourself.' Even the pitch of her voice was different. It was as if she'd just moved back into Hollywood reporter mode.

It changed the atmosphere in the air between them.

But he couldn't help but smile. 'I appreciate the sentiment. But no, I shouldn't. That film was terrible.'

He could tell she couldn't help it—her shoulders started to move and then her suppressed laughter bubbled over, her hand at her mouth. 'You think your own film was terrible?'

He laughed as he opened the front door for them just as the taxi pulled up outside. 'Sure, I do. At least, I was terrible. My co-star had a much better part than I did.'

'Then why on earth did you make it if you didn't like it?'

He wrinkled his nose. 'My agent told me to. He said the film was clever. He thought it was more *art nouveau* than anything else I'd made. He said it would widen my audience appeal.'

She rolled her eyes. 'Like that's what you need. Just about everyone in the world knows who you are.'

He opened the door on the taxi for her. 'And that's not always a good thing. Anonymity can be nice.'

She gave him a curious stare as she climbed in the taxi. 'If you say so.'

The journey in the taxi took less than five minutes. Javier was wearing dark trousers and a white short-sleeved shirt. The evening was warm so neither of them had a jacket, which meant that in the confines of the vehicle the dark hairs on his arms were practically tickling her skin. She was flustered and she hated being flustered.

It wasn't a normal state for Portia Marlowe. She spent most of her time in front of the camera, cool and un-ruffled.

She was about to go out to dinner with Javier Russo. The film star currently adorning a thousand teenagers' walls.

What on earth was she going to say?

Javier chatted easily in Italian with the taxi driver, asking him questions then taking a piece of paper and scribbling some notes before handing it back. She blinked as he pulled out his wallet and took out a wad of cash. 'What's that for?' She looked around—not quite sure what she was looking for—but almost as if it was some kind of clandestine act.

Javier laughed. 'The taxi driver lives next door to the builder's merchant. I've asked him to get me some glass for the conservatory. He's going to bring the de-livery to Villa Rosa tomorrow.'

'Oh, I see.' She gave a sigh and flopped back against

the cool leather of the two-seater. Her brain was spinning. What was wrong with her?

From the second he'd touched her cheek on the beach her brain had been filled with a thousand thoughts. She'd been straight with him. She'd been in Hollywood too long. She'd been propositioned by some actors, and seen others cheat and betray. She was jaded. And while the attention Javier was giving her was flattering, she also had the tiniest belief in the back of her mind that she could be being played. After all, wasn't Javier one of the best actors around?

The taxi driver opened her door and she stepped out. Javier had chosen a small restaurant overlooking the port. The waiter showed them to a table on the terrace without so much as a blink. Portia reached up to grab a strand of hair and twiddle it around her finger. It was a nervous habit—one she'd had since she was a child. But she'd forgotten her hair was coiled tightly into a bun at the nape of her neck.

Did no one else recognise Javier? She glanced around the restaurant. It was exactly as it should be. There was a large family at one table, and two other couples at tables on either side of them. Both couples were completely engaged in conversations with each other. No one seemed to have noticed their resident film star.

Javier pulled out a chair for her. 'Would you prefer inside? Will you be too cold out here?'

She shook her head quickly. Inside the restaurant was lit by flickering candles. Much too intimate. Javier gave her a nod. 'Would you like some wine?'

She nodded quickly. 'Rosé?' he asked as one eyebrow arched jokingly.

'No, white, please.' The waiter had placed a menu in front of her but her eyes had caught sight of a wooden board listing their special for the evening. 'I think I'll have the fish. White would suit better.'

Javier looked over his shoulder and nodded at the board too. 'Ah, yes, the fish looks good. We'll both have that.' He handed the menus back to the waiter and pointed to something on the wine menu. 'And this, please.'

The waiter nodded and disappeared. Portia felt her stomach do a little flip-flop.

She was out for dinner with Javier Russo. And those sexy grey eyes that usually graced the big screen were looking straight at her. Javier looked completely relaxed. He glanced around the port, watching the bobbing boats and fishermen packing up for the night. His head nodding slowly.

'Do you recognise this place?'

'Of course, I spent hours here as a kid.'

She was surprised. 'You did?'

He leaned forward and put his elbows on the table. 'You didn't?'

Portia shook her head. 'Hardly ever. We mainly just played at the house or on the beach.'

Javier gave a little smile. 'You and your sisters were obviously good girls. I couldn't wait to get a bit of freedom and wander into the town.' He pressed his lips together for a second, 'The house was either too quiet, or complete chaos.'

She was tempted to press for more. 'Didn't you enjoy spending time with Sofia?'

He looked out over the water. 'Well, yes, and no. The days could be long for a small boy.'

'You weren't playing with the Princes?'

He raised his eyebrows and she burst out laughing. 'That didn't quite come out right.'

He shook his head. 'No, I didn't play with the Princes. I didn't meet them at first. It was only when we had to stay for a bit longer that Sofia made the arrangements with the tutor. Even then, I always knew I was persona non grata in the palace. Alessandro was quite reserved to begin with—not like Nico at all.' He smiled and shook his head. 'Even now, every time I hear Nico's name, I wonder what crazy sport he's up to now.' He picked up the fork on the table and passed it from hand to hand. 'Alessandro would have been a good King.' He looked out over the port again. The sun was beginning to lower in the sky sending streaks of orange and red across the water. 'He loved L'Isola dei Fiori. He wanted the absolute best for this place and its people.'

He looked up and met her gaze for a second. 'Parents just shouldn't outlive their kids. There's just something so wrong about it.'

There was an ache to his words. A pain. Was he talking about Alessandro's death and the fact his father Vincenzo was still on the throne, or had Javier lost a child himself?

Almost instantly a cool breeze swept over her skin and she shivered. The waiter chose that moment to appear and pour their wine. She'd never been so glad to let the dry, sharp taste fill her senses.

Javier paused for a few seconds, sipping at his wine and staring at the horizon.

Her stomach did another flip-flop. If Javier had something deep and dark in his past she wasn't sure she wanted to know. She liked the Javier Russo that the world did. His sexy smile, the glint in his pale grey eyes and the way he could look at you as if you were the only person on the planet.

The flash of pain there had unsettled her.

She was looking for a headline. Something that could cause a five-minute frenzy, and let her get in her boss's good books again. But as tempting as that could be, she'd meant it when she'd told him that not every story made it onto her entertainment show.

Just being in Javier's company meant the questions she'd already been asking herself about her job seemed to be magnifying in her brain. He wasn't acting like the arrogant man she'd met on the red carpet in March. She'd brushed off his explanation—but maybe it had been true?

Javier turned his attention back to her. She could almost see him switch off—push the thoughts he was having away.

He leaned on the table again. 'So, Portia, what are your plans for the rest of this week?'

She smiled as the waiter set down their plates and she picked up her fork. That was a couple of times he'd done that with her. It seemed Javier had learned the art of changing the subject well. 'I haven't decided. I'm split between just cleaning in general or going up into the attic and starting to find out what's up there.'

'Knowing Sofia, it could be anything.'

She sighed. 'Part of me is excited, and part of me is dreading it.'

'Dreading what?'

Portia poked at the fish in front of her. It looked wonderful, it smelt fantastic, but her stomach was still doing flip-flops. She pressed her lips together and gave Javier a smile. She closed her eyes, seeing the villa in all its splendour in her head. Sofia in a beautiful long green satin dress, gliding down the staircase with a glass in her hand. Guests mingling all around her, spilling out through the conservatory and onto the terrace.

Others gathering in the flickering candlelight of the domed room. 'Dreading getting rid of all the memories of Sofia,' she admitted. She opened her eyes again. Javier was looking at her with the strangest expression.

She shrugged. 'When I first walked into the villa I just…just…*felt* her. You know? It doesn't matter that she's been gone two years. When Miranda walked up the stairs of the villa and opened the door of the wardrobe, revealing her spectacular clothes, it was like being five again. I kept expecting Sofia to walk in behind us and offer us a piece of her jewellery to match her clothes.'

'You were wearing Sofia's clothes?' He looked puzzled.

Portia nodded. 'Sorry, yes. Miranda got married on the beach below the house. It was kind of short notice. There was no time for bride or bridesmaid dresses. We all just picked something out of Sofia's vintage wardrobe.' She finally took a bite of the fish—it was delicious.

'You did?' He seemed genuinely surprised. 'I thought the wedding dress was a big thing for you girls.'

'Oh, it is.' She nodded. 'If you want it to be.'

She picked up her wine glass and took a sip. A smile crept across her lips.

'What? What is it?' Javier's eyes were sparkling.

She shook her head. 'I'm just thinking about some of the celebrity weddings I've covered.' She leaned across the table conspiratorially. 'Honestly, you have no idea. If an average woman can turn into a bridezilla, what do you think a Hollywood star with a million dollars can do?'

He wrinkled his nose. 'Bridezilla?'

She waved her hand. 'You know—a crazy lady.

Thinks the whole world revolves around her, and her wedding.'

He nodded and smiled. 'Okay, I've got it.'

'Let's face it. It doesn't matter how much money you spend on a wedding—or where it is. It's the person you marry that's important.'

He gave her a thoughtful glance. In the dimming evening light those grey eyes were mesmerising. People always said that every photo of a star these days was edited. And for the majority of them that was true.

But for some reason, right now, Portia had never seen a more handsome man in her life. The exposed skin on her arms prickled at the mere thought. The white shirt showed off his tan perfectly. She could see the hint of stubble on his jaw. Her fingers wanted to reach across the table and brush against it. The edges of his lips started to hint at a smile. 'So, what you're telling me is that you're a romantic at heart.'

She gave a conciliatory nod. 'I guess I am. I've never seen Miranda look happier. Cleve too. I guess a year ago he thought he'd never be happy again.'

'Why, what happened to him?'

'He lost his wife in an accident.' She ran her fingers up and down the stem of the wine glass. 'Grief can be a horrible thing.'

Javier was watching her closely. 'Do you think that people can have more than one big love in their life?'

She was surprised. Not many guys she knew would ask a question like that, and she wasn't quite sure how to answer. She nodded. 'If you'd asked me before, I would have said no. I would have said that I thought there's probably only one true love out there for everyone. But now? When I watched Miranda and Cleve say their vows together I could see the love in their eyes—

their devotion to each other. I think they're lucky that they've found it.'

Javier gave a slow nod. 'So, Portia—no big love in your life?'

She shifted a little in her seat. This conversation was getting very personal. Wasn't the shoe supposed to be on the other foot—wasn't she supposed to be getting information from him instead?

She sighed. 'In LA? Not a chance. Most of the time life feels unreal there. You must get that. I'm so busy with work most days that I don't really have time for dating. I cover all the parties but I don't actually *go* to them.'

She didn't want to seem too cynical, but the truth was her experience of Hollywood was a sham. After all she'd witnessed in the last few years she'd completely shied away from dating anyone around Hollywood. It all seemed so false. Why risk your feelings or your heart when it would end up broken anyway?

Javier laughed. 'Oh, come on. You're telling me that *none* of my fellow actors have ever invited you into one of the parties?'

She raised her eyebrows at him. 'Of course they have. And I don't need to tell you who they were—you could probably list them. But I'm not *that* kind of girl.' She took another sip of her wine. 'What about you? You get photographed often enough. Who is your latest flame?'

Are all your relationships fake too? That was the question she really wanted to ask.

He shook his head. 'No one—much to my agent's disgust. If I'm not photographed every few weeks with a different girl he seems to think my star will fade.' It was clear from the way he said the words that he wasn't at all bothered. That surprised her. She'd always thought there was a hint of arrogance around Javier. But here, in Baia di Rose, he didn't seem like quite the same person. Her curiosity was piqued again. He'd mentioned being at a funeral. Maybe the loss had affected him?

She filed the thought away and stuck to the conversation. 'So, how many of those photographs have actually been real?'

He winked. 'Let's see how good you are. How many do you think were real?'

She leaned back in her chair and tried to remember who he'd been seen with. After a few moments' contemplation she met his gaze. There was a twinkle in his eye. She counted off on her fingers. 'Okay, your co-star in the action film, Olivia Burns—no way. The comedy actress, Linda St John—' she waved her hand from side to side '—maybe. The female wrestler Jill Cacanna? No way, and last but not least, the up and coming Ms Ruby Delaware? Yes, I think that one might have been real.'

Javier started laughing. 'Oh, dear. Olivia, yes. But that was never going to last. Linda? No. We're just friends. Jill? Best blind date I ever had. She's one of the coolest human beings on the planet—but it's impossible to have a relationship when you never see each other. And Ruby?' He looked thoughtful for a moment and tapped his fingers on the table. 'That was odd. I think I might have been played.'

Portia was astonished. She thought her instincts were usually pretty good. But not with Javier Russo it seemed. What was it about him that just seemed to boggle her senses?

'What do you mean "played"?'

It was clear he was a little uncomfortable, and that reassured her a little that he wouldn't normally be indiscreet.

He reached for the wine bottle in the cooler at the side of their table and topped up both of their glasses. 'I'm not really a "drop a note to the press" kind of guy.'

She understood instantly what he meant. Lots of celeb photos on the beach, or coming out of restaurants, were staged—everyone in their industry knew that.

'But I think my agent is.'

She racked her brain trying to remember who Javier's agent was but came up blank.

'You think your agent was involved?'

He sighed. 'I'm not entirely sure. I think there may have been chat between my agent and Ruby's. All our time together felt kind of stage-managed. I didn't notice at first. But after a while, you realise that every time you go somewhere—even if it seems spontaneous to you—there are paparazzi waiting. It just didn't sit comfortably with me.'

Portia was amused. Ruby was a pretty enough actress. 'You think she wasn't actually interested in you?' It just seemed ridiculous. Javier was one of the hottest guys around. She just couldn't imagine that. But even more surprising was the fact that all his relationships hadn't been fakes. It seemed she didn't know everything about Hollywood after all.

'The truth is I don't know. She was nice enough but I always got the impression that underneath that sweet smile there was a streak of ruthless ambition. Once we started dating and had been photographed a few times she landed a couple of roles in upcoming blockbusters. It wasn't that she wasn't already being considered.' He stopped for a second, obviously trying to find the right words.

Portia finished the sentence for him. 'It's just that the exposure probably helped boost her up the list a little?'

Javier visibly cringed. 'I think so. It made me stop and take stock. Well, that and other things.'

He was doing it again. Fixing his gaze on the horizon while his thoughts obviously went elsewhere.

She didn't think she was boring him.

Please don't let me be boring him.

Javier Russo was more contemplative than she would have guessed. She'd only scratched the surface but was sure there was a whole lot more going on underneath.

She wanted to press. She really wanted to press. But her stomach gave an uncomfortable twist—almost as if it were acting as her conscience. It just felt…wrong.

'What about your agent?'

That caught his attention. He looked back at her again. 'What do you mean?'

She lifted her hands. 'On one hand, they're working well for you. You've had good roles.' She smiled. 'Or almost good roles, in back-to-back films. Isn't an actor's greatest fear not working?'

He nodded.

Just like mine, she thought.

'But, if your agent is involved in playing games with you—manipulating you—is that really what you want?'

Javier blew out a long slow breath between his lips.

She saw it as opportunity to continue. 'You said they wouldn't be happy about you having a break. Maybe not. You're probably the person they make the most money from. But, on the other hand, if you're their most bankable star, shouldn't they be looking after you *more* instead of less?'

He let out a gentle laugh and leaned across the table, his hand covering hers. The warmth shot up her arm like an electric shock. Someone at the next table was pointing at them, obviously recognising who Javier was.

'Portia Marlowe,' he whispered, 'you ask all the right questions.' He gave her arm a tug and pulled her up, throwing some money down on the table with the other. He was still smiling. She saw someone lift their phone at her side. Javier's hand was still holding hers, the other had casually snaked around her back, pulling her hip against him. His face was only a few inches above hers and he was grinning at her. 'But I like it. You're making me think. And that's exactly what I'm here to do.'

He glanced at the road between the restaurant and the port. 'Come on, it's a beautiful night. Let's walk a little.'

He didn't wait for her reply, just kept her hand in his as he led her out of the restaurant.

It was as if something had changed in the air between them. That physical contact was doing weird things to her brain. He'd taken her hand so easily, so casually, but should he really be holding it? All she knew was there was no way she was tugging it back.

As they walked along the port she noticed a few curious glances in their direction. Her heart skipped a few beats. Javier pointed out a few familiar places from his childhood. He seemed more at ease here, more relaxed. He nodded at the few people who said hello. Portia was trying her absolute best to be as casual as possible even though she felt as if there were a huge red arrow above her pointing to their entwined hands.

The breeze was warm, joined by the laughter of those drifting out from the nearby bars and cafés. The horrible tense knots that had been in her shoulders since she'd got here slowly started to unknot. L'Isola dei Fiori had a peaceful feeling around it. She hadn't really noticed it as a child.

When she was a child it had been a place of wonder and amusement.

Now she was an adult it was different. It was the first time in a long time that Portia had walked down a street where everyone didn't have a phone pressed to their ear. People were actually looking at each other, and talking to each other. In LA that was practically unheard of.

Javier was easy to talk to. He asked more questions about her family and her father's aviation business. He wanted to know where she'd gone to university and where her favourite holiday resort was. But as soon as he started to ask about work, she felt herself prickle.

'You were the one that broke the Jake and Meg affair, weren't you?'

She nodded. That particular story had been one of the biggest scandals in Hollywood a few years ago. Two of the biggest 'happily married' stars who'd had an affair together on set on their latest movie. Both of them were regularly talking in the media about how much they loved their partners, constantly talking about family values. The reality of their lives had been a little different and most of the world didn't believe it when the story first broke.

It was yet another nail in the coffin for love in Hollywood. It seemed that it just didn't exist out there.

'How did you find out, anyway?' His hand was still holding hers and as they walked he'd shifted his thumb so it was tracing little circles in the palm of her hand.

She gave a shrug. 'Would you believe a mistaken text message? It seems that Meg Malone and I had mobile phone numbers with two digits interchanged.'

His eyes widened. 'Do I want to know what the message said?'

She smiled and gave a shudder. 'Oh, no, absolutely not. The only reason I figured out who it was, was because they mentioned being interviewed together on a talk show that night. I did a little digging after that and…' She held up her hands.

He gave his head a shake. 'Well, I didn't know anything about it. I was just as surprised as everyone else.'

Portia let out a long slow breath as they kept walking. They'd reached the outskirts of the town and the villa wasn't too far away. 'I got offered the job at Entertainment Buzz TV permanently after that.' Her chest constricted. The thought of going back to LA in a few weeks with no story made her feel sick.

Her job would be no more.

What would she do next? Where could she find work?

That tiny little voice was rattling around her head. *Push Javier. Dig deep. See what you can find out.*

But the thumb making circles in the palm of her hand was stopping all rational thoughts.

She'd spent the last five years not being fazed by film stars, then, she'd arrived in L'Isola dei Fiori, spent one minute in Javier's company and felt like a star-struck teenager all over again. And that feeling wasn't really going away.

But part of her brain wasn't thinking about Javier the film star any more. It didn't matter that he could be the ticket to keeping her job.

Javier, the teenager that worked with his Uncle Vinnie, the young boy with the sometimes sick mother, was revealing a little more about himself every time they spoke.

He only let go of her hand when they finally reached the villa and slid the key in the lock. She couldn't help it, her feet led her automatically back outside, through the conservatory and out onto the terrace. The pinks and blues of the sky had vanished, leaving a navy dark sky dotted with little twinkling stars. The breeze here amazed her. Any time before she'd been on the coast the sea winds had always been fierce, no matter how mild the weather. But the breeze here was warm and welcoming, moving through the surrounding gardens with a mere rustle. The white sand in the cove gleamed beneath her, shadowed only by Neptune's arch. It really was the perfect place.

With the perfect person.

She heard his footsteps and felt his presence just behind her.

'Why are you so tense?' the voice whispered in her ear.

She stopped looking out over the horizon and closed her eyes for a second. She'd been tense since the first second she'd arrived here, first of all worried her sisters would figure out something was wrong, then, secondly, worrying about sharing a house with a Hollywood superstar.

She couldn't help the fact that the tension and anxieties in her head automatically translated their way into her body. She hated feeling like this, she really did.

She gave a little gasp as two firm hands found their way onto her shoulders. The fingers started moving straight away, finding the tiny knots around her neck and shoulder blades. She wanted to tell him to stop, but she could feel his warm breath at her neck and sense the presence of his body inches behind hers.

She moved her head from side to side as he continued. 'My goodness. What have you been doing? You're coiled tighter than a spring.' His soft Italian voice was like a soothing balm.

As he kept working his fingers she could visualise the picture from this morning, the bare chest and shoulders, the chiselled abs and dark hair. Then again from tonight, the twinkle in his grey eyes, his tanned skin and white smile. She moved without even thinking, leaning her body against his.

This time it was Javier that gave an intake of breath. His hands moved from her shoulders, one resting at the side of her waist. He rested his head just above one shoulder, taking his other hand and tracing one finger from the nape of her neck, painstakingly slowly across the top of her shoulder and down the length of her whole arm.

It was like a million little butterflies beating their wings against her skin. For a second she couldn't breathe. Then his fingers intertwined with hers and wrapped in front of her, resting next to her stomach.

His voice was low. 'I think that Villa Rosa has a little magic in it. Healing powers. It's a place to relax. To enjoy.'

She nodded, enjoying feeling his skin against hers. She couldn't pretend that her tension was gone. It had just been replaced with a whole other kind of tension.

She hadn't dated in so long. When was the last time she'd actually kissed someone? Sometimes, even though there seemed to be sparks flying, one kiss could reveal everything you needed to know. And right now her lips were tingling in anticipation. It didn't matter that Javier was behind her. It didn't matter that this probably wasn't the best idea she'd ever had.

He didn't seem to like false relationships any more than she did. He didn't want to be played—and she was still surprised he'd experienced it. It made him seem less movie star, and so much more human than the arrogant man she'd had in her head from months ago.

She leaned back a little more, letting her breathing

match the rise and fall of his chest. Were the healing powers Javier was talking about for her, or for him?

She still hadn't figured out why he was really here. Then again, she hadn't told him why she was really here either.

It seemed they both had something to hide.

But right now, with Javier's arms around her and their breathing in sync, staring out at the dark sky, the world seemed perfect.

'I could stay like this forever,' she whispered.

'Me too.' His reply sounded wistful and it sent little pangs throughout her heart.

So she settled her head back against his chest and they just stood, watching the dark sea stretching out in front of them, the glistening of the sand beneath them and the twinkling stars up above.

He'd almost kissed her. Two nights ago he'd almost turned her around and kissed her.

But as the warmth of her body against his had started to flood through his system he'd been struck by the fact that Aldo couldn't kiss a beautiful woman any more.

Aldo didn't get to do anything any more. And until he'd figured how to deal with that, he couldn't possibly get involved with anyone.

Which meant he had to apply his energy elsewhere.

The last two days Portia had continued to clean the upstairs rooms, emerging every now and then with smudges on her nose and cheeks. The glass had been delivered at the villa and he'd spent the last two days measuring, cutting and replacing individual panes of glass.

It was painstaking work but—as the plaster needed a few days to fully dry—it worked out well.

The conservatory was gradually beginning to take shape and regain some of its lost splendour. So far he'd only replaced the clear glass. The coloured glass he'd leave until last—because that was the glass that took the conservatory from elegant and sophisticated to dazzling and unique.

As he tidied his equipment he sighed. He needed to make a few calls. One of the deals he'd just reneged on was with a director he had a good relationship with. Javier knew he'd landed back in LA last night and would prefer to take the time to talk to him in person to explain why he'd backed out. He'd also like to talk to Aldo's parents—and the only way to do both of these things was to go into the village and find a phone.

Things were starting to take shape in his head. He had a few ideas. What he really needed to do was talk them over with someone he could trust. But there was only Portia here right now. And if he wanted to talk his ideas through, he'd need to give her the background.

Telling a reporter about Aldo's suicide seemed like the worst idea in the world.

'Portia?' He strode to the bottom of the stairs and shouted up to her. She appeared within seconds, wearing pink capri pants and a white shirt knotted at her waist. She had a list in her hand.

She waved it at him. 'I'd just been taking a note of a few cleaning products I need to pick up.' She wrinkled her nose. 'We need some food too. I was planning on heading into the village.'

He gave a guarded smile as a few more thoughts processed in his head. 'Great minds think alike. I have a few errands to run. Let's take the scooter.'

She narrowed her gaze for a second. 'Okay, but who gets to drive?'

'You want to drive?'

She held out her hands. 'It's sunny, I'm in Italy and there's a scooter sitting in the garage. Of course I want to drive.'

He shrugged. 'Then I guess I'm in your hands. Let's go.'

It had been a strange few days. The time on the terrace had felt magical—at least to her. But just when she'd thought something might happen, Javier had backed away as if he'd been stung.

She'd gone over and over the moments in her head. Nothing had happened. Nothing. Of that she was sure.

But it had still stung. It still felt like rejection.

She'd spent the last two days being polite and mannerly with Javier. Maybe she'd misread the whole situation? Maybe Javier had never even considered kissing her and it was all just a figment of her imagination.

That made her feel uncomfortable. She hadn't imagined the way he'd looked at her. She *hadn't*. Or the sparks in the air between them.

But for the last two days she'd cleaned. And cleaned.

Villa Rosa was finally starting to emerge from the clouds of dust.

She finished off her list and closed down her computer in the kitchen. Javier walked in at her back. 'Are you writing something?' He looked a bit uneasy.

She waved her hand. 'It's nothing. Just a story I've been working on for a couple of years. It helps me focus.'

He looked at her inquisitively. 'What kind of story takes two years to research?'

Something clicked in her brain. 'Oh, it's not a report. It's not *that* kind of story. It's fiction. I'm writing a book.'

His eyebrows rose. 'You're writing a story? What kind of story?'

The computer was closed now. She smiled and folded her arms. 'I'll let you guess. What kind of fiction writer do you think I am?'

He paced in front of her for a few seconds. 'Let's see. Thriller? No.' He shook his head and kept pacing. 'Historical? Hmm…no. Not that either. Romance?' He wiggled his palm. 'Maybe. Women's fiction?' He gave her a quizzical glance. 'Now, if I had my way, it would be science fiction or fantasy.' He turned to face her. 'But no, I think it's a romance. Am I right?'

She couldn't help but give a little smile. It felt ironic. 'You think I'm a romantic?'

His answer was automatic. 'Shouldn't we all be?'

She shook her head. 'It's not exactly romance. It's more Hollywood bonkbuster. I used to read them as a teenager and absolutely loved them. They've kind of gone out of fashion lately. But you know what they say.' She shrugged her shoulders. 'Write what you know.'

She picked up the keys to the scooter. 'Ready to go?'

He nodded and fell into step next to her as they left the house and headed to the garage. 'You are going to let me read this at some point, aren't you?'

She laughed as she slid her leg over the seat. 'Well, that depends how hard you work. Now, get on. The sooner we get to the village, the sooner we can get back. I've got an attic to tackle this afternoon.' She winked at him. 'Did I tell you that I crashed this once?'

'You what?' She was grinning, revelling in the fact he was horrified. 'What do you mean you crashed it?'

He looked over the vehicle again. There were no obvious signs of damage.

She shrugged. 'You know, teenage girl, sneaking out in the dark to meet a teenage boy in the village...' She laughed. 'I ended up in a ditch. But I was more angry about the fact I'd ruined my favourite dress and taken the toe out of one of my shoes.' There was a mischievous twinkle in her eyes and he wasn't quite sure whether to believe her or not.

He shook his head. 'And there are four of you? How on earth did your father cope?'

'If you think I'm bad you should meet my sisters. I'll have you know that I'm probably the best behaved.' She winked again. 'Come on, slowcoach, get on.'

With her dark eyes and tumbling locks—and if her sisters were anything like her—he was sure that the Marlowes must have been the most popular girls in town when they visited.

He climbed on behind her, then paused for a second, before moving closer and putting his hands on her waist. 'Why do I feel as if I'm going to regret this?' he murmured in her ear.

She laughed, gunned the small engine and took off.

By the time they reached the village Javier wasn't sure he wanted to get back off the bike. He was afraid he wouldn't be able to stand straight.

Portia drove as if she were being chased by a pack of man-eating zombies. It didn't matter that the top speed of the scooter wasn't exactly law-breaking, she zipped around corners and snaked between cars fearlessly. She laughed as she jumped off and took off her helmet. Her cheeks were tinted pink and her brown eyes were gleaming. Her shiny brown hair fell back over her shoulders. He almost sucked in a breath.

Portia was always a pretty girl. But sometimes she just glowed. Like now. He tried not to focus on her lips. Her pink, distinctly kissable lips.

It was easy to forget other things around Portia. Most of the time she was good company and light-hearted. He couldn't believe that she didn't have a boyfriend back home—especially with the kind of job she had.

And she could actually eat. In LA that was practically a miracle. Lots of people in TV or film had their own personal trainer and chef and spent the day eating unappetising seeds, drinking green smoothies and timing their next workout.

Portia seemed happy in her own skin. He was intrigued about her writing. Next time they were back at the villa he was going to try and persuade her to let him read her bonkbuster. He had a feeling he might recognise a few of the characters.

She pulled sunglasses from her cross-body bag and put them on. 'Will we meet back here in an hour?'

'Sure.' He glanced around the village. He was pretty sure he knew where he could find a phone. He watched as she strolled off towards the fishmongers, trying not to focus on the swing of her hips or the shape of her bottom in those capri pants.

He felt a huge pang of regret. He could have kissed her the other night. He *should* have kissed her the other night. But right now it just felt as if his timing was completely off.

He found a phone in the local café and made the calls he needed to. The director was disappointed but not upset. He understood that Javier needed some time.

Aldo's parents spoke briefly. They still sounded vacant and it broke his heart.

It made him more determined. More focused on what he should be doing. The work on the house was therapeutic, but what he actually should be doing was putting words into action. Bipolar disorder. How many people around the world were actually affected? How many families? Would the average person recognise the signs? After all, he'd missed them—or at least he felt he had. There were helplines all across the world. But was there something specific for bipolar disorder? Or was that something that he could do in Aldo's memory?

It was time to stop being distracted. It didn't matter how dark those brown eyes were. It didn't matter how kissable Portia's lips looked.

The ache and guilt in his heart were still there. It was time to put all his focus on one thing.

The trouble with trying to stay incognito was that curiosity drove her crazy. She'd been in the village less than half an hour, the groceries in a bag at her side, before she found herself in an Internet café.

She wouldn't look at her emails. She wouldn't. She'd maybe just have a five-minute browse of the Web and see what was happening in the world. There was a geriatric TV in Villa Rosa, but the signal was pretty rubbish and, with no phone line or Internet, there was none of the digital services that went along with most modern-day TVs.

So, unless something made it into the relatively conservative Italian newspapers stocked on L'Isola dei Fiori, or into the Italian TV news, she was essentially cut off.

It was a mistake as soon as she sat down. She knew that. She just couldn't help herself.

She pulled up Entertainment Buzz TV's website and Holly Payne's white teeth, blonde hair and size-six figure screamed back at her. She was covering while Portia was gone and it looked as if she was planning on making her mark.

Portia signalled to the waiter for a drink. She couldn't do this without coffee.

She flicked back over the last week. Holly covering the latest film premiere. Holly interviewing an unknown actor who'd just signed to star in the film of the biggest selling novel last year. Holly covering the death of an old-time movie star.

Portia breathed an audible sigh of relief. There was nothing spectacular there. Nothing that would draw attention to Holly as anything other than another Hollywood reporter.

Just to be sure she put Holly's name into the search engine on the Web.

It literally exploded.

So much for no attention.

Is Holly Payne about to become Holly Parker? screamed one headline. There were dozens more like it—all from last night. It seemed Entertainment Buzz TV's website needed updating.

Heading the article was a smudgy photo—obviously taken on someone's phone. It wasn't great. But there was no mistaking the people. Holly had her lips on Corey Parker, the latest pop sensation. He, in turn, was leaning her backwards and kissing her in the middle of an LA club. Portia recognised it immediately.

She let out a laugh. Really? Holly pretended to be twenty-two. But Portia knew exactly how old she was—

and that was seven years older than Corey Parker. She was just blessed with a youthful demeanour.

Portia peered at the screen again. Was that even a dress Holly was wearing? It looked more like a handkerchief. But the picture seemed to have caught one of Holly's best features—her legs—in all their glory.

Speculation was rife. There were hints at how long she'd been secretly dating Corey Parker. Rumours that she'd already met the family. Even more rumours that she and Corey had been seen checking out wedding venues. Really?

She blinked as she noticed something in the corner of her screen. What?

She sucked in a breath and sat back. Holly Payne's social media followers had just sky-rocketed to three hundred thousand. Oh, no. *Oh, no.*

Her fingers moved without her brain really engaging, pulling up her email provider and automatically typing in her email address and password.

She hadn't been in her emails since she'd arrived on the island for her sister's wedding. She didn't even glance at the total number. She just pulled up the name she was looking for. There were seventeen from her boss at Entertainment Buzz TV.

She pulled her hands back from the keyboard for a second and picked up the coffee the waiter had delivered, trying to ignore the shake.

This was pathetic. She hadn't even opened any of them and she wanted to cry.

Her boss had been succinct as she'd left. *'Don't come back without a killer story.'*

It had played on her mind ever since. And with each passing day the nerves and racing heart seemed to multiply like a killer virus. It was the hint as well. The implication. Almost as if she wanted something sordid. Portia hated that. Her boss was pushing her in a direction that she didn't want to go.

Ping. She opened the latest email from her boss. What was the point of reading the rest?

Due to recent events our executive director has suggested it might be time to review the arrangements for lead presenter on Entertainment Buzz TV. As per your contract, we are required to give you four weeks' notice. That is unless, of course, you can bring us a story that generates as much publicity as our current Holly Payne/Corey Parker headline. In those circumstances we would, of course, reconsider.

The breath left her body like a deflated balloon.

She was a has-been.

Was it even worth going home at all? Her stomach twisted. She loved her LA apartment. She loved her friends. Up until a few months ago she'd loved her job. She couldn't quite work out in her head what had happened. Maybe she'd always known her sell-by date would be coming up soon. Maybe she'd always known that there were some stories that shouldn't be told.

But how could she pay for her apartment if she wasn't working? Her salary at the TV station had been good— where else could she get paid like that?

Her skin started to prickle. Maybe she should reconsider the scoops she already knew. The Hollywood actress famous for her smile. She'd always been intensely private about her life. Her young daughter was terminally ill. That was why she was depressed. That was why she'd had to seek help at a private clinic. But was that really something Portia could share with the world?

No. She just couldn't. If she did something like that she wouldn't be able to look at her reflection in the mirror.

What about the nearly ninety-year-old Hollywood classic actor—married three times but thoroughly gay? She liked him. She really liked him. He was like one of the last true gents. It all seemed thoroughly unfair.

Then, something else came into her head.

Something so ridiculous she wasn't quite sure how it got there.

Holly had landed Corey. What if she could land Javier Russo?

Javier was a much bigger star. The highest earner in Hollywood this year. He'd topped every Most Eligible list for the last few years. Being seen on the arm of Javier Russo was much more newsworthy. Being seen in a clinch with Javier Russo could send the Internet into meltdown.

She winced. It was ridiculous. Of course it was ridiculous. He was the most gorgeous man on earth. He wouldn't be interested in her. He could have kissed her at any point the other night—and he hadn't. The humiliating part was he probably hadn't even contemplated it.

And she couldn't help but wish he had.

Her cheeks flamed with heat.

She hadn't filled Javier in on the rest of the 'crashed scooter' story. The fact that she'd never even got around to meeting that guy in the village. She'd thought she was going to get her first kiss. Instead she'd ended up in a ditch. It was fitting really. Her sisters had all managed to squeal about first kisses long before she'd finally been disappointed by hers. As she was the oldest they'd all just naturally believed she'd gone first. She would have hated them to find out she was last.

She closed the window on the computer in front of her—not even bothering to send a reply email. There was no point. She had nothing to tell. In another week or so she could kiss her job goodbye. She stood up, left some money and walked out of the café.

A realisation was creeping over her. When she'd been given the ultimatum before she left she could have held her ground and refused to leave. She didn't believe that Holly had 'accidentally' met the latest pin-up. Every part of the situation was contrived. The whole thing was just so Hollywood. Holly had seen an opportunity and taken it—just as Portia had five years earlier. It was just that Portia hadn't done it in quite so spectacular a fashion.

She should be in LA. That was where all the stories were. That was where she could find a story that would let her keep her job. So why hadn't she stayed?

Her stomach gave a little churn. How could she have missed Miranda's wedding? It didn't even bear thinking about.

The truth was she'd been having second thoughts about her job—she just hadn't wanted to admit them even to herself. And now she was having third thoughts. Or even final thoughts.

She'd fallen out of love with her job. She didn't have the hunger for it any more. She wouldn't do *anything* to get a story.

Her stomach was tied up in knots. This was it. This was when she needed to make a decision once and for all about her job. If it was over, she needed new career plans—rapidly.

Getting to know Javier had confused her. Discovering he wasn't the arrogant film star who had a string of false relationships had been news to her. And even though she'd had that tiny fleeting thought about using Javier for a story, the last few days had given her clarity.

She wasn't that person. She couldn't be that person.

Javier had reasons for being here she didn't know about.

But it didn't matter what they were—if he ever revealed them she already knew she wouldn't share them with anyone. It was his business. Not hers.

She couldn't be underhand. She couldn't be deceptive around Javier. Maybe he'd been right to distrust the press in the past. But she didn't ever want him to feel that way about her.

She was so caught up in her own thoughts that she didn't even notice Javier striding down the street towards her. He had a strange look in his eye. He looked just as tense and as distracted as she was. The charm that she'd glimpsed earlier had vanished. He held out his hand for a second, and it took a moment for her to realise what he wanted.

She pulled the key from her pocket. 'I take it you want to drive?'

He nodded.

He swung his leg over and started the engine. 'Ready?'

She swallowed the huge lump in her throat. What she really needed right now was someone to talk to. But Javier wasn't that person.

Something had upset him. Just as something had upset her.

And it seemed that neither of them were ready to share.

CHAPTER FIVE

THE NEXT TWO days were awkward.

It was clear Portia was unhappy about something. She was distracted and tired-looking. Sometimes she even looked as if she could burst into tears.

He'd love to use her as a sounding board. When it came to work and Hollywood she was completely sensible and, at times, frank. He respected her opinion.

But he couldn't tell her why he was reacting in an emotional way. He couldn't tell her how guilty he still felt about the death of his friend, and why he was so mixed up.

Because Portia was press. And he couldn't wipe his past experiences from his head—the press couldn't be trusted.

Part of it was pure and utter selfishness. What if she thought badly of him if he told her? There was a definite attraction simmering between them. Nothing like telling her he'd ignored a friend in need to squash it completely.

It didn't help that the reason he was shutting her out was because he still felt a pull towards her. Something he didn't feel as if he had any right to act on.

In the meantime a plan had formulated in his mind. He now knew what he wanted to do. Money was no problem. But he wanted to make sure that he did things well—not just throw a bunch of money at the project and walk away. He wanted to be involved and that would take business plans and commitment.

He looked around the painted drawing room. He'd plastered the crack again, skimmed most of the other rooms in the house. The conservatory glass would all be replaced in a matter of days. But he had to be careful and take his time. The frame was delicate. He couldn't manipulate and replace too many small panes at once. So far he'd completed all the plain glass and added some random red, blue and yellow panes. The green, pink and purple glass panes were sitting in a corner, waiting for their turn to be anchored in place and transform the conservatory into a rainbow of sunlight.

Up above him he could hear some noise. Portia had disappeared into the attic this morning. Maybe it was time to try and smooth the path between them.

He walked through to the kitchen and made some coffee, finding some pastries he'd picked up at the baker's this morning. He knew better than to go empty-handed.

Portia Marlowe didn't take her pastries lightly.

She could smell the coffee before she saw him. In fact, a steaming cup of coffee and a delicious-looking pastry laced with chocolate were sitting on top of one of the trunks near the entrance to the attic.

She crawled forward on her hands and knees, reaching the entrance to the attic and sticking her head out of the door. Javier was sitting on the floor outside, sipping coffee from a huge mug. He was wearing jeans and a white T-shirt that seemed to be smudged with bits of off-white putty. She scanned the floor around him. 'What—no pastry?' She wagged her finger at him. 'Don't think I'll give you half of mine. Ask my sisters. I've never been very good at sharing.'

He shook his head as he sipped at his coffee again. 'I ate mine before I even came upstairs. You forget, I've seen you in the bakery before.'

She sat back on her haunches and sipped her coffee. It was strong—just the way she liked it. 'This is different. Did you get something new?'

He smiled. 'I bought some beans in the village this morning and a cafetière. What I really want is one of those giant silver coffee machines and my own barista.'

'Is my instant coffee not up to your standards?'

He pulled a face. 'I don't think it's up to yours, either.'

She nodded as she took a bite of the pastry. It was delicious. The chocolate melted on her tongue.

'I'll make do. I'm just glad for the sustenance.'

He nodded towards the attic. 'You look like you're having fun in there.' There was a glint of humour in his eyes.

'I do?' She looked down. Her pale trousers were covered in grime, as was her pink T-shirt. She put her hand up to her head and brought it back down covered in a large cobweb.

She was on her feet in an instant, jumping around and shaking her hand furiously. 'Yeugh. Get it off.'

Javier started laughing, a deep throaty laugh that seemed to come from deep inside. When she eventually shook off her hitchhiking cobweb and ducked into the bathroom and washed her hands, one glimpse in the mirror made her wince.

Why, oh, why didn't she have the natural look like the female movie stars? Her hair was all over the place and she had a large black smudge on her nose. No wonder he was laughing.

She wiped her face and went back to the hall. 'There's not much point in trying to clean up. I've got a million other boxes to go through in there. Trouble is, I'm not sure what I should be dumping and what I should be keeping.'

'Would you like some help?'

'Don't you have the conservatory to finish?'

He gave a casual shrug of the shoulders. He had that expression on his face again, the half-smile that made a million women the world over go weak at the knees.

'It's a delicate operation. The frame is weak. I need to let the glass settle. I'll do the rest of the panes tomorrow.'

She gave a nod and folded her arms. 'So, are you going to be the brains of this operation—or the brawn?' She sighed. 'I have to be honest, I'm not quite sure what to do with some of the things—or most of the things—that I've found. I don't know if they're valuable or just junk. I think I've spent the last hour just moving things around.'

Javier took another drink of his coffee then set the cup down. 'Then let's get to work. I asked around. The waste-disposal trucks come tomorrow. If there's anything that we think could be disposed of, we can bag it.'

He pushed himself off the floor. She tried not to stare at his muscled biceps clearly defined by his white T-shirt. He walked towards her, stopping only a few inches away. She frowned and reached out and picked at the dried smudges on his T-shirt. 'What are these?'

He looked down. 'You're not the only one that needs a clean-up.' He pulled the T-shirt out from his chest. 'Some of it's silicone…some of it putty. Working with Uncle

Vinnie taught me some bad habits. I tend to wipe my fingers on my shirt instead of on a rag.' He let his T-shirt flop back against his chest and her hand fell back on his warm chest. The heat was instant. She hadn't really meant to get so up close and personal. Her eyes connected with his.

It was like being hit by a blast. The smouldering heat in his grey eyes could never be mistaken for anything else. It took her by surprise as the blood instantly raced around her system. This hadn't been in her head. It wasn't her imagination.

She pulled her hand back as if she'd been stung. She wasn't quite sure how to deal with all this.

Javier didn't move. It seemed like the longest time but it must have only been a few seconds before he finally spoke. 'Let's get started. We can always go freshen up at the beach later.'

He brushed against her as he moved inside the attic. Her brain was spinning. The beach. The place where they'd drunk wine and he'd touched her cheek. The place she'd first felt a real connection with Javier Russo. Her lips tingled in nervous anticipation as she gulped and followed him into the attic.

There were two tiny windows in the roof of the attic that let a little murky light filter through. Javier had to crouch down in the roof space to try and get inside. He glanced over his shoulder at Portia and gave her a smile. The place was stacked with boxes, trunks, plastic bags and cases, there was hardly any floor space visible and he had to pick his way over and around them to get even a little inside. 'Did you know Sofia was a hoarder?'

Portia shook her head. 'Honestly? I didn't have a clue. And from what I can see, nothing has a label. I've only checked a few bags at the front and one case at the door. It's full of china all wrapped in tissue paper.'

Javier held out his hands. 'Where do you want to start in here?'

Portia shook her head. 'Your guess is as good as mine. Why don't you take one side and I'll take the other? It's probably best if we keep to near the front—that way, if we find anything that can be dumped, we can take it downstairs.'

He nodded and moved over to the nearest trunk. 'Okay, then, let's get started.'

Portia got back down on her hands and knees. There was no point standing—this was going to take a long time. The first few bags were easy. They were mainly filled with ancient household appliances. Kettles, toasters, scales, all singed or with bits missing. Portia pushed them towards the attic door, along with the next bag that was full of similar items.

Next was a large leather trunk. She flipped open the lid and tried to ignore the cloud of dust that puffed into the air around her. 'Oh, wow,' she gasped.

'What is it?' asked Javier.

The trunk was full of clothes, all in individual clear garment bags. She lifted out the first. A long red evening gown. The next dress was black, the next green and so on and so on. Portia smiled. 'I knew that Sofia had a lot of clothes but I guess I didn't realise quite how many. I thought the wardrobes downstairs held all her dresses. I hadn't figured on her having more up here.' She pulled the neck of the garment bag down a little to feel the red dress. 'Oh, it's gorgeous. These are probably worth a fortune.'

Javier was smiling at her.

'What? What is it?'

'You,' he said. 'You look like you just won the star prize.'

She sighed and held the dress against her chest. 'That's what it feels like. If we push this trunk outside I can take the dresses downstairs and find somewhere to hang them.' The smell of lavender was drifting up around her. 'They all look in perfect condition. Posy will need to decide what to do with them.'

'Posy—that's the ballerina, isn't it? Will she be interested in a whole load of extra dresses?'

Portia smiled. 'Oh, yes. Posy and I have similar tastes. She'll love these.' She met his gaze. 'It's strange. Posy and I are very close. When I was young and the twins came along, it was almost like they had their own secret language. They didn't really need me. They were so close. They didn't seem to want anyone else around. When Posy came along it was such a relief. Finally, a partner in crime.' She sighed. 'I love my sisters. I do. But even in adulthood Posy and I are much more similar. Immi and Miranda both went into the family business and Posy and I, in some way, both went into show business—albeit very different aspects.'

He was watching her and smiling. 'Do you talk often?'

Portia licked her lips before she answered. 'Andie and I spoke a few times when she was contemplating the whole Cleve thing.' She smiled. 'Posy—I'm a bit worried about her. She seems a little distant right now. And Immi?' She pressed her lips together. 'We've not really talked in the last few days. I think something's going on but I don't know what.' She shook her head. 'I always worry about her—always. I can't help it.'

'Why?'

She bit her lip. Immi's condition hadn't exactly been a secret, she just wasn't sure how much to share. 'Immi was unwell. She had an eating disorder when she was younger.' She paused then added, 'Then she had some mental health issues and ended up in rehab. It didn't just affect her. It affected the whole family. In a way I'm glad she's in the family business. It means there is always someone to keep an eye on her.'

She felt exposed. She'd just told him about her sister. It was private. It was personal. She'd got so used to the Hollywood lifestyle of everything just being on the surface that she'd forgotten how tough it was to share.

It left her feeling vulnerable. Something she hated.

His hand brushed against hers. It seemed accidental, but then it stopped and his warm hand covered hers, giving it a gentle but reassuring squeeze.

He hadn't said anything out loud to acknowledge her words, but the squeeze sent a little shockwave through her system. The more time she spent around this man, the more he crept under her defences.

Javier stared at her for a few seconds. Then he lifted up a black and white photo in the trunk. It was a picture of his mother and Sofia laughing. They had their arms around each other and looked as if they'd just been caught sharing a private joke.

He looked into the trunk. 'Hey, what's this?' He pulled out something that was down the side of the trunk.

It looked like papers, but as he fanned them out she realised they were black and white photographs—all of Sofia. She picked up one after the other. 'Oh, look at her, isn't she so beautiful?' She kept flicking through in wonder. 'I never really remembered her like this. It's sad but you end up remembering someone the way they were the last time you've seen them.' Something about the pictures was familiar and it took her a moment to realise what it was. 'It's these! It's these dresses. Look, there's the black one. And this one is the red one—look how figure-hugging it is on her. And there's the green satin one all covered in sequins—look at the way it catches the light in the photograph.'

The pictures were fantastic. A little moment in time. Sofia was spectacular in them, so elegant and refined-looking. And while she'd always looked immaculate in real life, she also had a wicked sense of humour and raucous laugh that took those that didn't know her by surprise.

Javier's hand closed over hers again. Reaching for the photographs and looking at them slowly, one after the other. He gave a sad smile. 'You're right. You do remember people the last time you saw them. And Sofia faded a little, didn't she?'

Portia looked at his sincere expression. Sofia had faded. She hadn't taken well to growing old. She'd hated the fact she had wrinkles on her face, or that her hair had thinned. She would never let anyone take photographs of her in the last few years. Javier had found a way to say it nicely. It was obvious he had the same affection for her that Portia and her sisters did.

Javier ran his fingers over one of the photos. 'These capture Sofia in all her crowning glory.' Then he burst out laughing. 'No, I think that might have been an unfortunate choice of words.' He shook his head. 'She never got her crown, did she? I wonder if she ever actually thought that she would.'

Portia bit her lip. 'I don't know. She would never have discussed anything like that with us. But she might have with your mother.' She looked into the distance. 'I always thought of her as fiercely independent. I never really knew that Ludano had gifted her the house. I didn't find that out until I was much older.'

Javier gave her another grin. 'Do you want to see what I've found?'

She tried to glance over his shoulder. 'Why? Is it something good?'

'I think you might recognise it.'

She put the photographs back on top of the trunk, trying to remember she'd need to email Posy about them, then crawled on her hands and knees over to where Javier had another large case opened.

He pulled out one of the items at the top. It was an old Italian Monopoly game. Portia gave a little shriek. 'Really? That's what you found?'

She couldn't help herself; she immediately started scrambling through the case, finding a whole host of other childhood games she used to play with her sisters. She pressed the well-worn box to her chest. 'We couldn't understand parts of it. We loved the names of the Italian streets, but when it came to the Chance and Community Chest questions we just had to guess what they meant. I'm sure that Immi used to cheat. Every time she got one, she said it was her birthday and we all owed her money.'

She looked in the case. It was packed full of things she remembered. She pointed at a few. 'We had a huge fight over that chess set. Miranda and I both wanted to be black—the knight especially in the shape of a horse was really fierce and we ended up stomping off to other parts of the house rather than play each other.'

Javier was looking at her thoughtfully. 'You have lots of good memories here, don't you?'

She nodded. 'We had the best times here.' She tilted

her head to the side. There was something about the way that he'd said that. 'You must have had too?'

He opened his mouth and then hesitated. 'Well, yes, and no.'

She set the board game back down. 'What do you mean?'

She watched as he sucked in a deep breath. 'My mother wasn't always at her best when she was here. And I'm not sure Sofia knew how to relate to a young boy. She was kind. I was never neglected but—'

'But, what?'

He gave a tiny head-shake. 'I'm quite sure she had no idea how to entertain an eight-year-old boy. Then a nine-year-old, then a ten-year-old…'

He let his voice trail off then took a deep breath and spoke softly. 'My mother has bipolar disorder. At times in her life she's been quite unwell. In those days most people called it—what was it—"highly strung". But it was much more serious than that—particularly if she went off her meds. Sofia was good for her when she was like that. She would encourage her to take her meds and start eating again. Sometimes it took days, sometimes it took weeks.'

Her breath caught in her throat. It was the first time he'd ever really shared something so personal with her.

It was almost as if a wave of acknowledgement swept over her. 'How often was your mother unwell?'

It was the first time she'd seen him look kind of sheepish. 'She was at the height of her fame then. She was under a lot of pressure.'

He was making excuses for his mother. Even all these years on, as an adult he was still doing his best to protect her. She liked that about him, but it also made her ache for what he'd been put through.

She reached over and put her hand on his arm. 'And you were a young boy.'

He nodded. 'I was. But for some reason, even though my mother wasn't well, I still liked being here. This place. It's warm. And my mother always got better, and as she did she had more time for me. We walked on the beach. We took trips on the boats at the port.'

'What did she think of you being friends with the Princes?'

He laughed. 'Believe it or not, my mother wasn't too happy. She didn't like Ludano. She didn't think he was good for Sofia.'

Portia smiled. 'He probably wasn't. But it was different times then. There wasn't the same news reporting or social media that there is today. Sometimes I wish we could go back in time.'

'So do I.' His voice was wistful. He shook his head. 'Things were better here. On the mainland in Italy, my mother was hounded by the press. I can hardly remember a time when I could look out into the gardens and there wasn't a photographer hiding in bushes somewhere. Times were changing—even then.' He held up his hands. 'But here? Here was a little piece of paradise. A little bit of sanctuary for us all.'

She gave him a warm smile. 'It seems that Villa Rosa has lots of memories for us.' She looked around the cramped attic and held up her hands. 'This place. It's full of Sofia. Everything I see, everything I touch reminds me of her. How is Posy supposed to decide what she should get rid of? The other morning I woke up, and for a second, just for the tiniest second, I forgot that Sofia was gone. Then, in the blink of an eye I remembered again. It was like getting that phone call all over again. I know it sounds strange. I know it's ridiculous. But I wanted to sit in that split second—just for a while.'

She knew he didn't realise it—but it wasn't just Sofia she was talking about. It was everything. It was back to a few years ago when everything in her life had just seemed too good to be true. It had taken her until now to realise it had been.

Reality sucked.

Or did it?

The glamour had been fun. Some of the personalities had been fun too. She'd met a few of her all-time heroes. Some had disappointed. Some had lived up to and beyond her expectations. But times were changing for her too. She didn't feel the same fire, the same excitement about her job. She certainly didn't like the direction her boss had been pushing her in lately. She was spending longer and longer playing around with her writing. The words came easily—they just flowed. In a way she was glad that Javier was here. He was a welcome distraction. If she'd been here alone, her resolve might have crashed and she could have been back on a flight to LA by now.

She looked over at Javier. Something was wrong. He looked almost grey. As if he were unwell. He was staring blankly at the wall as if he were lost in his thoughts.

She sat up on her knees and cupped his cheek with her hand. 'Javier? Are you okay?'

He blinked. There was a sheen in his eyes. Was Javier going to cry? What on earth had she said?

He put his hand up over hers, sending little shots down her arm. His head gave the briefest of nods. 'Yeah, I'm okay. Or, I will be.' He paused for a second. 'Portia, how do you feel if we take a break? Cool off down at the beach for a while?'

Her stomach curled up. He was sad. She'd done something that made him sad. And right now she would do anything to change that. 'Sure, if that's what you want.'

He nodded. 'I do.' He put his hand into hers. 'Let's go.'

Things were starting to fall into place in his head. He was starting to almost find a way that he could feel as if he were doing something.

Some of the things that Portia had said today had really hit home. She didn't even realise how many of his buttons she'd pressed. But as he'd watched the sincerity on her face, he'd known she was talking from the heart. It didn't matter she was relating it all to Sofia.

Her feelings were true. Just as his were.

The walls of the attic had felt claustrophobic, as if they were closing in around him. He'd had to get out of there. But he knew exactly who he wanted to get out of there with. She'd revealed a little of the heartache about her sister. As he got to know her just a little more it was clear that Portia Marlowe had just as many chinks in her armour as he had.

For him it was a relief. Portia might be press. But slowly but surely the press walls around her were fading away.

She'd taken less than five minutes to get ready for the beach. He loved that about her. He'd spent days on set waiting six hours for his female co-star to get ready. This was a revelation.

He'd just pulled a different T-shirt on and grabbed a pair of swimming shorts that he'd purchased on one of his trips into the village. He might be Italian—but he didn't do trunks. As far as Javier was concerned they

were for competitive swimmers and multimillion-dol-
lar advertisements.

Portia came out with her hair around her shoulders
and wearing a hot-pink bikini and matching coverall.
It made his heart zing. She looked amazing, and it was
clear she was completely unaware of this.

She patted her stomach. 'This is when I'm especially
glad we're not in LA right now. A few weeks here, with
all the pastries and coffees, makes me lazy. I never want
to exercise again.'

'What do you do back home?'

'For exercise?'

He nodded.

She rolled her eyes. 'Same as everyone else. I have a
personal trainer. I try not to obsess. You'll know, there's
too much of that in Hollywood. Anyone who's bigger
than a size two over there is considered overweight. And
let's face it—there's history in my family that makes me
not go down that road.' She looked sideways at him as
he grabbed some water and a few beers from the fridge.
'What do you do?'

He pulled a face. 'Depends entirely on the movie. For
the action movie they wanted me to be pure muscle. I'll
not pretend. It was hard. Training six hours a day for
two months before filming began, and eating six weird
tiny meals a day. I was quite irritable. It didn't suit me.'

She smiled. 'Did your co-stars complain about you?'

'Who knows? If I was tense, I took myself out of the
way. Filming is full of coffee and donuts and if I wanted
to keep my physique on set I had to steer clear of all
that. When it's sixteen hours a day it's hard.'

They walked out onto the terrace then down the narrow path. Javier walking ahead and taking her hand
down the steep bits. He glanced back as they walked

down the path. She'd mentioned something back in the kitchen that made him curious. 'Your sister—Immi— is she well now?'

Portia nodded. 'She is. It took a few years. And I have to admit we all still have the signs tucked away in the back of our minds. Seeing your sister unwell is tough. We all felt as if we'd failed her—especially Mum and Dad. But Miranda, Andie, her twin, took it really badly too.'

Javier looked thoughtful. 'How did she get well again?'

Portia was watching her steps down the steep path. 'She had to be ready. She had to want to get better—and she had to have the right help. Some place that was a good fit for her. My mum and dad tried different therapists, different support groups and doctors. Finally, they found somewhere that specialised entirely on her condition. They were perfect for Immi because that's where all the expertise was.'

Something about her words made him smile. He'd made the right decision. The charity he wanted to start would focus entirely on bipolar disorder. There were various mental health charities and helplines in Italy. There were other helplines for those who were feeling suicidal. But he wanted his charity to specialise and focus entirely on the one disorder that had affected his friend, and still affected his mother. Portia's words just reinforced his decision even more.

The sandy beach was beautiful. Like a forgotten hidden private hideaway. Javier laid their towels on the beach and looked out over the clear azure-blue sea, rippling with tiny peaks of white. In the far, far distance there was a white yacht that looked as if it were moored for fishing.

Portia sagged down onto the beach and put her hands above her head and stretched out. He couldn't help but watch, appreciating her long legs and the look of pure and utter relief on her face. Once she'd finished stretching she turned on her side to face him.

She had no make-up on, there was still a tiny trace of grime in her hair and it made him reach out to wipe it away. He leaned closer. 'Hey, I never told you what my favourite type of exercise is,' he said softly.

She blinked and right before his eyes her pupils widened.

All of a sudden he realised what he'd said. He almost laughed. But he just couldn't do it. Not while he was here with her.

Portia was gradually sneaking her way under all the layers of armour that he had. She asked questions. But not like a reporter. She asked questions like a normal interested human being. He'd kind of forgotten what that felt like.

He knew what he had to do next. He'd finalised his ideas last night and his next steps would take him back to the mainland. But there was still time. Still time to tease out where this connection could take them.

He'd been making plans in his head. Some would need to be firmed up in person, and for that he'd need to go somewhere else. And he knew the perfect person to take with him.

'Is it a secret, or are you going to tell me?' she asked, then lowered her voice to a whisper, 'And is it exercise for one, or for two?'

So she hadn't missed the unintentional innuendo in his words. He actually wished it had been intended. He sat up and stretched his hand out towards her, inviting her to take it.

'My favourite kind of exercise is the entirely natural kind.'

She raised her eyebrows and slid her hand into his. 'Oh?'

He pulled her up towards him, letting her body collide with his, so he could slide his hand down her back to the small hollow where it seemed to fit perfectly.

She snaked her hands around his neck. 'Why do I think that you're teasing me right now?'

'Me?'

She tapped her hands at the backs of his shoulders. 'Yes, you.'

He laughed and lowered his lips so they brushed against her ear. 'Okay, then. My favourite form of exercise—at least, until we're better acquainted—is swimming. How about a race to the buoy out there? You wouldn't come swimming with me the other day.'

It was like two different people in his arms. Her cheeks flushed a little at his hint of something else, then paled instantly at the second suggestion.

She kept her arms tightly around his neck. He turned so they were chest to chest instead of sideways on. She stared out at the distant buoy in sheer unhidden terror. 'That? You want to swim out to *that*?'

Every muscle in her body had tensed against him.

He couldn't understand. 'Of course, it's maybe half a mile? It's an easy swim. We can do it together.'

She shook her head fiercely. 'Oh, no. No way. Not me.' Then she glanced at him. 'And not you either. You're not going out there.'

He started laughing. 'Portia, what on earth is wrong?'

She looked at him incredulously. 'What's wrong?' She swept her arm out towards the ocean. 'Look at it. All beautiful and blue. All tempting. All come-and-swim-in-me.'

'Exactly. Let's do it.'

She screwed up her face. 'Not a chance. Do you have any idea what could be out there?'

He pulled back to get a good look at her whole horrified expression. 'No. What?'

She stared back at him. 'Sharks,' she whispered fiercely.

He shook his head. 'You're joking, aren't you?' He couldn't believe it.

'Of course I'm not joking. Every time I see someone swimming in the ocean I hear the *Jaws* theme tune playing in my head. I like the sea. From a distance.'

'But just after we met you were in the sea with me.'

She gulped. 'I wasn't in the sea. Not properly anyway. I'll paddle. But that's it.'

Javier didn't hesitate. He swept Portia up into his arms and started striding towards the ocean.

'Don't you dare! Stop!' she yelled as she thudded her fists on his chest.

He laughed as he walked ankle deep into the waves. 'What about here? Is this where you want me to stop?'

She stopped panicking for a second and looked down. The water was barely around his ankles. 'Don't go any further.'

He smiled and took a few strides further. 'No!' she shrieked.

He stopped again. 'Watch out,' he said. 'If you keep struggling, I might drop you.'

She sucked in a breath and froze.

'How far would you actually go in the water?'

She still looked scared. 'Maybe my knees. Definitely not the chest.'

'Why not?' He couldn't help but be curious.

'Stop laughing at me. I'd never get in the ocean back

home. Sharks are all over LA. I've no idea if there are sharks around here.'

She did look panicked. He shook his head. 'I'm sure there are basking sharks, but none could come this close to shore. And they're quite harmless.'

She squinted at him as the sun's glare fell over her face. 'Do you really swim in LA?'

He nodded. 'Every day. Have done for years.'

She glanced down again warily. 'Well, I'll never go deeper than my knees. I've had a recurring nightmare about sharks for years. I heard that if you punch a shark on the nose it stuns it, and it goes away. And they can come quite close to shore. That's why I'd never wade out to chest height—too dangerous.'

He loved this. He loved that when he stripped back all the parts Portia Marlowe just made him laugh. She made him comfortable. She was fun to be around.

It didn't help that he also loved the way she screwed up her nose and squinted at him in the sun. He loved the way she wasn't obsessed about her weight.

'Would you feel safer if I held you? I thought you wanted to wash the cobwebs out of your hair?'

Her eyes opened wide. 'Oh, yes. That's right. I did.' She pulled a little closer to him as she looked at the clear sea surrounding them.

'Okay, you can take a few more steps, then that's it. You've got to stop.'

'Okay, then.' He couldn't stop smiling as he strode up to his waist. 'How about I just lean you back a little?'

She looked around again and loosened her hands just a little from his neck. 'Okay, but be quick.'

He let his legs bend and kept his hands under her back, so that she floated in the sea and her dark hair fanned out all around her. She stayed like that for a few seconds.

She was beautiful. Like a siren floating in the sea in front of him. That bright pink bikini enhanced all her curves and complemented her light tan. If she started singing any time soon he swore he would just give up and follow her wherever she wanted.

She gave him a signal and he pulled her back up. The water was dripping from her hair and her body. He took a few steps further back.

'What are you doing?'

'Making sure you stay in my arms.'

She gave him a curious stare, then wrapped her arms back around his neck and then her legs around his waist. 'Now, why would you want to do that?'

He didn't answer straight away. He wasn't entirely sure of the answer he could give. Instead he asked what was forefront on his mind. 'I need to do some business tomorrow. It means I have to go to Naples. Would you like to come with me? The business won't take long, and I love the opera in Naples. I've checked and *Le Nozze di Figaro* is showing at Teatro di San Carlo.' He gave her a wink. 'I might even know where you can find a dress you can wear.'

She gave a gasp and stared at him. 'You honestly think I should wear one of Sofia's dresses?'

He leaned back into the water. 'Why not? You'll look every bit as elegant in them as she did.'

He could tell she was a bit embarrassed, but also happy with the compliment.

'Hey, isn't it time you got me out of this water?'

Javier felt a little swell in his chest. The water droplets left on her body were virtually glistening in the sun. The feel of her body against his was having all the natural effects it should. He'd kind of hoped wading deeper, where the water might be colder, would have helped—but the fire inside was too strong. A few days of virtually not speaking had done nothing to cool the heat between them—instead it seemed to only have intensified the burn. Her dark hair and gleaming dark eyes were enticing him in ways he hadn't felt in years.

He tightened his grip on her hips. 'Maybe I just want to take you deeper into the ocean. Maybe I need some kind of persuasion not to.'

She lowered her gaze playfully. 'Oh, I think I can find a way to entice you.'

His pulse soared. 'How?'

She licked her lips and tilted her head to one side. Her lips met his. The smouldering fire ignited like a shooting firework. Her smooth lips moved over his with expert grace, coaxing, teasing and sending all sane thoughts floating off into the ocean around them.

And he was well and truly enticed.

CHAPTER SIX

SHE WAS NERVOUS. Her stomach had danced in knots all day. Last night they'd come up from the beach and drunk wine together in the painted drawing room by candlelight.

It was probably the most romantic setting in the world, and she wondered how often Sofia had sat in there with Ludano. Javier had kissed her as if she were the only woman on the planet and for a few hours she'd forgotten about everything else.

She'd forgotten about the job she didn't want any more.

She'd forgotten about being the oldest sister left on the shelf.

She'd forgotten about her experience of love in Hollywood.

She'd forgotten about all her curiosity about Javier.

And she'd forgotten about figuring out what to do with her life.

For that little bubble of time it had been just him, and her. And it had felt almost perfect.

Today had felt unreal. Javier had finished putting the coloured panes in the conservatory. She'd tidied out a bit more of the attic, labelling boxes that Posy would need to search through. It had been fortuitous. She'd found another trunk full of shoes and found a pair that would match the red dress perfectly. Javier had disappeared into the village for a while to arrange transport for them to the ferry and she'd packed her overnight clothes and evening dress in a light bag.

It was afternoon before they took the ferry to the mainland. As soon as they neared the Italian coastline her phone started to ping. She pulled it from her bag. Six voicemails. A few hundred emails. And numerous text messages.

Javier must have noticed the pained expression on her face. 'I'm not even looking at mine. There's someone I need to phone to finalise our meeting when we reach Naples—but that's it. Everything else can wait.'

She stared at him for a second. He seemed relaxed. He seemed sure. Almost as if he'd made up his mind about something.

She wished she could make her mind up about things. Maybe making a decision would make her feel better?

'Is there anyone you really need to call?' he pressed. 'Do you think any of it is an emergency?'

She had a quick scroll. There were a few messages from her sisters. She texted back some quick replies. Everything else seemed safe to ignore. 'No, I guess there isn't.' She put her phone on silent and stuffed it back in her bag.

She took a deep breath and leaned back against the railing of the ferry. If Javier Russo could ignore his phone, then she could too. The ferry was taking its time docking. She nudged Javier. 'Look around us. What do you notice?'

He glanced from side to side and frowned. 'I don't know. What is it?'

She gave him a smile. 'What's different about here, and what happens in L'Isola dei Fiori?'

He seemed puzzled but looked around again. After a few seconds he shook his head and turned back. 'Okay, you've got me. Is this a trick question?'

She laughed. 'No, silly. The phones. Most of the people on the ferry are all currently staring at their phones. We don't see that in L'Isola dei Fiori. People still sit at dinner tables and talk to each other. Have conversations. I'm beginning to think that humans are losing the art of conversation because we spend so much time with our heads in our phones. Weren't you twitchy the first few days you arrived? You get so used to having the world at your fingertips you forget how to manage without it.'

He leaned closer to her and smiled. 'Maybe these people should consider other distractions?' Something had definitely changed in Javier. He'd said he had some business to do but he also seemed more positive, more enthusiastic. The twinkle in his eyes that had dulled for a few days was definitely back.

His words sent a little shot of heat through her veins. She couldn't help but smile. 'Watch out, there are children about. Some distractions aren't for public viewing.'

'You think?' Before she got a chance to reply he lowered his lips onto hers. It wasn't a soft kiss. It was purposeful. As if he seemed certain of what he was doing. It was easy to put her hand up and run it through his short dark hair.

Something twigged inside her. A sense of belonging. Something she hadn't ever felt before.

As if, even though her rational brain told her otherwise, this seemed like the right time, in the right place with the right person.

Almost as if he were hers.

Something about that terrified her. Her stomach flip-flopped but her heart was practically swelling in her chest. Now, she got what Andie felt. She just wasn't entirely sure if this could all be real.

The ferry gave a jerk as it finally moored into place. They laughed as their heads clashed and Javier threaded his fingers with hers as he carried their bags from the ferry terminal.

It was busy here. There was instantly a buzz in the air that wasn't present in the more sedate L'Isola dei Fiori. And more people meant more chance of recognition. Not for her, but for him. Javier was Italy's biggest ever film star.

As they exited the terminal she saw a few curious glances. If they'd been in an airport she was sure that phones would have been whipped out and a million pictures snapped. But no one would expect Javier Russo to be coming off the ferry from the little-known kingdom of L'Isola dei Fiori.

He led her towards some waiting cars. He gave a nod to a uniformed chauffeur outside a long black limousine and threw their bags in the boot as the chauffeur opened the door for her. As the door closed behind her, Portia was happy to hide behind the black tinted glass.

She was starting to feel self-conscious. In Los Angeles she always took care of her appearance when she was out and about. Lots of people recognised her from the TV show and it would be bad publicity to be snapped looking frumpy and tired.

She hadn't even thought about it this morning. Even though she had the evening dress in her bag, she'd thrown on a pair of jeans, tied up her hair and not bothered with make-up. Her only partial saving grace was the sunglasses she was wearing.

'What's wrong?' Javier slid his hand over hers.

'Nothing.' She tried to push the self-conscious thoughts from her head. No one cared what she looked like. No one knew who she was.

He gave her thigh a squeeze. 'Have you visited Naples before?'

She shook her head. 'No. Never.'

His brow furrowed. 'If I'd planned ahead we could have stayed longer—done a tour of the city.' She could see him biting his lip. 'Do you want to see if we can stay an extra day?'

She shook her head. 'No, it's fine. To be honest I've been enjoying the sanctuary of Villa Rosa. I can't stay there forever and it's been a long time since I had a proper holiday. I'm learning that I can actually live without social media, and it's a revelation.'

His face broke into a broad smile. 'It is, isn't it? There's something nice about not living at such a frantic pace.' He rested back against the leather seats. 'Have you been to the opera before?'

She shook her head. 'Never. We weren't an opera kind of family. My parents—as you know—were Shakespeare nuts. We spent our lives seeing every production of Shakespeare. Then, when Posy was young she loved musicals. I've seen every one of those until they were imprinted in my brain. And the last fifteen years, it's been constant ballet. I've spent a lot of time sitting in a theatre—just never at an opera.'

He gave a nod. 'I can't wait until we get there. Teatro di San Carlo is magnificent. Like something from a bygone age. You'll love it.'

She smiled back nervously. 'I hope so.' She looked out of the window at the city flashing past outside. 'Where are we going to stay?'

'I've booked a suite at one of the hotels for the night. I've stayed there before. If you're hungry we can order some room service before we head out to the opera.'

She gave a nod and took a deep breath as she watched out of the window. Javier's hand stayed over hers. Naples passed by quickly. A suite. What did that mean? After what had happened last night between them, she couldn't help but think about what would come next. A suite in a luxury hotel somehow felt like the next step on the horizon. Nervous excitement bubbled in her stomach. It was like being a teenager all over again.

The limousine pulled up outside a grand-looking hotel. Everything was perfection. The foyer was all exquisite cream marble. They were shown to a private lift that took them up to the twenty-fifth floor.

As the elevator doors slid open Portia let out a gasp. The suite was huge, with spectacular floor-to-ceiling glass doors looking out over the Bay of Naples.

Javier tipped the concierge and took their bags, walking across the room and pulling one of the doors open, letting the warm air flood in.

He walked outside onto the balcony, resting his hands on the railing, and sucked in a deep breath. He gave her a smile. 'It doesn't quite have the tranquillity of Villa Rosa, but this place comes a close second for me.' He waved his hand downwards. 'On one side of the suite you can watch the buzz of the city, from the other you have this, the beautiful bay.'

She stood alongside him and admired the view. Vesuvius was in the distance, along with the coastline of Sorrento and isle of Capri. Underneath them was a whole array of million-dollar yachts.

She laid her head on his shoulder. 'I often wonder how long it will be before Vesuvius erupts again. I visited Pompeii once with my family. It was like stepping back in time. Everything about it felt so real. From the stepping stones, to the mosaics, and the amphitheatre.'

He nodded. 'We should go there again some day.'

Her mouth dried. That almost sounded like a plan. Something for the future. She wasn't quite sure how to reply.

Javier turned back towards her. 'I have a business meeting I need to attend.' He hesitated then pointed inside the suite. 'You're welcome to take any of the rooms, or you can share mine. And I'll order some room service while you get ready. Teatro di San Carlo is only five minutes from here.'

She gave a little nod. He seemed a little nervous too; he hadn't made the assumption she'd be sharing his room—that was up to her.

He bent down and brushed a kiss on her cheek. 'I'll see you in a couple of hours.'

She gave a nod as he disappeared back out of the door of the suite. Portia turned and faced the Bay of Naples again. She wasn't quite sure what the night would hold, but she couldn't wait to find out.

The meeting went well. Things were finally falling into place in his brain. He'd recognised something in the last few days. Aldo had left a message saying he wanted to talk.

Talk. It was the common theme for people with bipolar disorder who were feeling suicidal. Javier had done his research. There was no specific charity in Italy for people who had bipolar disorder. One of his biggest ambitions was awareness raising. There could be other families out there watching a loved one deteriorate and not recognising the signs. Not recognising the condition. And for people already diagnosed and experiencing the extreme mood swings that could come with bipolar disorder there would be somewhere they could call. A safe place when they were struggling. How many people could be helped if they had a place they could call when they felt at their lowest? Could it have helped Aldo?

He'd never really know. But it made him feel as if he were doing *something*. Something that might help others who felt the same way.

The charity was his starting point. He had more than enough money to fund this. He just had to make the right connections to make sure this could be set up safely, and well. And that was exactly what he'd been doing today.

He glanced at his watch. The details had taken longer than expected. He'd need to be quick to get ready for the opera. When the doors of the lift opened, he could see signs of Portia throughout the suite. A coffee cup. A plate of pastries. Her computer sitting on the desk.

Music was playing in one of the other rooms. His heart sank a little as he walked through to the main room and then stopped. Her bag was lying in the corner of his room. She might be taking time to get ready in another room, but it looked as if it was her intention to sleep here.

His heart gave a lurch in his chest. He could almost feel the blood quicken around his body. He strode into the bathroom and turned on the shower. His tuxedo was hanging in the wardrobe and the champagne that he'd ordered was sitting chilling in a bucket of ice.

It didn't take him long to shower, shave and change. He carried the ice bucket and glasses out into the main room just as the music in the other room was turned off.

The sun was beginning to set outside, filling the bay with streaks of orange and red. Javier glanced at his watch. They only had a little time before they would need to leave for the opera. Just as he thought about calling her, Portia opened the door from the other room.

He could tell she was nervous. She was taking tentative steps and had one hand on her stomach. The off-the-shoulder long red dress was stunning; it both hugged and complemented her curves, dipping slightly at the front. Her hair was curled, cascading over one shoulder. She had no jewellery on. She didn't need any. Instead, she wore long black gloves, completing her look of elegance.

'Wow,' was all he could say.

She looked over her shoulder as if he were talking to someone else, then her face broke into a wide smile. 'You think it will do?'

He popped the cork on the champagne and filled the two glasses, holding one out towards her. 'I think...' he paused '...that you're perfect.'

She was wearing make-up now. Black kohl around her eyes and red lips to match her dress. Her hand shook as she took the glass from him. 'I am?'

He nodded as he placed one hand at her hip. 'You are.'

The nervousness started to fall away from her face. Her dark eyes swept up and down him. 'You don't scrub up too badly yourself.' She winked at him. 'You should try and get a part that means you wear a tux in a film.' She sipped her champagne as she smiled. He got the hint about the world's most famous spy instantly.

He laughed. 'I think you'll find that particular part is quintessentially English.' He did his best impression of an English accent.

Portia laughed too. 'I've always thought that was a flaw.' She waved her champagne glass. 'They need to broaden their horizons. They're missing out on some prime candidates for the role.'

He guided her over towards the view of Naples bay again. She let out a little sigh. 'It's like someone planned this night perfectly.' She held out her hand. 'A stunning dress, a wonderful view, a luxurious hotel...' she turned and rested her hand on the front of his tux '...a handsome man and then...opera. What more could a girl want?'

She tilted her chin up towards him. 'What more could she want indeed?' he whispered as he bent to kiss her. He could taste the champagne on her soft, tempting lips. Her body turned towards his and it was easy to slide his hand down her back and press his hips against hers. Her perfume wound its way around him, pulling him in like the music of a snake charmer.

Nothing felt wrong. Everything felt right. For the first time since Aldo had died Javier finally had some peace. He could finally contemplate a future. And he knew exactly who he wanted to contemplate it with. Her breath was quickening, their kisses becoming more fevered, and he reluctantly pulled his lips from hers and pressed his forehead against hers.

'Ms Marlowe?' he said hoarsely.

She looked up through thick lashes. 'Yes?' Her voice was shaking.

He held out his hand to take her gloved one. 'Let me introduce you to the magic of opera. Let me introduce you to *The Marriage of Figaro.*'

It was as if she were in her own movie.

She was the heroine. And he was the hero.

In some ways she felt as if it were all unreal. As if at any moment she'd wake up from this wonderful dream.

The limousine whisked them to the Teatro di San Carlo. As soon as they stepped outside it was like being on the red carpet. Javier was recognised instantly. She could feel the electricity in the air around them. His hand stayed firmly at her back.

Cameras flashed intermittently. Javier shook hands with people and charmed his way along the row of staff who were standing outside the opera house.

As soon as they stepped inside her nerves increased. There were many hushed voices and glances in their direction. What a fool. She hadn't given this enough thought.

She'd got used to the anonymity of L'Isola dei Fiori. Of not looking over her shoulder and worrying about what she looked like. It was odd. The thought had flitted through her mind when they were on the ferry. But since they'd arrived in the hotel it had been like their own private world, and when she'd stepped outside the room and seen Javier's face, all she'd been able to think about was him and her.

Another glass of champagne was placed in her hand and she gathered Sofia's dress in one hand as they walked up the stairs.

Walking into the *teatro* was like entering another world.

It was breathtaking. The whole theatre was circular, set around the large stage. Red plush seats filled the stalls and sweeping around the walls were five tiers of individual boxes. White and gold gilt decorated the walls with sweeping red velvet curtains at each of the boxes.

Javier smiled at her and led her up a set of private

stairs. A staff member held the door open for her and she stepped inside. And then stopped.

They were directly facing the stage. The box had large sumptuous seats and gold gilt decoration all around. 'What is this?' she whispered.

He smiled. 'We're in the royal box.'

'The what?' It was almost as if the air had been sucked from her chest. Maybe this dress was tighter than she thought.

He gestured to her to sit down. The chair was almost like a throne, possibly the grandest chair she'd ever seen. She perched gingerly on the edge while an amused Javier watched. More champagne was waiting for them in the box along with strawberries. 'I thought you might be hungry.' he said with a shrug. Javier settled next to her as the lights started to dim around them.

'Do you know the story of *The Marriage of Figaro*?'

She nodded. 'I've never seen it though.'

He smiled and rested back in his chair as he clasped her hand. 'Then sit back and enjoy, let the magic begin.'

From the first beat of the music it was like a spell being weaved around her. Figaro, Susanna and the Count gripped her attention. Every one of Mozart's notes, every harmony, every element of comedy had her enthralled. The music from the opera filled every part of the huge theatre, reverberating around them.

In the dark of the theatre their box seemed ultimately private. So when Javier nuzzled at her neck she didn't object. He fed her strawberries, which trickled down her chin. The champagne made her hiccup, which set her off in a fit of giggles.

And he didn't let go of her hand the whole night.

She stopped worrying about her work and her life in Hollywood. Javier only had eyes for her. His attention was mesmerising. They whispered to each other. They kissed. She'd never been so connected.

Her heart was swelling so much it felt as though it would fill her chest. When the last beat of music had finished she leapt to her feet and applauded as loudly as she could.

Javier was at her side. 'Did you like it?'

She couldn't hold back the enthusiasm that was bubbling inside. She threw her arms around his neck. 'I didn't like it, I loved it.'

He looked so amused, but she felt safe around him, assured in his arms. That glint in his eye sent little shockwaves all around her body. No one had ever made her feel like this. No one had ever made her feel so special, and so loved.

She forgot about everyone else around them as they walked hand in hand to the limousine. She only had eyes for Javier. And it seemed he only had eyes for her.

By the time they'd reached the hotel she was breathless with anticipation.

The journey in the lift only took a few seconds and she held her breath the whole way.

Javier was quiet. Maybe he was feeling the same way. As the doors slid open she could see candles flickering all around the suite. Gentle music was playing in the background. It was magical.

But for some reason her feet couldn't move.

Javier stepped out of the lift and turned and held his hand out towards her. 'Ms Marlowe...' he bowed before her '...will you be my guest?'

Every part of her was trembling. But it wasn't nerves. It was excitement.

She'd never wanted anything more.

'I'd love to,' she answered as she put her hand in his.

Javier pulled her up against him. They'd never danced together before and this felt exactly how it should.

She slid her arms up to his shoulders and pressed her body against his, moving in time with the music. Javier's mouth trailed kisses down the side of her face and along her shoulder and neck. His touch so light, it was like butterfly wings against her skin.

Her skin was on fire. Every sense aching for his touch. His fingers traced a line down her closed eyes, past her mouth and over the delicate skin at her decoupage, stopping tantalisingly at the mound of her breasts. He moved it across her chest and down the length of one arm, spinning her around so she had her back to him and peeling her glove, oh, so slowly, so temptingly down her arm. It was like being part of an exotic and extremely private striptease. The next glove followed just as slowly. She could feel the planes of his chest and abdomen pressed against her back. She sucked in a breath as his hand slid between their bodies and rested in the arch between her shoulder blades. The noise of the slide of the zipper was achingly teasing. As the pressure of the dress released around her, she spun around, letting it fall on the floor at her feet and leaving her standing in only her underwear in front of him.

She didn't feel embarrassed. She didn't feel exposed. She just lifted her hands and started slowly pulling his bow tie apart. He stood still, not moving as she took charge. Instead, she relished him watching the candlelight dance over her body as she slowly undid each button on his shirt. Once she'd pulled it apart she slid her hands over the planes of his chest as he let out a groan. He pulled her bare breasts against his now bare chest.

'Do you know what you're doing to me, Portia Marlowe?'

She licked her lips as she lowered her gaze. 'Pretty much the same as you're doing to me, Mr Russo. How about we see where this takes us?'

She let out a whimper as his hands slid over the curves of her bottom. 'Let's see indeed,' he groaned as he lowered her to the floor.

CHAPTER SEVEN

HE WOKE UP with the sheets tangled around him and her bare body pressed against his.

In previous circumstances he'd always known there would be an end point in the relationship. He'd never been sworn on forever.

But with Portia he just couldn't picture how things would come to a natural end.

He didn't want to.

She smiled as she turned around, still sleeping, and reached out to press her head against his chest. He ran his fingertip down her nose. 'Hey, sleepyhead. We need to wake up at some point. We need to get back to our own private paradise.'

She let out a groan, still not opening her eyes. 'I like the sound of that.'

But she wasn't finished. She stretched, then swung one leg over his body, sitting astride him and brushing her lips against his. 'I love Villa Rosa, but I'm kind of liking it here too. Why don't we stay another night? Do a tour of the city like you said?'

He hesitated, trying to find the words. But they didn't come quickly enough. His mind was blank. Everything had gone well yesterday. But he was anxious to finish at Villa Rosa and get back to the real world. Get back to where he felt he could make a difference. He just hadn't had a chance to talk to Portia about it yet.

'How about we save that for another day? I'd like to finish up at Villa Rosa first.'

She frowned and sat back, placing her palms flat on his chest. Even though this was a little awkward, part of him loved that she wasn't embarrassed by their nakedness. She looked the tiniest bit hurt. 'Oh, okay, then.'

She sighed and swung her leg back from his body and stepped down onto the floor. She walked over to the wardrobe and pulled it open, reaching for one of the white luxury dressing gowns that hung inside. She wrapped it around herself and turned around. 'I think you should order me some coffee. It's time for you to tell me what's going on.'

He could tell by the tone of her voice that he wouldn't be able to brush her off with any made-up tales. And he didn't want to do that anyway.

They'd got this close. Maybe it was time to finally share the secret that had been eating away at him since he'd got the phone call to say that Aldo was dead.

It was surprising how quickly room service could arrive. Within ten minutes they were sitting on either side of a table with an array of food in front of them. Portia pulled one leg up onto the chair, revealing her bare knee as she reached for a croissant and tore it apart. Her dark curls from last night tumbled around her face. Not a trace of make-up was left.

He poured the coffee and left it black.

Portia didn't speak, she just studied him with her dark brown eyes.

'You know how we spoke about the funeral I went to just before the awards ceremony?'

She nodded. 'It was a friend, wasn't it? I just assumed

he'd died of cancer or something similar. You never really told me much about it.'

He nodded. 'I know. I never told anyone much about it.'

She narrowed her gaze. 'Okay, why?'

He felt his voice start to shake. 'Aldo was my oldest friend. I'd known him forever. He still lived in the village my mother's family came from. Aldo didn't die from cancer.'

She set down her coffee cup. 'What did he die from?'

Javier's eyes went to the bay, sweeping around the beauty of the view and glistening sea. 'Aldo committed suicide.'

Saying the words out loud was so harsh. It was like an admission of reality. The thing he really didn't want to talk about at all—but was trying to find a way to deal with.

'Oh.' Portia pressed her lips together. She was still studying him intently. 'I'm really sorry to hear that.' She waited a few seconds and then added, 'Had he been unwell?'

Bile rose in the back of his throat. There was an ache in his stomach. A real, physical ache. A gust of wind blew in through the open doors, carrying the aroma of all the food on the table, and he almost retched. Javier pushed his chair back from the table.

As he looked down he saw the goosebumps appear on his skin. 'Yes—but I didn't know it.' He ran his fingers through his hair. 'I didn't recognise the signs.' He shook his head. 'I wasn't there to recognise the signs.'

Portia spoke quietly. 'What do you mean?'

Javier's grey eyes met hers, pain etched through them. 'Aldo had bipolar disorder—just like my mother has.'

Portia's eyes widened. 'Oh.'

He shook his head. 'I spent my life around someone with bipolar disorder. If anyone should have recognised it—it should have been me. But I wasn't there. I didn't see enough of Aldo. I knew he was down. I knew he was depressed—but I thought that seemed like part of the grieving process after the breakdown of his marriage.'

'And it was more than that?'

Javier nodded. 'Yes. His sister told me later about the mood swings. The sleeplessness. The irritability. The erratic behaviour.' He leaned forward and put his head in his hands. 'All things I could have recognised.'

'And if you had—would you have been able to help?'

Javier threw up his hands in frustration. 'Of course I would have. I could have got him to see a specialist doctor, a therapist that could have helped with his condition.'

She gave her head a little shake. 'This isn't your fault, Javier. You weren't here. You were working.'

Javier clenched his fists. 'I know that. But still…'

Javier looked up and met her gaze. Those dark brown eyes were fixed on his. No judgement. No blame. His voice broke. 'There's more.'

Portia leaned across the table and squeezed his hand. 'What?'

He let out a long slow breath.

'I hadn't been good at keeping in touch. I'd called. I'd emailed. But we hadn't physically seen each other for seventeen months.' He shook his head and bowed it. 'That was far too long. Far too long for someone I'd known that long.'

Portia still had her hand over his. She stopped squeezing and started moving her thumb in little circles over his knuckles. 'But that happens with friends. Even the best of friends. I have friends from school that I only ever get to see every five years or so, and we just pick up from where we left off. Time doesn't matter to us. We're all leading our own lives.' Her hand came up and touched his cheek. 'But they're the kind of friends—almost like sisters—that I know if I picked up the phone to them in the middle of the night and told them I was in trouble, they'd drop everything to help me. And I would them.'

He could see the sincerity on her face. She absolutely meant it. Portia Marlowe was a much better friend than he'd ever been.

He snatched his hand back and stalked out to the balcony, putting his arms on the railing and stretching down, closing his eyes and willing the Bay winds to sweep away his conscience and regrets.

'Javier?' Portia stood beside him in her dressing gown, worry etched across her face. Her voice was quiet. 'What is it?'

She knew there was so much more to this. He couldn't pretend any more.

He started to shake. 'It was my fault, Portia. Mine. I was away—filming in the Arabian Desert. It was a terrible location. No phone signals. Sixteen-hour days on set. And even as I say that out loud I know exactly what a pathetic excuse that is.' His voice was getting louder. He couldn't help himself. He was so wrapped up in the emotion that he couldn't stop. 'He phoned me, Portia. He phoned me and left me a message saying he really needed to talk. And do you know what I did? I got back to the trailer, couldn't get a signal and fell asleep. *I fell asleep!*'

Portia had pulled back, her eyes wide. But she stood her ground next to him as her hair was blown around her face.

'What kind of friend am I? My best friend calls—tells me he needs me. And I'm too busy—too tired to call back. I was the last person Aldo called before he killed himself.' He thudded his hands down on the railing.

His breaths were coming in short, sharp bursts. He could feel his heart thudding against his chest.

There was a flicker to his left. Someone standing on the balcony of the neighbouring suite; a man also stood looking out over the bay.

Portia didn't speak. She just took one of his hands and pulled him back indoors. She pushed him firmly down onto one of the large armchairs and settled on his lap.

She wrapped her arms around his neck and dipped her head next to his ear. 'Don't, Javier. Don't do this to yourself. Don't blame yourself because you didn't answer the phone on one occasion. You have no idea if it would have made a difference or not. How could you? If you had spoken to him, and he'd still done it, would you feel better or worse?'

He was numb. But Portia was sitting in his lap, putting her cheek against his and letting the heat from her body reach through the robe towards him.

His throat was completely dry. Her fingers stroked through his hair. She was trying to offer some modicum of comfort.

His voice was throaty. 'He wanted to talk, Portia. That's what he said. He just wanted to talk.'

She gave her head the smallest shake. 'But you still don't know. You had no idea your friend was unwell. If you had done—I'm sure you would have called him straight away.' She closed her eyes for a second. 'We all have points in our lives where we'd like to turn the clock back and take different steps. But that doesn't always mean we've done something wrong.' Her hand was still on his face. 'What about his mum and dad? His sister? How are they doing?'

'I try and speak to them every week. I don't think his mum or dad will ever get over it. How do you do that? How does a parent get over losing a child?'

'And they didn't know either?'

He shook his head. 'That's just it. They didn't recognise the signs. He'd lost weight. He'd apparently mentioned he had trouble sleeping. His moods were erratic.'

She held out her hands. 'And because of your experience with your mother, you think you would have put the pieces together?'

He gave the briefest of nods. His emotions were bubbling beneath the surface. He'd never really spoken to anyone about all this before. He'd never really shared like this. It didn't matter that there was still that tiny voice in the back of his brain, telling him that Portia was a reporter. The woman he'd come to know in the last few days hadn't shown any cut-throat tactics that he'd seen in his childhood. None of the deviousness. None of the manipulative behaviour. The Portia Marlowe he knew had a good and honest heart.

She was nodding slowly as she looked out over the bay. 'So what is it that you want to do here?'

'You mentioned your sister needed specialist help. I want to do that for Aldo's condition—for bipolar disorder. The meeting yesterday—it was with a potential director for the charity I want to set up. I want to set up a helpline. I want to raise awareness of the signs of the condition. I want to organise support groups for those that need it—and specialist help.'

She gave a serious nod. 'That's a huge undertaking.'

'I know. But it's something I need to do. The money is easy—I have the money. I have more money than I can actually spend. I just need to be sure that I set up things to work well.'

Portia looked serious. 'It could be a minefield. You have to be prepared for anything.' She paused for a second. 'People will wonder why Javier Russo is so interested in bipolar disorder. You'll have to be prepared for the press you might get.'

'I know.'

He could see her concentrating. 'What about your mum?'

He nodded. 'She's well right now. She hasn't worked as a model in years. Times have changed. She's ready to talk about her mental health condition.'

He was overwhelmed by how understanding Portia was being. She was taking what he was saying seriously. She hadn't let him think—even for the briefest second—that she was disappointed he hadn't returned the call to Aldo straight away. She'd been kind. She'd been rational. And she'd shown him affection and love.

'Thank you,' he whispered.

She looked surprised. 'For what?'

'For being you.'

A soft smile appeared on her lips. 'Why would I be anyone else?' She leaned forward and dropped a gentle kiss on his forehead, her hair brushing against his face. 'You're a good man, Javier. I'm sorry about your friend—really I am. And I understand you wanting to look out for his family.' She slid her hand under his dressing gown and placed it over his heart. 'But you have to look out for yourself too. I get that you want to take some time. I think you're right to stop working so hard. But you need to think carefully about the next steps.'

Javier breathed slowly. It was as if a whole weight had been lifted from his shoulders. He'd shared. He'd said the words out loud that had haunted him for the last few months.

Did fate really put people in your path?

He looked up at the pale blue sky above and smiled. He'd come to Villa Rosa for solitude. For quiet. And instead he'd met Portia Marlowe. With her tumbling curls, perfect English accent and chocolate-brown eyes she'd taken him by surprise. Her intuitive questions. Her feisty attitude. Her laugh. The sometimes suggestive twinkle in her eyes. But most of all her good heart.

Slowly but surely, Portia had burrowed her way under his skin and into his own heart.

The gorgeous woman in his arms right now laughed as her stomach growled loudly. 'Oh, no! That's what happens when you distract me from breakfast.'

She walked back inside for a second, grabbed an apple then walked back out to his side. She looked back over the Bay of Naples and gave a little sigh. 'It's so beautiful here.'

Javier put his hands on her waist. The electric-blue bay was buzzing with activity. White million-dollar yachts and cruise ships bobbed beneath them. The area around the bay was packed with tourists, visiting the shops and heading in towards the city. The distant peak of Vesuvius looked crested in purple this morning with a white cloud misting around it. For lots of people this would be paradise.

Portia waved back in towards the suite. 'And this place is sumptuous. Won't you be sorry to go back to our crumbling Villa Rosa with its antiquated plumbing, dust-filled attics and barely functioning kitchen?'

He bent his head and whispered in her ear. 'Absolutely not. I can't wait.'

She twirled in his arms to face him. 'Really, why?'

'Because Villa Rosa brought me you.'

And he met her lips with his own and they forgot all about breakfast.

Any minute now she was going to wake up and discover this had all been some kind of wistful dream.

Even now it felt too *good* to be a dream.

When Javier had told her about his friend the anguish on his face had been heartbreaking. He truly believed he could have done something differently. The fact he hadn't returned the call straight away would probably haunt him for the rest of his life.

But she loved the fact he was trying to turn something tragic into something positive. Her stomach gave an uncomfortable twist. If she'd come here looking for a story—this was it. And depending on the mood of the press it could be spun either way. In one headline Javier Russo would be the tragic school friend of a man who'd committed suicide and was now trying to start a charity to help others with the same condition. In another, he would be the villain, the heartless Hollywood star who'd ignored the call of a suicidal friend.

But she didn't want a story any more.

She didn't want any of it any more.

All she wanted was Javier. The man who made her blood sizzle just by saying her name with his Italian accent. The man who could entice her to cross a room with one look. The man whose touch she would never tire of.

She wanted to help him. She wanted to support him.

She'd thought leaving Hollywood was a curse—instead it was a blessing. She'd had a chance to connect with someone who made her feel whole. Who made her feel complete.

She hadn't had a chance yet to tell him about her job. Or lack of it.

She'd toyed with the idea of just sending an email to her boss and quitting. But Portia wasn't that kind of girl. She'd meet her boss, have that conversation and walk out of the room with her dignity and pride intact.

She was professional enough to know she didn't want a bad reputation to follow her.

When she got back she would have to pack up her apartment and look for somewhere less expensive to stay. But she didn't care any more. Holly Payne could be the star at Entertainment Buzz TV. Her heart just wasn't in it any more.

Javier's hand stayed intertwined with hers on the car journey back through Naples and then on the ferry back to L'Isola dei Fiori. They talked through his plans for the phone line and she took some notes on questions he needed to ask. His phone rang a few times on the way back. Each time he took it from his pocket, checked it and put it away again.

'You don't want to take it?'

Javier shook his head firmly. 'No. I don't. It's my agent. I think he and I will be parting company soon.'

'You do?'

'I do. Let's just say it's time.'

She licked her lips and looked out at the coastline of L'Isola dei Fiori as the boat moved to dock. 'So, when are you due back home?' Asking the question made her a little nervous. It felt like putting a sign above her head saying, *Do any future plans include me?*

'Home? Oh, you mean Hollywood? That's not really home. I have a house in the hills and a house down in Malibu on the beach.'

'You have an original Malibu beach house?'

'And guess who helped me remodel?'

She laughed. 'Uncle Vinnie?'

'Yep. Uncle Vinnie. And guess what? He was the boss. I had to follow all his instructions.'

'Wow. I'd love to meet Uncle Vinnie. I bet he keeps you on your toes.'

'Oh, he does. He'd love you. Once he hears your accent you'll have him in the palm of your hand.'

A warm feeling spread across her chest. Javier said those words so easily—as if he was assuming she would meet his family.

He flung his arm around her shoulders as they disembarked the ferry. 'I also have a house at Lake Como. You should come and see that some time. I think you'd like it.'

Her footsteps faltered. '*The* Lake Como?'

He gave her an amused smile. 'Is there any other?'

'So, you're next door to George Clooney?'

He didn't miss a beat. 'Almost.'

It was as if someone had just sprinkled fairy dust over her. She'd spent the last few days thinking of Javier Russo, the man—the person. Because that was what he was to her. But it was Javier Russo the movie star that owned houses in the Hollywood Hills, Santa Monica beach and Lake Como.

Their time in Villa Rosa had been blissful. Private. The three weeks would be over soon. Could the connection they'd made here survive in the real world?

Just thinking about it made her stomach flip-flop.

Right now she wanted to direct her own movie. One

where she pressed a button and let time stop all around them. Not so much a *Groundhog Day* as a Groundhog Three Weeks. They could live in their own private bubble in the pink villa and let the rest of the world pass them by. If only.

Javier led her into one of the fishmongers at the port. 'Will we grab something for dinner?'

'Sure.' They picked up some fish, some vegetables and new potatoes. Then, they added some wine and took a taxi back to the villa.

This time, when Portia turned the old key in the lock and stepped inside the villa had a different feel.

When she'd done this first time around, she'd been sad, sensing the air of neglect and disrepair around her. Walking through the villa had almost made her feel like a ghost.

This time the air around her almost hummed. Javier was by her side, striding through to the kitchen to deposit their food. Now, she felt a sense of belonging. She wandered through to the painted drawing room. The plaster had dried in a long white crack snaking up the pale blue and mauve sky. The rest of the walls had been skimmed smoothly, ready for painting.

Javier appeared at her side again, sliding his arm around her waist. 'It's beautiful,' she sighed. 'Or at least it will be again once it's painted.' She tilted her chin up towards him. 'You've done a really good job.'

'Why thank you, madam.' He kissed her lips and her hand automatically went to his head, running through his hair and holding his lips on hers.

A sweep of anxious desperation that she hated flooded through her. She just honestly didn't want this time to end.

But it seemed neither did Javier, because he swept one hand under her legs and held her in his arms. His lips touched her ear. 'Your room, or mine?' he whispered.

CHAPTER EIGHT

SHE WAS TEMPTED to skip into the village the next morning, but instead she was happy to walk with Javier's arm around her shoulders. They parted at the top of the street. Javier had decided to buy something special at the fishmonger's for dinner tonight.

There was a crowd outside the newsagents and several faces turned as she approached, scowling at her and murmuring under their breath.

She almost didn't go any further, but one of them moved just enough for her to glimpse the billboard outside the newsagent and let her catch a glance at the headline and photo on the board. A flash of pink caught her attention. An achingly familiar pink bikini.

Her feet moved automatically. She shoved her way through the crowd and picked up the paper at the top of the pile.

She had no idea what the headline said but she could understand the photos—after all a picture spoke a thousand words. They were all of her, entwined around Javier. One from the private beach—he was holding her in the water and she had her legs and arms wrapped around him like some kind of limpet. The next was in the restaurant at the port, the third at the opera in Naples with her wearing Sofia's red dress and the final one—

the killer—was of the two of them wearing hotel bath-robes and standing on the balcony of the hotel in Naples.

She couldn't speak. Her mouth was dry. Who on earth had taken these pictures? And what did the story say?

She walked numbly into the Internet café and sat down at one of the computers. She winced as she searched for her own name and Javier's.

If she'd thought Holly had caused an Internet explosion a few weeks ago, then she and Javier had caused an Internet meltdown. At least in the US and in Italy.

But as she started to read the hairs on her arms stood on end as if chilled by an icy blast. A few headlines were just romanticising the relationship between herself and Javier. Some said they'd secretly dated for months, some claimed she'd seduced him on an aeroplane, others claimed they'd met by accident in Italy.

The same four pictures featured over and over again. How on earth had they got that picture on the private beach?

The boat. The boat moored in the distance. There must have been a photographer on board. She felt physically sick.

The picture at the restaurant or opera could have been taken by any of the other guests who'd recognised them. But the one on the balcony? She groaned. If they'd been recognised at the opera, it wouldn't have taken any reporter worth their salt long to figure out where they were staying. Years ago that reporter might have been her. That balcony looked over the whole bay. It was just that the picture was *so* close, *so* clear.

Her stomach lurched as she reached the next version of the headlines. There were video clips. She clicked on the first and her producer's face filled the screen. It was only a ten-second burst.

'Well, I told her she had three weeks to go and get a story and she certainly did that! We'll get the full exclusive when she returns from her break next week...'

But it was the next translated headline that stopped her breathing. *Ignored by the Billionaire.* She clicked and started to speed-read.

No.

There in the middle of the page was Aldo's name, followed by the fact that he'd phoned Javier—his old friend—pleading for help before he'd committed suicide.

It felt as if her blood had just turned to ice.

There was more. The reporter had tried to get comments from Aldo's family.

Oh, no. She glanced at when the report had appeared. It was only minutes ago in an Italian news website. It wouldn't take the US sites long to pick up the story and start to run with it. She knew how these things worked.

She grabbed the paper and ran out of the café. She had to find Javier. She had to warn him. She had to speak to him now.

Her chest was tight. She needed to find Javier.

But there was no sign of him around the port area and the more she looked, the more she got suspicious glances.

She flagged a taxi. She'd go back to Villa Rosa. It was safer there. Javier would appear eventually and she would have a chance to talk to him then.

But as soon as they pulled up outside the pale pink villa her stomach dropped. The front door was lying wide open.

She thrust some money at the taxi driver and rushed up the steps. 'Javier?' she shouted.

There was no reply. She ran up the stairs and headed for his room.

His room was in complete disarray. All his clothes were scattered across the bed, wardrobe still open and drawers askew. Javier's face was like thunder as he was blindly stuffing everything into his bag.

'Javier?' The air was almost black in the room. She was almost scared to speak.

The look he gave her almost cut her in two.

'Did you enjoy your story? Did I give you what you need? Do you know what's happened to Aldo's family in the last few hours? There are paparazzi camped outside their house—banging on their door and harassing them. How do you think they can deal with that?' He didn't even stop to draw breath, he just kept thundering on.

'I don't care that you used me, Portia. I don't care that all that you ever wanted was a headline to keep your job. Funny how you never mentioned that to me. But what I will never, *ever* forgive you for is the fact you used a grieving family to feather your own nest.'

The last item of clothing was stuffed in the bag. His face was red, his eyes blazing. She'd never, ever seen him like this.

'Wait, that's not what happened. I was going to tell you about my job—I was going to tell you that I was giving it up. That it wasn't for me any more. But I wanted to wait until I got back to LA and talked to my producer. I would never do something like this. Don't you know that?'

Javier grabbed his bag from the bed. 'What I do know, Portia, is that the woman I thought I knew doesn't exist at all. You knew, Portia, you knew what I experienced as a child. You knew how my mother was treated then. But you didn't care. You just wanted your story.' He glanced up and down her body and shook his head. 'Boy, you're good. You had me believing that this might actually be real.'

She was stunned. She couldn't find the words to speak. It was her that had had all the fears. The fears that she might be played. The fears that Javier Russo might not really be interested in her.

She tried to speak but he lifted his hand in front of her face. 'Answer me one question: your boss, did she or did she not give you three weeks to find a story or you'd be fired?'

The words stuck at the back of her throat. She knew exactly how this would sound. Her heart was twisting in her chest. In less than an hour her life had turned upside down. The love that she'd never been sure she'd encounter was right in front of her but slipping from her grasp in a way she hadn't even imagined.

'Javier...' It came out as a croak and he shot her a look of disgust as he shouldered his way past her and thundered down the corridor.

For a second he paused, then he shook his head and disappeared down the stairs.

She wanted to slide right down the wall onto the floor. But she couldn't. She had to see this through. She had to fight for what she wanted and who she believed in. Her heart was crumpling in her chest. The guy she'd lain next to only the day before. The guy who could make her skin tingle just by looking at her. The man she'd actually dared to picture a future with. The man she loved with her whole heart and she hadn't even had the chance to tell him.

It couldn't end like this. It just couldn't.

She pushed herself back from the wall and started down the corridor. There was a noise outside and every part of her body clenched.

No. Her feet moved faster, down the stairs and across the hallway to the main door, which was still lying wide open.

She reached the door just in time to see the taxi pull out of the driveway onto the road back to the village. He'd jumped in the taxi she'd just left. She started to run, shouting at the taxi to stop. But either the driver didn't see her, or Javier told him to ignore her.

One glance at her watch told her everything she needed to know. The next ferry left in ten minutes. The taxi would make it there just in time.

She—would not.

Her legs crumpled beneath her and she started to sob.

The job she used to love had just snatched away the life she was about to lead.

And she had no idea how to put it right.

CHAPTER NINE

NOTHING ABOUT THIS felt right. Everything about this felt wrong.

From the second he'd hit the mainland on his way to Naples airport his phone had pinged non-stop. His friends, relatives, newspaper reporters, showbiz contacts, acting contemporaries and…his agent.

He only replied to one message from Aldo's sister. His reply was simple.

On my way.

He had the luxury of being rushed through security and boarding the private jet he'd hired in under an hour.

But from the second the plane took off he had only one thing on his mind.

Portia.

When he'd seen the newspaper he'd been shocked. The pictures were intrusive. But they also made him feel like a fool. Over the last few years he'd got used to people snapping photos wherever he went. It seemed that every person in the world these days had a phone in their hand.

But L'Isola dei Fiori had felt different. He'd been more relaxed, let his guard down, and in doing so he'd inadvertently exposed Portia to something she might not have wanted to make front-page news with.

Or so he'd thought.

When one of the shopkeepers had gestured him in to look at his computer and watch the video clip of Portia's producer he'd felt physically sick. But more than that he'd felt betrayed.

He'd always been wary of reporters but he'd never contemplated the fact their relationship was contrived or false. It had never entered his head—the connection had just seemed so real. He felt like such a fool. She'd hardly mentioned work at all—and when she had she'd been a little evasive. Now he knew why. He'd trusted her with a secret that had kept him awake at night for the last few months and she'd revealed it to the world.

He'd known not to trust reporters. He'd known to keep them always at arm's length. To control how he appeared, and what he revealed.

But around Portia? His walls had been chipped away, until they'd finally tumbled down.

He'd trusted her. Trust wasn't something that came easily to Javier. And she'd betrayed him—just when he'd thought about taking their relationship to the next level.

He'd finally come to terms with how to move forward. And it had felt good. It had felt as if he could actually do something that might make a difference.

And it was freeing. Because he'd been able to recognise how he actually felt about Portia.

He loved her. Her English accent. Her dark brown eyes. The way she said his name. The way her clothes hugged her curves, and the way her smile could reach from ear to ear.

He was just glad he hadn't been fool enough to tell her.

That would have been an even bigger disaster than the one he faced now.

He absolutely didn't care what the newspapers and social media said about him.

What he cared about was the impact on Aldo's family. That was his priority. They were the people he had to sit down with, look in the eye and tell the truth to.

This was never the way he'd wanted this to happen.

He was trying to ignore the fact his heart felt as if it had been speared clean from his chest. He was trying to ignore the fact that he still couldn't really believe what had gone around about him.

His phone beeped. His agent and publicist were having a meltdown.

It seemed now that Portia's temporary replacement on Entertainment Buzz TV was being very uncomplimentary about her. Some of his fellow celebs were commenting on what a good match Javier and Portia were, and how they looked so happy together.

He was getting interview requests by the second.

His phone beeped again. This time it was the head of the film company for the action movie he was due to start promoting. The message was short and to the point.

Good work.

The irony made him shake his head. David McCurrie always said that all publicity was good publicity. Javier hitting the headlines a few weeks before the film premiere would be right up his street.

His heart weighed heavily in his chest. The betrayal was the hardest sting. He'd let Portia get under his guard. He'd believed what she'd said.

He closed his eyes for a second and leaned back

against the leather seat. Yesterday he'd been planning out his whole life in his head. A whole life that included Portia.

Today, he just felt empty. Empty, sad and betrayed.

The more he thought about those photos, the more confused he felt. There had been no one on the beach. He had no idea how someone had got the photo on the balcony in Naples. How sensible had it really been to walk out on a balcony overlooking the Bay of Naples? Was there really no privacy anywhere in the world?

But the thing that annoyed him most of all was still the news about Aldo's phone call. The only person he'd ever told about that was Portia. She was the only person that knew Aldo had told him he really needed to talk. Guilt washed over him again.

And now that was front-page news.

Was he really such a poor judge of character? Every cell in his body told him Portia would never do something like that. But it was front-page news. Along with the fact that she'd been given a deadline to find a story.

It didn't matter how he looked at it—in every version of this story, Javier Russo had been played.

CHAPTER TEN

GETTING A FLIGHT home from Italy was tougher than she'd thought. As soon as she'd hit the mainland her phone had pinged non-stop.

It was her sisters. It seemed it didn't matter where they were in the world—they'd seen the headlines too.

Naples airport was busy. And Portia was now in the unfortunate position of being recognised. Thank goodness her Italian was awful. She had no idea what the few reporters that were there were saying to her, and the girl at the check-in desk gave her a gracious nod, upgraded her and swept her up to the private lounge.

Portia was embarrassed. 'I'm not really famous,' she muttered.

The girl turned towards her—her English impeccable. 'No, but you're being harassed by the press and I won't leave you with those vultures.'

Those few words had been enough to let the tears that were brimming beneath the surface come flooding out. She'd been ushered into the lounge, then onto the plane. Eighteen hours later, after a touchdown in Munich, she finally arrived in Los Angeles.

She hadn't slept. Once she'd picked herself up from the driveway of Villa Rosa she'd contemplated opening a bottle of wine and losing herself in it.

Instead, a fire had burned inside her and she'd started to plot.

She'd emailed her boss. It had taken less than a minute to send her 'I quit' email. The press of a button had never felt so good.

LAX was notorious for paparazzi—but Portia had insider information. She knew a way to duck out avoiding most of the places the press would be waiting. At least her job had been good for something.

Her empty apartment had a stillness about it she wasn't ready for. She dumped her bag at the door and crossed the floor of her lounge. Her footsteps echoed on the wooden floor. A sob caught in her throat. She looked around.

She'd always loved this place. Loved being in the heart of Hollywood and only a short walk from Griffith Park. But all of a sudden it felt like a million miles from everyone and everything she loved.

Most of her friends were connected with work.

Her family seemed like a lifetime away.

She'd quit her job. She probably had enough savings to pay the next four or five months' rent and then she'd be out.

Her phone beeped again and she lifted it up. Immi.

Portia sagged down onto the sofa. She was sure something was going on with her sister—the last thing Immi needed was to listen to Portia's problems. But it was almost as if her sister had a sixth sense. As soon as the pictures had hit the press she'd kept texting, asking Portia to get in touch.

And it wasn't high-five texts like those she'd got from some Hollywood friends. Immi wasn't dazzled by the thought of her sister dating a film star.

Portia took a deep breath and pressed 'Call'.

Immi answered instantly. 'Tell me you're okay.'

It didn't matter that Immi sounded anxious; for Portia the familiarity of her voice was like a snuggly blanket. Comfort. That was what she needed right now.

'Tell me *you're* okay,' she replied quickly. 'Is something going on? I feel as if there's something you aren't telling me.'

There was a long sigh at the end of the phone. 'Deflection, deflection, deflection, Portia. And it isn't going to work. To answer your questions, I'm fine. We can talk about me later. Just know that I have everything under control. Now, tell me what's *really* going on.'

A tear snaked down Portia's cheek. She was so used to being the big sister. She was so used to being the one that had stuck plasters on her sisters' knees and stopped their squabbles.

'Portia? Are you crying? Talk to me. Tell me about Javier Russo. I don't need to ask what you've been doing because I've seen it. But I want to know how you are. I want to know what's happened.'

Portia licked her dry lips. Her case was still bulging by the door. She had half a mind to pick it straight back up and find another flight to somewhere else in the world.

Immi kept talking. 'I know he was in Italy this morning. I know he visited the family of the friend people are talking about. And if I believe what I hear on the news, he's currently on his way back to LA.'

Portia's heart nearly stopped. Javier was coming back here? Why? What for?

'Portia. Talk to me now. If you don't start talking I'm going to climb on a plane and shake you until you do.'

The words stuck part way in her throat. 'I… I don't know what to say…'

It was clear Immi was getting exasperated. 'Well, say something!'

The tears just started to flow. 'I've made such a mess of things. I've quit my job—'

'What?'

'And Javier thinks I've betrayed him. He thinks I lied to him. He thinks I broke the story about what happened with his friend. I would never do that. Never.'

'Well, of course you wouldn't. And why on earth would he think that?'

Portia sniffed. 'Because he hadn't told anyone else. Just me. Next thing it was plastered all over the news. He thinks it was me.'

She could hear the change in Immi's voice. 'What kind of a man is this Javier Russo? Doesn't he know you at all?'

Portia's voice broke. 'But I hadn't told him. I hadn't told him that my boss had given me an ultimatum to find a story.'

Immi's voice softened. 'Why not?'

'Because I didn't want him to think badly of me. He hated the press. They harassed his mother when he was a young boy. He didn't trust anyone in the press.'

'But he must have trusted you. I'm assuming from the way you were wrapped around him you got up close and personal?' Portia closed her eyes. She could picture Immi right now with her eyebrows arched as she asked the question.

She sagged a little further on the sofa. 'Yes.'

'And now—you've fought?'

'Yes.' It was all she could get out.

'Tell me what you think of him. Tell me what you really think of Javier Russo. And no holding back. Is this man really worth your tears? He's a film star, after all—aren't they all just smoke and mirrors?'

Portia blinked back her tears. It was a reasonable question. She'd moaned often enough to her sisters about the lies and betrayals in Hollywood.

She squeezed her eyes shut again and took a deep breath. 'I know that the man I met on L'Isola dei Fiori has the biggest heart on the planet. He's nothing like the arrogant man I've met on the red carpet. Most people watch Javier on a movie screen and just see the sexy Italian star with a twinkle in his eye. There's so much more to him than that. He's caring. He's hard-working. He wants to do his absolute best. I was lucky to spend time with him. I was lucky to connect with him in a way I've never connected with anyone before. He made me feel confident. He made me feel sure. He made me want to do better in this life.' She couldn't believe she'd actually just said all that out loud.

'Oh, no.'

'What do you mean—oh, no?'

Immi spoke in a voice that sounded so much older than her years. 'I mean, oh, no. You've fallen for him. You're in love. You never speak like this about anyone. Never. He's broken your heart—hasn't he? Right, that's it. Get me an address. Javier Russo is going to meet the Marlowe sisters in a way he could never even imagine.'

Portia choked out a laugh. She could only imagine her sisters stampeding Javier and letting him witness the full extent of the Marlowe sisters' ire.

She shook her head. 'Stop it, Immi. You can't do that. I don't know his address.' Those words made her heart squeeze. She hadn't asked Javier for his address. They hadn't got around to it.

'Why?' asked Immi, her voice wavering slightly.

'You'd do the same for me.' Her voice softened. 'What else are sisters for?'

Portia smiled. She wiped away her tears. 'Thank you, honey. It's good to talk. I need to take some time to decide what to do next.'

Immi was quiet for a second. 'Okay. You'll call me if you need me?'

'Only if you call me if you need me.' Immi gave a little sigh. 'Let's talk in a few days.'

'Done.'

Portia rang off, pushed herself off the sofa and walked over to the window. Hollywood wasn't for her any more. Not like this.

But there was some place she still wanted to go.

CHAPTER ELEVEN

His phone started buzzing as soon as he landed. Text after text after text.

His visit with Aldo's parents and sister had been short and sweet. Aldo's mother and father were upset by the press intrusion but the local *polizia* had moved them on. They'd known Aldo's last call had been to Javier. They'd known Javier hadn't got it. They hadn't known about the message.

But they'd handled it well. They didn't blame Javier. They knew he'd been filming in the middle of nowhere and working long hours. They'd been heartened by the news of his plans for the charity and the helpline. Their reaction had given him new vigour.

The paparazzi were waiting at the airport. Swarming around him. A private security firm kept them at a distance as their cameras snapped and their shouted questions all just merged into noise.

A car was waiting for him. He climbed into the back and leaned back against the cool leather seats. He was tired. He hadn't slept at all.

He ignored the texts and the messages on his phone, instead pulling up his browser, his fingers poised over the keys. He knew better than to do this. He did. But his fingers worked automatically.

The first hit surprised him.

Holly Payne lands Entertainment Buzz TV's top job after Portia Marlowe quits.

It was only a few hours old.

He straightened up in the seat. Why would Portia quit?

The horrible nagging feeling that had been in his stomach since he'd left Villa Rosa intensified.

His mind started to swirl. Portia had quit. That wasn't the sign of someone chasing a story. That wasn't the actions of a woman that was trying to entice someone into revealing details of their life.

He groaned and ran his fingers through his hair. It didn't matter that the car was air-conditioned, sweat started to break out on his skin.

He searched on his phone. There. A picture of the journalist that had broken the story. An Italian journalist. His mouth was dry. He recognised the guy.

The man from the next balcony in the hotel in Naples.

He'd heard every word.

Every part of Javier's body cringed. It was obviously intentional. The man had deliberately booked into the next suite to his. Hoping to find a story. And he'd got it.

He could feel his heart thud against his chest. Everything he'd hoped. All the plans he'd had in his head. Plans for him and Portia.

He groaned. He should have trusted her. He should have stopped to think. It didn't matter that he hadn't told anyone else—there was always a chance that an investigative reporter could dig deep. Celebrities' phones had been bugged before. Messages had been listened to. He should have realised. He should have thought a little harder about the glimpse on the balcony.

A trickle of sweat ran down his back. He had to speak to Portia. He had to find her.

He looked around. Hollywood. He hadn't even asked her where she lived. He had no idea where she might be.

Had she even left Villa Rosa—might she still be there?

The skyline changed in front of him and something came into view. Something that made his heart twist. His reaction was automatic.

He leaned forward and touched the driver's shoulder. 'Change of plan.'

The driver turned his head slightly. 'Mr Russo?'

'Take me to Griffith Park.'

The wind was whipping up a storm. When she'd changed and dashed outside she hadn't thought to bring a jacket. It was almost ironic. The outfit she'd grabbed from her case to put on was the pink satin dress she'd worn with Javier.

Normally when she came to the observatory she wore jeans, a T-shirt and running shoes. Today, she had the running shoes along with a satin dress. She'd already had a few odd stares. But she didn't care.

From here she could look out over LA. She could see the city beneath her.

Part of her loved it and part of her was tired of it. She just had to decide what to do next.

She'd been up here for hours. Her hair was tangled in knots with the wind and she was definitely feeling the chill. The crowds had thinned too. A lot of the tourists had vanished for the day. If she waited much longer, the place would be full of teenagers searching for a quiet corner. Nothing like young love to make you feel old. And broken-hearted. And useless.

She brushed her feet on the ground in front of her. It was time to move on. Time to make a change. Maybe she could finish that book? Maybe taking a complete break might do her some good. Help her re-evaluate. Help her decide what she wanted to do with her life.

Her eyes squinted in front of her. There was something familiar about the figure striding towards her.

She put her hands up to shade her eyes as he neared. There was a pitter-patter in her chest. She wasn't imagining things. She wasn't dreaming. The guy in the jeans and T-shirt really was who she thought it was.

Javier? Here?

His steps slowed as he neared and he pushed his sunglasses up on his head.

The steady grey eyes made her suck in her breath. 'Hi,' he said quickly, before he looked downwards and gave her a smile. 'Nice shoes.'

For a second she was stuck for words. Last time she'd seen him he'd yelled at her. Accused her of lying. Accused her of playing him.

She glanced around to check she wasn't hallucinating. Nope. That was definitely Javier Russo standing in front of her.

Her heart did that silly pitter-patter again. She wasn't usually lost for words. This just seemed surreal. Javier Russo at Griffith Park. The place she'd told him she loved the most in LA.

She glanced down at her red running shoes and wiggled her feet. 'Yeah, I think so. Come in handy around about here.' She pressed her lips together for a second. She couldn't help the next words that came out of her mouth. 'How are Aldo's family? Are they okay?'

Javier sighed and sat down next to her, taking off his sunglasses and turning them over in his hands. 'Yeah, they are. They aren't angry at me. They say they understand.'

He looked out across the skyline. There were lines around his eyes. He looked exhausted.

'You don't believe them?' she asked.

He shook his head. 'I do.' His head dipped for a few moments and he leaned forward with his elbows on his knees.

Portia nodded. 'I hope they're going to be okay.'

Javier looked straight back at her with those sincere grey eyes. 'But will we?'

It was as if something had struck her in the chest. It just seemed to cannonball out of nowhere. For a few moments there she'd thought they might tiptoe around each other for a bit. But it seemed that Javier had decided to go straight to the heart of the matter.

She followed his lead. 'Is there a "we"?'

Right now, she couldn't suck in a breath. A million thoughts were flying through her head. Not a single one of them made any sense. An imaginary fist felt as if it were clamped around her heart. She didn't want to believe that this could actually be real. He was actually here with her now.

He turned towards her, pulling one leg up on the bench seat so his chest was entirely facing her. They were in the middle of one of the most popular tourist destinations in LA. No one had noticed them. No one had commented.

She hadn't pretended when she'd said this was her favourite place and something about this felt so right. Whatever was going to happen to her life in LA, it seemed fitting that it should happen here. Javier reached towards her, his fingers stopping a few millimetres from her cheek. 'I never told you something.'

All the little hairs on her body stood on end. It wasn't the wind. It wasn't the temperature. It was every cell in her body preparing itself for what could come next. She tried to keep her voice steady. 'What didn't you tell me?'

His finger moved forward and brushed against her cheek. 'I never told you that in the last few weeks I discovered something about myself.'

'What was that?'

He met her gaze. 'I found out I'd met my soul mate. I met someone who made me happy. Who supported me. Who challenged me. Someone I could picture myself growing old with.'

Portia's heart thudded against her chest as he kept talking. 'Fate had put her in my path before, but it wasn't until I got to Villa Rosa that I understood why. I'm sorry, Portia. I'm so, so sorry. I couldn't think straight. I was so worried about Aldo's family.'

She shook her head, her voice shaking. 'Javier, you thought I'd betrayed your trust. You didn't even give me a chance to explain—not that I knew what the explanation was at the time. But you just upped and left. Is that how you treat your soul mate? Do you know what that did to me?' Tears were brimming in her eyes.

'I'm sorry, Portia. I was stupid. I was selfish. From the moment I left your side, you've been in my head. Nothing about this felt right. I jumped to a stupid conclusion. I know it wasn't you. It was the guy on the balcony next to us in Naples.' He shook his head. 'But I should have let you explain. I let my past experience with the press cloud my judgement. I've spent my life trying to protect myself, only revealing what I wanted to the rest of the world. The truth is I've never connected with someone the way I've connected with you. I am *so* sorry. So, so sorry I didn't take the time to stop and think. To believe in the person that I know you are—and always will be.'

The tears started to flow. 'And I felt the same. But you didn't trust me. You didn't give me a chance to explain. You walked away, Javier.' She shook her head. 'Do you know how much that hurt?'

He reached up and touched her cheek. 'And I'm so, so sorry. Portia, I went to Villa Rosa looking for peace. Looking for a place to regroup, and get my life back to a way I wanted it to be. And then...' he paused and smiled '...I found you. The crazy, unwelcoming Englishwoman who assaulted me and accused me of breaking in.'

The memories flooded back through her. 'You took me by surprise.'

'You took me by surprise too.' He ran his fingers through her tangled hair. 'And not just down on the beach.' He pulled her forward and rested his forehead against hers. 'I never expected to go to Villa Rosa and find love,' he whispered. 'I wasn't ready for it. And I didn't recognise it right away.'

She gave a little wheeze, her words caught in her throat.

'But for the first time in my life I've found a real connection. Someone I want to talk to, to share with—to fight with. Someone who can challenge me, and match me in every way. Someone I want to wake up with. And that's you, Portia. Every single day.'

A tear slid down her cheek as she pulled her head back and tilted her chin up towards him. 'I felt that way too. I stopped thinking about you as Javier Russo the film star. You were just Javier to me. The guy that wanted to help others. The guy that had a bigger heart than I could ever have imagined. The guy that stole my own heart away.'

His face broke into a smile. 'I stole your heart?'

She raised her eyebrows. 'You trampled it.' She shook her head. 'You don't get to do that again. You don't get to not talk to me. You don't get to walk away.'

He gave a slow nod. 'I promise.'

But she shook her head. 'Hollywood is full of promises. None of them I believe.'

He raised one eyebrow. 'The woman who doesn't believe in love.' He tilted his head a little. 'But you told me I stole your heart.'

'But can I trust you with it?'

It was bold. It was brash. But they'd come too far.

Javier didn't hesitate. He knelt down in front of her. 'You've quit your job?'

She nodded, wondering where this was going. 'Yes.'

'Have you found another one?'

She gave a little smile. 'Not yet. I may be considering other career plans.'

He took her hands in his. 'I want us to be together. Not just for now. Forever. What do you think, Portia? I love you. I want to find a way for us to plan for a future. Do you think we can find a way to stay together in this crazy world?'

Something surged inside her. She wanted to wrap her hands around his neck and cry with relief. But she wouldn't. She wouldn't let herself.

She straightened her back and looked him in the eye. 'So what comes next?'

'Whatever you want.'

She licked her lips. She wasn't going to tell him what she wanted even though she knew deep down in her heart. 'What do you want to do?'

He nodded slowly and pulled her up into his arms. 'I have three houses. Pick one. We can stay anywhere you want.'

'And?'

'And, I want to hire a plane. I want to take you back to Italy and introduce you to the Lake Como house first. But before that, we have something else to do.'

'What's that?'

He bent down and kissed her. 'I've wasted enough time. When you know, you just know.' He placed his hand over his heart. 'And believe me, Portia, I know. There's something that we need before we get to Lake Como. It's just a formality. Do you have your passport and birth certificate?'

Her heart surged in her chest. She almost thought she knew what he was hinting at. 'Yes, but why?'

He grinned. 'Then let's go to the Italian consulate before we get on the plane.' He swept her up into his arms and she let out a squeal. 'Hey, I'm doing things early.'

He leaned his forehead against hers. 'How about I promise to carry you over the threshold in Lake Como too?'

She smiled as she wound her arms around his neck. 'What about the Hollywood house and the Malibu beach house?'

'Mrs Russo,' he whispered, 'are you always going to be this demanding?'

She kissed him on the lips. 'Oh, believe me, Mr Russo, I'm only just getting started. Hold on for the ride!'

EPILOGUE

HE WASN'T NERVOUS at all. The paperwork was completed, the minister in place, the garden decorated and the families placated.

He'd surprised Portia with a huge engagement ring that she'd worn for five days. But Portia had assured him she was only interested in the thin rose-gold wedding band they'd picked together.

At the bottom of the garden, looking out over Lake Como, the florist had created their own Neptune's arch made entirely of pink and white flowers.

Portia was an uncomplicated bride. She didn't want fuss. She didn't want a million arrangements and the hint of press anywhere near them. She'd picked a dress from a local wedding shop that fitted perfectly and could be bought immediately. Pink flowers were threaded through her hair and in her bouquet. Her traditional wedding dress was cinched with a pink satin sash similar to the dress she'd been wearing a few days ago. Her dark hair tumbled about her shoulders and her eyes shone.

It was a simple civil ceremony with a blessing from the minister of the local church and two witnesses pulled from the luxury villa next door.

Portia's brown eyes brimmed with tears as they said

their vows. He'd never seen a bride look more beautiful. 'For better or for worse, in sickness and in health, for as long as we both shall live,' she repeated, sincerity emanating from every pore in her body. Then she smiled and added a few lines of her own. 'I never found anyone that made me feel complete, made me feel whole, until I met you, Javier. I promise to love you, respect you and challenge you, every single day for the rest of your life.'

He couldn't wipe the smile from his face. He repeated the vows looking into the face of the woman that he loved. When he finished he kept hold of her hands. 'Portia Russo.' He gave a little laugh. 'I'm going to love saying those words.' He shook his head. 'When I went to Villa Rosa I didn't expect to meet anyone. I wasn't ready to meet anyone. But then there was you. All English accent, twinkling eyes and very, very long legs. You made me smile, you made me laugh. You asked all the right questions. And before I knew it, I was in love. Hook, line and sinker. Don't ever let me go. Because I plan on us growing very old together.'

He bent to kiss her, her perfect lips on his, and then she wrapped her arms around his neck and whispered in his ear, 'I guess we should make this official.'

He swept her up into his arms, ready to carry her over the threshold of their home. 'It will be my pleasure, Mrs Russo.'

* * * * *

LET'S TALK
Romance

For exclusive extracts, competitions
and special offers, find us online:

f facebook.com/millsandboon

🐦 @MillsandBoon

📷 @MillsandBoonUK

Get in touch on 01413 063232

For all the latest titles coming soon, visit
millsandboon.co.uk/nextmonth

MILLS & BOON
Desire

Indulge in secrets and scandal, intense drama and plenty of sizzling hot action with powerful and passionate heroes who have it all: wealth, status, good looks… everything but the right woman.